Behind the Mask of
SPIDER-MAN
The Secrets of the Movie

Mark Cotta Vaz

THE BALLANTINE PUBLISHING GROUP
NEW YORK

A Del Rey® Book
Published by The Ballantine Publishing Group
Copyright © 2002 Columbia Pictures Industries, Inc.

Interior unit photography:
Zade Rosenthal, Peter Iovino, Peter Stone, Doug Hyun

Photo of John Calley as Zorro:
Photo of Antonio Banderas as Zorro by Rico Torres
Headshot of John Calley by Long Photography, Inc.,
    Los Angeles
Composite photograph by Dan Madsen

Visual effects and CG imagery: Sony Pictures Imageworks

Frontispiece:
Early movie concept illustration by Bernie Wrightson

Interior book design:
Michaelis/Carpelis Design Assoc. Inc.

www.delreydigital.com
www.sony.com/Spider-Man

Library of Congress Cataloging-in-Publication Data
   Vaz, Mark Cotta.
      Behind the mask of Spider-Man : the secrets of the
      movie / Mark Cotta Vaz.
         p. cm.

      1. Spider-Man (Motion picture : 2002) I. Title.
PN1997.2.S68 V39 2002
791.43'72—dc21   2001056457

ISBN 0-345-45605-X

Manufactured in the United States of America

First Edition: March 2002

10 9 8 7 6 5 4 3 2 1

"Am I more interested in the adventure of being Spider-Man than I am in helping people?? Why do I do it? Why don't I give the whole thing up? And yet, I *can't*! I must have been given this great power for a reason! No matter how difficult it is, I must remain as Spider-Man! And I pray that some day the world will understand."

—Peter Parker in *The Amazing Spider-Man* #4, September 1963

Contents

Acknowledgments

My appreciation to fearless editor Steve Saffel, who entrusted me with this assignment, set me off on a journey, and provided superb guidance throughout (may the comics gods award you a *mint* copy of *Amazing Fantasy* #15). And a ceremonial bow to those magicians of design, Fred Dodnick and Sylvain Michaelis, for the beautiful results. On the Sony side, I can't say enough good things about Cindy Irwin, who has a magical ability to overcome all obstacles. Whether it was providing a contact or coordinating the dispersal of hundreds of copies of selected visuals, she swiftly and expertly met every challenge. (Fun fact: Cindy *hates* spiders—but she loves that Spider-Man!) Similarly, *Spider-Man* associate producer Grant Curtis became an important resource who, despite the pressures of production, was unfailing in help, support, and good humor. And I'll take a couple swings on the spider's web in honor of Sony's Grace Ressler, who helped get things started.

A special thanks to Barbara Lakin in Sony photographic services for making me feel at home and giving me total freedom to peruse the *Spider-Man* visual record—I *did* raise a glass in your honor at Sam's! (And thanks to Jeffrey Stewart for the able assist.) My fond appreciation to all who gave of their time to be interviewed and a big Spidey salute to the folks who helped arrange it: Lisa Medwid, executive director for the office of the chairman, for time with John Calley; Heidi Fugeman, assistant for Ian Bryce; Lynn Padilla, producer's assistant for Laura Ziskin; Jeff Klein and Carlynn Chapman (executive assistant) for Avi Arad; Kelly Bush's I/D Public Relations and Dana Pucillo, Amy Thompson, and Carrie Byalick for Tobey Maguire and Willem Dafoe; Brenda Kelly and Hope Diamond at Shepley, Winings, Hober for Kirsten Dunst; Cory Richmond for Rosemary Harris; Jack Gilardi for Cliff Robertson; Robin Baum for James Franco; Steven Hirsch for J. K. Simmons. And to the masters of Imageworks: Yair Landau and Don Levy, Pamela Matthews (for facilitating questions for Don and Yair), Mary Reardon, and Chris Antonini, who ably arranged follow-ups and fact-checks.

A special salute to senior visual effects coordinator Lisa Zusmer, who, in the heat of post-production, took on the difficult task of preparing a superb sampling of Sony Pictures Imageworks' computer graphics images.

Victoria Shoemaker, my literary agent, was her usual font of wisdom and support. A blessing to my mother for her particular and expert insights. (And here's a filial kiss for padre and a hug all around for the clan. Hey, Peter! Now you get to dig into the secret stuff!) I'll also get Spidey to spell out in webbing a super "Thank You" to Denise Fitzer, Michael Kirk, Paige Brown, Tracey Tardiff-Hill, Laetitia May, Christiane Friess, Mike Wigner (master of "Happy Donut Land"), Bruce and Ginny Walters, Jesse Strauch at Infinity Color, Ozzy Inguanzo, Spider-Man Art Dept. coordinator, Ned Gorman, and Tom and Vita Blatchford.

Finally, I'm sure Sam Raimi's ears have been burning, what with all the good things said about him. All the testaments, freely given, speak to a talented guy with a good heart—as this writer can attest. Thanks, Sam. It was a pleasure.

—Mark Cotta Vaz

A Bullpen Bulletin
BY STAN LEE

Your friendly neighborhood Spider-Man almost never got born.

You see, in the wondrous world of comic books, a superhero can't see the light of day unless his adventures get published. Well, when I first proposed the idea of a teenage superhero named Spider-Man, my publisher thought I had lost my marbles. He hated the name, he hated the concept, and he hated the idea of a teenage superhero—and he wasn't the least bit shy about telling me so.

However, since this is America, truth and justice soon prevailed. No, I didn't finally convince him that Spidey would be a hit. Instead, I took the cowardly way out; I sneaked a story of Spider-Man into one of our magazines when he wasn't looking.

As proof of the fact that the good guy always wins, that issue became a bestseller. The readers kept clamoring for more, and suddenly my now friendly publisher told me how he had always loved the idea of our amazing little arachnid.

But let me tell you about the guy without whom it might never have happened. One of the luckiest decisions I ever made was asking Steve Ditko to draw the strip. He not only gave Spider-Man his uniquely different visual style, but he also made an enormous contribution in the plotting of the stories. In fact, as the series progressed, I relied more and more on Steve's plotting. He had such a great instinct for the way the stories should be presented that I often thought that he, too, must have had a spider bite somewhere in his mysterious background.

Y'know, there were many talented artists who might have drawn those early issues of *Spider-Man*, but Steve brought something to the strip that only he could have created, a certain compelling look, a "spidery" style that had to be seen to be believed. Spider-Man didn't move like any other comic-book hero, or villain, for that matter. His every movement, his every gesture, his every pose, whether in action or just standing around, had the feeling of a man whose actual gestalt had been taken over by a spider.

The fans went crazy. I couldn't count the hundreds and hundreds of drawings that readers all over the country, and later around the world, sent to our offices: drawings of Spider-Man, copies of Steve's action poses, various versions of webs flying all over the pages. Amateur artists everywhere seemed desperate to draw in the dazzlingly different Ditko style. I must shamefacedly admit that I myself received very few scripts from writers seeking to emulate the magic of my scriptwriting. But I sought solace by telling myself it was because they knew my style was so unique they wouldn't have a chance.

One of the things I've always enjoyed most when creating our fantastic little fables is writing about our deliciously diabolical supervillains. No matter how popular a hero may be, if you don't pit him against a colorful, exciting, unusual bad guy whom the readers will love to hate, then you've only got half a story—and I'm happy to say that we've never been accused of offering half stories.

Some of our Spider-Man supervillains became so popular that when Hollywood wisely decided to make a movie of everyone's favorite wall-crawler, it was apparent that, when it came to the most fiendish of foes, the filmmakers couldn't improve upon what had already been created—hence, a breathlessly waiting world is being treated to the senses-staggering impact of Spidey's battle with none other than that mad master of grotesquerie, that merciless merchant of titanic terror, that evil epitome of the Grand Guignol—the grim and gruesome Green Goblin!

The Green Goblin has always been a particular favorite of mine because he wasn't a typical master criminal. No, he was more a study in abnormal psychology, a modern-day Jekyll and Hyde, a man with many complex facets to his character. In other words, he was the furthest thing from the many one-dimensional villains who too often populated the burgeoning world of comics. I felt I knew the guy. What's more, I felt I could understand him. In a way, that worried me a bit!

Since I suspect there'll be sequels to the first Spider-Man movie, I can't wait to see the other fiendish foes who'll challenge our web-swinging wonder on the big screen. I'm kinda hoping that the next one will be another all-time favorite baddie of mine, that raging redoubtable rapscallion, Dr. Octopus. By the way, to me, a villain without a nickname is like a day without sunshine. The Green Goblin, of course, has always been Gobby to me. So what could be more natural than to refer to our many-tentacled terror as Doc Ock?

Of course, Spidey had many, many other memorable enemies, more than I can mention in this lamentably brief visit with you, but Sturdy Stevie Ditko (I suspect he always hated that nickname that I so generously bestowed upon him, but we're 3,000 miles apart right now, so I guess I'm safe from his righteous wrath), well, as I was saying, Steve and I really had a ball dreaming up a whole kaboodle of variegated villains. In just the first two years of the series alone, we brought the grateful flocks of fandom such stellar supervillains as Kraven the Hunter, Mysterio, the Lizard, the Sandman, the Chameleon, the Vulture, and the ever-electrifying Sultan of Shock, Electro! (And if you somehow suspect that, in seeking villains' names, I just thumbed through the dictionary and picked out nouns at random, you wouldn't be too far wrong.)

A reporter recently asked how it feels to know that Spider-Man has actually become one of the most readily recognized fictional figures on Earth. I told him it felt good. You should have seen the look of disappointment on his face. I imagine he was expecting some lengthy philosophical dissertation that would reveal many of my deepest and innermost emotions. But in all honesty, what else is there to say? Steve and I brought Spidey to life. Our creation has become world famous. Hey, it feels good.

Another question that's often asked is, what has made Spider-Man so popular and why has his popularity lasted for so many decades? Well, I'd have to base my answer on the countless comments I've heard from readers at different schools and colleges where I've lectured over the years. The one quality that has been mentioned over and over again is the quality of realism. The consensus seems to be that Peter Parker is the most realistic, the most believable of all superheroes. His flaws, his imperfections, his personal problems and hang-ups apparently make him seem like the guy next door to so many readers, especially those whose next-door neighbors are good at wall-crawling and web-shooting, I suppose.

Of course, nothing is perfect. Despite our costumed cavorter's burgeoning popularity, there's one great source of irritation that never seems to go away. I hate to burden you with this, but you brought it on yourself by staying with me so long. When I dreamed up Spidey, I wanted to be sure his name wouldn't be confused with another not inconsequential hero named Superman. So I purposely put a hyphen between *Spider* and *Man.* That made the magazine's masthead look totally different from the one featuring that cat from Krypton.

So what's my beef? This is it. Almost everybody now spells Spidey's name without the hyphen. It appears hyphenless in ads, in photo captions, in fan publications, and—worst of all—even some Marvel staffers themselves omit the critical, crucial, all-important hyphen when writing about Spider-Man. See, world? Didja notice how I just spelled it? That's how it should be. Spider-*hyphen*-Man. Now be sure to remember that. Don't get me mad!

Bob Kane, creator of Batman, was a very good friend of mine. We always used to joke about whose hero was the best. Bob would tell me the answer was a foregone conclusion because the Dark Knight had gotten to the big screen before Spidey. I'd reply that Batman was just the opening act, just paving the way for the big event. Man, how I wish Bob was still with us. The big event is now. *Spider-Man* has been one of the most eagerly awaited motion pictures of the decade. If only I could have seen it with Bob, so we could have continued our never-ending debate.

Speaking of Bob, I have to mention one of the greatest things about the comic-book business—the people. Sure, those who work for different publishers are competitors. And everyone hopes that his or her title will outsell all the others. But that's natural. The fact is, the artists, writers, editors, letterers, colorists, production people, and even the publishers are some of the most terrific people you'll ever meet. I've never met any artists who wouldn't offer to help other artists improve their drawings. Same goes for writers, editors, and all concerned. Comic-bookdom is like a small, intimate club, and once you become a member you've got friends for life.

Well, I'd better turn you loose before this page becomes too tearstained. But let me leave you with a personal message: I'm thankful for living in a wonderful world like this where a kid from a poor background can pull himself up by his bootstraps and finally amount to something. No, I don't mean me, Bunky! I'm talkin' about your friendly neighborhood Spider-Man!

Excelsior!

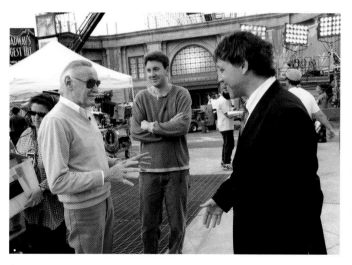

Stan Lee, creator of the Marvel universe (left), meets director Sam Raimi (far right) on the Spider-Man Times Square set. Looking on is associate producer Grant Curtis.

the amazing journey

The great comic-book superheroes were always a breed apart, distant and even aloof from their public. Some came out only after dark and moved like avenging angels through the darkness of the criminal underworld. Others were supersonic blurs streaking across the sky—suddenly seen and gone.

But there was one superhero who had people talking from the suites to the streets, and everyone had an opinion: Hero or Menace? He was a fixture of New York City, a celebrity sighting in either the light of day or the shadow of night. He might be seen clinging to the side of a midtown skyscraper at rush hour or glimpsed swinging on a silken strand above the crowds strolling Greenwich Village streets at evening. Often, a grainy news photo of the masked mystery man greeted New Yorkers from the morning paper's front page.

We're talking "the amazing" Spider-Man here, the first comic-book superhero who revealed himself to a waiting world—performing stunts on a nationally broadcast TV show. Of course, the Marvel Comics character, with his red and blue and web-lined costume and ability to shoot strands of webbing, became much more than a freak show to an awestruck public. In the comics, New Yorkers who loved him never knew who was behind the mask, only that he cared and would be there when innocent lives were in peril. The haters feared him for no other reason than that he *was* mysterious and powerful.

Forty years after he was born, the Spider-Man story would finally leap out of the lined borders of that two-dimensional comics world, coming to movie screens marked with the enduring icon of a tunic-clad woman on a pedestal in the clouds, holding high a torch for Columbia Pictures. Such was Spider-Man's appeal to a real-life public that Sony Pictures Entertainment—Columbia's parent company—entertained enthusiastic "franchise" expectations for their 2002 release.

And such were the expectations of that moviegoing public that fully a year before the film there was already a groundswell of anticipation. An authorized *Spider-Man* Web site was launched with millions of page

FAR LEFT: *Page one of the story that started it all says it all, with Peter Parker pictured in stark relief as the outcast with the secret shadow life. The fellow with the "cha-cha" comment is Flash Thompson, jock supreme, Big Man on Campus at Midtown High—and Peter's prime tormentor. Amazing Fantasy #15, "Spider-Man!" page 1 / Artist: Steve Ditko*

LEFT: *Spidey shocks his old foe Electro with a smashing left cross—packing the proportionate strength of a spider, of course! Electro was one of the villains considered for the movie, advancing through the early script development before being dropped in favor of the Green Goblin. The Amazing Spider-Man Annual #1, "The Sinister Six," page 16 / Artist: Steve Ditko*

BOTTOM: *When Peter Parker got his superpowers, he did what any self-respecting fantasy superhero wouldn't do—tried to cash in. His brief show-biz career included performing in the TV special pictured here. Indeed, Spider-Man may have been the first celebrity superhero. Amazing Fantasy #15, "Spider-Man!", page 7 / Artist: Steve Ditko*

views its first days, while a *Spider-Man* presentation at the summer 2001 Comic-Con International in San Diego packed a cavernous hall with thousands of eager fans. The June 29/July 6, 2001 issue of *Entertainment Weekly* magazine was a star-studded "It List" edition, with a cover splash featuring Spider-Man unmasked—actually, actor Tobey Maguire—and Kirsten Dunst, the "it" girl who plays MJ, Mary Jane Watson, the love interest of Peter Parker/Spider-Man.

Even as those portentous signs began appearing, behind-the-scenes creative forces were still deep into production. On the Sony lot in Culver City, California, director Sam Raimi sat in a cool, dark editing room, deliberating over every second of the recently completed principal photography film footage. A few blocks away, at Sony Pictures Imageworks, the studio's own visual effects house, one of the production's great acts of illusion—making audiences believe that Tobey Maguire *was* Spider-Man—was being conjured in the evolving images of a computer-generated web-spinner swinging through the steel canyons of Manhattan.

Spider-Man, slated for release the year of the character's fortieth anniversary, was to be the pinnacle for a superhero who had been building his pop cultural résumé ever since his 1962 origin in the comic book *Amazing Fantasy* #15. There'd been a 1967 ABC-TV cartoon series, a mid-1970s live-action television series and made-for-TV *Spider-Man* movie, and the 1981 unveiling of the *Spider-Man and His Amazing Friends* animated TV show. In 1987 the comic-book wedding of Spidey and Mary Jane Watson was reenacted before

FAR LEFT: *The Green Goblin has been around for some of Spider-Man's worst moments. In a classic early encounter, when Spider-Man overheard that his beloved Aunt May had suffered another heart attack, he ducked out of his battle with the Goblin—and got pilloried as a coward in publisher J. Jonah Jameson's Daily Bugle. The Amazing Spider-Man #18, "The End of Spider-Man!" page 1 / Artist: Steve Ditko*

LEFT: *This 1984 cover, an homage to the Jack Kirby and Steve Ditko cover art for Spider-Man's debut in Amazing Fantasy #15, presents Spidey reinvented, wearing a black costume from another planet that miraculously clothes him at a mental command. The costume was later revealed to be an alien symbiote using Peter's body for its host. Peter wisely rejected his new look, and the symbiote found a new host, returning to plague the webbed one as Venom. The Amazing Spider-Man #252, cover / Artists: Ron Frenz and Klaus Janson*

55,000 cheering baseball fans at Shea Stadium, in Peter Parker's home borough of Queens, New York, and the web-slinger was morphed into a 78-foot-long float for the Macy's Thanksgiving Day Parade. By 1999 one could retreat to Marvel Super Hero Island, a fantastical piece of the $2.5 billion Universal Islands of Adventure theme park, there to experience the Amazing Adventures of Spider-Man ride.

It's compelling stuff, this dream of Spider-Man. With a costume like a second skin—one of the only heroes whose outfit covers every inch of his body—the character boasts the proportionate strength of a spider, can crawl up the tallest building, and can swing above gravity-bound mortals on superstrands of spider webbing. It's the kinetic stuff of thrill-ride blockbusters—but that's *not* the Spider-Man that Sam Raimi wanted to bring to life.

Raimi's first encounter with Spider-Man was in the late 1960s, as a seven-year-old kid growing up in Detroit, Michigan. He'd seen a *Spider-Man* comic book in his older brother's bedroom—he doesn't recall the particular issue or even the story, but the memory has otherwise remained vivid. "My brother didn't always take a great interest in me, because he was six years older," the director recalled. "What was remarkable was he sat me down and began explaining who Spider-Man was, sharing something that was of interest to him. I grew to love Spider-Man and follow his adventures."

Young Raimi could relate to the spirit of Peter Parker, a character near his own age, a bright kid who seemed out of step with the in crowd. But Peter, an orphan living with his Uncle Ben and Aunt May, also had a secret side he was compelled to hide, the amazing truth that the bite of a radioactive spider had made him superhuman. "When I was in public school I read excerpts from the *Iliad* and the *Odyssey* but didn't really understand what it is to go on the hero's journey—but I did find that in Spider-Man, as I'm sure millions of other kids did," Raimi said. "It's not someone wearing a toga or sailing away in a ship. He's a teenager wearing the kind of clothes you wear and going to high school, a kid who lives in our world, who has to learn what it means to be a hero.

Two forces of the Marvel universe share a moment on the Spider-Man Times Square set: Avi Arad (left), prime mover behind Marvel's movie interests, and Stan "The Man" Lee, who, with the gifted artists of the legendary Marvel Bullpen, laid the foundations of the Marvel universe.

"Peter Parker's parents aren't around, like so many of the kids in America who come from broken families. He's kind of a geek; he's unnoticed by girls; he's on the outside. A lot of people can relate to that; they've got a secret side of themselves that's beautiful and heroic. They probably feel like Peter and Spider-Man—if only people knew who they really were! That's the beauty of Stan Lee and Steve Ditko's character. It's one of *us* who becomes a superhero. We weren't trying to make a superhero movie that had a lot of heart; we weren't even really trying to make a 'superhero movie.' We made the story of Peter Parker and how his life was affected by the curse or blessing of these powers. The Spider-Man stories are about how he learns to be responsible, and that's what our movie is about."

To unmask a superhero and find a kid struggling with all the insecurities that come with young adulthood . . . well, that was something new in the annals of the great comic-book superheroes. To understand how Spider-Man and his fellow Marvel superheroes broke the mold, we have to go back to the superhero genesis that began in the quiet of a warm summer's night in Cleveland in 1934.

The fevered imagination of a high school kid named Jerry Siegel was keeping him awake when—like a comic-book lightning bolt—there flashed the inspiration for a superpowered character who would be like Samson, Hercules, and all the supermen of legend combined into one mighty man. Come the dawn of a new day, Siegel was at the nearby home of his buddy, budding artist Joe Shuster, and the two dreamers were on their way to creating Superman, the caped and costumed superhero who rocketed to Earth from doomed Krypton to debut in 1938 in *Action Comics* #1. And thus began the Golden Age of Comics.

By 1939 Batman, a masked avenger of crime, was spotted on the moonlit rooftops of mythic Gotham City. Then a homeless boy named Billy Batson whispered "Shazam"—the magical word encompassing super attributes of Solomon, Hercules, Atlas, Zeus, Achilles, and Mercury—and transformed into mighty Captain Marvel. Wonder Woman arrived, strongest of the Amazons, and Captain America, an army reject, was juiced up by a superserum to become the star-spangled patriot who led the charge against the Nazi menace.

But there was a strain of mutant super-DNA embodied in a superamphibian named Sub-Mariner, who *hated* humans. Prince Namor, the Sub-Mariner, was a character created by Bill Everett in a tale for *Motion Picture Funnies Weekly*, a failed 1939 movie theater giveaway. His story was reprinted that year in Timely Publications' *Marvel Comics* #1. In those

days a legion of square-jawed do-gooders fought, without question, for justice, but the Sub-Mariner was imbued with complex emotions, a conflicted figure keen to wreak havoc on New York, but also harboring a longing for a surface girl named Betty Dean.

By the end of the 1940s, most of those once indomitable figures, among them Namor and Captain America, would fall victim to the comics' version of the Big Sleep, vanquished by anticomics crusades and plummeting sales as superheroes found themselves being replaced by humor, horror, romance, and western comics. The pillars of the pantheon shaken and cloaked in lengthening twilight shadow, the end seemed near even for the likes of godlike Superman. But a spark of creativity—maybe even that rebel spirit of the Sub-Mariner—remained, ready to be fanned into an unquenchable fire by a comics editor who had

ABOVE: Spider-Man *features some revisionary takes on the classic comic-book mythology—such as introducing Mary Jane Watson as Peter's neighbor and classmate at Midtown High—but the basic origin story was preserved. This is the gunman (played by Michael Papajohn) who murders Peter's Uncle Ben.*

LEFT: *Peter Parker pays his respects at Ben Parker's grave. Peter, who had already been blessed—or cursed —with his superpowers, had a chance to stop the thief who later gunned down his uncle. Haunted by guilt, Peter Parker learned the tough lesson summed up in the classic origin story: "With great power there must also come great responsibility."*

grown up with Timely and who, by the early 1960s, was tired of scripting monster comics.

Years later, in his *Origins of Marvel Comics*, Stan Lee would write of "the awesome affliction that threatens us all: the endlessly spreading virus of too much reality in a world that is losing its legends—a world that has lost its heroes." But Lee, along with such artists as Jack Kirby and Steve Ditko, began inoculating imaginations with the cure: the visions of a new breed of costumed superhero, unleashed under the aegis of the publishing house that began as Timely, now known as Marvel Comics.

Marvel heroes grappled with supervillains and inner demons, were as much cursed as blessed by the superpowers Fate bestowed on them. During a space launch to beat the Commies to the stars, the Fantastic Four were transformed by cosmic rays, particularly the pilot, whose misshapen form earned him the name Thing. Dr. Bruce Banner, blasted by Gamma-Bomb test rays, became the monstrous Hulk. Tony Stark was a millionaire playboy weapons manufacturer, but a booby trap in Vietnam left

shrapnel near his heart, forcing him to retreat into the life-sustaining transistorized armor of Iron Man in order to survive. Even a resurrected Captain America—preserved since the Golden Age in a block of ice!—was plagued by his adherence to patriotism in a time of flag burning. And the ice block that had entombed Cap was discovered by the Sub-Mariner, whose underwater homeland was ruined by nuclear tests and who again vowed vengeance against humans. Some things never change.

And then there was Spider-Man, a throwaway character for the final issue of *Amazing Fantasy*, one of those "monster mags" Lee had grown tired of writing. But it wasn't the finale for Spider-Man—skyrocketing sales saw to that. By 1963 the "amazing" Spider-Man had his own title.

The challenge for the production was making the transition from printed comics page to the big screen.

Right: Spidey and the Goblin pose atop a piece of soundstage balcony set built for the Times Square sequence.

Above: Here, first assistant cameraman Zoran Veselic measures Spider-Man's distance from the camera so he can focus the camera correctly. Director Sam Raimi and Don Burgess, director of photography, are below this set, watching monitors playing a video feed of what the camera is seeing.

WIL REES '00

The classic Spidey villain Dr. Otto Octavious—better known as Dr. Octopus—dangles J. Jonah Jameson outside the Daily Bugle offices in the first image artist Wil Rees produced for Neil Spisak's design department. When this artwork was executed, Dr. Octopus was being written out of the Spider-Man script, but Sam Raimi was so impressed by Rees's tableau that it earned Octavious another three months of creative life before the character was finally dropped and the production settled on the Goblin as sole antagonist. (The final film would include the scenario of the Goblin throttling the Bugle publisher.)

Maybe it was those first couple of pages of Lee's origin story and Steve Ditko's art that hooked fans, a narrative arc revealing a bespectacled kid beloved of his doting aunt and uncle, an honor student at Midtown High in Queens who could never get a date. Maybe readers saw themselves in the outcast kid who vowed that someday his tormentors would be sorry they'd laughed at him.

What the boy didn't know was that Fate awaited him in an "Experiments in Radio-Activity" science exhibit, that destiny had taken the form of a glowing spider whose venomous bite would change him forever. Transformed, Peter tested himself as a masked contestant in a wrestling ring. He then crafted a Spider-Man costume and shocked the world with a live-TV demonstration of his powers—becoming the first celebrity superhero.

It was then that Spider-Man refused to stop the thief who sprinted past him and escaped a pursuing police officer. From behind the mask, shrugging off the cop's angry tongue-lashing, Peter Parker proclaimed he was through being pushed around: *"From now on I just look out for number one."* But that thief was the finger on the trigger of the fatal gunshot that struck down his beloved uncle. For Peter, fame and celebrity became dross. The reward for his selfishness was a sudden death and guilt he'd bear forever. The shattering lesson he'd learned was summed up in the final panel of Spider-Man's first story:

"With great power there must also come great responsibility."

And somehow, through the years and despite self-doubts and endless tragedies, Peter has adhered to this code branded with searing pain on his heart. It's taken him through battles with such fantastic villains as Vulture, Dr. Octopus, Sandman, Electro, Lizard, the Kingpin, Venom, and deadliest of all, the Green Goblin—the foe destined to meet Spider-Man on the big screen.

"Every fan has a Spider-Man movie in their head, the one they would make, and our challenge was for audiences to suspend that and go along for the ride that was Sam Raimi's vision of Spider-Man," noted Laura Ziskin, who with producer Ian Bryce and executive producer Avi Arad formed the film's producing triumvirate. "There was so much potential story because there's forty years of comic books. We had to satisfy enough of the legend and legacy in a two-hour movie."

"This picture was a different beast from other films I've done," Raimi reflected. "I felt like Spider-Man's valet! This was less about me being a storyteller. It was about being at the service of a myth."

Part I

THE COMING OF SPIDER-MAN

Spider-Man as seen in the second movie teaser poster.

CHAPTER ONE

Web of dreams

Long before Columbia Pictures' *Spider-Man*, another Hollywood powerhouse had a Spidey thriller in the works. It was back in 1964, in the pages of *The Amazing Spider-Man* #14, and B. J. Cosmos of Cosmos Productions hired the web-spinner to star in a movie that would introduce . . . the Green Goblin! A fickle Hollywood type, though, by the end of the story, Cosmos was in the thrall of a potential development deal with the Hulk and reneged on his contract with Spider-Man, giving our hero only enough bus fare to get him from Hollywood back to the sanity of New York City.

"Oh well," Spidey said, shrugging, "that's show biz."

Of course, what self-respecting real-life movie mogul would walk away from an actual supercharacter, a walking visual effect? And, in truth, moviemakers *were* eager to tell the Spider-Man story—had been for years—but it was a long road back to Hollywood, and it would be nearly four decades before a flesh-and-blood film team would take up the challenge of turning this pen-and-inked figure into a transcendent silver-screen image, bursting with the illusion of life.

The *Spider-Man* production was largely made on the Sony lot and at nearby Imageworks, in the town that appropriately calls itself "the heart of screenland." The Sony lot in Culver City had once been home to Triangle, the short-lived studio of the silent era, which became Metro-Goldwyn-Mayer, the ultimate dream factory. Sony, which had bought fabled Columbia Pictures in 1989 and moved their moviemaking operations there soon after, settled into a lot filled with buildings from MGM's glory days and soundstages where productions such as *The Wizard of Oz* had been filmed.

RIGHT: Avi Arad, the president and CEO of Marvel Studios and director and Chief Creative Officer for Marvel Enterprises. Arad, who served as Spider-Man executive producer, combines business savvy with a creative understanding of Marvel characters. "What our universe brings to the table are characters mutated by various means, but the core is they're vulnerable human beings. They'd probably do anything to shed the powers given them, this awesome responsibility they live with."

LEFT: OsCorp World Headquarters, concept art by Francois Audouy . The corporation, headed by Norman Osborn (played by Willem Dafoe), builds the supersoldier suit and weapons-equipped glider that will be used as the costume and flying arsenal when Norman transforms into the maniacal Green Goblin.

In a pastoral, tree-shaded corner of the lot stands the white, four-story Thalberg Building, an elegant Art Deco structure built in 1937 and named for the MGM executive with the bad heart who died too young. On the third floor, in the very office space where Louis B. Mayer presided during Hollywood's own Golden Age, John Calley oversees the fortunes of Sony Pictures Entertainment as chairman and CEO. There's an eye-of-the-hurricane stillness here—no clattering office machines, buzzing and beeping, or sounds of stray voices. The atmosphere becomes Calley, a lean and dapper figure with a trim mustache and beard. He's coatless and tieless and bright and relaxed, with the confidence of a player who regularly makes the media's Hollywood power lists and the peace of mind of someone who could give a damn. "I was born in 1930, so I came in with talkies," Calley said, smiling. "I've been watching movies for sixty-five years."

And *making* them for an appreciable piece of that time. Calley at twenty-one saw a future of factory jobs ahead, until he landed a Christmas position delivering mail at NBC. Within four years he was director of nighttime programming and by 1957 was an independent producer at the old Columbia lot when Harry Cohen ran the studio. Calley was there when Harry died and the mogul's body was laid in an open coffin on a soundstage as thousands filed past in a wake that marked the end of an era.

By the late 1950s Calley was at old MGM, down the hall from his current office, working for prestigious producer Pandro Berman. "I was a kid from Jersey City who was very poor, looking at these people on the movie screen and having those dreams—and suddenly they were my friends and co-workers!" Calley said. "You're at the studio commissary and people like William Faulkner and Dashiell Hammett are walking past; you're eating with Cary Grant and Danny Kaye; you're seeing Judy Garland and Mickey Rooney coming in and out—it was astonishing, heart-stopping."

He became studio head at Warner Bros., but at fifty walked away from it all, tired of feeling "like a pinball bouncing." He embarked on a voyage of self-discovery, living like a hermit on an island during wintertime and sailing the Mediterranean in the summer. Years later he returned to producing with his friend Mike Nichols, then took the post of president of United Artists Pictures and in 1996 accepted the offer to run Sony's film studio. "What I discovered about myself is too subjective and personal to go into," he

The Green Goblin debuted in Spider-Man *comics with a high-concept plan for knocking off Spider-Man and then forming a global crime syndicate: pitch movie mogul B. J. Cosmos on a movie production as a cover to catch Spidey unawares. Spidey finally received the real-deal movie treatment in Sam Raimi and Sony/Columbia Pictures' 2002 production.* The Amazing Spider-Man #14, *"The Grotesque Adventure of the Green Goblin," page 3 / Artist: Steve Ditko* recalled of his earlier hermetic experience, "but it helped me, because I'm free of the constraints of those whose identity is tied up with their jobs. Those trappings had always been meaningless to me, anyway."

The world Calley returned to was as high-stakes as ever, and it was his finger that flipped the switch and greenlit *Spider-Man*—with its huge price tag. Calley explained, "There's no quantifiable essence that goes into a movie that will make it de facto succeed. Otherwise it'd be the golden calf! It's high risk and an arcane process that has a lot to do with an intuitive response to material. The rocks are covered with the ships of people who thought there was a formula."

There are advertising and marketing costs, which can outstrip production expenses. High-priced stars can jack up production costs. "A very dangerous game," Calley observed. "But I've learned that if you believe in an idea, you better back it."

During his tenure as head at Warner Bros., he had adopted that approach for such classics as *The Exorcist* and *Superman*, the seminal 1978 superhero movie that Sam Raimi points to as the film most like *Spider-Man* in spirit. "We didn't make *Superman* as an exploitative sci-fi, comic-book thing. It was done with a seriousness that said to audiences, 'We believe in this and we want you to, as well.' I'd always loved the Saturday matinee adventure serials, and I'd read *Superman* as a kid, but I hadn't awoken one morning with a number and a formula. I was making twenty-five to thirty movies a year, so I was scratching and looking all the time. *Superman* seemed plausible, then it worked because [director] Dick Donner was remarkable and inventive. He started a genre."

The closest thing to that golden calf is the franchise film capable

ABOVE: Director Sam Raimi surveys the moody Spider-Man/Goblin battleground he dubbed the "hulking ruin." "A picture like this is just gigantic," Raimi says, "and everything is done by hundreds of people. You create elements on set, and they have to be mixed and baked by the postproduction visual effects people. It's like a big factory, a long and complex process of which shooting is only the first step."

LEFT: Raimi sets up a shot with the superhero himself. "Most Spider-Man sequences were shot during daylight," the director explains. "I see Spider-Man, in his bright red and blue outfit, as a brighter, more daytime character—it's Peter Parker who's a little more tormented."

of generating bankable sequels. Movie history is rich with them, from Tarzan and Sherlock Holmes to James Bond and the *Star Wars* films. At Warner Bros., Calley worked with Clint Eastwood, and a *Dirty Harry* release was like minting money. He'd seen *Superman* sequels flow from that first production, and at UA he'd been involved in a James Bond release, while Sony sequels in the works under his tenure include *Stuart Little* and *Men in Black*. "If you're able to create a franchise, you know a very big piece of business is available to you every few years," Calley enthused.

The lure of franchise film possibilities is the biggest card that Avi Arad, the president and CEO of Marvel Studios and *Spider-Man* executive producer, plays as he expands Marvel's universe of characters from printed page to the movies. "*Spider-Man* was about finding the right people who were passionate, because this had the potential for being a franchise second to none," Arad said softly.

Arad sat in a brightly lit conference room at Marvel Studios in Los Angeles, surrounded by the iconic emblems of success, the walls emblazoned with posters of Marvel characters and recent movie adaptations, tables and shelves lined with toys and comic-book anthologies for the superheroes he calls "time-tested properties." He is a soft-spoken man, a successful toy maker with a swashbuckling penchant for dressing in black and a love of motorcycles—he founded and owns Harley-Davidson cafés in Manhattan and Las Vegas.

Arad summed up the recent successes, which began with the healthy $18 million opening in 1998 for Marvel's comic-book vampire killer *Blade* and its sequel, in the works at New Line. The next level was the mega international box office in 2000 for *X-Men* and its subsequent video and DVD success. He ticked off the productions in the works at studios from Twentieth Century Fox (an *X-Men* sequel and *The Fantastic Four*) to

ABOVE LEFT: Helming the logistics of the complex production was the producing team of Laura Ziskin, who concentrated on the script and casting, and Ian Bryce, who focused on assembling the crew and scheduling the filming.

ABOVE RIGHT: Costume designer James Acheson tends to a lavish costume worn by one of the extras for the World Unity Festival sequence. "My job is to support the characterization of the characters by what they wear," Acheson explains, "and that goes across the board from the leading actor to the last person in the crowd."

Universal (*The Incredible Hulk* and *Namor the Sub-Mariner*). The key, Arad contends, is the *first* film, making that difficult transition to the big screen. "Once you set up the origin and the character's world, we all want to know—what's next?" Arad said, smiling. "So, there is continuity. And if we tell the stories well, we can make three, four, five pictures."

Unlike DC Comics, an AOL Time Warner entertainment company whose characters, including Superman, Batman, and Wonder Woman, have a built-in connection to the Warner Bros. movie division, Marvel had no such synergistic relationship.

Over the last decade Marvel film properties had become mired in bad production deals, and comics sales fell into decline, the company problems reaching a nadir in 1998 when Marvel filed for bankruptcy. But Arad saw the golden lining behind that dark cloud. "Marvel has been successful despite bad management and bad economics, through transitions of good people and stupid people. It didn't matter—*the characters outlasted the humans!* You have fan loyalty, this community, that's built up over the years."

The turnaround came as Arad's division of Marvel Enterprises gained control over the process. "We now coproduce our movies with the studio or distributor. We have creative approval because we feel we have the best grip on this form of literature, which allows us to deal with what's best for the movies, whether it's changing a character's costume or adapting classic moments out of the books. The other issue is that people who grew up on the comics now have the clout to spearhead a movie. And they knew it was always more than a comic book. The *X-Men*, for example, is not about a bunch of people running around in costumes—it's about any civil rights movement."

Arad notes that Marvel's bankruptcy provided an opportunity to recoup some assets—including *Spider-Man*, which had been in development hell for years. Calley hails Yair Landau, currently president of Sony Pictures Digital Entertainment, with making the Spidey deal in his capacity as then executive vice-president for corporate development. Calley recalled, "The single person at this company most relentless in the pursuit of this property was Yair, who hung in with Avi for over a year and never quit, just kept making proposals until, finally, a deal was made that worked. Without Yair we would not have had *Spider-Man*."

What Arad sums up as a "real bad Hollywood deal story" was a truly tangled web of competing claims, with Sony, MGM, and Paramount claiming interests in Spider-Man. The ensuing negotiations and litigation over the property became serious during the 1998 Marvel bankruptcy,

Don Burgess, director of photography, whose work includes such recent Robert Zemeckis productions as Forrest Gump, Contact, and Cast Away. "We tried to make Spider-Man as realistic as possible, making the lighting, color, and sets look like New York," the cinematographer says. "It wasn't a gritty, hard-edged reality, but there weren't a lot of glossy images, either. It was a slightly stylized look. The challenge was the sheer scale. The sets were huge, the biggest sets at Sony."

The challenge for costume designer James Acheson's department was to create a Spider-Man costume that portrayed both musculature and the character's acrobatic athleticism. While many of costume concept artist Warren Manser's images pictured Spidey in dynamic movements, this series of static poses began working out the location of the muscle enhancements that would be further developed and incorporated into the final suit.

These images were based on photographs Acheson had taken of Tobey Maguire soon after the actor was cast, with Manser scanning in the Maguire photographs, as well as separate pencil drawings he'd made over the photos, which added the proportions of a padded suit. "Traditionally, my work has been drawing and painting, but recently the computer has been added," Manser notes. "I used a lot of Painter software, which allows you to paint with different brushes, so it wasn't pure cut and paste."

a time when Sony made a proposal to acquire the company. The proposal was rejected, but Sony had been active "strategically on multiple fronts," as Landau put it, and after losing their bid to buy Marvel, the focus became Spider-Man.

"A lot of people inside and outside the company asked why we were wasting our time, that we'd never unravel this mess with the Spider-Man rights," Landau revealed. "It became a matter of having the will, determination, and optimism to believe we could accomplish what other people didn't think we could.

"I've also been a Spider-Man fan since I was nine," he added. "There has to be a belief beyond something being a good business idea, because we had to endure a lot. Yeah, I'd say I felt very passionate about the character."

Landau continued his relationship with Arad, the two getting together at the Harley-Davidson café or a favorite deli on the Lower East Side whenever Landau was in New York. But Arad's support was only "half the equation," as Landau explained. "The other half was solving the situation with MGM and Paramount. The rights had been contaminated by a series of companies that had gone under. Some of the rights had belonged to Carolco, some to 21st Century. We had a home video output deal with 21st Century that they were unable to honor, so we ended up with their [Spider-Man] rights. We believed MGM had some valid interests because they'd bought a couple of libraries and ended up with the James Cameron [Spider-Man] treatment that Carolco had commissioned."

The key to breaking the deadlock was an exchange of icons: James Bond for Spider-Man. The famed secret agent of fiction—who made his movie debut the year Spider-Man was born—had been MGM's great franchise property until Sony acquired "a separate parcel of [Bond] rights and they sued and we were in lengthy litigation," Landau recalls. "At that point we each had a quarter of the rights [to Spider-Man]. As part of our settlement we essentially won half the rights. It was quite the win-win situation. They ended up with clarity that we weren't going to make a Bond film, and we ended up with Spider-Man."

The ability to get MGM's Spider-Man rights and negotiate a deal with Avi Arad helped Sony fight off a competing challenge from Paramount in court. "We ended up consolidating the rights," Landau said. "None of this had anything to do with the creative take, who would play Spider-Man or direct the movie. This put us in the position to have those conversations."

So the constellations began lining up, bringing into place the right director, screenwriter, actors, and technology. "I guess there is a God because the *Spider-Man* we made couldn't have been made even five years ago," Arad said. "There's this new word: CGI [Computer Graphic Imagery]. And you couldn't have a better Peter and MJ than Tobey and Kirsten. Sometimes these things fall into place."

The selection of the director had been *the* key decision early on for both Marvel and Sony. Raimi seemed a natural, with a kinetic visual style that began with 1982's *The Evil Dead*, the horror tale that earned him "cult" director status. By 1998 Raimi's *A Simple Plan* had garnered critical raves and a Best Supporting Actor Oscar nomination for Billy Bob Thornton. Raimi also had producing experience, including 1993's *Hard Target*, the American debut film for Hong Kong action director John Woo, and the *Hercules* and *Xena* sword-and-sorcery TV series. As a writer, Raimi had scripted his own productions, including *Darkman* and *Evil Dead*, as well as cowriting with Ethan and Joel Coen their 1994 film, *The Hudsucker Proxy*.

After hearing Sony was interested in him, Raimi read in *Variety* that the studio has its short list of potential directors down to three—but the

Raimi and John Dykstra, who supervised the visual effects produced by Sony Pictures Imageworks, refer to storyboards at the Times Square set in Downey, California. Although visual effects is considered post-production—coming after completion of principal photography—the new age of digital effects usually requires effects artists to be involved with the main production, particularly when it comes to the live-action "plates" that will be digitally composited with other separately created elements.

Images from the seminal Spider-Man wall-crawl test that Imageworks' Spencer Cook prepared to prove to the production and the studio that a computer-generated action hero was possible. The test also worked out such details as Spidey's trademark wall-crawling fingertip grip. "For Spider-Man we were paying attention to every little thing—the angle of each finger on every frame, where each knuckle was," animation supervisor Anthony LaMolinara says. "We were trying to push the limits—then push them a little more."

Raimi name was *not* among them. He was finally called to a high-level meeting that included Calley, Amy Pascal, chairman of Columbia Pictures, and Avi Arad. Days after the meeting, the press reported *two* potential directors—and Raimi still hadn't made the list.

"I thought that was too bad, but maybe a blessing in disguise, because I had no idea how I'd really make *Spider-Man*," Raimi recalled. "Then I got a call saying they were going to give me the job! It was exhilarating."

"We definitely met with a lot of people, but the press coverage had no relation to reality," Amy Pascal explained. "Nobody was inside our heads. The thing that sold me at our meeting was Sam said as a kid he'd had a picture of Spider-Man over his bed and he identified with Peter Parker, who is the heart of the movie. Also, Sam and I have known each other for twenty years; we came up in the business together. So there was a level of trust."

"Amy Pascal was very enthusiastic about Sam," Calley recalled. "When the focus switched to Sam, it just made sense. He was attuned to the character; he has a breathtaking visual sense; he's not an uncontrollable psychotic, but a wonderful man who is, nonetheless, an artist. He was so right, I thought."

When Raimi came aboard, the script in the works featured the classic villains Electro and Sandman. But the major concern, looming like a shadowy question mark, was the creation of Spider-Man himself. "We had to know, would a CG Spider-Man work?" Raimi says. "Could John Dykstra and Imageworks create a computer graphics character that would be believable?"

Helming the Imageworks effort was visual effects supervisor John Dykstra, whose career spans Machine Age "opticals" to the digital era. Dykstra supervised effects for the first *Star Wars*, in the process overseeing development of a repeatable motion-control camera system dubbed

A separate Imageworks swing test by Jason McDade presented Spider-Man characteristically swooping through the city on a strand of spider webbing. "Spider-Man is a realistic character that does unrealistic things," animation supervisor LaMolinara muses. "We first approached it with motion capture, but that's only good for doing things real humans or animals can do. So this was a new area of trying to make a CG character look exactly human, yet do things that are superhuman."

the Dýkstraflex. He had for years headed Apogee, his own visual effects house, and served as visual effects supervisor on films from *Batman Forever* to Sony's own 1999 release *Stuart Little*.

"In visual effects you have to take on challenges that you *don't* have solutions for if you want your film to be contemporary by the time you finish it," Dykstra explained. "Over the course of the one to two years it takes to produce a film like this, advancements come at such a pace that you have to shoot for the moon. Otherwise you'll find yourself stuck to the boardwalk."

Dykstra admits that starting out there was "no certainty" that existing technologies could produce a realistic computer graphics superhero. It was on the basis of the inevitable software and hardware advances and his belief in the Imageworks talent base that Dykstra assured the director that Spider-Man could be created. "I really didn't have any choice; we had to begin testing," Raimi recalled. "I began working with my storyboard artists Dave Stephan and Jeff Lynch on designs of Spider-Man crawling up a wall and swinging, getting an idea what it'd look like if they were to create a CGI Spider-Man."

Meanwhile, the colossal production machine was revved up by producer Ian Bryce, a Lucasfilm veteran whose producing credits range from associate producer on *Batman Returns* to producing *Saving Private Ryan* with Steven Spielberg. "I was largely responsible for the setup of the picture and the casting

ABOVE: Although Imageworks computer-generated and animated Spider-Man and the Green Goblin, many of the superaction shots were attempted as "practical" live-action stunts by stunt coordinator Jeff Habberstad's team. Special effects coordinator John Frazier assisted with some of the larger flying rigs for Spider-Man while concentrating on such mechanical effects as the live-action Goblin glider.

RIGHT: Kirsten Dunst, who plays Mary Jane Watson, stands against a bluescreen background, becoming an "element" in an effects shot. Filming a subject against a pure-color screen provides a neutral background that can be replaced with a separately filmed or digitally created image. (The color depends on the subject. The Green Goblin was filmed in front of bluescreen, while the red-and-blue-costumed Spider-Man was filmed in front of greenscreen.)

of the crew," Bryce explained. "I've done a number of big movies similar to *Spider-Man*, which Sam really hadn't. Sam and I talked about some of the people I've worked with who I felt would enhance our ability to make a great movie. I think casting of key crew is vital. Sam is a down-to-earth guy, so we tried to put people around him with that same sensibility."

Bryce brought aboard renowned special effects man John Frazier, Oscar-winning costume designer James Acheson, stunt coordinator Jeff Habberstad, and director of photography Don Burgess. The production design department was headed by Neil Spisak, who had done the honors for Raimi's *For Love of the Game* and *The Gift*, the director's two films immediately prior to *Spider-Man*.

The challenges and pressure were enormous, as John Frazier describes. "On a big movie like *Spider-Man*, if you're not ready, if you screw up on set and you can't shoot that day, that can get real expensive! You have to be prepared."

The balcony set for the World Unity Festival sequence at Sony soundstage 27, a piece of a mythical Times Square building designed by Neil Spisak's production design department and erected by the construction crew helmed by Jim Ondrejko. The set was a piece of a puzzle for a sequence that ranged from location filming in the real Times Square to the street-level portion of this building—erected outdoors on a parking lot in Downey, California. (Note, toward the middle, actors James Franco, who plays Norman Osborn's son Harry, and Kirsten Dunst.)

CHAPTER TWO

Spider, spider shining bright

Sam Raimi's nerve center on the Sony lot was an upstairs floor of the David Lean building, located just beyond the looming soundstages and off Main Street—several blocks of studio stores and offices done up like a small-town business district. Even into the summer of 2001, months after the end of principal photography and with postproduction in high gear, the office of associate producer Grant Curtis was filled with stacks and free-floating pages of storyboards, those drawings that graphically plot out a screenplay and establish action and camera composition.

One of Curtis's tasks was to disseminate the "boards" to the various production departments. "Every scene for every movie I've worked on with Sam is storyboarded and worked out before he steps out on stage," Curtis noted. Thousands of storyboards were produced over the course of the production. The storyboard department was also quartered in the David Lean building, with a visual storyboard team that included Jeffrey Lynch, David Stephan, Mark Andrews, and Doug Lefler.

The *Spider-Man* storyboarding began, Curtis recalled, while Raimi was still directing *The Gift*, with Stephan flying to the location shoot in Savannah, Georgia, in late February 2000 to start boarding David Koepp's script. It was a valuable head start, since the demands of *Spider-Man* would soon become all-consuming. "I'd never done a film with Sam where every single second he wasn't directing was taken up with meetings—it was bizarre," said Curtis, who began working with Raimi as his assistant on *A Simple Plan*. "But no matter how busy Sam's day got, part of it was always spent with the storyboard artists."

RIGHT: The fateful spider's web woven in a genetics lab by the mutant superspider that sinks its venom into Peter Parker. "The web we made for the lab was probably twelve inches in diameter," special effects coordinator John Frazier says. "We had a team of ten model makers making these spiderwebs out of monofilaments you could barely see, tying them together, strand by strand, on a wooden frame. It was beyond tedious! But those guys were the best I've seen."

LEFT: The superspider looks down on an unsuspecting Peter Parker in this eerie Wil Rees concept art.

Right: Kirsten Dunst brings Mary Jane Watson to life.

Below: Ka-CHING! Mrs. Anna Watson finally sets up that long-delayed blind date between Peter and her niece, Mary Jane, in issue #42 of The Amazing Spider-Man. *Artist John Romita, who did the honors for the 1966 story, describes the creation of marvelous MJ: "I tried to make her appealing and spectacular, but I never tried for flesh or sex. Some of the artists who followed me used to do nipple shots and all that kind of stuff—I wanted clean-cut. Yes, she was sexy, but she never looked like a bad girl."*

Bottom: Tobey Maguire as Peter Parker, ever ready with his trusty camera.

Lynch's background was feature animation, his résumé ranging from work at the Disney studio in the 1980s to being story department head on the 1999 animated feature *The Iron Giant.* "In animation you're basically acting with a pencil, which comes in handy when you're storyboarding," Lynch said. "With boarding you have to have a good story sense and focus on and capture the important emotions of a scene. The first pass will be totally conceptual. Then we hone in. We try to be as shooting friendly as possible, so when assistant directors get the boards they'll have an idea of how many setups might be needed and how many cameras they'll need. Sam might also get on a set or location for the first time and ask for a new pass on the boards based on what he'd seen. As Sam gets focused on what he's looking for, the boards get more specific."

"On a big visual effects movie like this you can have different units shooting at the same time, from principal photography to second unit to a separate unit for shooting stunts," director of photography Don Burgess added, "so storyboards are essential."

One of Raimi's visual concepts was to have audiences *soaring* with Spider-Man. But the director approached the rest of the film with more subdued camera moves. "In my *Evil Dead* movies the purpose was to make something outrageous for the audience, something they'd never seen before," Raimi explained. "Those movies were trying to capture the world of the supernatural, to have the camera take the place of an unseen entity that doesn't even exist in our world. So I came up with different ways to move the camera, different lenses. Those images really drew attention to themselves, and it was fine that they did, but I didn't feel that was the proper approach for *Spider-Man*.

"I wanted audiences to be pulled into the film by the performances. It's such an important character, with generations and millions of fans, that I didn't want to intrude with my flashy filmic business. I didn't want it to stand between audiences and the character they love. I think audiences wanted to see a translation process, to see the character come to life. And I felt if they were to take notice of the camera, it'd be an intrusion into that very special relationship. So I tried to be very reserved with the camera."

The challenges of mounting the production were also complicated because movie filming is, by necessity, shot out of sequence. A production schedule must account for shooting with cast members (the principal photography), working on locations and sets, and filming the live-action background "plates" into which computer-generated creations are composited. But that sched-

ule is dependent on everything from the availability of stars and locations to the readiness of sets. "Scheduling can be done a hundred different ways," Bryce, who began laying out the *Spider-Man* schedule in May 2000, noted. "In terms of the building blocks of scheduling, my preference is to schedule a big action sequence anywhere except right at the beginning. I think it's important to start off slowly, to let the cast

ABOVE: Maguire and Raimi confer in front of the house in Queens that served as the exterior for the Parker home. The location was what production designer Neil Spisak wanted, a humble, "house-proud" street in which Peter's good character could be rooted.

LEFT: The location street where Peter Parker lives, Queens, New York.

and crew settle in and get to know each other." For *Spider-Man* the first scene that was shot would be a dramatic post-spider-bite scene when Peter arrives home, feeling ill from the supervenom coursing through his bloodstream.

From the actors' point of view, making a movie is decidedly different from theater, where performances begin at opening curtain and end with the final bow. "We actors are like a band of gypsies; you could have an emotional scene with someone you just met," Cliff Robertson, the veteran actor cast as Uncle Ben, said, smiling. "In fact, I remember on *Picnic*, my first movie, we were filming out in Kansas with Josh Logan—God love him—and Bill Holden, Rosalind Russell, all these famous people. And I didn't know beans about the camera. And my first scene was the *last* scene in the movie! It was where my character turns on his father. I'm on set and this man appears and says, 'Hi, son, I'm your dad!' That was my first damn scene in a movie, with an actor I'd never met before. I said, 'Josh, this is crazy.' He said, 'I know, it's called movies.' "

"Movies are a filmmaker's medium," Tobey Maguire said. "It's all about their vision, how

ABOVE LEFT: Cliff Robertson and Rosemary Harris as Uncle Ben and Aunt May. "I actually wasn't that familiar with the comic book—but I am now!" the actress says, laughing. "I read the comics during my research for the part, and I loved Aunt May's laconic thing. She doesn't mince words; what she says is very to the point. When Uncle Ben dies, she tries to take his place, to be there for Peter."

ABOVE RIGHT: Robertson and Raimi confer during a break in filming. The Uncle Ben character was a small but pivotal part. The production felt the Oscar-winning actor had the all-American persona to instantly project the sage presence of the father figure and moral force at the center of Peter Parker's world.

LEFT: Peter and MJ were portrayed in the film as neighbors who had been friends as kids but drifted apart during their high school years. MJ becomes part of the in crowd at Midtown High, not knowing Peter's secret—that he's always loved her. "It's a big challenge taking something out of the two-dimensional medium of a comic book, especially when you're going for a world of reality," producer Ian Bryce notes. "Spider-Man is a strong character piece enhanced by groundbreaking effects from Imageworks. At its heart, as the character says in the movie, it's a story about a boy and a girl."

Harry Osborn (James Franco) would be a troubled figure in the complex web in which Fate ensnares the main characters. Longing for the approval of his dad—who seems to take a more fatherly interest in Peter Parker—he also makes major moves on Mary Jane.

they see it, what the tone is. I try to get a sense of how a filmmaker is seeing things in their imagination, and I try to fit to that. I see even good films that are uneven as far as performances because one actor might be over the top, another coming in under the radar—different colors. In real life, human beings are quite different, but in a film things have to fit together."

Although the *Spider-Man* screenplay underwent the inevitable revisions during production, it wasn't until the script was settled that the coveted roles could be cast. Discussions about whether Peter's movie love interest would be his great comic-book love, Gwen Stacy—the woman killed by the Goblin during a shattering encounter in the pages of *The Amazing Spider-Man*—gave way early on to Mary Jane Watson. On the villain side, Electro and Sandman fell away, and the Green Goblin was left standing.

"Would it have been fun to have had six villains? Yes! Could we have afforded that? No." So concludes producer Laura Ziskin, former president of Fox 2000 Pictures and an executive producer (including credits on *Pretty Woman* and *As Good as It Gets*), whose focus was the script and actors.

"Some people say the financial issues and the creative issues involved in making a movie are separate, but they're not," Ziskin noted. "Every financial decision is a creative decision and every creative decision is a financial decision. But I think it was more satisfying from a storytelling viewpoint to have one villain. The Green Goblin, and the complexity of his relationship to Spider-Man, was very appealing to all of us."

Raimi wanted Tobey Maguire to be his Peter Parker. Maguire was in his mid-twenties, with a boyish look that could pass for the high school senior. Most important, Maguire had starred in an impressive list of films, including *Pleasantville*, *The Ice Storm*, *The Cider House Rules*, and *Wonder Boys*. But Maguire had never before taken on the pressures of a potential franchise-film blockbuster. "It's now sort of folklore, but the studio was not completely convinced about Tobey," Ziskin said. "I think the studio was just being cautious. They wanted to make sure they'd made the right choice, because Tobey had never done a movie like this before. So I said to Sam, 'Let's do a full-blown screen test, not something on videotape, but like in a movie, with a set and makeup, wardrobe and music.' "

The test would be an emotional moment of Peter Parker and Mary Jane at the grave of Uncle Ben. But Maguire notes he'd already done a *Spider-Man* screen test on video and was loath to repeat the process. "I was sold on Sam's vision and wanted to be part of the film," Maguire said, "but it was discouraging to be asked to do another test. I guess sometimes my ego gets in the way and I was considering not doing it. I talked to Sam and he said, 'Listen, you're my guy, you're the one I want to make this film with. Without you I feel lost and I'm scared I might not have a movie.' It was nice to know I had a partner, someone who believed in me. Because of his passion for me, I decided to do the screen test."

It was also a "long way," as Ziskin put it, from the eventual selection of Kirsten Dunst for the MJ role, so a test actress played opposite Maguire. They pulled out all the stops, which included a separate fight sequence. Although the Spider-Man costume wasn't ready, Maguire was given a blue leotard, which he did up Hong Kong style for a little bit of kung-fu fighting. "I decided to pull this leotard down around my waist and go topless," Maguire said. "That was my call; that's how I did the fight scene—a Bruce Lee kind of thing. It was kind of cool, a good time."

"The studio was blown away by Tobey's screen test, and thank God, because he's so much the heart and soul of the movie," Ziskin said, smiling. "That's when you know you've cast something right, when you can say, 'Nobody else could have played that role—*he is that guy!*' "

If this was a comic-book origin story, there'd be rapid-fire panels depicting the young actor preparing to accept the mantle of comic-book superhero, his poring over the first four years of the classic *Amazing Spider-Man* comics, and embarking on a workout regimen that included gymnastics and martial arts. And that was exactly what happened. Maguire had

This night scene test was designed to see how closely an Imageworks CG building could match a real structure. A location plate was shot, with the real Hotel Roosevelt first overlayed with a wireframe and match-moved—a process for matching both live-action and CG elements of digital composite. The final test plate was ultimately replaced by a virtual copy of the building, with lighting and rendering by Ben Lishka.

been training for almost three months prior to the planned start of principal photography scheduled for November 2000, and even when filming was pushed to January 2001, he kept training.

"The gymnastics training was particularly fun," Maguire recounted. "I did a lot of basic stuff to get some air sense, because there was a lot of wire work and you've got to be aware. I started jumping and doing basic flips on the trampoline, climbing up ropes, trying to get a decent-looking handspring."

Maguire was a gamer, reports stunt coordinator Jeff Habberstad, who early on put the star in a harness and cables rigged to the Sony soundstage permanents—or "perms," as they call the soundstage roof—then dropped him the equivalent of a four-story building. "Tobey did real good," Habberstad said, and smiled, recalling that test drop. "When a guy he's never met before says it's safe to be hooked onto a wire and dropped forty feet, that's a pretty good leap of faith, I'd say."

While all this was occurring, production designer Neil Spisak was deep into preparing the look for Spider-Man's home turf, which, unlike other movies based on comic-book characters, would not offer up a strangely stylized world. "That's kind of the point, that Spider-Man isn't some dark, weird character with a secret lair—he's part of New York City," Spisak noted. "Sam told me he wanted to bring out the human emotions of this high school kid coming to terms with these amazing powers, so the environments couldn't over-whelm the character's emotions. We wanted the movie to be real, but heightened enough that the strange occurrences could fit."

Spider-Man's New York was an interpretation, pieces of a big puzzle

In this daylight test, two towering buildings were replaced with virtual copies. The first shot (left) is actual photography, as evidenced by the light spot—actual light—on the building. The final shot (right) is the CG replication needed for freedom of movement and the addition of reflections. Lighting and rendering by Francisco de Jesus.

ABOVE, LEFT AND RIGHT: The Columbia University Genetic Research Institute lab where Peter suffers that fateful spider bite was actually staged in the main rotunda of the Natural History Museum in Los Angeles. The gigantic microscope pictured here conceals three sixteen-foot-tall bronze centerpiece statues, with Jim Ondrejko's construction crew covering them with three layers of protective bubble wrap and then adding the shell of plywood rings, plaster and paint, and fiberglass top portion. Set dressing added the flat screens, computers, and other details that transformed a museum into a mythical genetics laboratory.

BELOW LEFT: The Midtown High field trip arrives for the lecture on the wonders of genetic engineering.

that included both location filming and what Spisak called "scenery New York"—soundstage and back-lot sets built in California. "Scenery New York" would also include the Imageworks digital re-creation of Manhattan. "Spider-Man and the Green Goblin are airborne characters, so a good deal of their arena is in the upper region of skyscrapers," Ian Bryce explained. "That altitude restricts what you can do, practically, with stunt people. And the city of New York doesn't like camera helicopters flying around in certain areas to shoot plates, so we had to create some of that environment in the computer, to create our *alternative* version of background plates."

While a virtual environment was needed for scenes of a soaring Spider-Man, much of the world was built on sets by construction coordinator Jim Ondrejko and a 150-person crew that labored almost a year on the production. "I start with [production] drawings and figure out how I'm going to do a set, what materials I might use," Ondrejko explained. "I'll estimate the cost, and if they don't have enough budget, there'll be a redesign. I order the materials, and we build the structure. And then the plasterers come to make the wall whatever texture. The painters come in and do their work. Then the set dressers add the furniture and details, and the painters might come back and age the set, or if it's supposed to be outdoors, the greensman will bring in trees and greenery. There's also the metal-shop guys, sculptors, the laborers. I had a great crew, but we had a big challenge—to build a lot of sets!"

The conjured New York was augmented with location filming, including shooting in Forest Hills, Queens, Peter Parker's comic-book neighborhood and the location of the mythical Midtown High School. While interiors of the Parker home were built on soundstages, the location exterior had to be the right street, the perfect house.

"Peter needed to be defined by simple, humble roots, a street that was sweet and wonderful," Spisak recalled. "I had a phrase for the neighborhood, which Sam liked: 'House proud.' It had to be a place where everybody took an interest in their homes, where things were tidy and neat. And toward the end of May [2000] we found it."

The house on Sixty-ninth Road, a two-story bungalow built in the 1940s, was located by John Fedynich, the production's New York location manager. It was the real-life happy home of an older couple whose children had grown up there. "The whole neighborhood was thrilled to have us filming," Spisak said, smiling. "The crew was very considerate, and we weren't there long enough to really annoy them. It worked out well."

Although the characters of Uncle Ben and Aunt May wouldn't have a lot of screen time, superb actors were needed for the critical roles, and the production filled the bill with stage and screen actress Rosemary Harris and Cliff Robertson, who won a Best Actor Oscar for the 1968 film *Charly*. "Rosemary Harris is a remarkable actress. She had the strength and decency of Aunt May," Ziskin observed. "Cliff didn't have a lot of scenes, so he had to make an impression very fast; audiences had to care about him. The dignity he brings is instantaneous. He felt all-American and iconic."

Indeed, Robertson was handpicked by President John F. Kennedy to portray him in *PT-109*, a 1963 movie based on the president's World

Peter Parker, taking pictures for the Midtown High school paper, prepares to snap a shot of the spider cage the moment before boorish Flash Thompson (Joe Manganiello) nudges him, ruining the shot.

BELOW: The spider man behind Spider-Man was arachnologist Steven Kutcher. Besides doing "bug work" in Hollywood, his mission is to educate people on the importance of insects in the natural world.

BOTTOM, LEFT AND RIGHT: Kutcher's assistant, Michele N. Pollack, places a spider in a cage as director of photography Don Burgess sets up a shot.

War II experiences. And in 1977, in the very American underdog tradition—and in a real-life drama straight out of a Frank Capra film—Robertson discovered that a senior studio executive was forging his name on checks, and went to the authorities. "That was an odyssey," he said softly. "An FBI agent explained to me that I'd broken the unwritten Hollywood covenant that for eighty years had been: 'Thou shalt not confront a major mogul on corruption.' But I think our God puts certain hurdles in our life and maybe that's good, maybe they're a test. I didn't work for three and a half years, but I'm prouder of that than any awards I've won.

"For this movie I wasn't the star; I was part of the mosaic. But Sam was wonderfully supportive. He encouraged you to keep reaching. Sam explained to me that Uncle Ben was an avuncular influence who, with his wife, has raised Peter as if he were their own son. Ben is the moral center of the boy's life, and Peter's basic civility and morals is a reflection of the environment in which he was raised."

The house-proud feeling of the Parker nest was replicated on a Sony soundstage, with windows looking out on a chroma-trans—a special, blown-up color photo back-drop—of the neighborhood. "I adored that little house. It felt like you could walk out the front door and be in Queens!" Rosemary Harris said. "There was the wallpaper and a little knitting bag for me and lots of machinery for Cliff to play with, and cooking utensils and aprons—all so believable. I think it's called retro now, but there was a 1950s and '60s feel to the place."

The Parker house was the first set attended to by set decorator Karen O'Hara, who headed a department that numbered forty at its height and worked under the umbrella of Spisak's design department. O'Hara, whose credits include *Philadelphia*, *What Lies Beneath*, and Raimi's *For Love of the Game*, described her job as "getting all the elements within the architecture."

As the field trip moves on, Peter Parker finally gets a chance to shoot some pictures for his school paper and happily does so, as MJ playfully poses in front of the spider's cage.

"We had over a hundred sets for this film," O'Hara explained. "Basically, I first read the script and meet with the production designer, and we go over ideas for each set. We also talk about the character, because that'll affect the production design. I'll work on problem issues, then I focus on the sets in shooting order. I always feel I have the chance to create a space that will hopefully facilitate the actors *becoming* their character.

"For this film we had a lot of things made. For example, I have a collection of old fabric material, and during my research I came across a piece with a spider-web pattern. I showed it to Neil and he decided we'd design it as wallpaper for Peter's bedroom. So we had a graphic designer scan the fabric and come up with a pattern. The wallpaper is a subtle hint of Peter's future."

While Peter Parker's home was a refuge of love and security, Midtown High School was, as in the comics, a place where Peter is plagued by school bully supreme Flash Thompson (played by Joe Manganiello). But the movie would also rewrite some classic *Amazing Spider-Man* comics lore, with Mary Jane—the love interest Peter wouldn't meet until his college years in the comics—appearing as literally the girl next door, and as Peter's high school classmate and distant dream girl.

In a further twist from the comics, it's not a solo trip but a high school field trip where Peter Parker has his date with Fate. And unlike the radioactive spider of comic-book lore— redolent of the nuclear fallout fears hanging over the Cold War years in which Spider-Man was created—the movie's superspider would be genetically engineered at a genetics research institute lab.

The "spider man" behind Spider-Man was arachnologist Steven Kutcher whose motto, "Bugs Are My Business," has the tag line "Solving Your Bug Problems," something he's been doing in Hollywood with his insect work on films from *Arachnophobia* to *Jurassic Park* and *James and the Giant Peach*. His first memory of what was to be his life's work is of fireflies flitting in the night. "What excited me was the *magic* of bugs," the trained entomologist said. "Particularly for kids, anything that flies and lights up is just amazing. Insects are the thermometers of the world. There are over a million different types of insects that have over a million different jobs to do.

"But there are only about thirty thousand different kinds of known spiders. I didn't know much

Genetics Lab 10-31-00

ABOVE: The genetics lab designs begun by Wil Rees were further developed by James Carson, with a gigantic microscope as centerpiece of what would become a location set.

RIGHT: When Rees rendered this concept the production was planning to build a set for the lab where Peter Parker gets his fateful superspider bite. According to Rees, production designer Neil Spisak wanted a "stab in the dark" image contrasting modern technology with classic architecture. Note, far right, the chandelier from which the spider has webbed down to where Peter Parker is photographing a spider display.

about spiders until I took a class in terrestrial arthropods. I learned about spiders that live underwater, spiders that make little domes, spiders that build trap doors, spiders that jump ten or twelve times their body length, spiders that make balls of sticky silk to spin and catch things out of the air—I was amazed! And like all insects, spiders hunt for food, find mates, build homes, do things with their tiny brains the most powerful computer chip can't do."

When Kutcher and his assistants Michele Pollack, Matt Moran, and Maia Wolff arrived at the lab set, the effect of a spider dropping onto Maguire's hand from the ceiling was being attempted with a plastic spider on a line of monofilament. "I was across the room watching them lower this plastic spider," Kutcher recalls, "and Sam asked me how fast a spider should drop. I thought I should be diplomatic, so I said, 'Well, you have to drop it fast enough that you don't realize it's plastic.' Sam is very perceptive; he understood exactly what I was saying, and he said, 'Let's use a real one.' "

Kutcher met both the art department's designs for a fantastic mutant superspider and the director's concerns that the spider be small enough to be unnoticed as it "webbed down" from the ceiling onto Peter Parker's hand. The real-life "hero" spider Kutcher selected was a brownish Steatoda, a nonlethal relation of the black widow. Then Jens Schnabel, an artist subcon-

ABOVE LEFT: In the Recombination Lab, superspiders have been produced from the genetic information from three spiders, each encompassing abilities ranging from strength and super leaping prowess, webbing with the proportionate tensile strength of steel, and reflexes bordering on precognition—"spider sense." The specific spiders posing here as the three test subjects are, from left to right, Agelenopsis funnel weaver, the Kukulcania, and Delana cancerides.

ABOVE RIGHT: The mutant superspider. The enthusiastic lab tour guide marvels at the possibility of this spider unlocking the secrets of the transference of genetic code. Of course, it's still too early to experiment on humans . . .

LEFT: Kutcher's assistants use a brush to place the superspider up in the monofilament strands from which it will web down.

BOTTOM: When Peter discovers his ability to produce sticky, silken webbing, the results are spectacular. The "organic" decision was a major departure from the comic book and, briefly, a controversial move among some Spidey fans. But Raimi reasoned it was too fantastic to imagine a high school kid, no matter how brilliant, creating a substance beyond the ken of major, multinational corporations.

BELOW, RIGHT AND LEFT: After a fevered night convalescing from the swollen spider bite, Peter discovers his amazing new abilities. His body has naturally buffed up and he doesn't need his glasses because he suddenly has 20/20 vision—"puny" Parker no more!

tracted from Warner Bros., meticulously painted on the red and blue design pattern, the colors of Spider-Man. "Just like [for] a person undergoing an operation, we put the spider to sleep and restricted the spider with tape," Kutcher explained, "and how I put the spider to sleep is one of my secrets."

The mutant spider's ceiling webbing was handmade by model makers working under John Frazier. From there, the production's spider man and his crew got up on a ladder with the painted live-action spider posed off camera on the end of a paintbrush, lined up to web down on its own spider strand onto Maguire's hand. "If you imagine the lightest feather floating in the air, that's how fast a spider webs down," Kutcher explained. "We used this web-down effect a number of times on the picture. Since the spider doesn't know how high it is, it'll keep putting out a line of silk until it reaches the ground. Tobey was a little nervous, because it was a real spider, but using the real thing gives an actor something to react to, as opposed to computer-generating it."

The spider dropped and bit the unsuspecting teen. Then it was back to the first scene filmed by the production, with Peter Parker going through the change.

"That first scene, Peter comes home and is feeling ill because his body is transforming, but he doesn't know anything other than he's ill," Raimi recounted. "He staggers into his bedroom feeling weak and pale, slightly dizzy. He wants to make it to the bed but realizes he can't and actually crawls on his knees across the floor and, shivering, pulls the blanket down over himself and passes out."

Little did he know what was to come.

ABOVE: Peter sets to work designing his homemade wrestling outfit. Note, above his desk, the inspirational photos Peter snapped of MJ during the field trip.

LEFT: Peter begins to come to terms with his powers, getting that web-shooting wrist action just right.

CHAPTER THREE

The evil that men do

Willem Dafoe recalls being in Spain working on a film when he got a telephone call from Sam Raimi. The director wanted to talk about *Spider-Man* and the role of the Green Goblin.

"Usually, when someone talks to you about a film, it'll be in broad concepts, or why they think you're good for a particular role," Dafoe recalled. "Well, Sam starts telling me the story of Spider-Man. He talked to me for two hours! Every ten minutes he'd say, 'Can you hear me, are you listening to this?' I'd say, 'Yeah, go, Sam, go.' I was just taken by the way he spoke in very smart, specific, and psychological terms. The comics spoke to him as deeply as the most sophisticated drama; he wasn't coming from a place that was cynical. I thought, 'Man, I want to do this movie.' Because we'd get it both ways. There'd be a lot of Big Movie payoff—we'd get to have fun with the hardware and melodrama—but we'd also get to go deeper with some of the relationships and the complex psychology."

Dafoe's roles over a long career have included sinners (Rick Masters in *To Live and Die in L.A.*), saints (Jesus in *The Last Temptation of Christ*), and even creatures of the night (an Oscar-nominated turn as Nosferatu in *Shadow of the Vampire*). The role of Norman Osborn, head of OsCorp Industries, presented a tortured character with an intriguing Jekyll/Hyde split that erupts into the maniacal, glider-flying Goblin. At the heart of the character was an emotional triangle, a conflict between his anguished feelings for his son Harry, and a fatherly interest in Peter Parker, Harry's best friend.

LEFT: Peter gets ready to rumble!

BELOW: As in the comics origin, Peter Parker tests out his powers in the wrestling ring, now going up against the bruising Bone Saw McGraw. The production imagined a thrown-together wrestling costume topped off with a stenciled and sprayed spider shirt.

As with Spider-Man, a computer-generated version of the Green Goblin was created, a process that involved full-body cyberscanning and digital photography to collect the raw data for the virtual replicants. "It was a whole-day affair," Dafoe recalled of the process. "You dress up in a suit and do these Muybridge studies against a grid so they get your movements. You do vocal sounds and facial expressions so they can [digitally] replicate your speech if they have to. Then they scan your body from all angles. I was really spooked when they scanned me: 'We've got him!' So, basically they can make a computer-generated Willem."

But while the film would boast dazzling effects, the attraction for its cast members, which also included James Franco as Harry Osborn and J. K. Simmons as *Daily Bugle* chief J. Jonah Jameson, was the character-based drama. And, as usual, the actors' preparation would take into

ABOVE LEFT: The OsCorp boardroom, a set built and shot on a soundstage at Warner Bros.

ABOVE RIGHT: Norman Osborn (Willem Dafoe) sits at the head of OsCorp, but one senses the intrigues swirling around him. Dafoe admits he came to the production green in comic-book knowledge. "I feel guilty, but I don't really have a connection to the comic book. But as an actor my job is to create a personal relationship to what I'm doing. Sometimes you're freed when you don't have a previous stake in the material. You don't have obligations to serve certain notions; you can deal with it in a very direct way."

BELOW RIGHT: Norman begins to hear the Goblin's voice in his head. "We like Marvel villains to have a point of view," executive producer Arad says. "Norman Osborn has tremendous insecurities; he has a mental illness. Here's a man raising his son alone—there must be a tragic story with his wife. She must have left him! Does Harry remind him of her? Does he love his boy or hate him? Then he meets a kid like Peter who he feels he can relate to better. Now we have a conflict!"

account the nonlinear nature of movie acting. "It's about actors doing their homework and knowing where they are from moment to moment in the whole of the performance," Raimi said of filming. "It's like being a musician and knowing the whole of a symphony and you're performing little bits at a time."

"That's an interesting analogy Sam comes up with," Cliff Robertson reflected. "I'd also compare the process of actors doing their preparation to a Duke Ellington rehearsal, where there appears to be disharmony and anarchy and everybody seems off on their own riffs. But that's not it at all; it's the spontaneous genius within these musicians, all working their way to a meeting spot. When actors rehearse, the air is filled with questions, a wonderful energy is generated. There's a creative process where, ideally, things emerge.

"And from that comes the knowledge of your character. Theoretically, if you've truly assimilated the character, you should be able to say what he or she would do in any given circumstance."

Willem Dafoe spoke to that point when asked about his working relationship with Tobey Maguire. "As on any film, we all worked with the script and saw how dialogue fit and made sure we knew the story. Tobey was insightful and perceptive and very, very good in his script analysis of the psychology of Peter Parker. That was very impressive."

James Franco came to the role of Harry Osborn fresh from starring as the true-life title character in *James Dean*, a 2001 Turner Network Television feature presentation. Although the young, doomed movie idol seemed a world apart from rich kid Harry Osborn, Franco noted a striking similarity. "Dean was neglected by his own father, just like Harry is. Norman's a father who's overwhelmed by his business interests, and his son, who is at the end of his priorities, suffers deeply because of that."

During the rehearsal phase, Franco quietly, subtly began stepping into the persona of the

BELOW RIGHT: Maguire, Dunst, and Raimi in the midst of setting up a shot in the Midtown High cafeteria set. "Acting for me is about being in the moment and being truthful to what your character has to say, being with the other actor and committing completely to what's going on in the scene," Dunst says. "Tobey and I would just feed off each other. You're on the same page and you inspire each other. You're not even conscious of what you're doing."

BELOW LEFT: The stars get set for the scene in which Peter uses his superreflexes to catch a falling MJ. She'll smile and notice his blue eyes—but then move on to Flash Thompson's table.

vulnerable son. "When we were together I tried to take on the admiration Harry has, to project that onto Willem. I already respected Willem as an actor, but I tried to add a shade of the admiring son, putting him up on a pedestal. It's not like I kissed his feet; it was in my own head, a way of getting the feeling going by letting my respect for Willem flow. When we were in the scenes together and all of a sudden he's Norman Osborn giving me the cold shoulder, it was easy to feel hurt because of the feelings of respect I'd let free."

Maguire captured the joy of the misfit kid who suddenly experiences "this miracle," as Robertson termed it, in an exhilarating sequence in which he leaps from building to building. That first burst of superhero energy was not only storyboarded, but was one of the sequences taken into an "animatics" stage by storyboard team member Andrew Jimenez, who began his work on the computer-animated storyboards in April 2000 and was done before actual filming commenced.

"Animatics, until fairly recently, was in the realm of feature animation where you're drawing everything by hand, so preplanning and working out camera angles is absolutely necessary," Jeffrey Lynch explained. "People were interested in using animatics on this film because it gives you an idea of pacing and how to hone things before principal photography. We didn't have time to do the whole movie as animatics, so we concentrated on visual effects sequences, which were going to be costly and had a lot of logistical demands."

These animatics were different from the video-game-quality 3-D computer graphics "previsu-

Director Sam Raimi carefully developed and prepared every sequence, from live-action to visual effects sequences, with hand-drawn storyboard art. Complex action sequences, which typically involved computer-generated effects, were further developed with early animatics prepared by Andrew Jimenez and, later in postproduction, through Imageworks' own CG previsualization.

ABOVE: In this image from the car-chase sequence, Mark Andrews' storyboard art showing Spider-Man swinging over a police car was scanned by Jimenez and the art separated into layers and combined with a rough, 3-D textured environment—a fusion of 2-D and 3-D that brought a static storyboard image to life.

RIGHT: Sony Pictures Imageworks' previsualization for the car chase utilized rough 3-D models to plot out the composition and dynamics for the effects shot. (During the early storyboard phase, the artists imagined Spider-Man giving chase in his classic costume. By principal photography it had been decided that Peter would be clad in his wrestling costume.)

ABOVE: A location stunt in New York utilized both Maguire and his stuntmen to give the live, in-camera illusion of the superpowered teenager making his incredible rooftop leaps. This shot illustrates the stunt's sheer scale, with cranes rising high above a six-story building and holding the track from which the performers will be picked up and flown.

TOP RIGHT AND ABOVE RIGHT: Maguire poised at the rooftop, with stuntman Mark Wagner (left) helping steady the star for the scene where Peter prepares to shoot his webbing and take his first death-defying swing. The multi-faceted athleticism intrinsic to Spider-Man necessitated a team of Spidey stuntmen. "Tobey had three or four stunt doubles because there are so many facets to his character's physical prowess," producer Ian Bryce says. "Early in preproduction we came up with the notion of multiple Spider-Man doubles: a tumbling double, an acrobat, a more typical stunt double."

LEFT: Up, up, and away! The rig that flew Tobey Maguire was controlled by a cable running down from the over-head track and attached to an air ram on the ground. With the operator keeping the stunt performer in sight, a push of the button at the end of the cable sent an electrical signal that pushed air pressure into a cylinder that pushed the piston attached to the cable rigged to the stunt person.

alization" models that Imageworks prepared. What distinguished the *Spider-Man* animatics was that they were created "in the early storyboard phase," Jimenez explained. "It was down and dirty—let's create a shot! We were essentially faking a 3-D camera move." Jimenez credits Brad Bird, director of *The Iron Giant*, with developing the innovative fusion of 2-D/3-D as a concept design tool, a bridge between tactile work and the three-dimensional imagery possible in the digital realm. Lynch, who'd worked on *The Iron Giant*, pitched the concept to Raimi, who liked the idea.

Jimenez scanned storyboards into a computer and then used Photoshop to separate out the drawings—for example, tracing out each drawing in a sequence of a leaping Spider-Man—and layered the sequential images over rough, 3-D mock-ups of the environment. The surroundings were simple, just detailed enough to provide a three-dimensional effect, such as pencil sketches of buildings "texture-mapped" over 3-D shapes. (This was a primitive version of the technique Imageworks used—at a vastly more sophisticated level—to create their photorealistic New York.) The elements were then composited using After Effects software, the virtual camera allowing for motion through a scene and rough animation. Added effects flourishes, from police searchlights to explosions, further enhanced the dimensional effect. Sealed with a temporary soundtrack, the animatic result was a virtual blueprint for a shot.

The actual effect of Peter Parker bounding from rooftop to rooftop involved stunt coordinator Habberstad's team and a rig built by John Frazier's special effects company, FXperts. A veteran of thirty-seven years in show business, Frazier has worked on movies

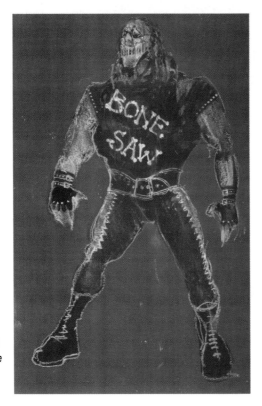

Wrestlers and costume concept art by costume designer James Acheson.

ranging from a roster of Clint Eastwood productions, including the Oscar-winning *Unforgiven*, to *Armageddon* and *Pearl Harbor*. Frazier has always had a thing for wire work, from flying Lucille Ball on an early Bob Hope TV special to a post-*Spider-Man* gig flying a foursome of Victoria's Secret lingerie models.

The rig that flew Tobey Maguire in his first burst of Spidey powers was an air ratchet, which Frazier described as "an air-operated piston. Stunt guys use air ratchets all the time for jerking guys up and down and into walls. We worked with Jeff Habberstad and designed some of the stunt rigs and collaborated on a lot of stuff."

The sequence had the unfortunate label "jump-jump-splat," with our hero ending his first super outing by flattening himself into a building wall. While a stuntman performed the splat, Maguire was swung over the twenty-five-foot-wide gap between two alcoves on the roof of a seven-story apartment building. The rig itself was a horizontal, motorized aluminum track thirty feet in the air and two hundred feet long, the length of the apartment building, held on each end of the building by cranes.

ABOVE: The wrestling auditorium set built on stage 27 at Sony. Suspended in the permanents, forty feet above the ring, was the 20' x 20' x 20' aluminum cage in which Peter and Bone Saw have their showdown. "We lowered the cage down with hydraulics and steel cables," John Frazier explains. "The scary thing was as it was coming down it had to close before it lowered over the ringside audience. It was a timing thing."

LEFT: Real-life pro Randy "Macho Man" Savage, who plays Bone Saw, discusses some of the finer points of the wrestler's art with an attentive Sam Raimi.

TOP LEFT: Spidey stuntman Chris Daniels did a lot of the ring cage stunts. Daniels, a fan of such "ground pounding" stunts as getting ratcheted through breakaway walls, got his chance for some physical stuff in the wrestling cage with Savage. "He's a big old boy," Daniels says, smiling. "It was pretty cool."

TOP, LEFT TO RIGHT: Peter seems down for the count—but never underestimate the proportionate strength of a spider! "Shooting this WWF-style wrestling ring was the most fun for me," cinematographer Don Burgess says. "I had the ring lit from the perms with what I called 'disco lights.' From a computerized dimmer board we could design different patterns and lighting scenarios."

MIDDLE LEFT: What's a little wrestling without a folding chair upside the head? Raimi stands in the background, setting up the shot—and staying out of the way.

MIDDLE RIGHT: A cameraman records a kick to the camera eye.

BOTTOM LEFT: Peter crouches down, steeling himself for a superpowered leap. Note the thin cables, attached on either side of a harness hidden under the costume.

"The difference between rigging in a soundstage and rigging at a location is that indoors we have this truss system built overhead in the perms of each sound-stage, and we hook all our cables and wires up there," Mark Wagner, one of a team of Spidey stunt doubles, explained. "Outdoors we have to use cranes, and it makes our job a little more challenging because we have to make sure the cranes aren't in the shot or throwing shadows into the shot."

In a later scene, as in the classic comics origin, Peter tests his powers by getting into the wrestling ring. In the comic book he fought Crusher Hogan, while the movie offered Bone Saw McGraw, played by real-life rassler Randy "Macho Man" Savage. In the comics Peter competes for $100, but forty years later the pot has grown to $3,000.

In the *Amazing Fantasy* origin tale, Peter Parker is green in the ways of the whole superpower/secret identity thing—he enters the ring dressed in old clothes and a mask to conceal himself from ridicule should he fail. In the movie, what emerges as the first Spider-Man costume was a similarly tossed-together affair. "We inferred this eclectic mix of things he finds in his closet," costume designer Acheson noted. "My associate designer Lisa Tomczeszyn came up with the idea of having a homemade spider stencil he spray-paints on a T-shirt, a ski mask and sweat pants, and old red and white sneakers."

The battleground was a wrestling cage lowered from the ceiling of

TOP LEFT: Peter Parker gets a rude welcome to the wide world of sports, as the fight promoter (Larry Joshua) stiffs him of the promised jackpot.

BELOW LEFT: The punk gunman gets the goods on the shifty promoter, much to Peter's delight—and eventual anguish.

TOP RIGHT: Location filming at the New York Public Library, site of Ben Parker's murder.

LEFT: *Peter finds himself in the path of a speeding truck but escapes—vertically (much to the confusion of the harried driver). Artist: Doug Lefler.*

BOTTOM: *This early Wil Rees mood shot shows Spider-Man poised at the corner of a building, waiting for the car driven by his uncle's killer. (The final script would have Peter Parker chase the killer in his wrestling outfit.) Production designer Neil Spisak specifically requested orange glows from windows and skylights to represent Spider-Man's rage, part of the subtle color palette used throughout the film.*

the auditorium, the first thing special effects man Frazier and his crew did on the film. "The cage idea was one of Sam's whims," Frazier recalled. "Sam is so cool, he comes up with things like that."

In a twist on the original story, even though Peter wins, an unscrupulous promoter stiffs him. So when that same promoter is robbed, Peter, who has a chance to catch the thief, does nothing. "Peter is not a selfish kid. On a normal day he'd have stopped this man, even if he didn't have any powers, but he was like a lot of people in this world who have been pushed around or never been

TOP: *Although rendered as quick, rough sketches, these storyboards pack the two-fisted power of raw comic book pulp fiction.*

Uncle Ben's killer seeks refuge in the Battery Maritime Building—but he can't escape the shadow of Spider-Man. The killer tries to break out of the old building, but Spider-Man grabs him. In this boarded sequence, which imagined Spider-Man in his classic costume, Peter Parker unmasks himself as he realizes the killer is the two-bit thief he once had a chance to stop. Artist: Mark Andrews.

BOTTOM: *In this production concept painting, the cornered killer fires at Spider-Man, a figure of dark shadow and reflected light in the rooftop beams where the bullets are ricocheting. "I do a black-and-white line drawing first," artist Rees explains, "and make a copy. I'll use marker inks and do all my highlight and midtones in gouache."*

noticed," Avi Arad said. "This promoter has just told him to get lost. 'I owe you nothing.' So, Peter's reaction is very normal, very human. Unfortunately, destiny is such you can never tell why you have to step up to the plate; you can never tell what's on the other side. And then he realizes that all he had to do was stop this man, and because he didn't, he loses the man he loves and respects."

Ben's death comes during a carjacking, and Peter, who has just had an argument with his uncle, arrives at the crime scene in time to hold his uncle in his arms as he dies. The death scene was filmed in front of the New York Public Library, and that day, when Cliff Robertson came to the set, he wasn't girding himself for a dramatic death scene. "You prepare yourself for the most unexpected thing that's going to happen to you by *not* preparing," he said. "You become so involved in the preceding scene that you're not thinking about it. You're not expecting to be shot."

LEFT: A greenscreen setup gives the illusion of Peter vertically crawling up a building to get a better vantage point from which to chase the car driven by his uncle's killer.

BELOW RIGHT: Peter shoots a strand of webbing—added later in CG—and prepares to truly test his powers in the desperate chase after his uncle's killer. In this first foray into crime-fighting, the production wanted to show a young man struggling to master his fantastic powers. "It's inconsistent in the comics, how strong Spider-Man is, how far he can leap and swing," Raimi notes. "We were trying to do what looked believable. Pulling myself into Spider-Man's world, maybe he can't leap four stories, but he can leap two stories, and maybe he lands badly, as the kid still learning to be Spider-Man. Maybe that'll help it look real. There was no general formula except we used our combined senses—the producers, myself, Tobey Maguire, senior visual effects supervisor John Dykstra, the Imageworks animators—to make him as believable as possible, a human being who's also a superhero."

LEFT: Uncle Ben's killer falls to his death in this Rees concept image. Although Rees recalls the circumstances of the scene as somewhat ambiguous, the unmistakable force clearly implies Spider-Man has thrown the killer out the window. The final film, however, would conform to the classic ethics of a superhero who doesn't kill. (The killer would indeed fall out the window, but by tripping over his own feet when cornered by Spider-Man.)

ABOVE: In this filmed image, Peter Parker surveys the death scene where the cornered killer has just tripped himself and fallen to his death. It's just sinking in: "With great power there must also come great responsibility."

LEFT: The killer gets the drop on the unmasked Spider-Man—but he's forgotten how many shots he fired in all the excitement. A fatal misstep—or is it a push?—and another perpetrator of violence meets a violent end. Artist: Mark Andrews.

TOP, LEFT TO RIGHT: Peter Parker, exhausted emotionally from his encounter with the killer, seeks solitude atop the Chrysler Building in these moody storyboard panels. Artist: Mark Andrews.

MIDDLE LEFT: Peter Parker broods atop a set piece that, when combined with Imageworks movie magic, will place him high above Manhattan.

MIDDLE RIGHT AND BOTTOM, LEFT TO RIGHT: The work of Neil Spisak's design department often overlapped with other departments. These shots for the Chrysler Building sequence, prepared by assistant art director François Audouy, illustrate how through digital previsualization (or previz) the art department could anticipate how other departments might realize the scene. "We used previz to help spawn conversation and determine how much set would need to be built," Audouy explained. "For this shot we also did a virtual camera move with a thirty-five-millimeter lens so we could show director of photography Don Burgess how a set would fit with the bluescreen."

The killing was a moment meant to echo throughout the movie, a tragedy that informs Peter's responsibility for his secret superpowers. "All Ben and May know is the boy seems to be going through an upsetting emotional experience," Robertson explained. "Then Ben and Peter have a little confrontation and almost immediately afterwards, Ben is shot. So Peter is not only confronted with the shock of his father-figure dying, but the remorse that their last time together he was unkind to Ben. Because Ben dies early in the picture, his memory had to be residual to Spider-Man's conscience whenever he was in a moral dilemma."

Peter Parker's first crime-fighting appearance as Spider-Man is the chase after the carjacked vehicle driven by his uncle's killer. Dressed in his wrestling duds of ski mask, sweat clothes, and sneakers, he scales an alley wall and flies through the night on his webbing, jumping from car roof to car roof. In the fantastic sequence, the production ran the gamut from completely CG animation and cityscape to the super-CG character interacting with live-action footage filmed in downtown Los Angeles of the killer's car and pursuing police.

The exterior place for where Peter corners his uncle's killer came from the Battery Maritime Building in New York's Battery Park, and the interior was a Sony stage 15 set of a gloomy, decaying place of rusted pipes and peeling paint. There, justice is served up by accident, a fatal misstep by the killer that sends him crashing through a window. Peter's shattering lesson learned—that with great power must also come great responsibility—would then take shape in the costume of a hero.

The classic costume faced an all-important test as the team confronted the question, in the summer of 2000, of whether or not they could make the CG Spider-Man look real. Laura Ziskin recalled the surprise that awaited Sony executives when she screened the completed test footage for them. "I called up John Calley and Amy Pascal and told them we'd put Tobey in the suit and had him crawling up a building and we'd shot a test and wanted to show them. We went to

Spider-Man takes a breather atop the Chrysler Building, having eluded the police helicopter at right, in this Wil Rees establishing-shot concept.

the screening room and I showed the test of the CGI Spider-Man—they thought it was Tobey! Then I told them that was the computer-generated Spider-Man."

"I was completely fooled by that test," Pascal said. "I was thinking that Tobey looked like he was in great shape. Then when I was told it was CG, it was, 'Oh, my God!' "

While Spencer Cook, Imageworks' lead Spidey animator, focused on a wall-crawling effect of the superhero in his classic costume, other animators worked on swing test animation, which was applied to the early teaser theatrical trailer. "My challenge on the test was to make it look like a real guy doing this, but one with enhanced abilities," Cook explained. "I tried to get the sense that he was pulling himself up a vertical surface, that he could stick to a surface and crawl up it. So I gave it a feel of spiders, some elements of lizards."

Convincing as it was, that CG Spidey was still the most primitive incarnation of the figure that would eventually be bounding and swinging across movie screens. In fact, the test model was based on a generic human character model found in the Imageworks digital library and had required a major overhaul.

Digital effects supervisor Scott Stokdyk noted that the test model required so much reconfiguring—adding

This establishing shot of OsCorp's underground lab—ultimately cut from the film—was originally planned to have Willem Dafoe striding across a catwalk set to his lab. The low-resolution computer-generated catwalk and figures are composited against Wil Rees's artwork.

the distinctive costume (complete with raised suit webbing to match the look of the practical costume), pushing and pulling muscle mass, replacing feet with boot-type shoe wear—that once the work was done, the original generic model had thoroughly mutated. And most important of all, that early wall-crawler would be a long way from the performance animation that would ultimately be required for the character.

But taking the test model out for a spin was the best way to figure out the superqualities the Imageworks modelers would have to build into the final model. "As I was animating that test model, I was thinking of ways we could improve on it for the real one we'd use in the movie," Cook said. "The test model had more realistic limitations to it, but we'd have to open up those physical limits because Spider-Man can move and bend in more extreme ways than a normal human. There were also little things, like getting the exaggerated look of Spider-Man's fingers when he grips a wall. The test was helpful in establishing a lot of the ways our Spider-Man would move and, from a technical standpoint, what we'd need for our real model."

The test shot of Spider-Man crawling up a wall would be significantly changed in the pace and mood of the animation and adapted for the scene where Peter begins the chase for his uncle's killer. The sequence begins with another example of the illusory power of the movies, when Tobey Maguire runs down an alleyway and, as he's tearing off his jacket and getting down to his ski mask and sweat pants wrestling outfit, he transforms into the supercharacter incarnate, his computer-generated counterpart who hits the wall and crawls up it.

Once at the top of the building, the character gains a vantage point on the car driven by his uncle's killer. "We see a wide view of the street, the criminal, and the cop cars chasing him," Cook explained. "There's a very cool shot where we did a greenscreen of Tobey, a close-up of his face, and as the camera rotates around him, we switch to the digital model. At this point the character is afraid, because he's not totally confident with his newfound spider powers. He shoots his webbing and then starts swinging and the camera starts traveling with him."

In addition to the CG Spider-Man, there would be many faces behind the mask of Spider-Man, from Tobey Maguire to a team of stuntmen versed in gymnastics and wire-rig flying. The stunt work itself was heavy on flying wire work ranging from outdoor swings to soundstage drops in front of a greenscreen. Stunt coordinator Jeff Habberstad, whose credits include *Mission Impossible 2*, *The Sixth Sense*, and *Men in Black*, brought to the production all the tools of his trade he could fit into a forty-eight-foot trailer, from an editing suite for preparing test videos to three industrial sewing machines for preparing the flying harnesses.

An invaluable part of Habberstad's stunt team and rigging crew—165 persons strong for *Spider-Man*—was Jake Brake, an outside vendor who built forty-three different harnesses for the show. "Jake

Concept views of the industrial-looking exterior of the OsCorp research facility. Art by François Audouy.

started with the military and got heavily into parachute harnesses and rigging on James Bond movies," Habberstad explained. "The harnesses he made for *Spider-Man* were of various types of nylon blended material, similar to parachute harnesses. We had harnesses that covered the whole upper body; others went around the waist; some were little wrist and ankle straps. What was great was these harnesses didn't show any bulging through that Spider-Man suit." Those that did—as well as visible rigs and cables—would be digitally removed.

But the one for whom the character truly got under his skin was stuntman Chris Daniels, who served as Maguire's Peter Parker double and a member of the *Spider-Man* stunt team. Lifecasts of both Daniels and a buffed-up Maguire helped produce a fiberglass suit that would be worn underneath the formfitting costume by the Spidey stunt team (with a special, custom Spider-Man suit also prepared for Maguire).

Daniels would also be scanned and used as raw data for the building of Imageworks' CG supercharacter. "Chris Daniels was critical to the creation of our CG model," Scott Stokdyk explained. "We had his body scanned to a T." Meanwhile, scans of Maguire concentrated on his face for use on the CG hero, notably the visible parts of the ski-mask costume and tears in the classic costume mask during the dramatic final battle with the Goblin.

For Daniels, who had wrestled and played football at Estero High School in Florida and spent years as a competitive jazz and hip-hop dancer, being part of the *Spider-Man* team had him recalling personal parallels to the Spidey legend. "It's funny, but when I was in elementary school I was kind of a dorky kid with glasses who always got picked on—just like Peter Parker. Then I had an eye operation and didn't have to wear glasses anymore and started working out and getting athletic and popular. When I was thirteen, I was part of a five-person team that won a gymnastics competition dressed as superheroes. The others dressed like Superman, Batman and Robin, Wonder Woman—I was Spider-Man. My mom made my costume, and I had to stand still as she drew every single black spiderweb line onto this spandex suit she'd made.

"When we started the movie, Sam took me and Mark [stuntman Wagner] aside and told us to do our homework, to get the comic books and watch videos of the old animated TV shows, to know all his poses. What was kind of weird was when I was in the costume I really felt like I was Spider-Man! When I had that mind-set, the poses flowed much better. It was a confidence thing—'Hey! *I'm Spider-Man.*'"

THE SPIDER SUIT

"The world of Spider-Man is this fantastic metropolis and the idea of this urban Tarzan swooping down into the streets of Manhattan," costume designer James Acheson says. Acheson, a native of England and a three-time Oscar winner, chuckles at the notion that with a résumé that includes *The Last Emperor* and *Dangerous Liaisons,* he was asked to create superhero fantasy costumes. "It was brilliantly incongruous, but I was thrilled. I didn't exactly grow up with it in England, but Spider-Man was a familiar icon to me, as was the whole world of Marvel Comics. Actually, it got me back to my fantasy roots because I started in television doing *Dr. Who.*"

Acheson was surprised that, unlike the heightened atmosphere and stylized look of Gotham City of the Batman movies, *Spider-Man* was set squarely in modern Manhattan. "Therefore, our early pitch was to modernize Spider-Man," Acheson explained. "We looked at modern plastics and synthetics, and I had this notion of a semitransparent mask so you could see his face, a kind of helmet, that wasn't part of a spandex suit. But the more we messed with it, the further away we got from the spirit of Spider-Man. Spidey had to have an athletic grace, not be trapped in a heavy latex mask. So, after this very elaborate journey, we came back to the idea of making the costume look as much like the comic book as possible. It looks simple, but it was the hardest costume I ever had to make."

"Even though Jim wasn't necessarily a Spider-Man fan growing up in England, he 'gets it,'" a smiling Warren Manser, who was brought on to the costume design

BOTTOM LEFT: Early James Carson concept art for the "helmet" mask proposed by James Acheson.

The more James Acheson's costume design department rethought Spider-Man's costume, the more inevitable became the return to the final result seen here—the character's classic look.

BELOW, BOTTOM RIGHT: The Spider-Man costume design emphasized a lean musculature; getting that effect in the physical costume was the hard part. The ideal was the look of the anatomically stylized Batman foam suit that grew in sophistication through four Batman productions. However, that suit was too cumbersome for the acrobatic web-slinger. What Acheson's team produced was a lightweight, anatomically stylized muscle suit underneath a sophisticated stretch fabric costume. Concept art by Miles Teves.

SPIDERMAN MASK CONCEPT 6.19.00
Material- hard shell semi- translucent polymer.
Vertical split for asses. Potential eye color/ opacity shift.

Peter Parkers eyes and vocal articulations somewhat visible through the mask.

team by Acheson, said. "He gets the strengths of these characters, the dynamics and boldness of the [costume] patterns. He was already familiar with the idea of escalating a look and a costume to a level of maximum impact. He adapted very quickly to not just the look of the Marvel universe, but the idea of the superhero."

Joining Acheson on the arduous five-month process were lead sculptor Ray Scott; Amalgamated Dynamics, Inc. (ADI), an L.A.–based animatronics and makeup company cofounded by Alec Gillis and Tom Woodruff Jr., specializing in the design and creation of characters; and John David Ridge, Inc., an L.A.–based company that creates clothing and provides costume fittings for movies.

The process began with top-to-toe lifecasts of Tobey Maguire and stuntman Chris Daniels. From a mold of the lifecasts, ADI prepared fiberglass copies. Ray Scott then applied clay

BELOW: Stuntman Mark Wagner gets tended to, revealing the muscle suit over which goes the silk-screened outer costume.

RIGHT, MIDDLE, AND BOTTOM: A Spidey stuntman gets suited up, with clip-on Oakley eyepieces the last to go on. Early in the production, black eyepieces were tested, and were abandoned in favor of the more traditional silver/white version. The costume was all one piece, with two zippers on each side and a U-shaped zipper in the back at the bottom of the belt. "The suits were all the same size, but stretchy enough to cover all of us," stuntman Mark Wagner says.

to the fiberglass and sculpted a subtly enhanced musculature.

John David Ridge described the classic costume itself as beginning with stuntman Chris Daniels wearing a white unitard, a one-piece stretch nylon fabric upon which Acheson drew muscle highlight and lowlight areas in heavy pencil, which were then air-brushed the appropriate red and blue. The one-piece suit was glued flat to a board, photographed, and sent to Imageworks, where it was scanned. Marzette Bonar of the art department took the lead in painting the grid patterns for the muscle definitions. "When the suit is off and in its relaxed state, it looks like nothing," Acheson explained. "But the textural pattern developed at Imageworks was a series of oval shapes, like a grid of shadings, which simulates the natural hills and valleys of muscle structure, and when this colored fabric is stretched over the muscle undersuit it tricks your eyes in a 3-D trompe l'oeil effect."

The resulting Imageworks pattern was produced as a computer disc that went to RC Communications in New York, which did the color separations by printing out the patterns on acetate. The process that began with such high technology would, Acheson noted, end with a process hundreds of years old—silk screen. "Silk screen is literally a wood frame with a piece of silk stretched extremely tight over it," Ridge explained. "This acetate was applied to the silk screen so when you pressed the ink with a squeegee, it only came through the holes for the particular pattern." The costume itself was made up of nine separate pieces, each of which required numerous separate silk screens—sixteen to eighteen just for the arm, Ridge estimated. The final stats: eighty-six acetate patterns

Scans of stuntman Chris Daniels in the classic Spidey costume, with resulting crude model heads formed from the raw cyberscan data. This rough version was "cleaned up for the real CG model," as digital effects supervisor Scott Stokdyk put it. This preparatory stage included stripping out the web lines to avoid carrying too much extra geometry through the animation process, with the web lines mapped back on in the final rendering phase.

These printing and muscle map patterns prepared in the computer by Imageworks worked out the textural and muscle patterns that would be realized in the final, silk-screened Spider-Man costume.

A gallery of classic Spidey poses. Key to the physical performance was emulating the way Spider-Man moved in the comic book. "I always lectured my apprentices that Spider-Man is not drawn like everybody else," classic Spider-Man artist John Romita says. "Spider-Man is all elbows and knees. He's always awkward, like a spider on the wall, with arms and legs all flexing."
"One thing Sam said was, 'When I ask you to do a jump or tumble, be able to show four or five ways of doing it—but still stay in character as Spider-Man,' " stuntman Mark Wagner recalls. "It wasn't like I was mimicking Tobey; we both had to kind of mimic Spider-Man."

RIGHT: An artist at ADI uses a heat tool to trim one of the hundreds of individual sections of webbing cast from metal molds for the Spider-Man costume.

BELOW: ADI's Eric Hayden inspects one of the vacuform shells that were assembled with custom foam rubber cushioning. The final undershell was used for the Spider-Man costume hood.

with the printing, turning the computer pattern into screens, was a new method."

SPIDER SENSE

One of Spidey's traditional powers is a heightened sixth sense, an ability to literally *feel* trouble coming, represented in the comics as tingling lines radiating in a halo effect. But in the movie the same effect could be achieved with changing camera speeds. "That image of tingling lines is fine in the comics, but in film we have on the order of a hundred times as many images to deal with the same storytelling," senior visual effects supervisor John Dykstra explained. "We could present the spider sense as more of a subjective thing, a temporal distortion of things slowing down if we're seeing it from Spider-Man's point of view."

SPIDER WEB

Another major divergence the movie would take from the comics lore was to be that, instead of whiz kid Peter Parker creating a sticky web fluid and homemade wrist shooters, his body would naturally produce the web substance, which would shoot out of glandular slits in his wrists. The notion was controversial among some Spidey fans—the "organic versus nonorganic" issue, as Grant Curtis recalled.

But in an interview that appeared in the March/April 2001 issue of *Cinescape* magazine, Raimi explained that having a high

silk-screened for each of the twenty-eight costumes produced.

The silk-screener Ridge hails as "a real artist" was Martin Izquierdo, owner of Izquierdo Studio in New York, who personally handled the intensive assignment. "Jim and I spent a week in New York watching paint dry," Ridge said, smiling. "We had to go there because no one in California silk-screens stretch fabrics because it's so tricky. What Martin did was amazing, because there are so many variables. You have to apply the same pressure, so one person has to do it, and there are so many silk screens. The color ink can just change in the air!" Ridge's company used the costume's webbing—a latex piece dyed black and painted with a silver highlight—to hide the seams, gluing and laying on the web with tweezers.

Each suit included gloves and specially

made flexible footwear, as would be worn by a dancer or high-wire artist, that were sewn all of one piece into the costume by Ridge's group. To hold the head in the character's classic comic-book shape, Acheson's head sculptor, Ray Scott, led the concept work and created the sculpture that was cast by ADI, a final vacuform headpiece with a soft inner cushion of foam latex covering the face and top of the head, which could be pulled over like a spandex hood with a zipper in back to close it up. The final touch was eye lenses made by Oakley, a custom sportswear company, with special urethane frames that allowed the lenses to be clipped on and secured with tiny magnets placed on the inside of the hood's eyepieces.

"We did things for the Spider-Man suit that had never been done before!" Ridge concluded. "The way the computer worked

FORGIVE THE FLAMBOYANCY, COUNSELOR...

BUT I'M JUST AN OLD *SHOW-MAN* AT HEART!

WHA..?? THE *SPIDER SIGNAL!!*

LET'S SEE... I'D BETTER CHECK ALL MY EQUIPMENT! I'VE GOT MY ANTI-MAGNETIC INVERTER WITH ME... AND MY WEB-SHOOTER IS POSITIONED AND READY FOR ACTION...

MY CAMERA IS IN ITS CASE, LOADED WITH FRESH FILM...

...I REFILLED MY WEB-FLUID CAPSULE--AND ALL DEVICES CHECK OUT... A-OKAY!

THIS WEB-SHOOTER IS THE COOLEST THING I EVER DREAMED UP! I CAN DO ALMOST *ANYTHING* WITH IT! THE VULTURE WON'T HAVE A CHANCE!

school kid create an adhesive that even 3M Corporation couldn't make was a little too fantastic, even for a teenager with the proportionate strength of a spider.

And in an interview with Bill Warren for the January 2001 issue of the horror magazine *Fangoria*, Raimi credited the early Spider-Man treatment, prepared by James Cameron, as having contributed several important aspects of the origin as it would appear in the movie. These included the organic webbing and the idea that the spider that bites Peter Parker was genetically altered—as opposed to the radioactive spider that appeared in the comics.

Raimi tips his hat to Cameron, noting that the director clearly linked the two concepts, taking to its logical conclusion the notion of rewiring Peter Parker's genetics. "Cameron must have been thinking, 'Look, if we're going to mutate him into a spider, let's go [all out].' " Raimi told Warren, "He sticks to walls, he can leap. Why does he then have to invent a web fluid? Why not just mutate him far enough into a spider to produce webbing?

"Cameron came up with a good idea that I can objectively judge, because it wasn't my idea," Raimi continued. "I like the mythos of the shooters, but when you finally get down to a scene where he's making this chemical concoction, it's hard to understand why he felt he would need it."

Conceptual artist James Carson, who worked under Neil Spisak's department and specialized in gadgets and hardware, worked on the web design, which was created as both a CG and physical effect. Over at John Frazier's shop, George Stevens was a key player in the design and development of the physical web look. "In the comics the webbing often looks beautifully ropy and swirly, but we were trying to get something closer to nature," Carson said. "John and his effects guys did some fantastic stuff, working with different urethane materials and even fishing lines." The webbing produced by Frazier's shop ranged from a twelve-inch-diameter monofilament web for the genetics lab set to thirty feet of fishing line stretched across a Manhattan street that had been closed for the production.

"The web had to do two things: look like the spider's webbing we all think of—this diaphanous quality—yet also be ten times as strong as steel, to support Spider-Man's weight as he swings through the city," Dykstra explained. "The beauty of a spider's web is that it will disappear against a background, so bugs fly into it. But ours had to be both visible and invisible."

The Imageworks CG webbing had helical strands ranging from that diaphanous texture, which could refract beams of sunlight, to numerous strands that could coalesce into a single, powerful strand. Ken Hahn supervised the work of effects animation head Theo Vandernoot, who created the web effects with Houdini software. Hahn described the webbing as composed of layered elements coming together in the digital compositing phase.

"There were four major layers to the web, multiple passes and looks the compositor balanced and finessed. One layer had a refractive feel, another specular highlights, the third an iridescence, and the final was a depth pass to integrate the web. Sometimes we needed that flexibility because the practical web might be more opaque and we'd need to match to that. As much as we like the freedom of CG, we have to adhere to what they do onstage."

In this finaled shot, Peter Parker discovers he has the ability to shoot out streams of organic webbing, snagging this tray of food in the Midtown High cafeteria. The practical webbing provided by the special effects department ranged from foam material to simple fishing line.

The CG webbing effect began with Imageworks' live-action plate. The scanned footage was then match-moved in preparation for the CG web element.

The cafeteria web element was, like all of the CG web shots in the movie, composed of separate passes comprising the web's individual properties. Beginning at top left, they include: iridescent, which gives the base color; dew, with droplets at the webline connection points; volume normal, for refraction to give a liquid look; specular, to give glistening highlights; and shadow, showing shadows cast by the web.

In addition, some shots may have a "depth" pass effects such as depth of field. Compositors would take these passes and dial them in as appropriate on a shot by shot basis

RIGHT: This James Carson web-net concept for catching bad guys was accepted by the production as a "final." In the ultimate in-joke, Carson placed himself in the web—JC's the one in the blue pants—along with fellow artist Jason Mahakian.

Part II

IN THE CLUTCHES OF THE GREEN GOBLIN

The Green Goblin glides in, preparing to toss a glowing pumpkin bomb. Unlike the fanciful comic-book costume, the movie Goblin's outfit was high-tech battle armor. Concept art by Warren Manser.

CHAPTER FOUR

Mask of the demon

A s with the home of Uncle Ben and Aunt May, the dwelling of Norman Osborn was a combination of soundstage interiors and a location exterior—the entire penthouse level of Tudor City, an apartment complex near the United Nations building. "In reality, that penthouse level is broken up into many different apartments, but we took that whole top of the building to be Norman's castle in the sky," production designer Neil Spisak said.

That exterior location, selected before Dafoe joined the production, also started a back story percolating in Spisak's imagination, a notion that Norman's company had Old World English roots, that the character's inner sanctum represented the culmination of the wealth of many generations. "That's how I was thinking of it, trying to get a handle on it," Spisak explained. "I felt that with this old family history I could elaborate on Tudor and Gothic styles, push these huge, weird shapes. But films are a collaborative medium, and when Mr. Dafoe came aboard he felt that he started the company, so Norman Osborn's penthouse home doesn't reflect old family heirlooms but became more contemporary, with modern furniture."

Norman Osborn's inner sanctum also reflects a subliminal visual element of that split personality that haunts him. "There's some wood and metal, but the room is green, the rug is green, the sofa's green—Green Goblin!" Spisak said, smiling.

LEFT: The mask of the demon.

RIGHT: In his inner sanctum Norman Osborn hears the Goblin's voice—and has a conversation with his split personality. The scenes were shot without visual effects or even camera tricks.

Meantime, it would be a *lack* of color that characterized Spider-Man's place in this designed world. "There were some basic, but difficult, concepts I wanted to adhere to for the overall look throughout the movie," Spisak said, "and one was that the red and blue of Spider-Man's costume not appear anywhere else in the movie—those colors were reserved for Spider-Man. We made the attempt, anyway. The idea was that when you see Spider-Man, he pops out."

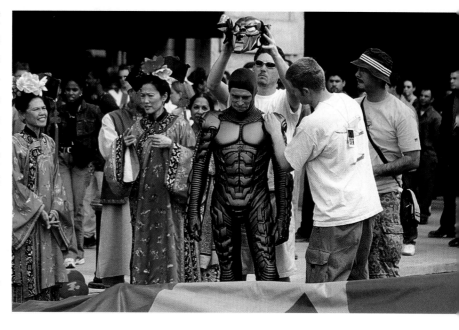

Although it wasn't easy selecting one villain from the pantheon of Spider-Man's classic foes, there were reasons Raimi wanted the Goblin. "I liked the Green Goblin not because of his powers, because I actually thought it'd be a nightmare to create this flying man on a rocket," Raimi said. "But the strength of Spider-Man for me has always been Peter Parker and who he is as a person. And because the Goblin is the father of Harry Osborn, Peter's best friend, I thought there was a greater chance for a dramatic interaction on a personal level than with Electro or Sandman, neither of whom know Peter Parker or ever relate to him. We also had a version of the script with the Green Goblin and Dr. Octopus, two great villains, but we felt there wouldn't be enough effects budget to do them properly. To tell three origin stories in one film would have compromised the different stories."

Yet the Goblin proved a difficult character to adapt to live action. One of the concept artists in James Acheson's costume department who wrestled with that challenge was Bernie Wrightson, a comic-book artist and illustrator known for his work on *Swamp Thing* comics and his elaborate illustrations for an edition of *Frankenstein*. Wrightson spent five weeks on *Spider-Man*, arriving early in the process as one of the "advance troops," a group that included James Lima, Warren Manser, Miles Teves, and James Carson.

"We all looked at the Green Goblin, and as a drawing he's fine, but as a real person dressed in a Goblin suit it'd be pretty silly looking," Wrightson said. "Another thing, in the comics he's clearly seen putting on a mask. But the mask has expressions; it smiles and frowns and blinks its eyes! So, what's it going to be in the movie? Is he wearing a mask or does his face

Willem Dafoe suits up prior to wreaking more havoc at the World Unity Festival. The actor's dedication to both the physical and performance aspects of his character earned the admiration of cast and crew. "He's awesome," Maguire says, smiling. "He's a workhorse. He wants to do everything. I'd be a little tired, and they'd be shooting something on the sleeve of the Goblin costume and Willem wanted to do it himself, to make sure the movement was exactly right. It was good to watch that example and learn from a great actor."

LEFT AND BELOW LEFT: Artist Miles Teves's takes on the Goblin face ranged from a ghoulish countenance to an overlay of circuitry inspired by Norman Osborn's high-tech background.

FAR RIGHT: In the earliest stage of preproduction the costume design department—the "advance troops," as artist Bernie Wrightson described the group—struggled with how to adapt the menacing but fanciful character to live action. In this drawing Wrightson tried to find some logic to the character's peaked cowl, that "maybe it was an extension of his mask or a helmet, that it wouldn't just be hanging down as a useless thing but might be a mechanical tentacle with an eye."

GREEN
GOBLIN

ABOVE: Artist James Lima's Goblin concepts range from rough sketch to polished final drawing (note the circuitry theme that pervades the designs).

RIGHT: This series of poses by artist Warren Manser explores the Goblin's look and the notion of a fearsome Goblin supersuit.

transform? Then we had the idea that since he's wearing this green, scaly suit in the comics, that the scales could become circuitry, because Osborn is an electronics whiz. We just played with that idea of different kinds of armor. No matter how wild we got with this stuff, it always came down to it having to work as a suit on a real person."

Wrightson left the project before the Goblin look was finalized, but getting to a final costume design proved as complicated as the psyche of Norman himself. Costume concept artist Warren Manser noted that he was initially brought on by James Acheson for six weeks, which became a six-month process based on the strength of their productive collaboration and the way in which they met such challenges as the Green Goblin's costume.

"Somehow the process seemed to make more sense for Spider-Man," Neil Spisak said with a sigh. "You have this crazy high school kid who's been bitten by the spider, he's going through this dramatic change, and there's this intermediate step, which was the costume he makes for the wrestling ring.

"But with the Goblin the intermediate step wasn't as clear. It proved to be a difficult char-

The concept artists had no trouble infusing their Goblin drawings with the character's trademark menace. Art by Bernie Wrightson.

ABOVE LEFT: This dramatic James Lima concept art proposed that the Goblin literally take wing.

ABOVE RIGHT AND BOTTOM LEFT: These Miles Teves sketches ranged from a leather look—complete with six-shooters!—to intricate layers of circuitry.

acter to translate in that we didn't want to go [too far into] unreality. Obviously, it's based on a comic book, so it's pushed some, but the idea that there was a human being there was important to Sam. What was clear was that there wouldn't be a change in the way Norman Osborn looked when he became the Goblin, that it had to do with a mental change and putting on a costume."

"Spidey wound up in his traditional Marvel suit, but the biggest challenge for the Goblin was we had to define him as a character," Manser explained. "In the comics he was more of a Halloween goblin. But we

Goblin mask, front and side profile.
Concept art by Warren Manser.

began considering what devices and costumes a wealthy arms manufacturer would use to commit his evil deeds. Is his costume purely aesthetic, or totally teched out?"

Since much of the early Goblin artwork had referenced Osborn's electronics background, Manser noted, the idea of integrating a technological look led Acheson to a decision that this was the way to

Left: Goblin and glider concept art by James Lima.

Top: Chrome-plated mask receiving a layer of translucent green tint by Amalgamated Dynamics' Eric Hayden.

Far right: A polyester resin casting of the Goblin mask is polished by ADI's Brent Baker.

Above: Polished mask casting ready for the chroming process.

go. While traces of that "Halloween goblin" of the comics remained, the costume itself began evolving into a supersoldier suit built at Osborn's company, the perfect complement to the military glider.

"At a certain point there was the realization that a clean direction for the Goblin would be that the suit fit with the glider, potentially made by the same company," Manser recalled. "This manufactured look means there's potentially less chaos in him, since it's built by a corporation, not a crazy person. It's not a maniacally crazy, Halloween idea of him running around and scaring people, but the insanity of it is him *using* this power! It gave the Goblin a different edge."

But while the supersoldier suit and glider went together, there was a piece that didn't fit—the mask. Gillis and Woodruff were working under James Acheson to develop a mask during a time when it was all "a blank page," as Tom Woodruff, Jr., recalled. They proposed doing a mask that would actually emulate the facial-changing dynamics of the rubber pullover comic-book mask, but the director and producers were uncer-

ABOVE: Goblin mask sculpture, front and side profile, prepared by Amalgamated Dynamics, Inc. This "wicked witch" look featured a prosthetic makeup and radio-controlled brow to bring to life the animated quality of the character's comic-book mask.

RIGHT: Green Goblin full-body armor sculpture, prepared by Martin Smeaton.

tain as to whether or not they wanted to go in that direction. Then Gillis and Woodruff suggested an articulated prosthetic makeup, and Raimi gave his blessing for the company to work up a test.

The result was a prosthetic appliance makeup using silicone, as opposed to more traditional foam latex, which would allow an actor to freely work the makeup, while an exaggerated, articulated brow could be manipulated via radio control receivers hidden in the character's peaked cowl. But to their disappointment, the production opted for a more static look. "Sam's concern was that if we saw Norman Osborn putting on a rubber mask, how we'd justify it being able to change expressions," Woodruff recalled. "Was it a new, lifelike material or some kind of hybrid synthetic flesh? He decided that approach would require too much back story."

The key to unlocking Norman's psychology—and that intermediate step to the Goblin mask—was Osborn's own mask collection. "It was proposed that Norman has a collection of ancient ceremonial masks," Woodruff explained. "The idea is that he's picked up this Goblin mask somewhere along his travels. So we took the look we'd developed for the articulated prosthetic and began developing something in the context of tribal masks."

The Goblin suit takes form. The final spandex and vinyl pieces were dyed a pearlized iridescence.

Meanwhile, production design and set decoration began developing the idea of masks displayed in Norman Osborn's home. "Originally, the idea was Norman would have a large collection of masks and elements of war, like battle armor," set decorator Karen O'Hara recalled. "But there's a scene in the first *Batman* movie where Bruce Wayne has a room of armor, and we thought that'd be too similar, so we came back to just masks."

In O'Hara's research, she'd come across *Masks of the World*, a museum catalogue published in conjunction with an exhibition at the Heritage Museum of Santa Monica. She brought the book to a meeting with the director, producers, and costume designer James Acheson. "This catalogue showed some Brazilian carnival masks that were very much like the Goblin in the comics, very menacing, and one was even green, with protruding teeth," O'Hara described.

O'Hara had a Los Angeles dealer and a friend and former dealer in primitive art in New York's Soho district collect some seventy masks for the production, an international sampling from Africa to China to the Americas. The masks had different cultural significance; some were new and others valuable antiques, some rented and others bought outright, with prices ranging from $150 to $4,000. But all the masks had one thing in common: "We chose masks that were fierce or frightening, as opposed to fertility masks," O'Hara said. "A lot of masks from Latin America, for example, had the theme of Diablo, the Devil."

For the final Goblin mask design, Gillis and Woodruff managed to keep the original rubber mask concept of large ears, long chin, crooked nose—the "classic goblin look," as Woodruff describes it. The sculpture itself evolved from sculpted teak wood and other materials, which proved too literal an interpretation of a tribal mask. Acheson finally proposed that they move in the direction of a manufactured design with a smooth, pris-

ABOVE: What Wrightson called the Goblin-ettes were inspired by flying robot "Goblin women" unleashed in the 1996 Spider-Man/Green Goblin magazine Spider-Man: Legacy of Evil. Goblin-ette art by Miles Teves.

ABOVE LEFT: Goblin-ette art by Bernie Wrightson.

tine finish. The result was a fiberglass mask covered with copper and bonded with a chrome-plated surface—fiberglass can't directly bond with chrome, Woodruff explained. "The final mask has the look of refined metal," Woodruff said. "It's no longer 'tribal' because of the technology, but the look evokes a sense of battle armor. But it is the essence of the Goblin. It's the opposite of the OsCorp supersuit he wears. The mask is something he grabs in his madness to conceal himself."

The fateful step Norman takes in letting the demon out comes as company intrigues and competition drive him to enter his lab "gas chamber," strip bare-chested, and use himself as the first human subject for his experimental "human performance enhancers." The vapors, meant to unlock the secrets of human evolution, have increased the strength of rodent test subjects 800 percent. But there's a downside: violence, aggression, and insanity. Thus does the Goblin manifest the superstrength that allows him to go toe to toe with Spider-Man.

The madness is manifest immediately as Osborn kills his hapless assistant, Dr. Mendel

ABOVE: The masks decorating Norman's home were not of the "happy angel" variety, production designer Neil Spisak notes. They represented an odyssey in themselves, with dealers in Los Angeles and New York supplying the production with masks collected from around the world. "The masks were mostly human scale, like faces around the room," Spisak noted. "It was purposely to give his Goblin mask a logic."

LEFT: In production designer Neil Spisak's original conception, Norman Osborn was a product of old money and lived in a baronial Manhattan mansion. In this Wil Rees interpretation, Osborn's manor includes what the artist calls "the Green Goblin's closet," a retreat where Norman keeps his mask collection and where his Goblin psychosis finally manifests.

Stromm (Ron Perkins). Originally, the script called for Norman to stagger out of the chamber, but Raimi and Dafoe decided it'd be more dramatic to have Norman immediately exhibit his superpowers with a huge leap toward camera. The director and star went to the stunt coordinator with their sudden inspiration. "The camera was over thirty feet away, and Willem had no shirt on," Jeff Habberstad said, "and the problem was we had to ratchet, decelerate, and land him in front of the camera. If we picked him with the cables around the waist, there was the potential he could flip upside down and land on his head. But Willem is into yoga; he has great stretching ability and a natural sense for flying through the air. To be honest, he was probably as qualified as any stuntman to do his own stunts."

From that morning, when the request was made, Jake Brake, the harness maker, went to work, configuring a harness with cable pick points behind the back and down low, so the actor could remain bare-chested. Later that morning, on a stage adjacent to the lab set, the stunt crew worked out the rig and tested it with Dafoe, rigged it during lunch, and shot the stunt in the afternoon.

"We had Willem jumping thirty feet and landing literally six inches from the camera lens," Habberstad said, and smiled. "And later that day, Sam comes up and says, 'I pretty much put you under the gun,

The OsCorp supersoldier suit and glider, the latest in high-tech warfare, are unveiled in OsCorp Lab C35. "The idea for OsCorp Lab was that it was a modern company with a secret underground facility out on Long Island and nobody knew what was going on there," Neil Spisak explains.

Conceptual illustrator James Carson concepts for the isolation chamber where Norman Osborn subjects himself to the white vapor that causes his physical metamorphosis into a superpowered being.

LEFT: The OsCorp lab chamber where the military glider would be built underwent numerous designs, including this fantastical —and very early—Harald Belker design.

According to assistant art director François Audouy, Spisak wanted to provide the chamber with a wind tunnel. The idea never went anywhere because of budget concerns, although the final lab set was designed so it could be redressed and converted to a wind tunnel.

ABOVE: The OsCorp lab set erected on Sony stage 15 was an estimated 60 feet across, 220 feet long, and 32 feet high. "Spider-Man rides a fine line between science fiction and reality," set decorator Karen O'Hara says. "For example, you want Peter Parker's house to be real-looking, while the OsCorp lab is where this corporation is designing high-tech warrior suits and vehicles for the government. For the OsCorp lab we did some research at Lawrence Livermore Lab [in the San Francisco Bay Area], and the rest was conceptualized by Neil Spisak."

LEFT: The OsCorp isolation chamber where Norman Osborn makes himself his own test subject for his controversial vapor inhalation "human performance enhancers." The 16' × 24' chamber was constructed of steel and tempered glass. "We built the structure, and special effects coordinator John [Frazier] rigged the doors to open and close hydraulically," construction coordinator Jim Ondrejko explains. "The bed of the chamber was also raised a couple feet off the ground, and we had holes in the floor where the gas effect could come up through hoses. You can run hoses and cables across the floor because it all looks like a lab."

Strapped to a gurney in the isolation tank, Osborn hopes that when he emerges he'll have unlocked the secret to human evolution. Some second unit pickup shots needed in this "transformation sequence" were filmed by storyboard artist Jeffrey Lynch, who reveals Raimi asks all his board artists to serve some camera duty. "This set had already been struck, but we had the gas machine," Lynch says. "Willem came in; he was always great that way, even if you just wanted to shoot a portion of him. We put in a wall and dressed it and stayed tight so we could grab that moment."

didn't I?" I said, 'Well, yes!' And he said, 'You did good. Plan on me doing that all the way through the show.' "

Dafoe had the challenge of having to perform with a mask that exposed only his eyes and mouth and with the encumbrance of the elaborate Goblin costume. "I had to find a physical way of being expressive without being too stylized," Dafoe explained. "You don't want to be inhibited; you look for a gesticulatory language. But I feel my tendency has always been to work from action and through the physical body, which probably comes from the fact that most of the time I'm working in the theater where you're not necessarily bound by naturalistic behavior."

But the eeriest Goblin scenes are several Dafoe played without the mask and within the mask-lined walls of his inner sanctum. There, his split personality emerges and his dual characters have a conversation. The sequences were meticulously prepared in rehearsals between Dafoe and Raimi before the cameras rolled. Both a storyboard artist and associate producer Grant Curtis were in on those rehearsals, Curtis to take notes because any performance decisions and shooting setups affected departments from props to cinematography. "I feel lucky because I had a front-row seat watching Willem get that character in his head from Day One," Curtis recalled. "Acting is a very interesting craft and it takes a lot of talent that most people don't see. To see Willem get his head around his character to such a phenomenal degree raised the hairs on the back of your neck!"

"There's no physical change, but there's a change of attitude," Dafoe explained. "It wasn't a conventional scene, so we had to figure out how to separate these two characters, Norman and the Goblin. Sam and I would go to the space and I'd act out some of my ideas, and Sam would react and then tell me how he could support me with the camera. Sam is like a fabulous audience and he gives you a good setup and all the tools you need to play around. It was real simple show-and-tell between us, but he made me feel very inventive. One of the scenes was done entirely in the mirror *without cut*, without fancy special effects or even camera wizardry. So, Norman's back can be to us, while the reflection in the mirror is the Green Goblin! It allowed me to slide between the two characters within the same time frame."

ABOVE LEFT: Cinematographer Don Burgess notes that in scenes where Dafoe played both Norman and the Goblin, the camera "played tricks with time and space." What helped the setups was that once the camera rolled, Dafoe never changed what had been arranged in rehearsal. "The angles selected are so important, it affects everything if an actor changes things," Burgess says. "But Dafoe is a fantastic actor. He did it exactly the way we rehearsed it; he nailed it every time."

ABOVE RIGHT AND LEFT: Sam Raimi preps actors Dafoe and Franco for an intense exchange between father and son. "I always knew Sam was proficient with the camera, but I found that he was very attentive to the actors," Franco says. "More than a lot of directors, he works with actors to personify their roles. One of Sam's specialties is that even the smallest character can stand out. It was refreshing, particularly on a big, technical film, to have the director care so much."

It's been said that the psychology of acting is its own kind of psychic split, an atavistic impulse. "Some actors take things to ridiculous extremes; they cross the line," Cliff Robertson said with a shrug, recounting the famous story of the performer who had to play scenes of an exhausted character, so he sat up several nights straight in Central Park, arriving at the set each morning in an increasingly bedraggled state, until his costar politely asked him, "Have you tried acting?"

"I always feel that when actors say they can't escape a character that there's a degree of will in hanging on to that," Dafoe mused. "We actors always have to fight hanging on to what we've done, what we think something should be. My feeling is to always discard, discard, discard, and let in the fresh impulse, the fresh impulse, the fresh impulse. Of course, it depends on the role, and what supports the character, but I'm always eager to let go, because if I extend it beyond its proper borders, it'll become dissipated and common. I prefer to work with it in that heightened state.

Goblin ascendant.

"Basically, the camera activates the character, and when it stops rolling, the character ceases to be because the conditions that allow the character to be disappear. The second the camera stops and everyone agrees not to come together to create that moment, it recedes back inside you."

CHAPTER FIVE

The heart is a lonely place

"Mine is a tale of pain and sorrow, longing and heartache, anger and betrayal, and that just covers the high school years. But let me assure you, this, like any story worth telling, is all about a girl.

"The girl next door, Mary Jane Watson."

And so goes Tobey Maguire's voice-over as he sits in the school bus rolling through Queens to Midtown High School, gazing at MJ sitting next to Flash Thompson. Mary Jane seems tight with the in crowd, but there's something haunting her, something screenwriter David Koepp underlines in his script as he describes her gazing out the bus window: "MARY JANE WATSON, knockout pretty but sad eyes, too sad for seventeen."

Although in the comics MJ marries Peter and shares his secret life, there had been other potential love interests. Peter Parker's great love of the early comic-book continuity was Gwen Stacy, the curvaceous blonde who died in 1973 in issue #121 of *The Amazing Spider-Man*, the story climaxing with the Green Goblin tossing her from the top of the George Washington Bridge. Spider-Man's superstrand of spider webbing caught Gwen, but couldn't stop the shock of the fall from killing her. On the next issue's cover, with the Goblin flying in on his attacking glider, Spider-Man had Gwen in his arms and was vowing, "You murdered the only girl I'll ever love—and today's the day you're going to die!!"

The Goblin did die within those pages, but impaled on his own remote-controlled flyer, not at Spidey's hands. And, in the epilogue,

RIGHT: Mary Jane in the outfit she wore to the World Unity Festival.

Left: Mary Jane holds on to the super-powered masked man who has swooped down to rescue her during the bedlam unleashed by the Goblin.

Mid-Air Collision
CONTROL TOWER TO BLAME
PAGE 16

Catastrophic Weather
POLAR ICE CAPS MELTING
PAGE 20

DAILY BUGLE

REWARD!
FOR PHOTOS OF
THE SPIDER-MAN

THE DAILY BUGLE ALWAYS GIVES YOU MORE · EXCLUSIVE STORY INSIDE!

EXTRA, EXTRA! The Bugle *tracks the continuing Spider-Man phenomenon.*

readers took their leave with a poignant scene of Mary Jane, the famous party girl, ready to learn her own lesson in responsibility, as she stood by to comfort a grieving Peter Parker.

Avi Arad noted that, at one point, the film was contemplating including Gwen Stacy but then, "she went away. She was never that interesting. It was my personal belief that in an origin movie you couldn't deal with both Mary Jane and Gwen Stacy. And Gwen was too dry, too straightforward, too single-dimensional.

"I liked Mary Jane, an abused child who cries on the inside but has to look perfect on the outside. But she has optimism galore—she's going to be somebody! She's miserable at home, so she craves company, which is probably why she wants to be with the in crowd. She lives in Queens, but wants to make it to Manhattan. Now, that's an interesting girl."

The search for a young actress to play MJ turned out to be the production's toughest casting call. It was December 2000, principal photography a month away, and the pivotal role still hadn't been cast. "First we had to cast the Peter Parker role, and then we had to find an actress, and there had to be chemistry between them," Ziskin explained. "When there's a romantic relationship in a story, you have to see the actors together. And Tobey was very generous, a great trouper, because we had him read with twenty-five actresses. However, you can be a great actress, but you can't manufacture chemistry. It either happens or it doesn't."

Kirsten Dunst, whose roles range from the vampire child in 1994's *Interview with the Vampire* to a rebellious, upper-class high school senior in 2001's *Crazy/Beautiful*, hadn't read for the part but had met with Sam Raimi. However, a commitment to play Marion Davies, William Randolph Hearst's mistress, in director Peter Bogdanovich's *The Cat's Meow* conflicted with the original *Spider-Man* start date. "I'd really clicked with Sam," Dunst recalled. "Then I didn't hear from them and I was doing my movie in Berlin. I thought they didn't want me."

When principal photography was pushed to January (there was "still so much to do" before the cameras could roll, Ziskin explained) the production saw a window of opportunity to do a reading with Maguire and Dunst. The only problem was Dunst was still in Berlin finishing *The Cat's Meow*. "Tobey was in L.A., and we called and told him he had to get on a plane and come with us to Berlin, that Kirsten was there and that we wanted them to read together," Ziskin recalled. "We wanted to tape them to see if the magic would happen. Things were getting hairy because we'd just have two hours to see Kirsten and we couldn't wait; we had to make a decision."

But there was one problem. Maguire had strep throat and his doctor advised him not to travel. "I talked to Sam and he talked to me about sacrifice," Maguire said, laughing. "So I jumped on the plane."

TOP RIGHT: Betty Brant, Peter Parker's first love in the comics, senses the turbulent shadow life Peter keeps hidden. Betty was the first person to whom Peter contemplated revealing his Spider-Man secret. The Amazing Spider-Man #9, "The Man Called Electro!" page 5 / Artist: Steve Ditko

BOTTOM RIGHT: Fans sometimes talk of the curse of the spider powers. And even in the early comic-book continuity, people sometimes died around Spider-Man. In the case of Bennett Brant, his hard-luck life—from top of his class in law school to jailbird flunky for mobster Blackie Gaxton—earned a martyr's redemption when he took a fatal bullet to save his sister Betty. But that stray bullet also earned Spider-Man the everlasting enmity of his first love. The Amazing Spider-Man #11, "Turning Point," page 13 / Artist: Steve Ditko

Feeling, as he put it, "miserably sick," Maguire flew to Berlin with Laura Ziskin, Raimi, and storyboard artist Jeffery Lynch (so the director could continue apace the all-important storyboarding prior to the start of filming). The party arrived in Berlin at six o'clock in the evening and was scheduled to meet Dunst at her hotel after nine-thirty, when the actress would return from a long day on the set of the Bogdanovich production. Waiting for Maguire at the hotel was a note from the actress. "This message said something like, 'I know you're very sick and I appreciate your coming, it wouldn't have been the same without you,'" Maguire recalled. "I thought that was very, very sweet and it made me feel a lot better about being there."

The script reading was scenes of Peter Parker and Mary Jane talking in the backyard after MJ has had a bitter argument with her father, a later meeting on a Manhattan street, and a final scene at Uncle Ben's grave. The group set up in a little conference room with a video camera, the makeshift set illuminated by as many lights and lamps as could be grabbed from the hallway and adjacent rooms. And the two actors—one sick and exhausted from a transatlantic flight, the other tired from a long day playing Marion Davies—began the reading.

And the magic happened.

"You drop all your other

thoughts away and just get involved in the scene," Maguire explained, "and it's nice when you have a good partner. We just had the best time."

"It's indescribable, the 'magic,'" Ziskin said, smiling. "You just know it when you see it. But you can't beat it and they have it. The camera doesn't lie. You have to be feeling the emotions; it has to be real because the camera can see everything. We were feeling really good about it, and, ironically, on the plane ride home the next morning they were playing Kirsten's film *Bring It On*. And we're all saying, 'That's it—she's the girl!'"

Mary Jane and Peter Parker follow parallel paths in the movie, from neighbors and high school classmates in Queens, to life in Manhattan.

ABOVE: In this introspective concept, artist Wil Rees pictures Peter Parker in the boiler room of the hospital where Aunt May has been hospitalized after a Goblin attack. As he often did in the comics, Parker contemplates consigning his costume to the flames and turning away from his super responsibilities.

BOTTOM LEFT: Sometimes the pain of a double life has left the man behind the mask aching with angst in that dark waiting room of the soul, such as in this scene, the aftermath of another anguishing encounter with the Green Goblin. The Amazing Spider-Man #17, "The Return of the Green Goblin!" page 22 / Artist: Steve Ditko

The gang's all here in this dramatic comic-book moment as a bedridden Peter Parker receives the ministrations of his love, Gwen Stacy, with Mary Jane and troubled roommate Harry Osborn hovering in the background. Marvel Super-Heroes #14, "The Reprehensible Riddle of . . . The Sorcerer!" page 9 / Artists: Ross Andru (pencils), Bill Everett (inks)

And while the central theme of the story was Peter Parker's journey, Kirsten Dunst noted that the movie was also about MJ's journey. "There was definitely that bubbly, sexy fire thing to her, but she goes on this journey of being insecure and trying to get out of her hard family life. So she covers up by dating Flash, the cool football player, and later she starts dating Harry because he has money and seems the kind of guy to date, but she's not happy with him, either. She's making decisions about her life and not being true to her heart."

MJ doesn't see the truth, that the one who truly loves her was always just a backyard away. "Peter has loved her from the beginning for who she is, not the mask she wore," Dunst said. "How we played the relationship between Peter and MJ is they were childhood friends and kind of broke off when high school came and everybody got separated into their little groups."

From the old neighborhood in Queens to a new life in Manhattan, Raimi encouraged Maguire to provide feedback from Peter Parker's perspective. "Sam wanted me to stay on top of my world; he gave that to me as my responsibility," Maguire related. "He wanted me to go through the script and the sets and tell him if something didn't feel right. Ultimately, it was his decision, but he wanted me to be his partner on Peter's journey."

One major Maguire contribution was during the conceptual stage for the Manhattan apartment Peter Parker and Harry Osborn share. Maguire recalls looking at concept art and a model of a two-story, two-bedroom apartment that seemed too big a leap from that house-proud neighborhood in Queens. "That kind of apartment in Manhattan seemed too extravagant for Peter," Maguire recalled. "I mean, as an actor I couldn't afford this place! I just thought it'd be weird having people all over America and the world looking at Peter Parker living in this superrich apartment. So I brought that up with Sam. But they were already thinking along those lines and they brought the space down."

The look of the *Daily Bugle*, the Manhattan newspaper where Peter Parker gets hired as a freelance photographer, also changed from a grander initial vision. That famed newspaper from the comics, which publisher J. Jonah Jameson uses as a bully pulpit to decry what he perceives as the

Spider-Man menace, was conceived as the top three floors of an old Manhattan skyscraper—an image of power. Then the concept shifted toward the *Bugle* becoming "a real New York subway paper," as Raimi explained. "Our *Daily Bugle* office became a little less fantastic and more like a modern-day tabloid newspaper. Our art department researched what places like the *Daily News* or the *Post* were like. Neil Spisak and I wanted to make it seem that Peter Parker was trying to get a job at a real newspaper in New York."

The on-site research ranged from studying what was pinned to the newsroom walls to typeface styles. J. K. Simmons, who played Jameson, also visited a newsroom to get a feeling for the world his irascible character would inhabit. "I spent a couple afternoons at the *New York Post*, getting a sense of the general level of hysteria," Simmons said, smiling. "J. J. operates at a two-minutes-to-deadline stress level at all times."

Simmons's character was practically lifted from the *Spider-Man* comics, with a flattop wig and prosthetic teeth emphasizing J. J.'s perpetual snarl. For costume designer Acheson, the comic-book character come to life was a chance to have fun. "We certainly pushed things with Jameson," Acheson said. "You look at his wig; it's that wonderful flattop. He has too-wide stripes on his shirt; his cufflinks are a little bit vulgar; the suspenders a bit too bright."

In 1994, writer Kurt Busiek and artist Alex Ross imagined what it would be like if ordinary humans and superheroes actually coexisted, with fictional photojournalist Phil Sheldon documenting the resulting Marvels. Here, Sheldon hopes to record a moment of triumph, but instead witnesses Spider-Man's greatest defeat as the Goblin hurls Gwen Stacy to her death. The Spider-Man production debated whether to introduce Gwen Stacy in the first movie. Marvels Book Four, "The Day She Died," pages 34–36 / Artist: Alex Ross

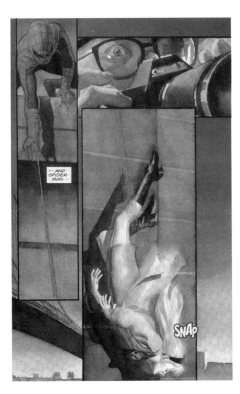

In a life passage, Peter Parker takes a bow as "outstanding science scholar" during Midtown High School graduation ceremonies.

J. K. Simmons played the stoic Detroit Tigers manager in Raimi's *For Love of the Game* and had brought to that character some compelling back story, the idea that the manager's wife had survived cancer (which didn't make the final film). "I think Sam keeps hiring me because I come up with stuff on my own," Simmons, who was also in Raimi's *The Gift*, said. "Sam knows what he wants, but is open to what happens. That's rare, that quality of preparedness and spontaneity." Simmons said that for J. J. a little touch was that the harried publisher keeps getting calls at the office from a wife perpetually mired in home renovation issues.

Simmons was also determined that his character not just be a cartoonish caricature. "J. J. is the classic blowhard, ill-tempered boss," Simmons said. "But when I'm playing someone who's not a good guy, there has to be something compelling about the character. In Jameson's case, he's a good newspaperman in the old-world sense and in the 1960s was a big civil-rights advocate. And he treats people equally—he screams at *everybody*!"

Of course, there's Jameson's personal war against the web-slinger. In fact, Raimi and Simmons discussed the matter when the script was in development, particularly the introspective panels way back in issue #10 of *The Amazing Spider-Man* in which Jonah reveals the secret of his Spidey hatred—he's *jealous* of him!

"That particular comic is the sole reason in the entire history of the comic for this vendetta against Spider-Man," Simmons said. "I tried to come up with other motivations, like he hates spiders because of a childhood incident where his favorite uncle got bitten by a black widow. But it goes with J. J.'s political leanings that he wouldn't approve of vigilantism. Basically, he's *terrified* of this superbeing. And what follows is the assumption that Spider-Man and the Green Goblin must be in it together. After all, they're both hiding behind masks!"

But even as Peter settles into life in the big city, the Green Goblin lurks in the wings, ready to literally glide into action. Bernie Wrightson recalls heated discussions in the early preproduction days about how the Goblin's glider—without even a seat, its pilot having to stand up with feet locked into stirrups on the wings—was even practical. "We took a board with a tennis ball underneath and tried standing on it," Wrightson said, smiling, "and you can't steer something that way. It'd be like riding a surfboard—sideways. If he was going to fly around on something, it'd be more like the Silver Surfer!"

ABOVE: The two kids from the old neighborhood cross paths in the big city in this scene shot on Warner Bros.' famed New York street back lot. "Sometimes I felt like an old Hollywood, little glamour girl in my trench coat—I felt very Marlene Dietrich, and it felt like Tobey could be Cary Grant," Kirsten Dunst says, smiling. "I love that glamour and romanticism. It should have been shot in black and white."

LEFT: News on the March! Daily Bugle headlines from yesteryear.

BOTTOM: New Yorkers eager to read up on the mysterious Spider-Man sightings are going to get an anti-Spidey slant in the Bugle.

RIGHT: Sam Raimi and Jameson actor J. K. Simmons debated the motivation for the Bugle publisher's hatred of Spider-Man, referring to this never-to-be-repeated confession from Amazing Spider-Man #10. The Amazing Spider-Man #10, "The Enforcers!" page 22 / Artist: Steve Ditko

But that fantastical comic-book glider was exactly the approach Neil Spisak's production design department began honing in on, although in the beginning it was all "blue sky," conceptual illustrator James Carson recalled. "I did one concept of a glowing disk; someone else did a big rocket engine with little wings. But in the end it was more like the comic-book glider, this flying machine in the form of a bat. We also didn't want to conflict with any of Batman's gadgets, so we made sure our look was separate."

ABOVE: J. K. Simmons plays Jameson from low boil to boiling over. "Even though our movie takes place in 2002, there's a sense of the 1960s or '70s with Jameson," Simmons notes. "He's a postwar kind of guy."

RIGHT: Peter Parker makes the grade with the gruff publisher himself.

ABOVE: An abundance of reference photos for the downtown Los Angeles Daily Bugle location set helped give Neil Spisak "a very clear vision of the set for publisher J. Jonah Jameson's office," Wil Rees says. "We worked on the feel of the set, which is more run-down than the rest of the Bugle office." The design work reflected the personality of the hard-bitten publisher, a tough and savvy newspaperman of the old school. (The implied persona included the notion of the legendary hard-drinking newsman—note the ready bottle in easy reach.)

RIGHT: Bugle publisher J. Jonah Jameson's office and newsroom, pictured here, was built on the vacant floor of a building in downtown Los Angeles.

The construction crew doubled the set's construction materials, including making two sets of walls, so the Bugle could be exactly reassembled in a warehouse in Downey, California. Jim Ondrejko's crew even re-created a real building visible across the street at the L.A. site, complete with a blue sky backing.

One major departure from the comics was that instead of having the villain fumbling in a grab bag slung over his shoulder for nasty gadgets to toss, the flying glider itself was a weapon. The final design accounted for missiles, machine guns, and new-look pumpkin bombs that popped up into the Goblin's eager hands. The director was involved throughout this and every design stage. Carson's first step was "finding the design" in rough pencil sketches—with help from Harald Belker and Jim

Martin—for Raimi's approval, then honing in and tightening the renderings with tracing paper overlays. Once Raimi approved that stage, sketch art was scanned into the computer and further developed with Photoshop image-processing software.

The glider concept design team, which included Harald Belker, Jim Carson, Jim Martin, and Jason Mahakian, spent a month and a half designing what John Frazier's shop would build, which, in turn, could be duplicated in the virtual realm at Imageworks. For the final detailed schematics Carson prepared illustrated top, side, and back views, which gadget model maker Paul Ozzimo built using Rhino modeling software at the Sony *Spider-Man* art department. In addition, a scale clay model based on that final design was sculpted and converted into digital data. "Once we had the basic architecture, it got refined quite a bit," Carson explained. "It got a meaner look; the edges got sharper; it had a stronger attitude. Even though it was a rough bat-shape, we

In this storyboard series Peter happily sights MJ—and is quickly crestfallen as the girl of his dreams drives off with another. (Note the passing bus in the last panel that Peter, with his newfound Spidey powers, will catch up with—running at fifty miles per hour.)
Scene 18/Panels 4-11 / Artists: Doug Lefler and Jeffrey Lynch

ABOVE: This scanned photo of the completed practical Goblin glider formed the template for Imageworks' computer-generated model. "We definitely also used the data from the manufacture of the real glider," Scott Stokdyk explains, "but it had to be slightly modified for our use. We had to clean up and define surfaces to be renderable. We also added a few things that didn't exist in the real model, such as flaps that open to reveal machine guns."

ABOVE LEFT: Imageworks' wireframe construct for CG Goblin glider model.

RIGHT: While Peter settles into life in Manhattan there's a storm cloud ready to blow in—a green storm cloud. OsCorp "military scout glider" concept art by Jim Martin.

(A) RETRACTED "NORMAL" MODE

(B) HOUSING UNIT PROTRACTS

(C) DEPLOYMENT. SIMULTANIOUSLY TELESCOPES OUT AS SPEAR SLIDES FORWARD

(D) FIRES WITH A GOOD OL' "PFFFFFFTTTT" (OR OTHER APPROPRIATE SOUND EFFECT)

SPEAR DEPLOYMENT CONCEPT
J CARSON 8.21.00 - SPIDERMAN

Goblin concept and details for "spear deployment," one of the nasty little devices considered for the flying weapons system. Art by James Carson.

j carson 8.17.
goblin concep
SPIDERM

BOTTOM LEFT AND RIGHT: Quest Aerospace, rival company to OsCorp, also produced its own version of a military exoskeleton—the Badger. This James Carson Badger concept was realized by John Frazier's special effects shop.

LEFT: Early Badger concepts included this scuttling, creaturelike design by James Carson.

BELOW: In this early Photoshop-processed Badger image, Carson imagined the military device as a tank rolling across a dramatic wasteland. (The inferno-like backdrop is a scanned photo of the oil fields that burned during the Persian Gulf War.)

also incorporated the sense of an open, outstretched clawed hand ready to grab someone. We worked into it a lot of different axis of positions; everything moves and twists; its wings can spread out—it looks like a living creature."

At John Frazier's shop, Mark Noel supervised the glider's construction, including the motion-control system and gimbal. The construction of the glider itself was generated from the digital model produced by Paul Ozzimo. "Once we'd created the whole 3-D architecture, we sent a file to John Frazier's shop and they cut out the practical wing with a mill," Carson explained. "Imageworks could also take our architecture, but because they had so many more requirements for their animation and image resolution, they converted our Rhino program into Maya software."

The Goblin finally unleashes his power at the OsCorp-sponsored World Unity Festival in Times Square. For Peter Parker, there to shoot pictures for the *Bugle*, the day already proves heart-wrenching, as he sees MJ and Harry Osborn together. But Peter Parker doesn't have time to nurse a heartache. Before the celebrants see it, they hear it—the drone of the approaching Goblin glider. Norman, betrayed, is giving full vent to his ghoulish Goblin side.

CHAPTER SIX

The green goblin attacks!

When producer Ian Bryce worked with Steven Spielberg on *Saving Private Ryan*, that film's re-creation of the D-Day invasion at Normandy was staged on a beach in Ireland complete with a thousand trained soldiers, restored landing boats and guns and gear, and tens of thousands of rounds of ammunition fired. But staging D-Day was simple compared to the complexity of setting the stage for the Spider-Man and Green Goblin face-off in Times Square.

RIGHT: Director Sam Raimi sets the stage for the centerpiece OsCorp-sponsored festival. The dramatic sequence, with the attacking Green Goblin and Spider-Man battling for the first time, had to re-create Times Square in production pieces ranging from soundstage and back-lot sets to Imageworks' CG workstations. "The tough part was getting everything to match up!" associate producer Grant Curtis explains. "It was a very intricate puzzle to figure out."

LEFT: The Green Goblin prepares to toss a pumpkin bomb in this effects shot by Sony Pictures Imageworks. The computer generated imagery includes the Goblin and glider and World Unity Festival balloons. The buildings were based on photographic location elements. "Using our pan and tile system," explains Scott Stokdyk, "we could apply a move to the image and replace the background."

"The Times Square sequence was the single most complicated sequence I've ever been involved in," Bryce concluded. "It was more complicated than the D-Day invasion in *Saving Private Ryan*, which was largely a matter of logistics.

"This was a nearly eight-minute sequence that was one of the structural centerpieces of the picture in terms of story and action, and it was complicated because we had to shoot in four separate components. There was filming in the real Times Square; we built a huge outdoor set in a parking lot in Downey, California, that represented the lower two or three floors of a portion of Times Square; we had an enormous balcony set piece for greenscreen photography; and there were computer graphics in postproduction at Imageworks. And all of these already complicated elements had to be cross-referenced and matched, so it was enormously challenging for all the production heads. If you aggregate all the time we spent, it took us about four weeks to dissect and figure out how to shoot that sequence."

TOP: World Unity Festival set, Downey, California.

BOTTOM: Stan Lee makes a cameo appearance in the World Unity Festival scene.

Set decorator Karen O'Hara pinpoints the sequence's exact location as the block of Forty-seventh and Broadway. But the production's plans were "not something they let you do in Times Square," associate producer Curtis observed with wry understatement, noting that for the movie a rock concert and festival would be in full swing until the Goblin glides out of the sky and all hell breaks loose, with panicked crowds and falling debris from pumpkin bomb hits, including a hanging piece of crumbling balcony where Mary Jane is trapped, all of the action topped off with Spider-Man's first battle against the Goblin.

The sequence had originally been planned against the backdrop of the Macy's Thanksgiving Day Parade, with a lot of the action taking place in the parade route bleachers. But the first unit wasn't ready to shoot at the annual parade, according to Laura Ziskin. Regardless, production principals felt the festival idea was an inspired change and provided more leeway for designing action. "Sam wanted more of the action to be up in the sky, where Spider-Man could be up in the buildings and the glider could fly around," Neil Spisak added. "The ideal is to have everything locked down but, particularly on a movie like this, you add or enhance things if it'll make the movie better. It's such a kinetic, organic, and unwieldy thing, making a movie."

Thus, the importance of storyboards. Working from both Spisak's production designs and with the guidance of Sam Raimi, the Times Square sequence was one of the first scenes David Stephan, Jeffrey Lynch, and Doug Lefler worked on. "The animatics were also an absolutely neces-

In the story the World Unity Festival essentially closes down bustling Times Square for the world's biggest block party. For the sequence, the production design department researched everything from the look of real Times Square to international festivals.

What represented essentially the street level and first two floors of the area (with Imageworks filling in the cityscape with CG set extensions and background buildings) was staged outdoors, on a parking lot in Downey. After the construction crew laid out the street, poured the concrete, and erected the building facades, the set decoration department added touches ranging from newspaper vending machines to garbage cans. A festival touch were the twenty-two tents built on-site atop wheeled platforms that could be moved for varied camera angles (although it took ten people to push them).

TOP: Downey set view toward the bottom floors of the centerpiece building that includes the balcony from which the OsCorp party watches the festivities, a piece of the puzzle built as a soundstage set.

MIDDLE RIGHT: This part of the Downey set encompasses the band shell and some of the international-flavor concession tents.

MIDDLE LEFT AND RIGHT: Director of photography Burgess's team put up these two giant silks as high as eighty feet above the Downey set, each one hundred feet by sixty feet, to take out the sunlight and emulate natural shade conditions. The "sunlight" was created with banks of forty or fifty "par lights" of some 1,000 watts each. The look was also crafted from Burgess's nearly twenty-five years' experience and a natural feeling for "sun, light, and silk."

sary part of the equation for all the big action sequences like Times Square," Curtis explained. "Most productions don't utilize animatics, but it's a huge cost saver, because Sam could work with Andrew [Jimenez] and see his action sequences animated before he started filming them."

"Many of the great visual ideas for the Times Square sequence were developed by Doug Lefler, although all the storybook artists contributed" said Raimi.

"I remember big meetings in the art department around the middle of November [2000] that Neil had for Times Square," Andrew Jimenez recalled. "They were deciding what they needed to build and whether they could move the balcony set over to a certain building. And [director of photography] Don Burgess had his laptop and could look at the animatics in continuity where it all fit in versus having all this paper everywhere. The laptop was sitting right there next to a model of Times Square."

From the start there were some obvious puzzle pieces, from the Goblin flying in on his glider—a no-brainer Imageworks visual effects assignment—to the crumbling balcony, which became a set piece on Stage 27 at Sony. The balcony itself was part of a bigger puzzle piece representing a made-up Times Square building, the bottom floors of which were at the outdoor festival set erected on what was a parking lot in Downey.

This centerpiece building and balcony emphasized Beaux Arts, an architectural style that provided a touch of the unreal while

The World Unity Festival gets off to a rocking start as Macy Gray takes the mike.

faithfully adhering to reality. "That's where I was at, not just for Times Square, but for the city," Spisak explained. "Whenever I could use that style, I did. It's very New York and represents an interesting period of architecture, but it's also slightly fantastical; the details in some of those actual buildings are almost unreal. The Beaux Arts style lights in an interesting way; there's carved pieces of enormous stone, and by backlighting and cross-lighting, you get all these details. It gave Spider-Man and the Goblin a fantastic world they could be a part of and operate in, surreal yet perfectly real."

One of the keys to unifying the separate shot elements was director of photography Don Burgess's selection of an optimum time of day in which to stage the action and replicate lighting conditions. "We did a light study in

LEFT: The director instructs the OsCorp elite who will soon be victimized by the Green Goblin's vengeful attack. (Note the greenscreen dividing line to allow Imageworks to digitally composite in the bottom floors as needed.) Although shot indoors, the balcony set had to look outdoors. "All the different elements had to be shot under the proper conditions to go together," Raimi says. "The direction of the light had to be the same; it had to be the same optics so it looked like it was shot together."

BOTTOM LEFT AND RIGHT: The Times Square balcony set, Sony stage 27, represented the nineteenth floor of an estimated eighty-story building. "The balcony is part of a building that's completely made up," production designer Spisak explains. "I did some initial rough sketches for what I thought it'd look like. Then our set designers and art directors went crazy with it. They did a beautiful job."

BELOW LEFT AND RIGHT: The beautiful balcony set gets blasted by the Goblin. "We did the big explosion below the balcony with all the windows blowing out," special effects man John Frazier says. "That was propane through air mortars, which blew out Styrofoam pieces and balsa wood, all the stuff you couldn't get hurt with."

BOTTOM: Prior to the Goblin attacks, Harry Osborn and MJ, his festival date, seem to gaze uneasily out across Times Square. Do they see the Goblin coming?

Times Square, shooting still photos from sunrise to dusk," Burgess said. "We then picked the most interesting time of day we could make work, which was late in the day, when there's still shade and a hard sunlight giving depth to the images, carving out the skyscraper canyons.

Burgess, aided by his longtime gaffer Steve McGee and his fifty-person crew, would also do more than just point a camera at Spider-Man and the Goblin in action. The Spider-Man costume itself required prep time with James Acheson, regarding the proper color saturation of the suit so it could photograph properly. Burgess's preproduction tests even worked out the optimum lighting and camera angles for avoiding reflections in the character's eyepieces. "We also had to figure out how to photograph Spider-Man in action," Burgess added. "The two different things were having him climb up walls like a spider and then swing through the city like Tarzan. For my part, that meant figuring out ways to move the camera. We also subtly manipulated camera speed, under- or overcranking.

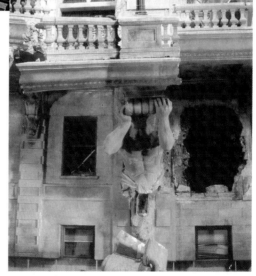

TOP LEFT: *Aftermath of the balcony set pyrotechnics.*

TOP RIGHT: *A very hands-on director assists with balcony set damage control.*

BOTTOM LEFT AND RIGHT: *Neil Spisak's department created a model for the balcony element. "It was all figured out how the balcony would break apart," Spisak explains, "what happens to the statue. Each movement was calculated as to how the hydraulics would move and the statue crumble." The lower windows shattered with pyrotechnics, while a chunk of the balcony, anchored by a plaster and fiber-glass Hercules statue, was engineered to break away. The set also featured curved end pieces that could be dismantled and laid on their sides to film the illusion of Spider-Man crawling across them.*

TOP LEFT AND RIGHT: Kirsten Dunst is stationed on her perilous perch. Her actual fall would be a wire-rig drop shot against greenscreen for Imageworks to composite against a background. The stunt was shared between the actress and stuntwoman Jeri Habberstad, along with a little save-the-day Spider-Man stunt action.

Before Peter Parker suits up, he saves some innocent bystanders from the debris dislodged from the balcony by the Goblin attack. The action, filmed on the Downey set, has Tobey Maguire alternating between web-shooting action (added later as a CG element) and practical web effects.

TOP LEFT: In the story, the Goblin gets knocked off his glider and falls onto the Chinese tent located in front of the balcony building. Note the vivid red lanterns, selected by the set decoration department for their simple, graphic shape. "In a film you just get glimpses, so we went for large and graphic objects which could read well," set decorator Karen O'Hara explains. "Instead of lots of stuff, each tent had a few items. The Chinese tent had red lanterns; another only had kites and puppets."

TOP RIGHT, MIDDLE LEFT AND RIGHT: Goblin stuntman Kim Kahana is positioned and dropped over the tent, one of the rare times Willem Dafoe did not do his own stunts. Those exceptions were usually reserved for the most dangerous stunts, and in this instance there was concern the suit could cause compression on the spine from being dropped from this height. (Everything turned out fine, but, kids, don't try this at home.)

LEFT: After the Goblin's fall, his out-of-control glider punctures a gigantic balloon that threatens to crush "little Billy," played by proud stuntman Jeff Habberstad's eight-year-old son, Shane.

*Times Square sequence
concept art by Wil Rees.*

"The Goblin outfit was difficult to shoot, a real dark green. To bring it to life, we used colored cards, like yellow and green, and reflected those lit surfaces onto the Goblin surface. We'd put these cards on stands, or sometimes people held them in position. So you'd have a crane arm and dolly grips, someone holding a fluorescent light, a couple of guys with these colored cards, the sound man with the microphone, all moving with the action—it was like a ballet!"

Imageworks had its own criteria for animating its CG supercharacters. "The freedom of digital is also its limitation, because the respective character comes with its own set of body language as defined by Tobey Maguire and Willem Dafoe," John Dykstra explained. "For example, we had to bring those components into the animation of our CG Goblin, to get the particular way Willem bends his knees to absorb shocks, where he puts his head, how he anticipates and reacts. The different personalities of the Goblin—whether he's enraged, happy, a trickster—affect how he performs on the Goblin glider. That's all body-language stuff, but it's also personality-defining movements and storytelling components."

Times Square sequence concept art by Jim Martin.

The internal digital skeletons for both characters required *physiquing*, an Imageworks term for the setup required to make any CG model ready for animation. "It's basically the animation controls the animators need, the muscle system that drives the muscles under the model's CG skin, everything that takes a model to something that can be animated," Peter Nofz, the CG supervisor who oversaw both the building and physiquing of the models, explained.

The Goblin model, however, was more complicated than his web-suited adversary because of the geometry required to digitally duplicate the hundreds of separate pieces on the real suit. "The Goblin costume is like a hard exoskeleton, individual pieces connected on top of a spandex type of suit," Scott Stokdyk noted. "For our CG character we had to balance between sliding those pieces on top of the surface and giving a bit of stretch. It's a challenge when you have different materials with different kinds of gives and stretches."

TOP: Cyberscan of Willem Dafoe in the Green Goblin suit, scan data taken at Gentle Giant. (The Spider-Man scans of Tobey Maguire and stuntman Chris Daniels were done at Cyberfx.) The scan data was used to build the wireframe computer model, which was then set up for animation with a special muscle system designed to move the CG skin—a process Imageworks calls physiquing.

RIGHT: With his superstrength, the Goblin tosses cops las if they were rag dolls. Although some of the steel stunt cables were thin enough to not be picked up by the camera, visible wires had to be digitally removed, a process of tracing out the form frame by frame with "rotoscoping" software.

Imageworks' Alberto Menache came up with a system by which the Goblin's exoskeleton costume moved with the underlying model animation. "We went through Alberto's setup for each piece of the Goblin's costume, balancing how each piece slid and how much they bent and stretched depending on different movements," Stokdyk said. "Once the system was put into place, it required less tweaking."

For an establishing shot from the balcony at Times Square, the visual effects artists saved themselves the trouble of creating a complex 3-D computer graphics cityscape by digitally seaming together a mosaic of live-action shots. "One of the things that has come into vogue is called 'pan and tile,'" Stokdyk explained. "Just about every big effects movie has a little pan and tile in it."

John Dykstra likens pan and tile to a series of still photographs pasted together to create a bigger picture. The effect involves location shooting with a special motion-control camera, so-called because it's computer programmable for exacting, repeatable movements. "We went to Times Square with our camera and from the balcony of the Marriott Hotel photographed twenty-six individual tiles," Dykstra explained. "Essentially, our locked-off camera was looking at a portion of the world, or tile, and because of the motion control we could accurately reposition the camera between each adjacent tile. We came back and took out the distortion in the lens. Then we brought all the motion-control tiles into Maya software where we knew exactly where each tile was and what was in them, which tiles included street activity or sky. Once all those tiles were seamed together, it gave you a version of the world you could move in on a little bit—that's why they call it pan and tile."

The balcony, where doomed OsCorp executives get fried by the Goblin, is also where innocent Mary Jane gets caught in the cross fire. The ensuing chaos, with MJ stranded on a broken chunk of the bombed balcony, was designed to feature a giant piece of supporting Hercules statuary cracking apart as the balcony begins to break away. Special effects guru John Frazier and Jim

TOP LEFT: Stuntman Chris Daniels practices the rescue sequence. "There's definitely a camaraderie and trust among stunt people built on years of experience and knowing how this stuff works," stunt coordinator Jeff Habberstad says. "But rehearsal time is the most dangerous time. Then, when the testing is done and it's time to film, it's just a matter of going through your checklist and making sure everything goes as you tested it."

TOP RIGHT AND BOTTOM LEFT: The rescue of little Billy included a greenscreen element shot on a Sony stage of Chris Daniels as Spider-Man swooping in and picking up the boy and flying into the air. The final piece was shot at the Downey set, with Daniels landing and handing the boy off to his mother (Deborah Wakeham). "We rehearsed it and the timing was crucial because we'd pull Shane on a wire as Spider-Man gets him," Habberstad notes. "But Shane couldn't flinch as Spider-Man flies in. It worked great, and Shane's comment right after was, 'Let's do it again!'"

TOP: Imageworks conjured up a virtual version of New York in several ways, including using "pan and tile" techniques to create this establishing view of Times Square. The process began with a motion-control film camera programmed to capture predetermined pan and tilt angles shot at the location. The few seconds of footage for each angle—or tile—were scanned into the computer, the resulting jigsaw mosaic seamed together in "a virtual geodesic dome," as Scott Stokdyk explains.

ABOVE RIGHT: Times Square tiles with borders showing how the images were seamed together into a continuous environment.
ABOVE LEFT: Placed tiles without borders.
BOTTOM RIGHT: Seamed image with color correction.

Ondrejko's construction team worked closely on a special effects piece that Frazier likened to the mechanics of "a theme park ride."

Ondrejko's crew cast the statue, four of which were made for the sequence. Frazier then cut the statue into almost thirty separate sections, each designed for the cut-on-cue action. Frazier's team then engineered a computer-programmed hydraulic ram hidden behind the breakaway piece of balcony and mounted it to the statue.

"The construction crew built on either side, and we filled in the middle with our piece," Frazier explained. "There was a specific order Sam wanted this Hercules statue to crush, which we controlled through the computer. With the hydraulics we could crush it down a little bit and go back up again. The balcony piece was hinged to fall against the building and shake. All the I beams and exposed understructure look like steel but were made of lead so they could bend and twist."

Meanwhile, the building's bottom floors and surrounding street level were constructed on the vast Downey parking lot by Jim Ondrejko's crew as a freestanding forty-foot set, a facade of raised

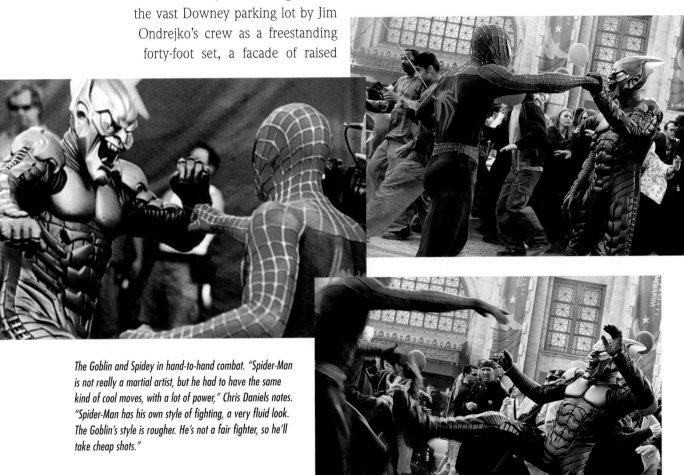

The Goblin and Spidey in hand-to-hand combat. "Spider-Man is not really a martial artist, but he had to have the same kind of cool moves, with a lot of power," Chris Daniels notes. "Spider-Man has his own style of fighting, a very fluid look. The Goblin's style is rougher. He's not a fair fighter, so he'll take cheap shots."

scaffolding and plywood glued and plastered over with trowels. "The first thing we did was reasphalt that parking lot area, make it nice and smooth," Ondrejko said. "Then we did all the concrete work, poured all the cement for the curbs, and built our facade on top of that. The plaster skins were made to look like stone, and behind our main building they'd computer-generate more buildings."

Yet another piece of the puzzle was a shot of MJ finally falling from the collapsing balcony and Spider-Man swooping to the rescue. The sequence included a dramatic outdoors drop at the Downey location, an area of

Top: Spider-Man meets Spider-Man! A number of Spidey stuntmen were on hand to provide the variety of specific stunts required for the action-packed Times Square sequence.

Middle and right: In this elaborate stunt, an acrobatic Spider-Man has flipped over these tables, careful not to dislodge even a napkin, but a super Goblin punch sends him flying back, with explosive results.

the parking lot painted green for a neutral backing, with stuntman Mark Wagner the man behind the mask and Jeri Habberstad, the stunt coordinator's sister, doubling for Dunst. Wagner was well versed in swinging from wire rigs and performing at great heights, having spent years as a competitive gymnast who later toured as a flying trapeze artist with a circus troupe. For the drop, Jeri Habberstad was rigged to flail away in a horrifying fall while Wagner took a dramatic 160-foot dive—just another day at the office for those who live the stuntman's code.

"I'd say more than 60 percent of our job is mental," Wagner reflected. "We have to keep cool in high-pressure situations. You not only have to keep your focus and do action, but bring character and performance to a stunt."

The jump began from a crane raised 160 feet above the ground. The cable for the aptly named "descender" rig was wound up in a big spool, with Jeff Habberstad controlling a manual braking system. "We hung from the cables with no mats

BELOW LEFT: The punch-propelled Spider-Man smashes into a breakaway light post, a stunt rigged with the aid of an overhead track. "He's hanging from a pull wire that runs through a pneumatic cylinder, which, with the compounding, gave forty feet of pull and acceleration, so he was really screaming in there," Jeff Habberstad explains. "Another wire decelerated him before he got too far into the post. Then we released the overhead wires so when he smashed into the light post he'd fall to the ground."

Greenscreen element and final Imageworks composite of Spider-Man swooping in to rescue MJ, who has fallen from her precarious perch on the crumbling balcony.

below; we fell toward solid concrete," Wagner recalls. "She fell first, but I was falling at a faster rate so that I could catch up to her before we hit our mark. It was a major adrenaline rush, but I also had to focus because I had to make a clean dive, grab her around the waist, and then make the motion like I'm slinging a web, which was added later in the computers. So I had to concentrate to make sure I was hitting every action I needed to do before Jeff put on the brakes and we hit our end mark."

According to Wagner, the fall was shot some fifteen times that day.

The battle in the air shifts to a ground-level duel between the two superpowered combatants, staged amid the frenzied extras at the Downey set. In another of the dramatic stunts, the Goblin has fallen off his glider, which, out of control, punctures a large inflatable balloon globe of Earth, which crashes onto the festival band shell and threatens to crush a little boy until Spidey swings in and saves him. This was the "Spidey saves little Billy" sequence, and the boy was played by Jeff Habberstad's own son, Shane.

To create the sphere, set decorator Karen O'Hara contracted Aerostar International, Inc., a South Dakota firm expert at balloon work and parade floats, and the result was a 600-pound, 40-foot cold-air inflated balloon. "It's bigger than it sounds—that's as tall as a four-story building," O'Hara noted. "John Frazier rigged the glider on wires from a crane to hit the balloon, which was suspended from a crane."

In yet another stunt, Spider-Man does a clean gymnastic flip over tables, including one stacked with a pyramid of filled champagne glasses. For that, gymnastic expert and Spidey team member Alex Chansky got the call to suit up in the red and blue.

"We built a spring floor into the asphalt and these tables—just like the spring floors that give more bounce when Olympic athletes do their tumbling runs," Jeff Habberstad revealed. "It was a precise thing. Alex had to go from table to table and do tucks in between. The tables were only three feet wide, so he had a fairly small target to land on. Then, after his running and flipping ordeal, he lands and fights with the Goblin on the other end. The Goblin punches Spider-Man in his super way, and Spider-Man crashes back through all of this stuff he just missed and smashes into a light pole, which falls over."

One of the standout stuntmen throughout was Willem Dafoe, the actor earning raves from stunt and special effects crews for his dedication and desire to do *everything*. "I love doing physical stuff; it's the purest

Top: Team Spidey stunt double Zack Hudson gets raised up at the Times Square set.

Bottom: Spider-Man survives the Goblin's attack—to fight another day.

kind of performing for me," Dafoe said. "It's exciting, athletic. But there were times Kim Kahana doubled for me, either on a couple things that were a little too dangerous or when they had to shoot double units and needed to film two Goblins at the same time. But it was very important—how the Goblin moved—and as good a stuntman as Kim is, he's not me. I didn't want anyone else doing my movements."

One of Dafoe's greatest athletic challenges was simply standing up on the glider built by John Frazier's special effects squad. "Willem was a natural; he seemed born to it," Frazier said with unreserved awe. "Actually, we were all taken aback; our jaws were dropping. He was so cool up there—like he was surfing. He had the moves, but he was also unafraid of it. He made us look good."

Spidey takes a break from the action while Ric Spencer, key set costumer for the second unit, checks the costume's eyepiece.

"Riding the glider was like surfing or snowboarding; it was about balance and shifting weight," Dafoe said. "There were a couple of power moves where you had to let your weight go forward. One of the tricky things was that your feet are locked into this glider, so there was always some concern that if you didn't zig when it zigged, you could break your ankles. That was a little hairy, but it was programmed on the computer so I'd have some sense of what the pattern was; I could anticipate those weight changes."

The glider included snowboardlike bindings in which the Goblin could stick special shoes. The tension on the springs of the shoe bindings was adjustable to accommodate either Dafoe or his stunt double. "That was real tricky to work out," Frazier noted, "having the wings dip from side to side yet keeping these bindings level so Willem could stay upright and not break his ankle. But that's why it was done hydraulically, through a computer, so we could program specific moves."

The physical glider was fixed atop a shaft that raised it two feet above a six-axis, 500-pound motion base. The specific and repeatable move data could also be passed to Imageworks. "In this age, everything has to match with what the computer guys are doing," Frazier said. "We could program a move on our glider and then give Imageworks a disc with a copy of the move."

One of Dafoe's most dangerous stunts was riding a "machine gun" glider for a live-action scene of the Goblin strafing the World Unity Festival while a beleaguered Spider-Man dodges the pyrotechnic hits. The setup involved hanging the glider from the crane of a camera car at the Downey location. The stunt department was planning to use a Goblin double—but Willem Dafoe wasn't going to sit on the sidelines for this one.

"We were going to do this machine gun strafing, and Willem came out and said, 'I need to be doing that,'" Frazier recalled. "And it was real dangerous. We're hanging this guy off the side of the camera car as he's chasing Spider-Man and we're driving thirty miles an hour! But Willem was such a professional, he made sure it would not only look good but be safe. His concern about doing the stunt himself was *he* was the Goblin. And nobody could match Willem's look. There wasn't a stuntman or photo double that could do what Willem could do."

THE GOBLIN SUIT

Costume designer James Acheson realized a challenge lay ahead when Willem Dafoe came in for his first Goblin costume fitting and did the splits. "Willem is a yogi of some twenty years' experience, with not an ounce of fat on his body, and he wanted to play the Goblin in a more acrobatic way," Acheson said. "We realized we needed to have a costume as flexible as the actor, because the actor wears the costume, not the other way around." As with the Spider-Man suit, John David Ridge, Inc., and Amalgamated Dynamics, Inc., helped bring Acheson's design off the drawing board and onto the actor.

Since Dafoe had been cast so late in preproduction, the Chris Daniels lifecast taken for Spider-Man had been used as the starting point for the Goblin suit, which was composed of strips of spandex and vinyl sewn together by Ridge's company. "The spandex gave it the stretch, particularly in the crotch and inside of the legs, so Willem could hunch down like a surfer on his glider," Ridge explained. "Each piece was different, some padded or folded."

Martin Smeaton, another sculptor working with Acheson, sculpted the separate panels for the look of segmented armor. Then ADI cast the pieces that went over the suit. Those costume pieces were covered with vinyl by Ridge, the vinyl "pearlized" with a dye that provided an iridescent finish, as Ridge described it.

In all, some 580 separate pieces went into each of nine final Goblin suits.

It was a rush to get the costume fitted properly, since Dafoe was set to go before the cameras as the Goblin on January 23, Ridge recalled. The suit was too ill-fitting and baggy in places—but that was the point of the fittings, to make those discoveries and deal with them. "It looked *awful* that first fitting," Ridge groaned, "but we learned a lot, because we didn't know how much it would stretch. We took out fabric by the handfuls to get it skintight. We had six more fittings, honing in each time. It was a real madhouse, but we made it."

in Glider   Jim Martin

The Goblin's glider went through numerous designs.

RIGHT: This Jason Mahakian schematic, dated May 2000, works out an early design for a Goblin "skyboard."

ABOVE RIGHT: Early skyboard concept by Jim Martin featuring step-in bindings and a rotating foot mechanism so the Goblin could ride like a surfer.

ABOVE LEFT: Goblin "flyer" concepts by Harald Belker.

LEFT: *For this glider shot featuring Dafoe in costume, the close-up's the thing. Dafoe's stunt double Kim Kahana looks on.*

BELOW RIGHT: *Dafoe and J. K. Simmons practice for a scene in which the Goblin and glider burst into the Bugle office.*

BOTTOM: *The Goblin in all of his glory.*

BUILDING THE GOBLIN GLIDER

After the art department prepared a digital blueprint for the Goblin's glider, special effects coordinator John Frazier could convert it to a special computerized system for controlling a device that precision-cut all the glider pieces out of foam—some fifty different parts. The actual computerized device, which Frazier calls a "five-axis overhead router," was truly cutting-edge technology, recently built by Frazier's shop and used for the first time on *Spider-Man*.

"We could make a car with this," Frazier said. "This technology is certainly out there, but this is new for the motion picture industry. Normally, everything at a studio is done by hand. It takes someone like us to come along and say, 'Hey, look! This is the New Age of computers.' We're that New Age shop."

In the final construction phase, fiberglass molds were made of the foam pieces. Ultimately, Frazier's shop turned out six gliders, each about six feet in wing span. Although each represented the same "hero" machine, one was rigged with machine guns, another with pumpkin bombs. "You couldn't get all that stuff into one machine, so each glider we built was a specialty glider," Frazier said. "It's all movie magic."

Imageworks reconstructed the glider in CG using reference material, notably photos of

the physical glider scanned into a computer. Although the moves of the physical—or "practical"—glider programmed by Frazier could be supplied to the effects artists, the data that built the practical glider wouldn't necessarily directly convert into the CG model. "We had to set up our glider with certain textures and ways it moved," CG supervisor Ken Hahn said. "Sometimes a production will rely on [a CG prop] to go further than with a practical one."

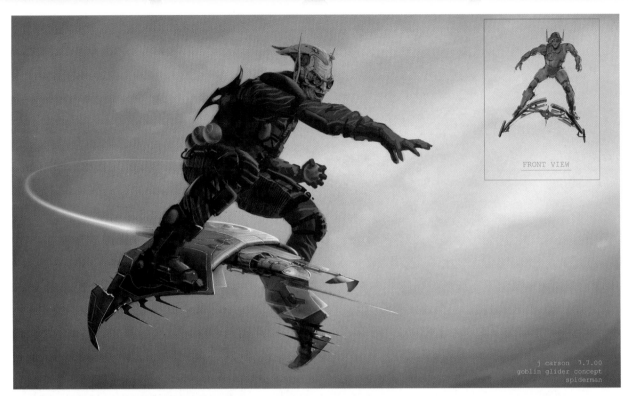

FRONT VIEW

j carson 7.7.00
goblin glider concept
spiderman

TOP: *James Carson glider concept art.*

ABOVE: *The Goblin takes his place on the glider for a bluescreen visual effects shot.*

ABOVE RIGHT AND BELOW: *Goblin glider rigged for OsCorp lab scene and World Unity Festival location filming.*

LEFT: Goblin glider model with steel support structure highlighted in red, with orange pumpkin bombs visible in their launch chutes. John Frazier's shop took the digital data of this Ozzimo model and converted it to a special computer-controlled device that cut out of foam the exact pieces for the final physical prop.

BELOW LEFT: Goblin glider, front view, art department rendered design. Concept includes "laser o's" for blasting deadly laser rings.

ABOVE: Spider-Man glider blueprint, top view, prepared by the art department. Note the machine gun doors and pumpkin bomb launch hole. Glider team development by James Carson, Paul Ozzimo, and François Audouy.

BOTTOM LEFT AND RIGHT: Top and bottom views of 3-D Goblin glider model built by Paul Ozzimo from James Carson's design. Ozzimo took Carson's illustrations and sculpted a detailed clay model, which he then photographed and scanned into a computer. With Rhinoceros (or Rhino) modeling software, Ozzimo built in details, from the glider's steel structure to the machine gun barrels visible in the upper, leading edges of each wing.

SPIDER-MAN ART DEPT. 9.25.2000
GOBLIN GLIDER
DESIGN: JIM CARSON
3D MODEL: PAUL OZZIMO

SPIDER-MAN ART DEPT. 9.25.20
GOBLIN GLIDER
DESIGN: JIM CARSON
3D MODEL: PAUL OZZIMO

GOBLIN GLIDER GADGETS

When the Green Goblin of the comics was ready for a night of mayhem, he always had his bag filled with nasty tricks, including mechanical bats able to emit blinding black smoke, and bombs shaped like miniature pumpkins. But the bombs designed by Harald Belker for the movie departed from the cartoony contraptions of the comics. "Sam wanted the Green Goblin to be a believable character, so his actual weaponry had to be more functional, yet still look cool," James Carson explained.

Each specialty glider required particular setups by Frazier's effects team. The machine gun glider was radio controlled, with three guns on each wing able to trigger a mixture of acetylene and oxygen, creating little explosions and the illusion of real guns firing. The pumpkin bomb glider was also operated

TOP LEFT AND RIGHT: Glider boots and bindings, with special Goblin footwear.

MIDDLE: Boot mount concept design by James Carson.

ABOVE AND LEFT: Goblin trident concept art by James Carson and final prop.

via radio control, with an internal mechanism that allowed each baseball-sized prop to pop straight up. "We could load six at a time, fed by air pressure, like balls in a pinball machine, through a chute built inside the left wing," Frazier explained. "A pumpkin bomb would pop straight up, about three or four feet in the air, so Willem could catch it. Willem was great with it, because he'd be in the costume and mask and it was hard for him to see. But we'd time when they'd pop up and how high each bomb was, so when he heard the noise he could reach out and grab a bomb without even looking at it." The pumpkin bomb props themselves were made of fiberglass, with buttons on top that Dafoe could press to set off a sequence of blinking lights, as if the device had been activated.

Harald Belker and Paul Ozzimo teamed up to work out the ingenious and deadly ways the Goblin's various pumpkin bombs—from bat-shaped to boomerang devices—would unfold. "Harald did line drawings and I transformed them into 3-D shapes in the Rhino modeling program," Ozzimo explains.

BELOW RIGHT: *In this Ozzimo model of a Belker design, a laser pumpkin bomb is pictured in its final, ready position.*

MIDDLE RIGHT: *This 3-D "solid model" pumpkin bomb design was transformed from digital data to physical object in a process Paul Ozzimo called "rapid prototyping," a method by which Squid Prototyping, an outside vendor, used its Pattern Master machine to "grow" a three-inch-diameter prop. "The 3-D model data is imported into this machine, which breaks the model into tiny slices, reinterprets those layers, and grows material to form the object by using a 3-D printer to print out the parts in a wax and plastic mixture," Ozzimo explains, noting many industries utilize this and similar devices to create product prototypes.*

BELOW LEFT: *Pumpkin bomb laser gun design by Harald Belker, 3-D model by Paul Ozzimo.*

BOTTOM RIGHT: *Boomerang design by Harald Belker, 3-D model by Paul Ozzimo.*

BOTTOM LEFT: *Spider-Man* art *department pumpkin bomb concepts. Concept art by Harald Belker.*

Pumpkin-bomb (Laser gun)

Spider-man Art Dept.
08-24-00
Design by Harald Belker
3D-Model by Paul Ozzimo

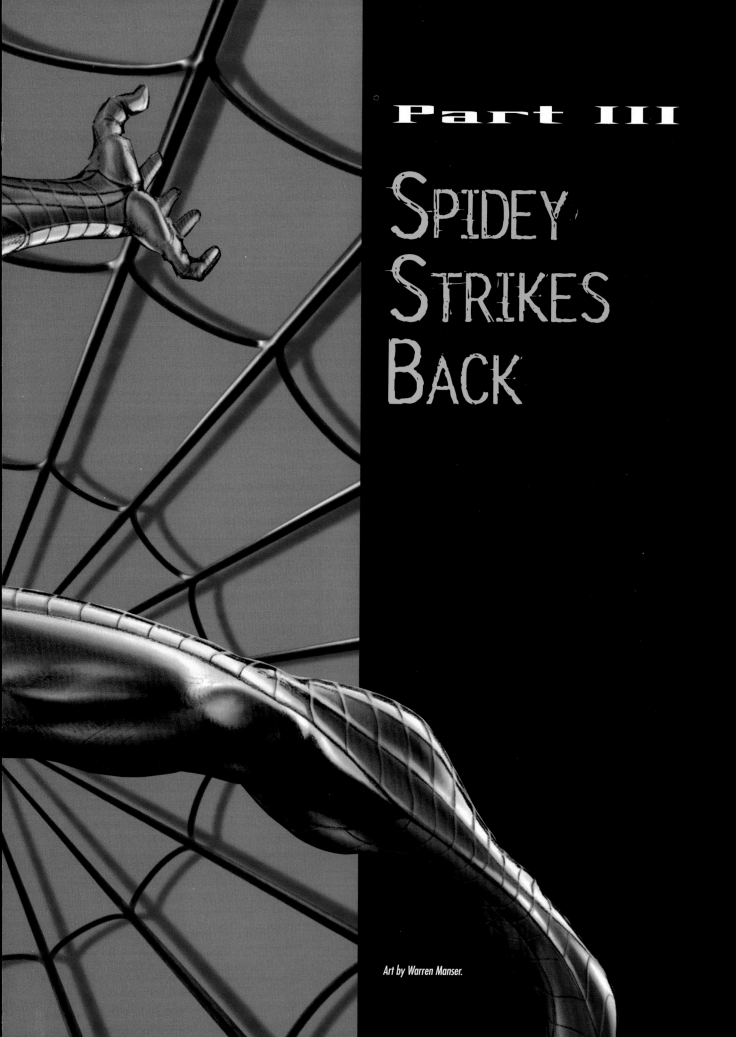

Art by Warren Manser.

Part III

Spidey Strikes Back

CHAPTER SEVEN

Your friendly neighborhood spider-man

The room is cool and dark, except for the high-tech glow of a monitor, but there's a whisper of distant, wide-open spaces in the Moroccan rug that hangs on a far wall and the candle flickering in a jar. Sam Raimi is leaning forward on a couch, deep in the muse of postproduction, watching as editor Arthur Coburn works on the digital Avid editing machine. Unlike the days of Moviolas and cutting and splicing film, a click of this machine calls up any piece of digitized footage. It's a medium where not only principle photography, but visual effects shots in progress—elements of animated characters and synthetic cityscapes—can be combined with the live-action footage.

On the phosphorescent screen, a computer-generated Peter Parker, dressed in his wrestling costume, drops out of the sky onto the roof of the car driven by his uncle's killer. Then the killer is firing gunshots through the roof as the scene plays out with temp music, screaming police sirens, and screeching tires taking hairpin turns.

"Spidey is no fool," Coburn mentions, wondering if maybe Peter should be out of there before too many bullet holes crack through the roof.

"I think all we need is one shot to show he's got a gun and is firing," Raimi replies.

Then, in his leap from the car, the masked man seems to stay up in the air too long for Raimi's taste. "At the top of that shot he doesn't want to come down."

Left: Final Imageworks "slick costume" Spidey model, test image pictured against the film's final "hulking ruin" battleground (note the shadowy Goblin in the background).

ABOVE RIGHT: Spider-Man and Mary Jane take a breather following the World Unity Festival assault.

TOP: *The effects artists at Sony Pictures Imageworks get to vicariously emulate Spider-Man's web-swinging heroics. Let's hope John Dykstra and crew haven't taken their assignment as seriously as did their colleague Mysterio, one of the wizards of special effects who decided to simulate Spider-Man's superpowers. The Amazing Spider-Man #13, "The Menace of . . . Mysterio!" pages 15–16 / Artist: Steve Ditko*

ABOVE: *Spidey is set up for a greenscreen shot. The dramatic shots of Spider-Man soaring through Manhattan utilized a computer-generated character composited into a synthetic New York backdrop.*

"You want another shot for this?"

"Maybe there's one where he descends quicker."

The two debate the entire chase sequence from where Peter Parker takes his still fledgling superleaps, the sequence featuring a rough, computer-generated figure swooping down over both live-action plates and an entirely computer-generated cityscape. Looking like a video game figure (and long, long before the final high-resolution detailing and animation will be done) this is Imageworks' previsualization, 3-D animation that allows the filmmakers to create a rough composite, to better ascertain how live action and CG animation are matching up.

"The previz basically replaced the animated storyboard panels, but those early animatics were important—before shooting started, the whole movie existed," Bob Murawski, who shared editing duties with Coburn on *Spider-Man*, explained. "Once we got the shot, with the previz we had a CG Spidey we could put into the live action. The previz gives a feeling of the overall pace of a shot, whether it's too fast or slow. While we're editing we can speed things up or slow them down, move that animated figure around in our live-action plate. We sped up the CG figure of Peter in his wrestling suit 20 percent when he's jumping from rooftop to rooftop. There was a lot of back and forth between us and Imageworks. What was cool was every week there was a progression. We saw more and more refined versions of the CG work; it became more textured and realistic. Also, with a lot of CG shots coming in, there was the potential of making things different, a lot of options and the ability to manipulate the story and action."

The Imageworks facility is located in Culver City near the historic old Selznick movie lot where once stood the gates that kept out King Kong, and where antebellum Tara stood and Atlanta burned. Imageworks had been pushing the art of visual effects on such productions as *Stuart Little* and *Hollow Man*. Not only did the effects house have to create a realistic, athletic Spidey, but it usually had to place the superhero within a synthetic New York City.

"Whenever Spider-Man had to do more radical web swings with radical camera moves following him, that dictated where we'd have our synthetic environment," digital effects supervisor Scott Stokdyk explained.

The Imageworks approach for creating its virtual cityscape was texture mapping, with scanned textures applied to basic CG forms. "Texture mapping means we generated our synthetic buildings with photographs of real buildings," John Dykstra explained. "We could take still photographs of real buildings from different angles, and use survey data so we'd know exactly the positions of those buildings. We could then build a piece of geometry to match that building, varying the data depending on how close we had to come with our virtual camera. Then we created a projection in the virtual environment that matched the position of the taking camera position, and projected the textures from the building back onto that geometry."

The process was coordinated with production

After the completion of the greenscreen effects shot of Spidey swinging in to rescue MJ, the production cut to live-action filming of the web-slinger setting Mary Jane down on a garden rooftop at Rockefeller Center.

The red lines over the images of these Times Square buildings indicate the laser path traced by Imageworks' surveying devices, while the green lines show CG building model wireframes based on the information. "The red line encompassed every single point captured by the laser surveying equipment," digital effects supervisor Stokdyk outlines. "This is a preliminary connect-the-dots step. The green lines for the modelers are then used in match-moving, for previsualization, and in the lighting phase to cast and catch shadows from the CG elements we added into the environment."

designer Neil Spisak, who selected fifteen specific "hero" buildings in Manhattan, which Kerry Nordquist, Imageworks' lead texture painter, spent more than a month photographing, along with supplementary buildings. "I selected the buildings that formed the working library, very specific buildings scouted all over New York," Spisak says. "There was the idea of the Beaux Arts buildings mixed with a little bit of the more modern buildings."

Nordquist shot his still photos from both street level as well as from adjacent buildings, aiming at the skyscraper heights with his telephoto lens. He returned to Culver City with some 8,000 photos, Stokdyk estimated. Some photos weren't acceptable for texture mapping; others were purely reference shots for different times and lighting conditions. The detailed survey data—taken using the same measuring devices as used by road construction crews—provided essential information concerning key points in the buildings.

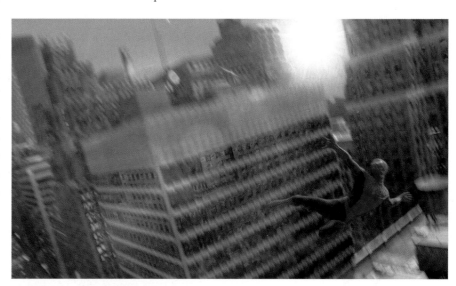

"One of our concerns was whether fifteen hero buildings was going to be enough, because we wanted to [maintain] the integrity of the buildings the production had selected," CG supervisor Ken Hahn, whose focus included the 3-D environments, said. "But we found that if you looked at a hero building from a different angle, particularly the older ones, there were enough architectural differences, say stone work or glass,

The CG Spider-Man's first appearance, in a July 11, 2001, theatrical trailer, which included this dramatic sunshine "flare" shot, also featured an entirely synthetic city as backdrop. The "building pipeline" team included lead technical director Francisco de Jesus, lead texture painter Kerry Nordquist, lead modeler Alex Whang, and early R&D supervisor Sam Richards. The "hero" building models were created in Maya, with Houdini software essentially "gluing together the texture maps to the models," Ken Hahn, CG supervisor for the building R&D, says. The CG cityscape was also designed so Imageworks' technical directors could have their computers program the types of rooms assigned from a digital library, automatically calculating such random details as the percentage of rooms with lights off or on. The city views were also embellished with a variety of CG props, including birds, pedestrians, building heat vents generating smoke, and moving traffic. "Anything to keep the shot alive and in motion," Hahn observes.

ABOVE LEFT: Imageworks' animation previsualization of Peter Parker for the chase after his uncle's killer.

ABOVE RIGHT: After animation was accepted, the cloth simulation program for the wrestling costume, developed by Daniel Kramer under CG supervisor Daniel Eaton, could be run. "We render our cloth tests with a checkerboard pattern because it makes it easier to see wrinkles, movement, and surface stretching," Scott Stokdyk notes.

RIGHT: CG Spidey performance animation, with cloth simulation.

that it was tough to tell that it was the same building. We mixed and matched the various hero buildings, and we also shot midlevel buildings we could intersperse."

Ultimately, the virtual cityscape was formed using those fifteen high-resolution foreground buildings that would be closest to camera, with twenty to forty midlevel and background buildings that would be created at varying resolutions. Imageworks further extended the digital cityscape to the distant horizon. At that distance objects would be too far away to betray perspective shifts, and digital matte paintings and still photos would provide the distant skylines.

For the reflections on the building windows themselves, Imageworks technical directors converted their shaders—the algorithm for determining the shininess and color of a surface—to work with Mental Ray rendering software, which allowed for realistic motion-blurred reflections as Spidey, and the virtual camera, flew past.

Author Terrence Masson, in his 1999 book *CG 101*, has called rendering "the cinematography of computer graphics." Rendering involves the actual creation of a digital picture in terms of its lighting, surface quality,

Test photo scan of a suited-up Chris Daniels (left) and CG model replacement; Dafoe in the Goblin suit poses for test scan (left) and CG model replacement. As with Imageworks' test replacement of real buildings with computer-generated copies, these photo scans provided a sure way of ascertaining how accurately the digital doubles matched the real-life performers. "Without this kind of proof-of-concept test, we're reduced to subjective judgments and making the characters look 'cool,' " Stokdyk notes. "We had to prove we could cut back from CG characters to the real thing."

After having saved Mary Jane from a pack of muggers, Spidey drops in to share the moment with the fair lady. That's Tobey Maguire suspended upside down for the romantic interlude.

and other aspects. For *Spider-Man*, digital reflections and shadows were "ray traced," a rendering technique different from "radiosity," a technique that calculates the ambient qualities of reflected light throughout a scene. While some consider radiosity a more realistic approach for lighting a 3-D scene, the lighting for *Spider-Man* was "cinematic lighting," Hahn explained. "Radiosity looked too real-world, too monochromatic. We did try to light our virtual environments realistically, but that wasn't the aesthetic the production was looking for."

Hahn cites as an example of cinematic lighting the first *Spider-Man* theatrical trailer, which featured shots of a computer-generated Spider-Man swinging through the city. The trailer, showing Imageworks' virtual city during Spidey's fly-through, began with a specific sun position requested by the production, which produced a dramatic lens flare over a swinging Spider-Man—and was one of the first CG Spidey shots Imageworks developed. But if that sun position had remained consistent throughout, it'd have put everything in shadow.

"It's subtle, but we basically cheated the sun position three times throughout that sequence," Hahn said. "Actually, we cheated the sun position a fourth time—to light Spider-Man. He's brighter in those shots then he'd be normally. But in movies you want to light the main character to stand out, not fade into the background. That lighting was particularly important to Avi Arad. He wanted audiences to see Spider-Man, not have their gaze drift off him."

Creating the CG superhero was a case of déjà vu all over again for supervisor John Dykstra. As the overall visual effects supervisor on the 1995 release *Batman Forever*, Dykstra had watched over the creation of a computer-generated Caped Crusader, the beginning of a learning curve that reached fruition in the CG web-slinger. "I began doing our CG Spider-Man when we began doing that figure of Batman, no question about it," Dykstra admitted.

One of the first synthetic stuntmen was the lawyer who was eaten by a T. rex in 1993's *Jurassic Park*. For the next level, in *Batman Forever*, the "breakthrough" CG Batman took a 600-foot fall with a dramatic virtual camera move, and "our CGI superhero allowed us to give the character the graphic quality of the comics," Dykstra said at the time (in an article for issue #63 of *Cinefex* magazine).

But while that CG Bat-hero might have been super in its day, it'd be no match for today's super-CG Spidey. "That was six years ago!" Dykstra said, smiling. "*Spider-Man* is *multiple* light-years beyond! It's fair to say that the Batman character was terrific for his time, and had a panache you wouldn't have gotten out of a stunt guy. And, in a sense, you could call our Spider-Man a digital stunt person, because it's a surrogate for the actor, Tobey Maguire.

The Kiss of the Spider-Man. "One thing I always thought was funny," Dunst giggles, "is what if Mary Jane pulled down Spider-Man's mask and he was some kind of weird old creepy dude? That was very risky of MJ to pull down his mask and kiss him."

"But there's a physical performance and physiognomy that's critical to our character. Today we have hugely, hugely higher resolution figures and more experienced animators, so our character can live more in an anthropomorphic world of real people. It has all the subtleties of motion, down to the slight tremors that go through people when they shift their weight. The ability to interpret athleticism is another step up. And there are more factors: Is our Spider-Man excited, happy, or unhappy? Those emotions have an impact on how he moves. The key is the CG guy is indistinguishable from the live guy, with the exception of the feats he can perform."

"The Spider-Man model we built was very complex, but very efficient," Peter Nofz noted. "It's a process of computers getting faster and faster and us being careful not to add anything that wasn't absolutely necessary. The entire computer model is built up of patches [each a four-sided 3-D geometric surface], and a model can 'break' if one patch stretches differently for one motion than another. Gaps can become apparent. They can be stitched together, but it's better to have them stay together from the get-go. In fact, normally we put limits on all our models to discourage animators from doing something that a human being couldn't do. But with our Spider-Man model we definitely allowed animators to go beyond what a human being can do."

The CG Spider-Man model required two costumes, one the classic spandex costume—his "slick" costume as Imageworks called it—the other Peter Parker's outfit of sneakers, sweat pants, and a sprayed spider-pattern shirt. Instead of the normal cloth-simulation program for adding clothes, Imageworks' Daniel Kramer, working under CG supervisor Daniel Eaton, came up with a method for taking the cloth patterns from the actual wrestling costume into the computer and projecting them over the slick-costume model figure.

Key to the animation was the setup of the classically costumed Spidey figure. Imageworks had created computer-generated muscle, bones, and skin for the anatomical reveals of the invisible man character becoming visible in the 2000 release *Hollow Man*, a breakthrough that helped effects artists produce a CG Spider-Man with a believable physique. "We treated the slick costume like human skin, but with slide and stretch in different areas," Stokdyk explained. "When we worked on *Hollow Man* we learned a lot about how to get good representations of muscle underneath the skin—this was the next step.

"Koji Morihiro, one of our physiquers, spent almost eight months looking at all the videotape we shot of the people in the costumes during the cyberscan, balancing how that costume should realistically stretch over muscles," Stokdyk added. "Then he'd basically bind the surface to the animation skeleton, going through a range of motions and doing different weightings on the surface to make it look right, dialing in how much every point on that surface would move relative to the motion of the whole. From there, when the animators were animating the slick-costume model, they could just apply their animation to the system Koji had set up."

The Spider-Man animated character itself lived in a strange, subjective area of having to look realistic while performing fantastic feats, and that was of constant concern for animation supervisor Anthony LaMolinara. "At first glance it doesn't feel right to see a character jump thirty feet up on a wall. The most challenging shots were just having him crawl up a building, because it involved so many sub-tleties [that had] to look right. There's the angle of his fingers, the shift of weight as he pulls himself up the wall, the movement of his hips and shoulders. So you're always playing around with this fine line between doing fantastic things, yet still having audiences accept it as a real person doing them.

"Spider-Man had to evolve, in terms of his ability. In the beginning, when he's first using his powers, he's a neophyte, and when he's swinging from his webbing he moves like a layman acrobat, clumsy and afraid. As the film progresses he becomes more adept at using his powers, and by the end, he's quite slick."

The animation itself first blocked in the action, establishing the general "motion and emotion of a shot," as lead animator Spencer Cook explained. "When that was accepted by the director and John Dykstra, we started adding the detailing, paying attention to what Spider-Man's fingers were doing, the exact twisting of his body.

"There's a lot that goes into it. When they shoot a background plate on stage or location, that has to be imported into the computer and an exact 3-D representation is made of that world by our match-move department, to literally match the point of view of the plate photography. With that 3-D environment, we do the animation, evaluating how the character interacts with the environment. If it's a completely CG environment, we'll have simple 3-D representations. In Maya software we have these things called shelves, a series of buttons to click on to activate different commands. Then, another team of modelers adds details to the buildings, the texture painters add even more detail to that, and the people who do the lighting, compositing, and rendering all add their specialties."

"There's this whole part of the movie that gets made in postproduction," producer Laura Ziskin said. "So we were always at Imageworks to see shots and address issues. Someone asked me, 'Do you go every day?' Well, it's like, why would I go to the shooting of principal photography every day? It's where the shots are being made that are going to be in the movie. *Of course* I had to be there."

That soaring figure of Spider-Man, as rescuer and protector, is what entrances Mary Jane and, ironically, further separates her from Peter Parker. "MJ has this obsession/crush thing with Spider-Man," Kirsten Dunst said, smiling. "He gives her feelings she's never had before. He makes her feel like a woman, instead of a girl. All girls love mystery, and it's a fantasy thing with Spider-Man—what's under that mask?"

CHAPTER EIGHT

Duel with the devil

Roosevelt Island, a strip of land between Manhattan and Queens, holds upon it a rotting corpse of a building, the remains of a pre–Civil War smallpox hospital—the perfect setting for the fateful encounter the production called "Spidey and Goblin Square Off." "It's a shell of a building; it's condemned," Neil Spisak said. "But beyond is the skyline of Manhattan, which Sam was interested in. What's funny is people don't really know about it. But it's not hidden—you can stand by the East River and look at Roosevelt Island and see it, it's right there! Sam called it the 'hulking ruin,' and that name always stuck."

Ever since their first encounter in the bedlam of the World Unity Festival, the encounters between Spider-Man and the Goblin have become darker, each more desperate, leading to that battle in the hulking ruin. "The Goblin doesn't hate Spider-Man. In fact, he respects him!" Dafoe said, smiling. "The only reason the Goblin wants to destroy Spider-Man is because he rejected him—he's hurt!

"There's a logic to the Goblin. It's not some abstract world-domination thing," Dafoe continued. "With Spider-Man he makes a case for an elitism he believes in, the seeds of which are in the Norman Osborn character. Norman is a self-made man, a man driven to pull himself up by the bootstraps and make something of himself. In our culture this is the good news, but the Goblin is the perversion of that. He says to Spider-Man, '*We* are the special people; those other people are the drones which it's our obligation to control.'

RIGHT: Spider-Man confronts the unmasked Goblin in the "hulking ruin" set.

"That's what he presents Spider-Man with, which is an interesting proposal because here you have a kid who's rejected constantly, who's talented but they're not the talents celebrated in the society. Then, suddenly, he has these newfound powers and it's like an adolescent coming into his sexuality—he doesn't know what to do with it! And here's this powerful figure saying, 'Look, kid. *This is the way!* This is our obligation.' There are all these interesting psychological underpinnings to this comic-book face-off."

The Goblin tries to get at Spider-Man through Peter Parker, bursting in on J. Jonah Jameson's *Bugle* office to demand the whereabouts of the kid who takes the pictures of Spider-Man—trying to shake out the answer as he literally has Jameson by the throat. "J. J. is the foul-tempered boss, and it's fun to see that kind of character in a tough situation," J. K. Simmons said. "But here's the thing that makes this character. Peter Parker has just left his office and the Goblin bursts in on his glider, lifts me up, and asks, 'Where is Peter Parker?' I should say, 'There he is!' But I say the noble thing, 'He's not here.' I risk my life to protect him."

The Goblin finally realizes that Peter Parker and Spider-Man are the same, and wages a campaign against him by attacking those dearest to him. The Goblin doesn't spare Aunt May, even as she kneels by her bed to say the Lord's Prayer. "I get as far as 'lead us not into temptation but,' and the next line is 'deliver us from evil,' and at that moment the Green Goblin crashes in and I stop, in horror," Rosemary Harris recalled. "And he goes, 'Finish it, finish it!' I say, '*from evil!*' And he says, 'Amen, lady!' He's trying to give me a heart attack, to kill me, I think. But I'm too resilient. I wake up in the hospital saying, 'Those eyes, those horrible yellow eyes!' But I survive.

"I teased Willem because we made a wonderful movie together called *Tom & Viv* [1994] and he was my son-in-law, and my char-

The Goblin lurks in the skyscraper heights. Although the production went for a realistic design, the airborne action lent a surreal touch, as did the Beaux Arts architecture Neil Spisak favored, evident here in the elaborate stone carvings of this set.

In this elaborate sequence, filmed in the Bugle set erected in the Downey warehouse, the Goblin throttles Jameson, demanding the whereabouts of Peter Parker, the kid who takes the Spider-Man pictures. The webbed one appears—and gets a whiff of Goblin knockout gas. (Throughout the film any visible wires or rigs—such as the glider motion base visible here—were digitally removed.)

BOTTOM RIGHT: In this reverse angle, note the blue sky backdrop and half-scale re-creation duplicating the building visible at the original Bugle set in downtown Los Angeles. "The real downtown building was visible about fifty feet away, but for our indoors set we built at half size and in perspective," construction coordinator Jim Ondrejko explains, "so it looks like the same building."

acter gives him a very hard time. So, I called this scene the 'son-in-law's revenge,' because now he gives me a hard time. I'm saying my prayers one moment and the next the bedroom wall crashes in and there's flame and smoke and Willem arrives. And everybody knew what was expected of them. People were shaking the bed, throwing bits of cork and debris around from the blast. The man on the wind machine was getting the wind at the right speed—he's an important guy, the man on the wind machine. Action pictures are difficult but wonderful!"

Harris marveled how, within the whole of the massive production, there was such attention to detail. Prop master Robin Miller even asked Harris what kind of book Aunt May would be reading during her hospital convalescence. "I called Robin back and said I thought Aunt May would probably have a little book of daily meditations. So I looked through my bookshelves and found this old, dusty volume of Marcel Proust's *Swann's Way*. I must have had that book for forty years, but never read it. But it just looked right, like it was an old book, a favorite book. I read it and I was enthralled! So that's the book I have with me in my hospital bed."

TOP LEFT: The director and stars share a moment during a break in the shooting.

TOP RIGHT: The Bugle trumpets J. Jonah Jameson's brave encounter with the dueling supercharacters. You didn't think the jovial one would let this headline-grabbing opportunity pass, did you?

BOTTOM RIGHT: The Goblin proposes a partnership to Spider-Man, a scene shot on the rooftop set built on Sony's stage 15, complete with a background photographic chromatrans. "You have to sell that it's nighttime New York," Don Burgess notes, "so I used a certain amount of smoke to create diffusion between the subjects and the trans. I usually don't like to use a lot of smoke, but New York outside you'll usually get that feeling of atmosphere, so it feels right."

TOP LEFT: Aunt May prepares to kiss a photo of Uncle Ben good night before saying her prayers. In a few moments, all hell breaks loose as the Green Goblin arrives.

The Goblin appears, terrorizing Aunt May. Actress Rosemary Harris later joked that this scene was Dafoe's revenge for an earlier movie they did together where she gave him the hard time.

In an echo of the dramatic comics fight between Spider-Man and the Goblin on the George Washington Bridge—that dramatic battle in which hostage Gwen Stacy dies—the Goblin kidnaps MJ and brings her to the top of the Queensboro Bridge. That face-off culminates with the superpowered Goblin breaking the cable for the Roosevelt Island tram and dropping MJ. Spider-Man's superheroic response—diving down, shooting his web at the bridge, and then catching MJ and the tram cable—required a practical stunt performed by Mark Wagner and Jeri Habberstad that the stunt coordinator called "the big fall and swing scenario."

The fall and swing was shot outdoors at the old Marineland park in Palos Verdes, California. The stunt performers would become matte elements in an Imageworks visual effects shot, but the scale of the shot would have been difficult to perform against the usual bluescreen backing. So the production used a technique that went back to the earliest live-action matte photography, using blue ocean

and sky as natural bluescreen. "It was shot on a bluff overlooking the ocean and blue sky," Jeff Habberstad explained, "a camera angle from the ground looking up, so the CG guys could pull a matte off the sky."

The stunt involved two 220-foot, sixty-ton cranes, with Habberstad and Wagner wired so they'd fall together. They began atop a crane that served as the platform, their cables strung to the opposite crane and rigged with a decelerator system, a pneumatic cylinder tested and preset to allow for

ABOVE: Aunt May says her prayers, blissfully unaware the Goblin is swooping in for a smashing entrance. Art by Jim Martin.

RIGHT: In this Wil Rees concept of the Goblin invading Mary Jane's apartment, the image was created while the glider was being considered as a telescoping device that could cleanly contort and glide through a narrow opening. However, in the final film, the glider makes a smashing entrance whenever the Goblin is on the attack. (Alert Spidey watchers will spy the webbed one in this picture.)

TOP: The Green Goblin on the attack, Queensboro Bridge sequence, art by Warren Manser. "For this image we were exploring the idea of the Goblin suit being based on product technology," Manser explains. "It was like the suit had integrated circuitry and was automated to do certain functions. This design showed that off [the circuitry beneath the suit].

RIGHT, BOTTOM RIGHT: The Goblin's terror campaign against Spider-Man includes kidnapping MJ and placing her on the precarious heights of the Queensboro Bridge. The scene was a dramatic echo of the Spider-Man and Goblin comic-book duel on the George Washington Bridge in which Gwen Stacy fell to her death.

The bridge set was based on drawings and photographic reference of the real bridge. The scale set was erected out of a steel framework, with molded fiberglass rivets and wood in the upper part textured with paint. "The painters are very important to a set. They make it look real," construction coordinator Ondrejko says.

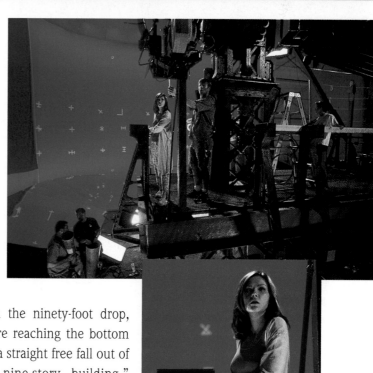

thirty-six feet of deceleration from the ninety-foot drop, absorbing the shock of the fall before reaching the bottom and then swinging them out. "It was a straight free fall out of a crane basket, equivalent to a nine-story building," Habberstad explains. "At the point where he shoots his web out to the bridge, the fall translates to a swing where the arc brings them another ninety feet. The total of their fall and swing was one hundred eighty feet—in one take."

A combination of Sony soundstage greenscreen shots allowed

ABOVE: The Green Goblin dangles a captive Mary Jane high above the waters of the East River.

LEFT: Kirsten Dunst prepares to be terrorized on the bridge set. "I told Kirsten, 'damsel in distress,' " Laura Ziskin says. "And it was scary—she was hanging from high places. But she was a good girl. She's also nineteen years old, so she has that going for her. But Sam told her very clearly at the beginning, 'There are things you're going to have to do.' And she was game."

"Once, I got dropped and swung too much and hit the side of what was supposed to be the bridge," Dunst says, grimacing. "I got a big black and blue mark on my arm. But I knew I wasn't in any danger. Jeff Habberstad, our stunt guy, was amazing. He showed and explained everything to me. He was so calm it made me feel calm."

for close-ups of Spidey and MJ dangling under the bridge, with Kirsten Dunst doing the honors. Raimi and Ziskin had both forewarned the actress that she would be placed in numerous damsel-in-distress situations.

"Kirsten was fantastic," Habberstad said. "Early on, we did the same thing with her that we did with Tobey, a test drop where I hoisted her up forty or fifty feet and dropped her on a decelerator wire. She spent a lot of time in the harnesses, and although they were as comfortable as they could be, she had to hang in ways that were not comfortable. But she didn't complain and she'd talk to me about any problems. She started out being a little afraid of heights, but she put a lot of faith in us and was willing to do what it took to make the shot. I can't say enough good things about her."

The bridge sequence also afforded a rare opportunity for the production to stage a dangerous stunt shot at the actual location, with New York authorities allowing Mark Wagner and Jeri Habberstad to be rigged and dangled from a crane parked underneath the bridge some 150 feet above the water. "But we couldn't hook anything to the bridge," Jeff Habberstad explained. "So we had to get the tip of the crane where we hung the wire—which was actually dressed with practical spider webbing, a kind of epoxy material—right up near the edge of the bridge."

Following the dramatic bridge battle above the East River, Spider-Man finally corners the Goblin one-on-one in the hulking ruin. Jim Ondrejko's construction crew built the interior at Sony stage 15, the set taking up almost half the stage and rising some forty feet high, the walls constructed of plywood backing nailed with sheets textured with simulated old bricks formed from different molds, with additional bricks plastered on in traditional bricklayer style. For a crawling ivy effect, Ondrejko's greensman used old grapevines with added leaves fashioned from silk.

The Roosevelt Island tram greenscreen set. In the bridge sequence, the Goblin severs the tram cables and drops MJ, forcing Spider-Man to perform a daring double rescue.

Fight choreographer Chuck Jeffreys worked with the stuntmen and the principal actors a couple of hours a day for about a week preparing for the hulking ruin face-off. Chris Daniels recalls that Dafoe did almost all his fighting in the final battle, with Tobey Maguire doing his share, as well.

As the final battle approached, it was apparent that it would be far more to the film than just another fight scene. Despite all the superhero action, the production never lost sight of the man behind the mask, that young man nursing his grief for his lost uncle, a fragile person coming to grips with his great power and awesome responsibility. The others of the pantheon—Superman, Wonder Woman, Captain Marvel—had about them the rarefied air of golden gods. Even Batman had a regal air, flying through the Gotham night as if he had wings, *forgetting* he was mortal—one of us.

And mortals know there's something called redemption.

"Visual effects, given enough time and money, can do anything—but that's a temporary satisfaction," Arad noted. "The main thing is seeing Peter and Mary Jane afraid, in love, disappointed, in love again. *Then* it becomes an awesome thing when the hero is flying in the air and you're

Conceptual image of the Queensboro Bridge sequence by Wil Rees.

flying with him. It's the ultimate wish fulfillment of the kid who couldn't, but now can, and you're watching him as a superhero and you're going, 'Good for you, Peter—wow!'"

And all the elements came together—from the soaring Spider-Man to the tense moments of character drama—in the cool, dark editing suites located off Main Street of the Sony lot, in the Gene Autry building. There, film editors Arthur Coburn and Bob Murawski created their individual versions of the picture in a highly unusual working method.

The process for a Raimi production began on *A Simple Plan*, with Coburn and Eric L. Beason doing the honors and each wanting to edit the entire picture, neither satisfied with having to divide up the sequences. Thus each editor provided Raimi with his own cut, leaving the director free to select what he liked from each, ranging from wholesale use of one editor's work on any given sequence to

TOP LEFT: A greenscreen shot with Dunst's double, Jeri Habberstad. "One of the physically challenging things was to hang from a cable and hold positions that aren't normal for a human being," Mark Wagner notes. "You end up using muscles you never knew you had. By the end of the day you're completely wiped out."

ABOVE AND LEFT: Dunst up in the air with Spidey, rigged for the bridge fall. Although computers have become omnipresent in filmmaking, the technology isn't used for actual stunts, according to Jeff Habberstad. "It's not the best deal to have a computer suddenly have a glitch in the middle of a sequence when you're relying on it for somebody's life. There's a great old seat-of-the-pants philosophy of watching it happen, you know? We can watch a stunt and slow things down or stop them manually, but a computer is preprogrammed."

what Murawski calls a "Frankenstein stitched-together version," combining the best of both.

"We each cut our alternate universe versions, but this system works because Sam likes choices," Murawski, who finished up when Coburn had to leave the production in mid-July 2001, said. "A good thing about Sam is, the shots have an inherent logic because he plans everything out. His coverage is thoughtful, as opposed to some directors who shoot from every considerable angle and sort it out in the editing room."

Raimi could work with either editor or both editors for eight to ten or more hours a day. With the nonlinear freedom provided by the Avid digital editing machine, the takes a director requests

are digitized and ordered by *bins*—an Avid term for a system that organizes all the printed and digitized takes in any given sequence. Murawski noted that Raimi's *Army of Darkness,* on which he was editor, was the first studio film to use a "nonlinear" digital editing machine. It was crude but "cool what these machines could do, like a word processor for film images. I get nostalgic for film, but on flatbeds with Moviolas it was very labor intensive, the cutting and splicing. Actually, after we digitally edit the whole movie, the work print is used to physically cut the final film together."

But whether it's cutting raw film or digital files, the editor's challenge is always the same. "Editing is like being a sculptor," Coburn related. "You get to work in a dark room and play with story and visuals—to re-create a story. To a degree, editing is creative problem solving. For this movie the wrestling sequence was tough, because a lot of footage had been shot. The Queensboro Bridge sequence was hard because it wasn't all there [because of later CGI that was added]. Other scenes might be a challenge because

ABOVE: Foiled again! The Goblin registers his frustration as our friendly neighborhood Spider-Man rescues both MJ and the tram full of passengers.

RIGHT: MJ suffers a deadly fall in the Queensboro Bridge sequence, in this greenscreen and final composite shot. (Fans of the Spider-Man comics, recalling Gwen Stacy's fatal fall, were doubtless relieved that history did not repeat itself, as the webbed one makes a successful rescue.).

Stuntman Chris Daniels makes a smashing entrance into a burning apartment set where the Goblin awaits. The rough plywood exterior will not be filmed; cameramen will record the action from inside what is a furnished set.

maybe they should have shot a certain angle but didn't have time to get to it, so you have to do without. By changing one shot you can change the whole meaning of a scene. Good editing is taking the images and coming up with creative solutions. And sometimes the best solutions come out of the deepest part of your consciousness, which, in my view, is the most creative part of your being.

"Leaps of discovery come from an intuitive place in your psyche, but you also can't have wonderful solutions without the freedom to fail. If you try to make everything a great suggestion, you're going to fail because you're trying to be too safe. Sam is a very creative person who isn't threatened if you try something. That's all you have at the end of the day, your instinct."

For both editors there would be a natural logic as to how a sequence could be structured, but often there were those intuitive ideas each brought to their individual cuts. For a flashback scene Peter experiences, recalling when he didn't stop the killer who ran past him, Coburn *reversed* the flashback footage.

Murawski had a sequence showing Norman Osborn leaving a disastrous Thanksgiving dinner party and having a violent seizure in the elevator, a cut Murawski himself moved to the *beginning* of the scene, when Norman arrives for the dinner, changing the whole mood of the sequence.

Coburn keeps his imagination charged, he said, by travel and encounters with different people and places. And so, when he comes to a new work space, he likes to bring in personal artifacts, a "nesting" touch to fill the space with "atmosphere and memories." For *Spider-Man*, a dominant piece of his nest was a rug from Morocco, purchased during a trip there to edit a TV movie, a memory artifact that reminds him of a town on the desert's edge, moonlit dunes, and crowded bazaars and mosques. "I find that the richest part of this work is the experience of being in a new place, meeting new people," Coburn said. "It's a mind- and spirit-changing experience."

RIGHT: Conceptual image of Spidey and Goblin battling in the "hulking ruin," by Wil Rees. Note the Queensboro Bridge visible outside the window, far right.

BOTTOM: Interior, hulking ruin set. Neil Spisak's location of the exterior site— an old hospital on Roosevelt island— inspired the scenes for the big Spider-Man/Goblin battle. "We knew the basic beats of what had to happen, but we were in the process of figuring out the specifics of what to do," producer Ziskin explains. "But that location became an inspiration for us; that's where the story went."

Moviemaking has been likened to a magic act, a circus, a dream state—it's all those things. Like any magic act, things disappear, the circus moves on, the dream dissipates but can linger in memory.

And so, the soundstage sets come down, the ensemble of talent go their separate ways, the months of action staged for the cameras remain as recorded, emulsive textures that will become visions of light when projected.

"That's what I find so amazing about movies," conceptual illustartor James Carson said, smiling. "A movie is a vast pool of knowledge and talent. Overnight a production forms a working company that basically designs and builds products, a functioning entity that lasts about a year's time—then goes away."

For Dunst, the chance to film on the Sony soundstages—the old MGM domain—was part of

LEFT AND MIDDLE LEFT: The fight in the hulking ruin was choreographed by Chuck Jeffreys and John Medlen in a week of rehearsals with the principal actors and stuntmen.

The duel ranged from fisticuffs to the Goblin wielding his deadly trident. "For a scene like the hulking ruin, it's a fine line between making something look dark and dramatic, yet introducing enough light to let the performances come through," cinematographer Don Burgess says. "The look of the hulking ruin is much more stylized than other parts of the movie. It's mano a mano in an old, dusty building."

BELOW: In a dramatic turn of the battle, Spidey webs and pulls a wall down onto the Goblin, who emerges unscathed.

In the final face-off, the defeated Norman Osborn asks for mercy.

the excitement of doing the movie. While she had been involved in playing Marion Davies, she'd looked at vintage footage of MGM and Hollywood's Golden Age, and she found herself appreciating that she was walking, literally, in the footsteps of the stars of old. "When you're making a movie it's like you live in this fantasy world they build with all these sets, and it's sad, at the end, when they tear them down. But I think a piece of that history, its spirit, kind of lives on in that studio soundstage. People say there are ghosts at the old MGM lot, and I'm sure there are.

"You know, when I go to certain sets I can feel the ghosts, particularly at Warner Bros. and at Sony, which feel the most like old Hollywood to me. When I was at the costume department and walking down the different streets at Sony I felt *something*—it was creepy, but comfortable creepy. I think I felt the energy of past movies, the presence of those legends from the past. And the fact that we shot our movie in those places makes me feel like a part of that history."

Months after the wrap of principal photography, Rosemary Harris was at her country retreat, sitting on the porch swing of a historic log cabin, watching an electric storm roll in, and reflecting on the *Spider-Man* experience. "My last scene in the movie, Tobey is there with me, doing his homework on my hospital bed. I tell him it's time for him to go home, that I'm fine now, 'You've done enough.' And then I say, 'Why don't you tell Mary Jane that you love her? She's waiting for you.'

"I'd never been in a visual effects film before and it was all intriguing and exciting. I looked around at all these grown-up people, all believing so completely in this wonderful fantasy and believing it with every fiber of their being and giving every ounce of their artistry to it. And we all believed that Tobey could hang upside down on the ceiling! It was wonderful, the dedication, because it certainly helped the credibility of all these extraordinary things happening. And Sam was a joy to behold directing the scenes, his commitment. It was wonderful childlike behavior on his and everyone's part, yet very adult and concentrated. It was all about using as much imagination as possible. But what is acting but make-believe? It's all 'let's pretend,' isn't it?"

CHAPTER NINE

If this be my destiny . . .

When Sony executive Yair Landau, a key player in bringing *Spider-Man* to Sony, became president of Sony Pictures Digital Entertainment, he had a front-row seat to watch the superhero emerge from Imageworks' computers. "I'm thrilled to be a part of the life of this character," Landau said, smiling at the thought of coming full circle.

Landau also was overseeing the Spider-Man Web site (http://www.sony.com/Spider-Man), the official place where, a year before the film's release, fans could begin to experience the character. According to Landau, when the first teaser trailer was put on-line, 1.9 million people downloaded it in less than a week. The launch of the Web site itself generated "six million page views the first few days," Landau recalled.

The flip side of the new media age were the unauthorized Spider-Man chat rooms and Web sites eager to dish even the crumbs of insider knowledge. "I have to assume there aren't a lot of productions like *Spider-Man* that have been scrutinized by such a large fan base from Day One," associate producer Grant Curtis said. "What was kind of a bummer was trying to keep things under wraps, like what the Green Goblin suit looked like, and then filming the World Unity Festival sequence and going home that night and seeing on an Internet site that one extra had taken an Instamatic picture of Willem standing there in full costume. That was tough. But not too many projects have forty years of anticipation built up by people who grew up with these characters.

LEFT: Spidey to the rescue!

RIGHT: A new generation of artists has been reimagining the classic exploits of Spider-Man, as in this Alex Ross image that freeze-frames a deadly encounter between Spider-Man and the Green Goblin. Marvels #0 (one-shot), cover / Artist: Alex Ross (based on a John Romita sketch)

There's so many people who have a personal investment in them."

The production was eager to reach out to its core audience far in advance of the film's opening, and a major venue for doing just that was the summer 2001 Comic-Con International in San Diego, the thirty-second annual gathering where, under one massive roof, gathered the forces and free-floating ephemera of pop culture. Through the downtown streets and historic Gaslamp Quarter, signposts decorated with signs proclaiming "Celebrating the Popular Arts" pointed the way to the San Diego Convention Center. More than 53,000 fans, guests, and exhibitors followed the lead, crowding more than 300,000 square feet of space.

In the modern world of media synergy, these conventions are fertile ground to plant the seeds that will flower into future movie attendance. Thus, the actual time machine used in the Dreamworks production of H. G. Wells's classic *Time Machine* novel sat in all its glittering simulated Machine Age glory, in a special carpeted display area. On an upper level, preview presentations for the future theatrical releases of *Spider-Man* and *Star Wars: Episode II* were held in meeting halls seating thousands.

On the floor, tattooed slackers walked alongside parents pushing infants in baby strollers. The true fanatics came costumed like their favorite heroes and villains: a green-haired, nattily dressed Joker strolled

Willem Dafoe rides the glider suspended from a camera car crane in this kinetic action scene, as the Goblin zeroes in on Spidey during the bedlam in Times Square.

These gunmen think they can make off with the take from a humble grocer's cash register. But that ain't gonna happen if your friendly neighborhood Spider-Man is around!

MIDDLE LEFT AND RIGHT: In this behind-the-scenes shot, a nifty wire rig serves the illusion of Spidey bringing down the bad guys.

Spiders also come out at night, particularly when there's a chance to thwart an armored car holdup.

with a woman costumed as Harley Quinn; Trekkies appeared in the guise of Klingons; cameras clicked as the towering, black-caped figure of Darth Vader swept by with a contingent of uniformed stormtroopers.

There was even a "real" superhero: Lou Ferrigno, the former Mr. America and Mr. Universe bodybuilder who played Marvel's green-skinned Hulk on the late-1970s CBS TV series. "I'm still a superhero in real life," he said, smiling, still possesing a body that looks straight out of a comic book, with biceps the size of an infant's head, arms as big around as a normal person's thighs. "As a kid, my two favorite comics were the Hulk and Spider-Man. I related to what the Hulk was going through, because people classified him as a monster, but he was basically a good guy. I understood the Hulk—the sensibility, the fear, the rejection, the aggression."

It was light-years beyond the sword-and-sorcery gatherings of old or the flea markets where fans rummaged through boxes of old comic books. At the booth for Neat Stuff Collectibles of New Jersey, a back wall displayed a lineup of the touch-

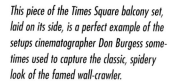

This piece of the Times Square balcony set, laid on its side, is a perfect example of the setups cinematographer Don Burgess sometimes used to capture the classic, spidery look of the famed wall-crawler.

stone comics that began the Golden Age, including Superman's first appearance in *Action* #1—priced at $43,000—and Batman's debut in the 1939 *Detective* #27, on sale for $42,000. And the prices would only get higher for this vanishing ephemera of the Golden Age, seller Oliver Hochron promised. "Every year it's fewer and fewer comics. It's just paper. One of these days it'll all be dust—unless these comics can be stored away like the Dead Sea scrolls."

But author Michael Chabon seemed to hold the key to the appeal of the old artifacts. The author of such novels as *Wonder Boys*—the movie version of which starred Tobey Maguire—was a featured guest and panelist on the strength of his 2000 Pulitzer Prize–winning novel *The Amazing Adventures of Kavalier & Clay*.

Set in New York during the birth of the great comic-book superheroes, the saga told of how two cousins, Joe Kavalier and Sammy Clay, create the superpowered Escapist, Nazi scourge and leader of the League of the Golden Key, a team of super freedom fighters operating out of their "secret mountain sanctum at the roof of the world." Chabon sat in a far corner of the professionals' area dubbed "Artists' Alley" and signed copies of his novel, drawing alongside his signature the outline of a key—the Escapist's iconic emblem. "Now you're a member of the League of the Golden Key," he said, and smiled as he handed the copy back to an admiring fan.

"Comics are tied up with childhood innocence and first experiences—it's been said that the

Being a superhero isn't about the glamour of fighting famous supervillains—it's about protecting the innocents. Here, Spider-Man does just that, rescuing a child from a burning building.

Golden Age is actually age eleven," Chabon reflected during a break. "I guess the concept of a Golden Age is always a question of looking backward."

And Chabon told the origin story of *Kavalier & Clay*. Many years ago he'd sold off his once vast childhood comics collection, except for a box of Jack Kirby comics from the late sixties and early seventies he couldn't bear to part with, comics that explored a mythological universe summed up in the titles *New Gods* and *Forever People*. "I taped up this box of comics and never opened it, just dragged it around with me wherever I moved—and I moved *a lot* in the next fifteen years. Finally, I'd just finished *Wonder Boys* and was thinking of what I was going to do next. I was also moving again and there was that box! So I got a knife and finally cracked it open.

"Now, some of those comics were in bags and others weren't, so they'd moldered a bit. When I opened that box this smell of moldering comics just came pouring out, washed over me, along with associations and memories and feelings about comic books I'd had since I was a kid, of being alone in my room reading comics, lonely but not necessarily unhappy. That feeling of traveling through space and time in my imagination while lying on my bed in the suburbs of Maryland, that amazing feeling of being in two places at once. A little bit of nostalgia and regret for the passing of time. That's when I realized, 'There's something in this box I need to write about.'"

At another booth, crowded by conventioneers and decorated with space suits, was Unobtainium Ltd., a collectibles company formed in June 2001 to make replicas of moviemaking artifacts. There, fans found *Spider-Man* movie props provided by Sony. Heading the enterprise was president Rick Cigel and his partner Christopher Gilman, a prop master with twenty years' experience in the movie business. The two were kindred spirits in their love of outer space stuff, the booth itself decorated with Gilman's special art, from an exacting replica of the Apollo 11 space suit worn by astronaut Edwin "Buzz" Aldrin, Jr., to screen-used astronaut suits made for *Space Cowboys* and *Deep Impact*. As Cigel explained, his love for prop replicas comes from his love for space memorabilia. "I can't be an astronaut, but to actually hold something that's been in space, that a real astronaut has used, thrills me no end—it's a piece of history and it's wonderful."

The *Spider-Man* props had arrived from Sony the day before, Cigel explained. He picked up what he called a screen-used pumpkin bomb that the Green Goblin had tossed. Cigel touched a top button, and the heavy, baseball-sized prop began glowing.

In the display case rested other *Spider-Man* items: the Goblin weapon the production called the trident, and a small Goblin glider model representing the full-scale and one-sixth replicas Unobtainium modelers planned to make of the original

flying machine. "Chris and I decided there's a great demand for high-quality, legitimate movie licensed prop replicas, so we met with the studios and they were all very interested," Cigel explained. "Most fans can't own the actual prop, so a replica is an extension of the love fans have for a movie and the items them-

Despite just making a daring rescue, the masked superhero is still confronted by two wary cops, one with a hand on his holster. Talk about being misunderstood! It'd probably help if the Daily Bugle wasn't keeping up that editorial drumbeat about the Spider-Man menace.

selves. For them to hold and display something just like what their favorite characters held is very important to them."

Spider-Man was born the year AT&T launched *Telstar*, the world's first commercial satellite, and seven years before the first lunar landing. The character had grown into a future once only dreamed of in science fiction or comic-book fantasies, a time of Earth-orbiting space stations and space shuttle flights, personal computers and the Internet, mass media and global satellite communications. Somehow, through all the decades of evolution and revolution, the character survived.

"There's a reason Spider-Man has lasted forty years—I think Stan Lee and his collaborators were geniuses," writer Brian Michael Bendis, a Comic-Con guest and honored comics writer/artist, said. "Peter Parker is very much like I was in high school. I related to him and felt like him."

Bendis, writer of Marvel's *Ultimate Spider-Man* comic-book series, is part of a new wave of Spider-Man comics creators, and was even asked by the *Spider-Man* movie production team for his notes on the movie script. It had been Bendis's *Torso*, a true-crime graphic novel, that was one of the reasons Marvel editor-in-chief Joe Quesada picked him. "I write characters," Bendis explained as he signed an *Ultimate* comic for a fan wearing a black T-shirt imprinted with the first *Amazing Fantasy* Spider-Man cover image. "Joe saw *Torso* and thought I'd be great for Spider-Man because he looked past the genre and thought, 'This guy writes people.' I always loved Spider-Man. I drew him from when I was a four-year-old. The lesson Peter Parker has to learn—'With great power comes great responsibility'—was like a mantra to me. I think it was my first philosophical thought as a child.

Tobey Maguire, unmasked, exhibits the intensity he brought to the role. Although he'd known of the famous comic-book superhero, he'd never understood Spider-Man until he got deep into the mythology. "When I try to flesh out a character I go to the source; that's why I read the first four years of the comics. I went back to get a sense of the comics as a whole, how people relate to Peter Parker, and who he is to me. And then, how all that fit into the movie Sam wanted to make and what I could do to make my part fit his vision. I never thought, 'This is a comic-book movie.' I approach everything real-istically: What if this really did happen?"

"When you think of all the recent pop-culture characters, almost all of them have about a two-year arc and then they fall by the wayside. So when I began working on updating the Spider-Man characters to a modern setting, I realized it's like when people take Shakespeare and put his characters in a new setting. The story still works, all the humanity rings true. And the reason is simple—Stan Lee was a genius."

Also at the convention was John Romita, one of the most fabled of Spider-Man creators and an artist who not only took over the *Amazing Spider-Man* comic after seminal Spidey artist Steve Ditko left, but worked on some of the great early stories, from the first appearance of marvelous Mary Jane to inking Gil Kane's art for the dramatic two-part tale in which Gwen Stacy and the Green Goblin both die. Romita, a veteran of a half century in the comics biz, has watched his son, John Jr., follow in his footsteps as a Spider-Man artist.

"I can't describe what that feels like," Romita Sr. said, and smiled. "A lot of my colleagues had kids who wanted to get into comics and couldn't make it—I'm blessed! I'm so proud of him, I can't tell you. Actually, I tried to talk him out of the business. I once asked him why he'd take a job that was liable to lead to a seven-day work week with long hours through the night. He used to come in and sympathize while I was working. 'Gee, you've been working all night while we were sleeping!' He'd rub my neck and check and see if I was all right. But he couldn't resist; it's a calling that's irresistible."

Sam Raimi included himself in that proud lineage of Marvel creators as he took the stage to present a first-time look at a scene from *Spider-Man*. Using an old Marvel Comics catch phrase, the director saluted the thousands of assembled fans as "True Believers." After this appearance, he noted, he had to race back to the editing room to work on the rough cut of the film he'd soon be showing the studio.

Almost forty years after his first appearance, Spider-Man gets a retrospective updating in Ultimate Spider-Man. *Here, Peter Parker's everlasting, agonizing regret—his failure to stop the thief who killed his Uncle Ben—haunts his dreams.* Ultimate Spider-Man #8, "Working Stiff," *pages 16-17 / Artists: Mark Bagley (pencils), Art Thibert (inks)*

CONTINUED AFTER NEXT PAGE

Whatever Peter Parker's travails, the regrets and burdens of his secret life or defeats and loss of loved ones, the guy possesses an indestructible spirit. Consider this classic scenario of a battle-weary Spidey, trapped under tons of steel as leaks in an underwater citadel keep getting bigger and, just out of reach, a precious serum that could save the life of his dying Aunt May. It's more than just his proportionate spider strength that will save the day—it's his proportionate heart. The Amazing Spider-Man #33, "The Final Chapter!" page 4 / Artist: Steve Ditko

Hands went up for a Q&A session, and to one Raimi explained the story was set in the classic origin years when Peter Parker was in high school. To another question he answered that he wanted Tobey Maguire for the lead because "he had that true good soul that I always thought that Peter Parker was." A fan of Raimi's old *Evil Dead* horror films asked about those beginnings, and the director recalled starting out in 1979 with a Super-8 movie camera to shoot a short he called *Within the Woods*, the film that helped him get financial backing. To another fan he explained he wanted audiences soaring with Spider-Man, but grounded in the story of Peter Parker who "was a loser, like all of us; that's why we're here, face it," Raimi concluded wryly as the audience laughed.

But what about the *curse* of Peter Parker being Spider-Man, another fan asked. Would the movie go into that?

"Maybe we did touch on the curse," Raimi reflected. "But more it's about how a young boy grows to be a responsible young man. In fact, why don't I show some of the picture right now?!" A huge, cheering ovation rolled through the vast hall. "We haven't shown anything to anyone, including Sony Pictures, so this is . . . a little treat we prepared for you guys."

The lights dimmed, the hall hushed as the stage screen lit up with the scene of the Midtown High field trip to the genetics lab. Flash and his cronies pick on Peter, bumping him the moment he tries to snap a picture of the spider display cases. Peter watches his pal Harry sidle up to Mary Jane, making a conversational gambit of the arachnid knowledge Peter has just shared with him. And only MJ notices that one of the superspiders seems to be missing. Then comes the fateful moment when their classmates file out and Peter and MJ are alone and Peter asks her to pose. Peter happily snaps away even as the escaped spider webs down, lands on his hand—bites him. He watches the strange spider fall and scurry off, looks at his hand where an ugly welt is already forming. "Parker, let's do it," an offscreen voice echoes.

And the clip ended with a single cut of a costumed Spidey swinging through Manhattan's skyscraper canyons. The lights came on as the crowd roared and whooped its approval. And some fans shook their heads, obviously thinking to themselves, *we have to wait a year for this movie!*

The movie the fans saw ended with a poignant encounter between Peter and MJ—the culmination of "any story worth telling," as Peter Parker's voice-over noted at the beginning. It's a scene in the best movie tradition of the guy and the girl who finally find themselves with no room left to run from each other. In the sweet agony of that precious moment, with the ferocious demands of the world mercifully at bay, MJ and Peter each find the next best thing to peace.

"Sam and I wanted to create a superhero for the girls," Dunst said, smiling. "We wanted them to watch MJ and realize that they can be true to themselves, that they don't have to pretend for anybody. It isn't until MJ faces death at the hands of the Green Goblin that she realizes Peter loves her for who she is, that he believes in her and not the facade she was putting on to please other people. I think Mary Jane is freed at that moment."

For Peter, his journey has simply brought him full circle to an understanding of his personal legend: "With great power there must also come great responsibility."

"The angst of Tobey as Spider-Man is he realizes that the closest people to him are the most in danger because of who he is," Avi Arad reflected. "That takes just as much courage as it takes to be a hero, to say to someone, 'I have to go.'"

And when Peter and MJ finally kiss, the production staged it with several meanings, one a magical memory awakened. "He kisses her and she realizes she's felt like this before—she knows it's *him*," Dunst said.

The end of the movie marked the end of a long creative journey. For years Stan Lee had been philosophical about the poor track record of Marvel characters as movie properties, but the fact that the creations of the Marvel universe were now bounding, leaping, flying off the comics page and onto the silver screen was a point of deep personal satisfaction. At least that was the thought *Spider-Man* associate producer Grant Curtis had the day he gave Lee a tour of the Times Square set.

Peter and MJ meet at Uncle Ben's grave for a precious moment of peace and understanding between them.

"Stan Lee came to do a cameo for the World Unity Festival, and Sam was in dailies and the extras were all eating, so the set was empty when I greeted Stan. Walking onto that set with Stan Lee and bringing him into the world he'd concocted in his head forty years ago was one of the most bizarre and gratifying experiences I've ever had! I'm basically telling him, 'Here's where the superhero you created is going to come down and battle one of the most famous villains you ever created.'

"I think he was impressed to see it all finally come to fruition, because *Spider-Man*, the movie, had been stalled for so long, and here it was finally being filmed and with a high degree of respect and craftsmanship going into his characters and his world. I was standing there with him, looking out over the set, and out of the corner of my eye he'd be smiling. I think that's what he was smiling about, just seeing it all finally coming to fruition."

The man behind the mask.

A dream had come to fruition for Sam Raimi, as well. The immense demands and pressures had not, by all reports, changed him. He had coolly taken on the blockbuster assignment as if he were back in the woods with his Super-8. "Sam has a sensitivity to people, not just the actors but the technical people around him," Cliff Robertson concluded. "I never saw him show any meanness, and under that kind of pressure it's almost expected that there be *moments*, lapses. There was a consistency about Sam that was so decent."

"Sam never wavered in the story he wanted to tell," Neil Spisak added. Throughout the production Raimi held fast to his passion for the heart and soul of Spider-Man—that emotionally vulnerable youth behind the mask.

"I'd like audiences to leave the theaters absolutely identifying with Tobey Maguire and his character and conflicts," Raimi revealed not long after the wrap of principal photography. "The character of Peter Parker has gone on a journey of learning what it takes to be a responsible young person, and having experienced that journey with him, it'd be nice if they gleaned some insights into that journey for their own lives. That's what stories can do."

Well, it took four decades, but finally Spidey and the Goblin got before the cameras, just like they did way back when in the comics. Say, isn't this where we came in?
The Amazing Spider-Man #14, "The Grotesque Adventure of the Green Goblin," page 7 / Artist: Steve Ditko

Several months later, on the Sony lot, Raimi sat under an umbrella at a table on a deserted patio off Main Street, taking a break before returning to the cool, dark editing room in the Gene Autry building. He was reminded of his comment about *Spider-Man* being a hero's journey story. Well, what about the journey of *making* the picture? Had it been his own hero's journey?

"I didn't feel like I was on a hero's journey while I was making the picture—I was fighting for my life!" Raimi said with a laugh. "I was more on the journey of a mother fighting for my baby, trying to see that it gets the nourishment, attention, and care it needs to grow."

When asked what kept him going through the years of preproduction and production, what kept his energy and enthusiasm high throughout the creative challenges, he got quiet. He paused, looked off into a middle distance, and said quietly, "It was just the desire to make a really great picture."

John Calley sat in the quiet of his office on the third floor of the Thalberg Building and reflected on the heart of *Spider-Man*, spoke of the young man "inflicted with a power he could never have imagined and the struggles of dealing with that power, of using it appropriately and not being a bad person. It's a metaphor for growth and maturity, I think."

It still was almost a year before the film's release date, but Calley had a cool confidence about its chances. "It's been as low maintenance a giant project as I've ever experienced. Sam is an angel; the producers are amazing; the Imageworks guys

are breathtaking; Yair has been something; the marketing has been
great. We're very excited about it and think it'll have a long and
fruitful life." He credits Amy Pascal as the "dominant figure in the
creative realm of the moviemaking universe" at Sony, who did the
hard work in the trenches.

John Calley's dream.

For Calley, *Spider-Man* is a piece of a large and intricate puzzle, part
of a global operation with managers running everything from TV channels
in India to DVD operations and Imageworks itself. "But my love is
movies," he said, smiling. "I've been in this business for fifty years now."

One of the things Calley fondly remembers about the movies are the
Saturday matinees, the fantasy and superhero serials. "I still watch those [old
serials] when they sometimes come on television. Now they're treated like
jokes, but they weren't back then—I used to lose myself in them. Audiences
today have been culturally altered in the sense that technology has moved
along, but there's an enormous afterburner on it for me because it's evocative of
a time and a place and poverty and getting out of it and moving on to this. So, it's
highly charged for me. For others it's a gag, a joke.

"But it's not a joke."

Calley gets a mischievous gleam in his eyes and walks across his office to a
closed door. He opens the door and motions his guest to come over.

There is a life-size standee of a promotional photograph of actor Antonio Banderas
as Zorro, taken from the 1998 Tristar/Amblin production *The Mask of Zorro*. The classic swashbuckler is dressed in black from hat to boots, a frozen image of a swirling cape

and a slashing sword
extended in a black gloved
hand. But behind the
mask, replacing Banderas's
face, is John Calley's own
bearded visage.

Thus someone living a
story straight out of a Hollywood movie—that struggling
kid from the mailroom who
became head of the dream factory
—still retains a love of those fabled
heroes of yesteryear, can relate to
the myth of those who wear the
mask. Maybe the hero myths are a
lingering dream, the reflection of a

The legend looms large . . .
The Amazing Spider-Man #11, "Turning
Point," page 21 / Artist: Steve Ditko

piece of our-selves we lost along the way. Maybe that's the secret Peter Parker discovered when he was blessed—or cursed—with his superpowers. It's a notion bigger than the comics, bigger even than as grand an illusion as the movie medium itself.

"The superhero myth is found in literature; it goes back to the most primitive storytelling," Calley mused. "We love myths because we're trying to soften our lives and face the fact that we are the missing link. We need mythology to support our hopes and dreams, our hereafters, our glorious fantasies. And I think we're just another stage in the evolution of that species requirement. We soften the blows with our imagination."

Every completed film has within it the echoes of an alternate universe, the tantalizing possibilities of what might have been. In this parallel film dimension Ronald Reagan, not Humphrey Bogart, might be the world-weary café owner presiding over the intrigues of *Casablanca*, while Frank Sinatra, not Clint Eastwood, could wield Dirty Harry's .44 Magnum. Decisions on character and casting, story and dialogue, and a myriad of other production concerns can alter the subtle creative chemistry.

Spider-Man is full of its own "what if" scenarios. As we've seen, originally the Green Goblin was to be joined by Dr. Octopus to bring mayhem to the web-slinger's world, but in the end the moviemakers decided to focus on a single villain. In this and many other cases it would be the challenge for Raimi's production team, indeed, the creative challenge for any film and filmmaker, to make certain that all the creative decisions would be the right ones—that the story be served.

For a well-prepared director like Sam Raimi, many of the key decisions were made even *before* filming began. The storyboards proved integral to that process, during which scripted and even unscripted ideas could be explored, then finalized or discarded. "We're like the Marines, the first ones in and usually the last ones out," said *Spider-Man* storyboard artist Mark Andrews laughingly.

And storyboarding remained inextricably linked to the filming schedule established by producer Ian Bryce even before the cameras rolled. The allotted schedule sometimes provided de facto answers on what could and couldn't be filmed. Further creative decisions arose in the heat of principal photography, as was the case in the final Spider-Man and Goblin confrontation staged in the hulking ruin set. Storyboard supervisor Jeffrey Lynch revealed, "That sequence was going to be an extravagant and involved battle, three or four times as long as what's in the final film. A large set had been built, which was predetermined by the story boards. Unfortunately, it was shot toward the end of principal photography and [the production] realized there wasn't enough time to do everything that was planned. So, the scene had to be truncated in a way that still got the story point across, while maintaining a visceral impact.

"Someone once described moviemaking

as like planning a battle," he added. "Once it begins, anything can happen, so sometimes you have to make adjustments."

The following are three sequences that were boarded and scripted—and dropped. Don't expect to see them in a future "director's cut," as they were never even filmed. But each of these ideas, developed in the pre-filming phase, provides an insight into the fluid dynamics of motion picture storytelling.

THE SCHOOL BATHROOM SCENE

Peter Parker's organic webbing has just spurted out of his wrists in a scene set in the Midtown High cafeteria, the sticky strands catching a tray of food and sending it spilling over school bully Flash Thompson. As the shooting script notes, when Peter sees this, he gulps "one of those swallows you can actually hear... Horrified, Peter turns and races out of the cafeteria."

Parker stops at a row of lockers, where he notices the almost invisible slits in his wrist. Then, suddenly, his spider sense activates, and he turns just in time to duck Thompson's flying fist.

But before the fight with Flash, another scenario was planned and scripted. Let's pick up that screenplay passage just after Peter's swallow of dread:

Horrified, Peter turns and races out of the cafeteria.

School bathroom scene. Artist: Jeffrey Lynch (Scene 17B/ Panels 1-8)

Interior library scene. Artists: Jeffrey Lynch, breakdowns; Mark Andrews, final art (Scene 18B/ Panels 1-8)

CUT TO: INT.   SCHOOL BATHROOM   DAY

Peter is at the sink, staring down at the under-sides of his wrists, trying to figure out what the hell is going on.

His wrists are oozing a pearly white fluid from almost invisible slits about a quarter of an inch long.

Peter pushes on the skin next to one of the slits, to relieve the pressure. A dark shape, the size and color of a rose thorn, emerges from beneath the skin and shoots a jet of liquid silk straight up in the air, where it SPLATS onto the ceiling and adheres there.

Peter, panicked, breaks his hand free of the strand, turns, and bolts from the bathroom.

"The idea with the bathroom scene was to play that moment where he's trying to figure out what's happening to him, to amp up the anxiety before the fight with Flash," explained Jeffrey Lynch, who boarded the sequence. "We isolated him in the bathroom to show that he's freaked out, so by the time he gets back out into the hallway and encounters Flash, he's clearly rattled.

"When looking at [the animated story-boards], you can get a feeling when some-thing might not be necessary. I think Sam felt the bathroom scene was a bit of a double beat, that you started to feel that anxiety at the end of the scene in the cafeteria, and by the time Peter's in the hallway you see it clearly written on his face. So [the anxiety in the bathroom] was folded into the other scenes."

THE INTERIOR LIBRARY SCENE

After Peter has vanquished Flash with an inexplicable knock-out punch, the shooting script describes how the confused teen bolts from the school grounds. Peter pauses at an alley and observes a spider web, sunshine glinting off the freshly woven strands, and suddenly realizes there's a connection between the spider bite back in the genetics lab and the strange things that are happening to him. He puts his hand to the alley wall and tentatively "begins to *walk up the wall*, his hands clinging like suction cups."

But in another scripted scene, illustrated by the storyboards, Peter would have kept walking after seeing that spider web, and would have gone to a public library to research spider lore at a computer terminal.

"The idea in the library scene was [that] Peter is putting the pieces together," Jeffrey Lynch explained. "We were also thinking he might even be pulling research on OsCorp from the Internet, that what happened to him at the genetics lab might also tie into OsCorp."

As Peter clicks on the computer key-board, images of various spiders and their capabilities appear on the screen: "…can leap up to forty times body length…reflexes so fast they border on precognition…web strands with tensile strength of high-tension wire…." Peter's epiphany is emphasized in the boards by Mark Andrews and Jeffrey Lynch, which zoom in to Peter's astonished

eyes, the notation below one panel announc-ing: "Peter now *knows* what has happened to him. He is mutated."

But the library scene—literally just a few scripted sentences—was cut. Given the time and effort it would have taken to set up and shoot in the main public library in Manhattan, the moviemakers didn't feel it was going to further the story enough to jus-tify the strain on the schedule. "That location was scouted and planned out, but producer Laura Ziskin and Sam realized the time it'd take to light these beautiful, huge rooms would be crushing, and would compromise the shooting schedule," Lynch recalled. "At that point, they weren't shooting yet, but pro-ducer Ian Bryce was planning the shot demands and how many days they'd need in each location.

"The idea became to achieve the same concept in another location. So, when Peter leaves the school in a panic and runs into the alley, he puts it [all] together there. It's done visually, when he sees the spider web. You get the same idea in less amount of time."

THE SAVING FARGAS SCENE

In another what-might-have-been sequence, artist Mark Andrews was asked to storyboard a follow-up to the Green Goblin's Times Square attack. The scene featured Mr. Fargas, a wheelchair-bound OsCorp board member and Norman Osborn's corporate foe,

Saving Fargas scene. Artist: Mark Andrews (Scene 98/ Panels 1-2; 3-5; 9-19; 22-32; 35-39; 43-45)

as he's attacked by the Goblin and rescued by Spider-Man.

Not only was the scene planned to be the second encounter between Spidey and Goblin, it represented a plot thread in which OsCorp board members who'd escaped the initial World Unity Festival attack were tracked down by the vengeful Goblin.

"We knew, as we were boarding, that cuts had been made in some sequences that were already boarded," Andrews noted. "The big car chase, where Peter Parker pursues the guy who killed his uncle, was one of the sequences pared down because of scheduling. So I purposely boarded the Fargas scene very lean, keeping in mind the practicality of how fast they could shoot it."

Despite Andrews's best efforts, the Fargas scene didn't make the final cut. "Another

sequence that was cut, which followed this line of the Goblin getting back at OsCorp, was the 'OsCorp Weapons of the Future' sequence," Andrews added. "It's an industry show attacked by the Goblin, which featured all these top-of-the-line OsCorp weapons: guys in jet-packs, remote drones, robots with big Gatling guns on them."

Still another scene boarded by Andrews, with an eye toward making it practical for shooting, was a dramatic subway hostage sequence in which Spider-Man comes to the rescue—and almost bollixes it. "We were considering a montage sequence, where Peter Parker is learning to use his spider skills, and making mistakes," Andrews recalled. "In the subway hostage sequence I boarded, Spider-Man takes out the bad guys, but a SWAT team comes in and sets off tear gas that

Spider-Man succumbs to. He's handcuffed and is being taken away to the police van, where his head finally clears and he breaks the cuffs and manages to escape."

Despite Andrews' extensive work on the subway sequence—some twenty-five pages of storyboards—it was cut. "Boarding allows you [an effective way] to explore sequences," Andrews said with a shrug. "We put time and effort into something, but it's a 'good idea at the time' kind of deal. In the end, we board artists are story guys. We understand that a sequence has to work with all the other scenes around it and the full sense of the story. And if a sequence doesn't work—cut it!"

Behind the Mask of Spider-Man™

Photo Gallery

Mark Cotta Vaz has authored thirteen books, beginning in 1988 with *Spirit in the Land*, an investigation into America's traditional and New Age spiritual practices. He has specialized in works documenting popular culture, including *Tales of the Dark Knight*, the authorized fiftieth-anniversary history of Batman, and *Industrial Light + Magic: Into the Digital Realm*, a chronicle of the second decade of George Lucas's effects company. Vaz is a longtime contributor to *Cinefex* magazine and a past board member of the Cartoon Art Museum of San Francisco. He's currently finishing a first novel and is working on a history of two of the most distinguished of the segregated units of World War II.

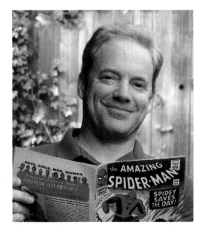

SPIDER-MAN

THE SCREENPLAY

BY DAVID KOEPP

BASED ON THE MARVEL COMIC BOOK BY STAN LEE AND STEVE DITKO

A BLACK SCREEN

SPIDER-MAN: *(v.o.)* Who am I? You sure you wanna know? The story of my life is not for the faint of heart.

EXT. PARKER HOUSE—DAY (1987)

A cab pulls up to an average house in Queens.

SPIDER-MAN: *(v.o.) (CONT'D)* If somebody said it was a happy little tale, if somebody told you I was just your average, ordinary guy, not a care in the world...

A SOCIAL WORKER gets out, holding the hand of PETER PARKER (4). Tears streaming down his face, he lugs a small suitcase. The cab motors away showing Peter—

—his new home. AUNT MAY and UNCLE BEN stand on the porch, smiling. The Social Worker leads Peter up the steps. Uncle Ben extends his hand. Peter looks up at the Social Worker. She nods. Peter looks back at the loving hand before him, takes it. Uncle Ben and Aunt May lead Peter inside. Peter turns, looks at the Social Worker. The door closes.

SPIDER-MAN: *(v.o.) (CONT'D)* ... somebody lied.

EXT. A SCHOOL BUS—DAY

A yellow school bus roars through Queens.

SPIDER-MAN: *(v.o.)* Mine is a tale of pain and sorrow, longing and heartache, anger and betrayal. And that just covers the high school years.

INT. A SCHOOL BUS—DAY

A bus full of teenagers. We float down the center isle, drifting from face to face—

SPIDER-MAN: But let me assure you—this, like any story worth telling, is all about a girl...

—holding on MARY JANE WATSON, knockout pretty but sad eyes, too sad for seventeen, looking out the window of the bus.

SPIDER-MAN: *(v.o.) (CONT'D) That* girl. Mary Jane Watson. MJ, to her friends. The woman I've loved since before I even *liked* girls.

An arm drapes around MJ's shoulders, FLASH THOMPSON, self-assured, handsome, the high school Big Name. He's looking across the bus, out the window, HOWLING with laughter.

SPIDER-MAN: *(V.O.) (CONT'D)* I'd like to tell you that's me next to her.

We pull back, toward the front of the bus. Another KID.

SPIDER-MAN: *(V.O.) (CONT'D)* Or even that.

Further back. Another KID, messily eating a jelly doughnut.

SPIDER-MAN: *(V.O.) (CONT'D)* Heck, I'd even take him.

We turn, look out the window, see what they're laughing about. PETER PARKER, 17, bespectacled and book-bagged, chasing after the school bus, to the derision of everyone aboard.

M.J. can't take it anymore. She jumps up, hurries to the front of the bus and SHOUTS over the laughter, to the DRIVER.

MJ: Stop the bus! He's been chasing us since Woodhaven Boulevard!

There is a collective AWWWW as the bus slows down.

AT THE FRONT,
Peter climbs onto the bus, breathless, limping.

PETER: Thanks... sorry... sorry... thanks...

He eyes an open seat next to a GEEKY GIRL with a mouthful of braces. She makes eye contact with Peter, moves her books to occupy the vacant space.

GEEKY GIRL: Don't even think about it.

Peter moves on. As he makes his way down the aisle, MJ sits down next to Flash again, next to the window this time. When she's not looking, Flash slides his foot out in front of Peter's beat-up sneakers. Peter trips and falls, hard, facedown in the aisle. More laughter. M.J. looks sharply at Flash—did you do that?

FLASH: *(outraged innocence)* What?

On the floor, Peter lifts his head, looks up at Flash and MJ Flash is grinning, MJ is staring down at him with pity. Peter looks up at her, helpless, glasses dangling from one ear.

SPIDER-MAN: *(v.o.)* That's me. Peter Parker.

EXT. QUEENSBORO BRIDGE—DAY

The yellow bus crosses the Queensboro Bridge and heads for the spectacular skyline of Manhattan.

EXT. COLUMBIA UNIVERSITY—DAY

A stressed out TEACHER, with a clipboard, enters frame. The students are gathered around the steps. Teen energy. Peter, his camera hanging around his neck, stands alone. M.J. is with her girlfriends.

TEACHER: Okay, people, no wandering! Proceed directly up to the KNOCK IT THE HELL OFF! up the steps and into the building.

They all move slowly to steps. They turn to see:

A CHAUFFEUR-DRIVEN BENTLEY—PULLING TO THE CURB
Inside, HARRY OSBORN, seventeen, sits in the back seat, next to NORMAN OSBORN, mid-forties. Norman exudes power and anger. Harry is slowly acquiring both.

INT. BENTLEY—DAY

HARRY: Dad, could you drive around the corner.
OSBORN: Why? The door's right here.
HARRY: These are public school kids. I'm not showing up to school in a Bentley.
OSBORN: What? You want me to trade in my car for a Jetta because you flunked out of every private school I sent you to?
HARRY: They were not for me. I told you that. It wasn't me.
OSBORN: Of course it was! *(reaches for Harry's door)* Don't ever be ashamed of who you are.
HARRY: Dad, I'm not ashamed, I'm just not what you...
OSBORN: What, Harry?
HARRY: Forget it, Dad.

Harry gets out of the Bentley.

EXT. COLUMBIA UNIVERSITY—DAY

PETER: *(big lovely grin)* Hi ya, Harry.
HARRY: Hey, Peter.

Behind them the car door opens. Norman emerges holding Harry's book bag.

OSBORN: Won't you be needing this?

Osborn hands Harry the bag.

HARRY: *(moving around car to sidewalk)* Peter, this is my father, Norman Osborn.
PETER: Great honor to meet you.

Harry is looking off at MJ, who is making conversation with her girlfriends about the arrival of the Bentley.

OSBORN: I've heard a lot about you. Harry tells me you're quite the science whiz.
PETER: Well, I don't know about that.
HARRY: He's being modest. I told you, he's won all the prizes.
OSBORN: Anyone who can get Harry to pass Chemistry shouldn't be modest.
PETER: Harry's really smart. He didn't really need my help.
HARRY: We have to go, Dad.

Norman lays his paternal hand on Harry's shoulder, squeezes too hard.

OSBORN: I'm something of a scientist myself, you know.
PETER: I know. I know all about OsCorp. You guys are designing the guidance and re-entry systems for the first shuttle mission to Mars. Really brilliant.
OSBORN: Impressive. Your parents must be proud.
PETER: I live with my aunt and uncle. They're proud.
OSBORN: What about your folks?
PETER: My parents died when I was little.
OSBORN: I lost my parents as a young boy as well.
HARRY: Which no doubt strengthened your iron will to succeed, huh, Dad?
TEACHER: HEY, YOU TWO, I'M CLOSING THE DOOR!
PETER: *(moving away)* Nice to meet you, Mr. Osborn.
OSBORN: See you again.
HARRY: *(moving fast up steps, passes MJ, smiles)* Hi.

They walk in. Harry smiles at MJ, now in front of Flash.

PETER: He doesn't seem so bad.
HARRY: Not if you're a genius. I think he wants to adopt you.

Harry discretely calls Peter's attention to MJ, primes him to say something.

HARRY: *(cont'd)* Hey. *(nods to MJ)* Say something.

They approach. MJ waits, feels the energy. Nothing comes. Harry steps in to fill the awkward moment.

HARRY: *(cont'd)* Hi. How ya doing?

M.J. smiles.

MJ: Hey.

Peter does nothing. They continue on.

HARRY: Why didn't you say something?

PETER: I was about to. It wasn't the right moment.

Peter manages to look back over his shoulder to where Harry's father still stands beside his car.

CLOSER SHOT OF NORMAN
Looking off. He seems a lonely figure. Over him, we hear:

TOUR GUIDE: *(o.s.)* There are more than 32,000 known species of spider in the world.

INT. COLUMBIA GENETIC RESEARCH INSTITUTE—DAY

Thirty-odd students and their teacher are led around a cavernous laboratory by a TOUR GUIDE. They pass a number of large spider exhibits.

TOUR GUIDE: They are in the order Araneae, which is divided into three sub-orders—Mesothelea, Orthognatha, and Labidognatha. All spiders are carnivorous, ravenous eaters who feed on massive quantities of protein, in liquid form, usually the juices of their prey. Arachnids from each of the three groups possess varying strengths which help them in their constant search for food.

Peter, the camera around his neck, keeps an eye on MJ who is joking around with her friends. Flash moves to MJ, puts his arm around her, nuzzles her neck. Peter winces and turns away, back to the tour. MJ sees Peter's reaction. She pulls away from Flash, embarrassed.

TOUR GUIDE: *(cont'd)* For example, the jumping spider—family Salticidae, genus Salticus—
TEACHER: Excuse me. Is anyone paying attention to the genus Salticus? *(to Guide)* I apologize, go on.
TOUR GUIDE: The genus Salticus can leap up to forty times its body length, thanks to a proportionate muscular strength vastly greater than that of a human being.

Peter catches the eye of the Tour Guide and gestures to his camera—okay to take a few pictures?

PETER: For the school paper?

The Tour Guide nods. A few STUDENTS around Peter roll their eyes, one or two mutter "geek." Peter ignores them, raises the camera. Behind him, one of Flash's CRONIES bumps Peter's elbow on purpose, ruins the picture. Other kids laugh.

TOUR GUIDE: The funnel web spider—family Hexathelidae, genus Atrax—one of the deadliest spiders in the world, spins an intricate, funnel-shaped web whose strands have a tensile strength proportionately equal to the type of high-tension wire used in bridge building.

Peter raises the camera again, gets bumped again. He turns. Flash's Crony steps forward, threatening. A VOICE mutters from nearby.

HARRY: Leave him alone.

Flash's Crony turns, sees Harry Osborn staring at him.

FLASH'S CRONY: Or what?
BOY: Or his father will fire your father. **HARRY:** *(alt.)* Or my father will fire your father.

Laughter.

TEACHER: *(loud & clear)* The next person who talks is going to fail this course. I kid you not.
TOUR GUIDE: The crab spider—family Thomisidae, genus Misumena—spins no web to catch its prey, but hunts instead, using a set of reflexes with nerve conduction velocities so fast some researchers believe it almost borders on precognition, an early awareness of danger, a "spider sense."

WIDER SHOT
They reach the center of the rotunda floor, where RESEARCHERS work at computers surrounding an electron microscope. Large video screens around the room display giant images of the microscope's area of scrutiny—spider DNA.

TOUR GUIDE: *(cont'd)* Over five painstaking years, Columbia's genetic research facility has fully mapped the genetic codes of each of these spiders.

UP ABOVE THEM,
in the high arch of the rotunda, a single spider sits at the center of a magnificent web, glistening in the light.

TOUR GUIDE: *(o.s.) (cont'd)* Armed with these DNA blueprints, we have now begun what was once thought impossible—inter-species genetic transmutation.

DOWN BELOW
TOUR GUIDE: *(cont'd)* In this Recombination Lab, we use synthesized transfer-RNA to encode an entirely new genome, combining genetic information from all three spiders into these fifteen genetically designed super-spiders, the first mankind has ever produced.

The class checks it out. Creepy-looking mutant spiders crawl about in a glass tank.

MJ: *(wide-eyed, loving it)* Disgusting.
HARRY: Hateful little thing.
MJ: I love it.

HARRY: Really? Me, too.

TOUR GUIDE: Just imagine—if one day we can isolate the strengths, powers, and immunities in human beings and transfer that DNA code among ourselves. All known disease could be wiped out. Of course, we're nowhere near ready to start experimenting with humans, so for the moment we're concentrating on these fifteen spiders. Any questions?

PETER: *(whispering)* Fourteen.

HARRY: Fourteen?

TOUR GUIDE: I beg your pardon?

PETER: There's only fourteen spiders.

TOUR GUIDE: No, there's fifteen. Aren't there?

As he and the others turn their attention to the tank and start counting the spiders, we drift up to the ceiling.

UP IN THE ROTUNDA ARCH,
a spider's web. The mutant spider is on the move, fingering its way across its web. It begins to drop.

DOWN BELOW,
the tour group has given up on the mystery of the missing spider and is following the Tour Guide. MJ lingers for a moment, to check out her reflection in the glass of one of the tanks. By herself, looking particularly beautiful in her light. Peter stares, mesmerized, snaps up the opportunity.

PETER: Can I take your picture? *(she turns, surprised)* I need one with a student in it.

She hides a smile. Poses, having fun. She loves the camera.

MJ: Don't make me ugly!

PETER: Impossible. Right there. Good!

Above him the spider descends. He snaps the picture of MJ

PETER: *(cont'd)* And one more.

He snaps again but she has turned away moving to her waiting friends.

PETER: *(cont'd)* Thanks.

The spider continues to drop, straight down upon Peter's right hand.

PETER: *(cont'd)* Ow!

He shakes his hand, hard, flips the spider off of him. Peter looks at his hand. There are two tiny red marks where the spider sank its fangs into his skin. Peter bends down, looks at the spider on the floor. It's dead. Peter stands again, rubbing his hand. From across the lab, we

see him, silhouetted before the huge electron microscope display screens, where swirling strands of DNA molecules combine, detach, and recombine.

EXT OSCORP INDUSTRIES—DAY

A gigantic industrial complex out on Long Island. Smokestacks belch black nastiness into the air. Huge red neon letters that spell OSCORP tower over the gate. A VOICE comes over:

SIMKINS: *(O.S.)* General Slocum and the others have already started—

INT ENTRANCEWAY TO SUBTERRANEAN LABORATORY—DAY

An elevator door opens to the OsCorp R&D headquarters, a sprawling lab complex hundreds of feet below ground level. Norman Osborn quickly strides across a massive catwalk as he is briefed by SIMKINS, his aide, whose voice continues from outside:

SIMKINS: —the inspection. Mr. Balkan and Mr. Fargas are with them.

OSBORN: Why wasn't I told about this?

SIMKINS: I don't think they wanted you to know, sir.

INT LAB—DAY

A work area where a strange object is mounted on a servo-pole, being worked on by TECHNICIANS. It looks like an aerodynamically perfected boogie board, with upturned fins on each side, footholds carved into the wings, and a center tube that looks like a jet engine.
Next to the device, a TECHNICIAN wears a lightweight, super tight-fitting electronic suit. As he moves his head, arms and legs, the boogie board pivots on the pole—up, down, left bank, right bank.
The Pentagon delegation, a group of UNIFORMED OFFICERS and several MEN and WOMEN IN SUITS, observe the device with DR. MENDEL STROMM, the project director. BALKAN and FARGAS, two exceedingly grumpy septuagenarians, look on. Fargas is in a wheelchair.

STROMM: Individual Personnel Transports are moving along splendidly.

GENERAL SLOCUM: I've seen your glider. That's not why I'm here.

Norman Osborn and Simkins enter.

OSBORN: General Slocum, good to see you again. Mr. Balkan, Mr. Fargas, always a pleasure to have our board of directors pay us a visit.

Slocum nods to Osborn, keeps talking to the delegation.

GENERAL SLOCUM: I want a progress report on Human Performance Enhancers.

ACROSS THE LAB,
they stand next to a glass-walled isolation chamber, within which several SCIENTISTS work on a bank of equipment.

STROMM: We tried vapor inhalation with rodent subjects. They showed an 800 percent increase in strength.

Fargas rolls forward.

FARGAS: 800 percent? That's excellent.

GENERAL SLOCUM: Any side effects?

STROMM: In one trial, yes, the—

OSBORN: *(cutting him off)* It was an aberration. All the tests since then have been successful.

GENERAL SLOCUM: *(still to Stromm)* In the test that went wrong, what happened? What were the side effects?

STROMM: Violence, aggression and, eventually, insanity.

GENERAL SLOCUM: What's your recommendation?

OSBORN: With the exception of Dr. Stromm, our entire staff has certified the product ready for human testing.

STROMM: We need to take the whole line back to formula.

OSBORN: Back to formula?!

Back to Stromm. He could kill him with his bare hands.

GENERAL SLOCUM: Mr. Osborn, this department has missed seven consecutive delivery dates. After five and a half years of R&D, the United States government has a right to expect the super-soldier you were contracted to deliver.

OSBORN: These are quantum leaps in science, gentlemen. We are unlocking the secrets of human evolution. I never said it would be cheap or fast, only groundbreaking.

GENERAL SLOCUM: I'll be frank with you, I never supported your program. We have my predecessor to thank for that.

BALKAN: The General has given the go-ahead to Quest Aerospace to build a prototype of their exoskeleton design. They test in two weeks.

GENERAL SLOCUM: If your so-called Performance Enhancers haven't had a successful human trial by that time, I will pull your funding and give it to them.

FARGAS: Norman, we are not going to lose this contract.

All eyes turn to Osborn. So what are you going to do about that?

EXT PARKER HOUSE—LATE DAY

The Parker house sits indistinguishable among other lower-middle income houses on cozy Franklin Street.

INT. PARKER HOUSE—LIVING ROOM/KITCHEN AREA—LATE DAY

BEN PARKER, a kindly man in his sixties, is changing a light bulb, standing on a chair, reaching high, stretching precariously. MAY PARKER, a frail woman the same age as Ben, moves into the doorway to the kitchen.

AUNT MAY: Why aren't you using a ladder? You'll fall and break your neck. Wait for Peter to do that.

UNCLE BEN: *(the light bulb in, the light comes on)* "God said let there be light." Voila, 80 soft glowin' watts of it.

Starts getting down, still holding burned out bulb.

AUNT MAY: Good boy, God'll be thrilled. Just don't fall on your ass.

UNCLE BEN: I'm already on my ass. When the plant senior electrician is laid off after thirty five years, what else would you call it... Of course I'm on my ass.

AUNT MAY: Hand me that bowl. The green one.

Ben hands her a pot, looks at classified page open on the table.

UNCLE BEN:
Corporations firin' people left and right so they can have a few billion more. What do they know about standing on a stool, screwin' in a light bulb?

AUNT MAY: Ben, you'll get another job somewhere.

UNCLE BEN: *(gesturing to paper—moves to dining room, sits)* Well, let's see. *(reading from paper)* Computer analyst, computer designer, computer engineer, computer... *(he sighs)* I'm sixty-eight damn years old. I have to provide for my family.

AUNT MAY: *(moves to him, embraces him, kisses his cheek)* I love you. And Peter loves you. You're the most responsible man I've ever known. We've been down and out before but somehow we survive. Where is Peter, anyway? He's late.

Aunt May starts for the kitchen as the front door opens. Uncle Ben quickly flips the paper away from the want ads.

UNCLE BEN: Here he is.
AUNT MAY: Just in time for dinner.
UNCLE BEN: How was the field trip?
PETER: ...don't feel well...gonna go to sleep...
AUNT MAY: *(moves to table)* You won't have a bite?

Peter looks at her, surprised. Is she psychic?

PETER: *(staggering upstairs)* ...no thanks...had a bite.
UNCLE BEN: Did you get some good pictures, Peter?
PETER: ...gotta crash...everything's fine...

His bedroom door SLAMS.

UNCLE BEN: What's that all about?
AUNT MAY: *(moving toward the base of the stairs)* He's a teenager.
UNCLE BEN: He's depressed.
AUNT MAY: He's a teenager.
UNCLE BEN: I better go up.
AUNT MAY: Stay put. He'll let us know if he needs help.

INT PETER'S BEDROOM—LATE DAY

Peter drops to his knees in his bedroom and clutches his abdomen in pain.

PETER: *(gasping)* Help...

He falls to the floor, writhing in agony. He looks at the spot the spider bit, which is now completely red and swollen.

Drenched in sweat, he starts to shake uncontrollably with chills, trembling violently, face pale, eyes black and sunken, teeth chattering. His eyes roll up into the back of his head and he passes out. Under the lids, his eyes flicker crazily.

EXT PARKER HOUSE—DAY

Morning of a new day. A very new day.

INT PETER'S BEDROOM—DAY

Peter wakes up, morning sunlight streaming through his window. He hasn't moved from the position he collapsed into on the floor. But as he orients himself, he seems to feel better. Carefully, he stretches his legs, takes a few deep breaths.

Definitely better. He sees the alarm clock. He's late. He grabs his glasses. Puts them on—

—and walks right into his chair, stumbling to the floor.

He gets up, puts his glasses on again. Looks into a mirror on the wall. He squints, everything's fuzzy now. He takes them off, it's 20/20. He tries once more—on, off. He can see.

PETER: Weird.

He shrugs and takes off his T-shirt. He walks away from the mirror. Hold on the empty mirror, then:

Peter jumps back in front of it, aghast. His chest is that of a Greek god. Nothing overdone, not a body builder's chest, just a perfect one. Peter tries something, flexes his pecs. They jump like cheerleaders.

Peter SCREAMS.

He checks out his body. Incredible. Puny Parker no more. There's a KNOCK at his bedroom door.

AUNT MAY: *(o.s.)* Peter? Are you all right?
PETER: Fine! I'm fine. Just fine!
AUNT MAY: *(o.s.)* Any better this morning? Any change?

Peter tosses his glasses in the trash can.

PETER: Change! Yes! Yes...big change!

He turns to grab his clothes. Through the window sees MJ in her bedroom finishing brushing her hair. She picks up a purse and darts out of view.

Peter throws on his shirt and moves quickly out his door.

INT. KITCHEN—DAY

Peter comes bounding down the stairs and leaps over the banister, landing with acrobatic grace behind Uncle Ben. He sees the breakfast Aunt May has prepared on the table, goes for it, eats what he can get as he grabs his backpack.

PETER: Hi. Gotta go.
UNCLE BEN: We thought you were sick.
PETER: *(mouthful of food)* I was. I got better.
AUNT MAY: Sit down, dear.
PETER: Can't. See you later.
UNCLE BEN: Don't forget, we're painting the kitchen today. Home right after school, right?
PETER: Sure thing, Uncle Ben, don't start without me.

He's out the door, full of energy, hoping to meet up with MJ

AUNT MAY: What was that about?
UNCLE BEN: He ate my bacon.

EXT. MJ'S HOUSE—DAY

Peter comes out his front door just as MJ leaves hers. Her father, MR. WATSON, a hungover guy of forty or so, SHOUTS after her. Mrs. Watson behind him.

MR. WATSON: I don't care what your mother said. It's not okay with me. You're trash. You'll always be trash. Just like her.
MJ: I have to go to school.
MR. WATSON: Who's stopping ya?
MRS. WATSON: Leave her alone.

MJ runs to the sidewalk, holding back tears.

Peter hurries after MJ

EXT ANOTHER STREET—DAY

Peter paces her, on the opposite side of the street. She doesn't see him.

PETER: Talk to her... talk to her...

But he doesn't, because he notices MJ is wiping away tears.

A HORN honks and a car full of her girlfriends pulls up next to her. Peter watches as MJ's face transforms. She puts on a mask of happiness and jumps in.

Peter watches as the car ROARS away. She eludes him again.

Peter runs, top speed, chasing the bus again. He reaches out to the side of it, to pound on it, get them to stop.

His hand touches a "GO WILDCATS!" school banner that's pinned on the side of the bus. But as the bus accelerates, his hand sticks, tears the banner right off the bus.

What the hell? He tries to unstick his hand from the banner, but every time he frees one hand it sticks to the other. He tries everything. Wrestles with it, wads it into a ball to throw it. Nothing doing. Frustrated, he bends down, puts a foot on the banner and stands, thus freeing his hands.

He looks at his hands, confused but happy to be free of the banner. He takes a step and quickly learns otherwise. The banner is stuck to his foot. He tries to shake it free, but his feet get tangled in the banner and he crashes to the ground.

EXT. MIDTOWN HIGH—DAY

KIDS hang out. The BUZZER continues, they move inside.

INT. CAFETERIA—DAY

Peter approaches a table with an absurdly overladen tray of food. He sits. MJ moves past him on her way to her group. As she passes, she slips, her feet fly out under her. She's about to crash hard.

Peter's spider-reflexes are at work and he moves—lightning speed—up and out in front of her, catching her tray with his left hand, and dropping his right shoulder just enough for her to grab onto. It's one of the most graceful moves we've ever seen.

She regains her balance, looks at him, impressed.

MJ: Wow. Great reflexes!

Peter shrugs, freaked out, he can't believe he did it either. She takes her tray back from him.

MJ: *(cont'd)* Thanks.
PETER: No problem.
MJ: Hey, you have blue eyes. I never noticed without your glasses. You just get contacts?
PETER: Uh-huh.

She waits for more. Nothing comes.

MJ: Well, see ya.

He blew it again.

She turns and walks off, across the cafeteria. She looks back over her shoulder, smiles—

—and then sits at a crowded, popular table, right next to Flash Thompson and her girlfriends.

Peter sits back at his table. He begins to eat. Actually, he begins to chow. Thirsty, he sets his fork down. But it sticks to his hand.

He tries to pull it free with the other hand, but a long gooey strand stretches from his hand to the fork. It dangles. Peter tries to separate fork from strand. Nothing doing.

He tries harder. ANOTHER STRAND shoots out, from his other hand. This one flies out, to the table across from him, and SMACKS onto a GIRL's tray. She doesn't notice, as she's talking to the FRIEND on her right, and wouldn't touch that gross food anyway.

Shocked, Peter stands up and backs away, whipping his arm back, trying to pull free of the strand. But his movement yanks the girl's tray off the table, sending it flying toward Peter, who ducks, and it sails over his head.

Finally, the strand comes free. Relieved, Peter turns—

—and sees Flash Thompson wearing the girl's lunch. MJ is covering her mouth, laughing at Flash, but trying to hide it.

Peter swallows, and it's one of those swallows you can actually hear.

FLASH: Parker?! *(have you gone insane?)*

Horrified, Peter turns and hurries out of the cafeteria.

INT. HALLWAY—DAY

Just outside the door of the cafeteria, Peter stops next to a row of lockers, breathing hard, surreptitiously checking out the undersides of his wrists, trying to figure out what's going on.

For the first time, he notices two almost invisible slits in his skin, one on each wrist. Those were not there yesterday. He drops his arms and pulls his shirt sleeves down over his wrists as far as he can.

Suddenly, his features jolt as he's slammed with the strangest feeling he's ever had. He doesn't know it yet, but—

PETER'S SPIDER-SENSE
has kicked in. Everything and everyone surrounding him slows to a crawl and it is as if he is suddenly seeing outside himself—360-degree peripheral vision.

And what he sees in back of him is a FIST, Flash Thompson's fist, closing in on the back of Peter's head in slow motion. As quickly as it turned on the Spider-Sense switches off and

BACK IN REAL TIME,
Peter whips around and darts to the side, a split-second ahead of Flash Thompson's thrown punch, which BANGS into a locker where Peter was standing.

FLASH: Think you're pretty funny, don't you, Freak?!
MJ: *(running in)* It was an accident!
PETER: I'm sorry. It really was.
FLASH: My fist breaking your teeth, that's the accident.

Two of Flash's cronies close the classroom doors on either side of the hall, to block the view of the teachers within.

PETER: I don't want to fight you, Flash.
FLASH: I wouldn't want to fight me neither.

A crowd forms around them. Flash takes two more swings, but again Peter evades them—and fast. Flash is puzzled.

Sensing an attack from behind, Peter suddenly ducks. One of Flash's cronies, who was sneaking up on him, is left grabbing air. Peter stands, flips the guy off his back.

A crowd forms to watch. Harry Osborn, coming down the hall from the other direction, joins them.

Enraged, Flash ROARS and lunges at Peter. Peter ducks one, two, three, four punches, never even moving his feet, just darting his torso around so fast he creates a motion blur.

Harry, impressed, gives a look to the person standing next to him, who happens to be MJ Harry turns back to the fight, then does a double take back at MJ She returns the look.

MJ: Harry, please help him.
HARRY: Which one?

Flash lunges at Peter. Peter throws a punch that lands solidly on Flash's jaw and sends him sailing back against the lockers, hard. He slumps to the floor, unconscious.

CRONY: Jesus, Parker, you knocked him out!

Peter GASPS, shocked at his own strength, but thrilled. A STUDENT arrives on the scene, steps forward for a better view.

STUDENT: *(motioning toward unconscious Flash)* Parker did that? Yeah right.

Flash MOANS, lifts his head up, revealing a face covered in blood. The crowd GROANS. A few kids go to Flash, suddenly a sympathetic figure.

Peter looks at Flash's battered face, then to his hands. He starts to back away, aware and terrified of his newfound strength. He turns on his heels and takes off, down the hall.

EXT. STREET—DAY

Peter is walking along, looking down at the fading spider bite. What's happening to me?

EXT. ALLEY—DAY

He turns, sees—

—a glorious spiderweb that's been spun between a Dumpster and the alley wall, the sun glinting off its fresh strands.

Peter looks around. He's alone. He reaches out to the alley wall, and as his fingers draw close

WE GO IN SUPERTIGHT ON HIS FINGERTIPS,
as tiny, microscopic hairs leap out of his pores and cling to the wall.
Slowly, tentatively, Peter begins to walk up the wall, his hands clinging like suction cups.

EXT. ROOFTOPS—DAY

Peter leaps with abandonment, over alleyways from rooftop to rooftop.

EXT. ROOFTOP—DAY

He pulls up short at one rooftop. It is too far to the next one. He looks down at his wrist, sees the narrow slits. Gets an idea. He turns, points his wrist at a taller building across the alley.

He wiggles his wrist, tries to get the goop to spray out. But it doesn't come. He makes a fist. Nothing. He closes his thumb and little finger together. Nothing. He rotates his hand so the palm faces up, extends all five fingers, and brings his ring and middle fingers toward his palm, together.

THWIP!

A single strand of webbing shoots out from his wrist, straight up. Peter frowns, tries to direct it more. This time the webbing flies across the alley and sticks to the side of the other building.

Peter tugs on it. It's tough. He pulls harder. Can't break it. He wraps one hand around it, double strength, closes his eyes, mutters a prayer—

—and jumps off the roof. He sails through the air, comes in for a landing on the side of the other building—SPLAT!

He clings there with his hands and feet, face crushed against the brick. Learning hurts.

INT. PARKER KITCHEN—NIGHT

Peter comes into the kitchen at home, late, exhausted, confused. He sniffs the air, smells something funny.

He touches the wall, comes up with paint on his fingers, and notices the buckets and drop cloth folded in the corner of the room. He sees a note on the ladder:

> "Meatloaf and vegetables in the oven. Cherry pie on the shelf. We've gone to play bridge at the Anderson's."

PETER: Ah, shoot...

A SHOUT from next door distracts him. He goes to the window.

THROUGH THE WINDOW,
he can see MJ's house, just across the narrow driveway. He can see silhouettes moving in their windows, a man, a woman, and a teenager, SHOUTING at one another.

EXT. MJ'S HOUSE—NIGHT

Outside, MJ BANGS through her screen door and walks into her postage-stamp back yard, trying to ignore the chaos inside that house. Inside her house.

She's angry, ready to cry, yet able to hold it back. She turns and SEES Peter standing in his yard, other side of the fence. He's caught watching her.

PETER: *(embarrassed)* Oh. Hi.
MJ: Were you listening to that?
PETER: *(rattled)* No! Yeah! I heard something, but wasn't listening. To what?
MJ: I guess you can always hear us.
PETER: No. I was just taking out the trash.
MJ: You always do your chores, don't you, Peter?
PETER: Well...
MJ: I'm sorry we do that all the time. Your aunt and uncle never scream.
PETER: Oh, they can scream pretty good, y'know.
MJ: So...where to after you graduate?
PETER I thought I'd go into the city, get a job as a photographer, work my way through college. What about you?
MJ: Headed for the city, too. I can't wait to get out of here. I thought I'd...Oh, I don't know...
PETER: Try me.
MJ: I want to...act...on stage. Be an actress.
PETER: Hey, that's great. You were really awesome in all the school plays, Mary Jane.
MJ: Really?
PETER: Yeah. I cried like a baby when you played Cinderella.
MJ: Peter, that was in first grade.
PETER Well, even so, you know how sometimes you can know something, like what's going to be. Like feel what's around you, what's coming?
MJ: Sometimes.
PETER: And you can just see things coming that aren't exactly there, but you just believe.
MJ: What do you see coming for you?
PETER: I'm not sure, but it feels like something I never felt before, whatever it is.
MJ: And what for me?
PETER: You? You're...why, you're gonna...light up Broadway.

Silence between them.

MJ: Y'know, you're taller than you look.
PETER: I hunch.

She reaches out, puts her hands on his biceps. Wow! She straightens him up.

MJ: Don't. Hunch.

His heart is going a million miles an hour.

Suddenly we're interrupted by loud shouting again from MJ's house. A horn honks.

In the driveway, Flash in his new car. MJ peers around the corner of the house.

FLASH: Hey MJ Come take a ride in my birthday present?

She's torn, turns back to Peter.

MJ: Thanks, Pete. I gotta go.

She grins, waves and goes.

Peter watches as Flash shows the car to MJ, oohs and aahs. Flash puts down the top. They hop inside and SQUEAL away. She laughs, her hair blowing in the wind.

Peter watches the car disappear. Looks downcast. He thinks a moment, then raises his arm and makes a muscle. A GREAT, BIG MUSCLE. Lowers his arm. So what?

INT. PETER'S BEDROOM—NIGHT

His bulletin board with snapshots he's taken at school events and of his aunt and uncle. A framed PHOTO OF HIM AS A 4-YEAR-OLD WITH HIS MOTHER AND FATHER. A newspaper CRINKLES open to a big ad for used cars. Peter looks at them wistfully. He turns the page, sees another ad:

> Attention Amateur Wrestlers!
> THREE THOUSAND DOLLARS
> For just three minutes in the ring!
> Colorful Characters a MUST!

Peter RIPS the ad from the paper. He has a plan. As he contemplates it, we FEATURE behind him two other snapshots: MJ at the museum—one posing, the other of her walking away.

INT. PETER'S BEDROOM—NIGHT

On a sketch pad, Peter's hand draws the outline of a human figure and various costume possibilities.

He draws a pair of wings on the figure.

PETER: A spider with wings?

He crumples it up, starts over. He tries antennae, hates it, crumples that up too.

He draws some web-type lines over the face and arms, draws the eyes. Large, jack-o'-lantern ovals, with upturned edges.

INT. PETER'S BEDROOM—NIGHT

Two empty glass bottles stand on a bookcase on the far side of Peter's bedroom. SPLAT! A web strand fires toward them, misses by a mile.

Peter, sitting on the opposite side of the room, frowns and tries again. SPLAT! Another wild miss. He looks down at his wrists, thinking.

INT. HALLWAY—NIGHT

Aunt May at his door with a bunch of laundry. She knocks.

AUNT MAY: Peter? What's going on there?
PETER: *(opens door a crack, peeks out)*
Exercising...not dressed.
AUNT MAY: Well, don't catch a cold.

INT. PETER'S BEDROOM—NIGHT

He closes the door revealing the room is full of webs. He decides to make the web shooter. Takes a pad, sketches it.

ANOTHER DAY,
Sparks fly. Peter has dismantled several Zippo lighters, watches, and assorted old jewelry and is silver-soldering them back together in a new way. He picks one up, blows on the solder. Happens to glance out the window—sees MJ's silhouette. She's dancing, acting, being free.

LATER, IN THE BEDROOM—NIGHT

Peter picks up the finished contraption and puts it around his wrist, right over his biological spinnerets.

He turns his chair, aims his wrist across the room, now with the bracelet. He takes aim and—

—SPLAT! Scores a direct hit on a can of Jolt Cola on the nightstand. He spins around, fast, in the chair, and fires a web under his arm, as if snuck up on from behind.

SMACK! Hits a plaster lamp, snags it. Yanks it towards him, he ducks. It hits the wall. SHATTERS!

He spins again, fires a double-barreled blast at those two glass bottles. Both of them hit, sending the bottles flying against the wall, where they SHATTER noisily.

Peter is thrilled. But there's a POUNDING on the wall.

UNCLE BEN: *(o.s.)* What are you doing in there?!
PETER: Studying! Hard.

EXT. OSCORP INDUSTRIES—NIGHT

Even at night, OsCorp's stacks spew foulness into the air.

INT. OSCORP LAB—NIGHT

—the OsCorp lab, deserted, dark at this hour, except for one area. It's the glass-walled isolation chamber we saw earlier, glowing ominously in the middle of the floor. Inside it, we see a man moving furtively, anxiously, preparing for a test.

INSIDE THE TANK,
Stromm and Norman Osborn making preparations for something—an experiment.

STROMM: Mr. Osborn, please, I'm asking you for the last time...

OSBORN: Don't be a coward. Risks are part of laboratory science.

STROMM: Let me reschedule this with a proper medical staff and a volunteer. If you just give me two weeks...

OSBORN: In two weeks this project, this company, will be dead. Sometimes you have to do things yourself. Give me the barium phosphate.

STROMM: Sir?

OSBORN: Decreases nausea when the vapor hits the bloodstream.

Stromm sighs, gives him the phosphate.

OSBORN: (cont'd) Forty thousand years of human evolution and we've barely even tapped the vastness of human potential. (he drinks) To the final realization of man's true physical and intellectual capability. (nods to Stromm)

Osborn lies on the gurney.

ZIP! A restraining strap is tightened across his leg.

CLICK! A restraining buckle SNAPS across his waist.

Dr. Mendel Stromm hits switches, a motor HUMS, and the steel gurney slides into the tank and is rotated up to vertical.

OUTSIDE THE TANK,
Mendel Stromm pops switches and levers on the vast console outside the glass tank, making last second checks on the battery of monitors in front of him.

He grabs hold of a set of controls.

A thick, noxious green gas rises up from the petri dish. Heavy, but still lighter than air, the gas creeps up, swirling around Osborn's feet. Over his legs. Over his groin.

Creeping up his chest. Tickling over his chin.

In spite of himself, Osborn holds his breath.

The green cloud envelops his head and he forces himself to open his mouth. He draws just a tiny bit of air—

—and the gas seems to leap into his mouth, as if it had a mind of its own. Osborn panics, chokes on it for a moment

But then he calms, lets himself breathe normally. The gas flows, in and out of his nostrils, we can see it move.

Stromm peers through the glass, monitoring every second.

OSBORN: (cont'd) I—

And suddenly, his entire body begins to convulse, seized by spasms, his fingertips, his teeth, his eyes show only whites.

ON THE MONITORS,
his body functions go crazy. Stromm works the controls frantically. Flat line. All across the monitors. Stromm SLAMS a hand down on a red button and—

IN THE TANK,
— giant vacuum vents in the ceiling ROAR to life, sucking the green gas up and out of the room.

Stromm races to the door, as soon as the gas is gone the security latches CLUNK open, he shoves his way inside, goes to Osborn, unstraps him, rips open his shirt and frantically begins emergency procedures.

Suddenly, behind him, he hears a SHRIEKING sound. Stromm turns as

THE MONITORS,
go crazy, heart rate leaping up to 226, blood pressure, BANG, respiration, POW, every single graph and scale and chart registers at or near its peak, BEEPING AND WHOOPING.

INSIDE THE TANK,
Osborn's eyes pop open and he leaps to his feet, terrified. He RIPS the sensors off his chest. Stromm tries to restrain him, Osborn ROARS—

—and bats Stromm across the chamber with just one arm.

But not just across the chamber, he hurls him through the glass wall of the chamber, which explodes in a shower of glass as Stromm's body hits it. Stromm keeps flying, sailing across the lab and SMASHING into a pillar on the far side, some fifty feet away.

He sags to the floor, blood pooling under his head.

Osborn staggers through the broken wall of the tank, steps across the rubble, and towers over Stromm's lifeless body.

FAR AWAY ACROSS THE LAB,

we see Osborn's hulking figure standing over Stromm. We keep pulling away until we see something in the foreground, two items sitting patiently, waiting for someone to finish them, to make use of them. Mounted atop two poles—

—that strange single-winged flying platform and the remote control suit that controls it.

In the distance, Norman Osborn throws his head back and HOWLS in pain, confusion, transformation. His primitive cry echoes over—

EXT. OSBORN'S APARTMENT—DAY

—an opulent Tudor Hill apartment building, crowned by an imperious townhouse. Inside—

INT. OSBORN'S DEN—DAY

This room in Osborn's lavish apartment. A collection of masks of all kinds. Ancient, tribal, hideous, garish masks. The essence of violent warfare. Norman sits bedraggled, dressed in yesterday's clothes. Disoriented. Dazed.

Harry, ready for school, a backpack over his shoulder, walks past the room, looks in, stops and enters.

HARRY: Dad? What is it, Dad?
OSBORN: *(blurry)* Harry.
HARRY: You look sick. What's happened?
OSBORN: *(sincere)* I don't know...
HARRY: *(kneels before him)* Where were you last night? I didn't hear you come in.
OSBORN: I was...last night I was...
HARRY: What?
OSBORN: I don't remember.

Voices come from the hallway.

INT. HALLWAY—DAY

Simkins briskly walks down the hallway, argues with Osborn's HOUSEMAN.

SIMKINS: I have to see him.
HOUSEMAN: He can't be disturbed now.

INT. OSBORN'S DEN—DAY

OSBORN: Who's there?
SIMKINS: *(o.s.)* This can't wait. *(calls)* Mr. Osborn!

Simkins enters the room.

HARRY: My father's not well, Mr. Simkins.

SIMKINS: Mr. Osborn. Dr. Stromm is dead.
OSBORN: What?
SIMKINS: His body was found this morning in the laboratory. He was murdered, sir.
HARRY: Murdered?
OSBORN: *(on his feet)* What are you talking about?
SIMKINS: And the flying wing prototype, sir...
OSBORN: What about it?
SIMKINS: It's missing. It's been stolen.

Silence. Osborn shocked. He moves quickly out of the room.

OSBORN: Take me there.

He exits. Harry remains behind for a moment, then goes after them. We're in the empty room. Camera lands on one of the masks.

INT. PARKER HOUSE—LATE AFTERNOON

Peter moves quickly down the stairs into

LIVING ROOM,
Uncle Ben and Aunt May are there. Peter holds his shoulder bag, moves quickly to the door. Starts to open it.

PETER: *(fast)* Goingtothedowntownlibraryseeyoulater.
UNCLE BEN: Hold on! I'll drive you.
PETER: It's OK. I'll take the train.

As Uncle Ben grabs a jacket and his keys.

UNCLE BEN: I said I'll drive you. Get in the car.

Peter moves out. Ben follows, turning to wink at Aunt May.

EXT. NEW YORK PUBLIC LIBRARY—DUSK

An Oldsmobile Delta '88 pulls over at the curb in front of the New York Public Library.

INT. OLDSMOBILE DELTA '88—DUSK

Uncle Ben is at the wheel, Peter beside him, moves to get out.

PETER: Thanks for the ride.
UNCLE BEN: Hold on a minute...We need to talk.
PETER: Talk about what?
UNCLE BEN: You're not the same guy lately. Fights in school, shirking your chores, you barely say a word to me or your aunt—what's the story?

Peter unconsciously pulls his sleeves down over his wrists. He just can't tell him.

PETER: There's no story.

UNCLE BEN: You're changing, and that's normal. This is the age when a man becomes the man he's going to be for the rest of his life. Just be careful who you change into. Okay?

PETER: I feel all this, all this power, but I don't know what it means, or how to control it, or what I'm supposed to do with it, even.

UNCLE BEN: You'll figure it out. You're one smart cookie, always have been.

UNCLE BEN: *(cont'd)* But knowledge is power. And with great power comes great responsibility. Don't ever forget that.

PETER: Yeah, yeah, I know all that, it's not what I'm talking about. You wouldn't understand.

UNCLE BEN: Wanna bet? When I was your age I went through exactly the same things.

PETER: No you didn't, that's my whole point. It's just possible that something unique is happening to me, isn't it?

UNCLE BEN: Believe it or not, it passes. You grow out of it.

PETER: I'm not gonna grow...just drop it, I'll figure it out myself.

UNCLE BEN: Look, if you won't give me so much as a clue, I can't help you.

PETER: I didn't ask for help.

UNCLE BEN: I know I'm not your father, Peter...

PETER: Then stop pretending to be.

There are some things you say that you wish you could pluck right back out of the air. This is one of them. And it's too late.

Uncle Ben's feelings are deeply hurt. He looks away.

UNCLE BEN: I'll pick you up on this corner at nine o'clock.

Peter wants to say something. But can't.

ON THE STREET,
Peter climbs out of the car, holding a brown paper bag, and closes the door. He starts up the steps of the library and watches as the Oldsmobile pulls out into traffic.

PETER: *(to the disappearing car)* I'm sorry.

He turns around, goes back down the steps of the library and heads off in the other direction. A deafening ROAR comes over and—

INT. ARENA—NIGHT

—we see a costumed AMATEUR WRESTLER, CONTESTANT #1, SLAM into the floor of a wrestling ring in the middle of a small, hot, dusty arena. The crowd goes wild as BONE SAW McGRAW, six feet nine inches, three hundred pounds of pure muscle, climbs to the top turnbuckle. He leaps and delivers a crushing flying elbow to his opponent's chest.

Peter grimaces.

INT. ARENA HALLWAY—NIGHT

A line of colorfully dressed wrestlers. A spunky CHECK-IN LADY sits behind a table taking information. A wrestler, clad in Robin-Hoodesque garb, stands before her.

CHECK-IN LADY: Down the hall to the ramp...and lose the hat.

"Robin Hood" removes his hat, gives the lady a dirty look.

CHECK-IN LADY: *(cont'd)* Yeah, yeah, nice tights tough guy. Next.

Peter Parker steps forward. She gives him the once over.

CHECK-IN LADY: *(cont'd)* There's no feather-weight division here, small fry. Next.

PETER: No, no, I know.

CHECK-IN LADY: Okay...you understand the NYWL is not responsible for any injuries you may...*(looking him over)*...and probably will sustain while participating in said event and that you are, at sub 150 pounds, indeed participating under your own free will.

PETER: Yes.

CHECK-IN LADY: Down the hall and up the ramp. May God be with you.

Peter turns exits. A male wrestler dressed as "Xena," steps up.

CHECK-IN LADY: *(cont'd)* *(taking it in)* Let's go princess.

INT. ARENA—NIGHT

Bone Saw pulverizes a new victim, CONTESTANT #2. He hurls him into the ropes, sending him careening back to the middle of the ring. Bone Saw grabs him, chucks him into the stands.

The crowd goes nuts. Bone Saw ROARS with rage. A HECKLER rises in his seat.

HECKLER: Hey Bone Saw! You big fake! You suck!

Bone Saw's eyes zero on the Heckler. He balls up his fists, GROWLS, leaps from the ring.

Bone Saw pushes his way through the crowd. The Heckler's eyes go wide as Bone Saw bears down on him, grabs him by the throat, pops him one.

Bone Saw grabs his folding chair, starts to make his way back to the ring, mumbling as he goes.

BONE SAW: Fake my ass.

Bone Saw drags the chair toward the ring, finds CONTESTANT #2 trying to crawl away. CONTESTANT #2 looks up just as Bone Saw rears back, WHACKS him across the face with the chair.

That's it for #2. He's out. The crowd howls.

RING ANNOUNCER: *(o.s.)* "Are you ready for more?"

The crowd demands more.

Bone Saw climbs back into the ring, sits on a stool in his corner. His bikini clad ring maidens, THE BONETTES, are quick to sponge him off, give him water, massage him.

RING ANNOUNCER: *(cont'd) (louder)* "I said, are we ready for more?!"

CROWD: MORE, MORE, MORE!!!!!

Bone Saw's had enough pampering, rises, flexes, whips the crowd into a frenzy.

BONE SAW: Bone Saw's ready!
RING ANNOUNCER: *(o.s.)* Will the next victim please enter the ring at this time! If he can withstand just three minutes in the cage with Bone Saw McGraw...

Two pendulously breasted CARD GIRLS strut around the ring with a banner reading "3:00 for $3,000."

RING ANNOUNCER: *(o.s.) (cont'd)* ...the sum of three thousand dollars will be paid to...

We find the RING ANNOUNCER standing behind a curtain on a ramp leading to the ring. He covers his microphone with his hand, turns to someone off screen.

RING ANNOUNCER: *(cont'd)* The Human Spider? That's it? That's the best you got?
SPIDER-MAN: *(o.s.)* Yeah.

The Ring Announcer huffs.

RING ANNOUNCER: Nah, you gotta jazz it up a little. *(back into microphone)*...the sum of three thousand dollars will be paid to...

The curtain opens, spotlights search through the crowd, swing to the top of the ramp where we find Spider-Man partially hidden by a black scrim.

RING ANNOUNCER: *(cont'd)*...the terrifying...the deadly!...THE AMAZING!!...

The scrim starts to rise.

RING ANNOUNCER: *(cont'd)*...SPIDER-MAN!!!

The scrim is gone, revealing Spider-Man, clad in a baggy, homemade costume made from old sweatpants, sweatshirts and a Balaclava.

SPIDER-MAN: *(to Ring Announcer)* That's "The Human Spider."
RING ANNOUNCER: Get out there, dipstick.

A PA gives Spider-Man a shove. He takes in the arena, the crowd for the first time. He's frozen, paralyzed by the spectacle before him.

Spider-Man cautiously makes his way toward the ring. The Bonettes wait like hungry wolves on the ramp. They mercilessly heckle him as he goes, feel his muscles, taunt him, egg on the crowd to do the same.

A gurney with CONTESTANT #2, groaning in agony, wheels by.

CONTESTANT #2: I can't feel my legs...I can't feel my legs...

Spider-Man watches them wheel him away, cautiously continues. He crawls into the ring, looks around. All of a sudden—

CROWD: CAGE! CAGE! CAGE!

Spider-Man scans the crowd. Cage?

WIDE SHOT,
A flat structure with metal bars drops from the ceiling. Its sides fold in, form a cage that sets down on the ring.

RING ANNOUNCER: *(o.s.)* Will the guards please lock the cage doors!

CLANG!! Stage Hands wrap huge metal chains around the corners of the cage, lock in the combatants.

SPIDER-MAN: Hey, wait a minute...

Spider-Man tests the cage.

SPIDER-MAN: *(cont'd)* This thing's locked.
BONE SAW: *(o.s.)* Freak show!

Spider-Man turns around, sees Bone Saw standing center ring.

BONE SAW: *(cont'd)* You're going nowhere! I've got you for three minutes...three minutes of playtime with Bone Saw.

Spider-Man flattens himself against the bars.

SPIDER-MAN: What am I doing here?

Bone Saw rushes Spider-Man, lunges at him. Spider-Man leaps out of frame. Bone Saw crashes into the cage wall, bounces off, crumples to the ground. He looks up, sees Spider-Man clinging to the top of the cage.

The Heckler, bloody faced and back in his chair, is shocked.

Bone Saw gets up, looks at Spider-Man.

BONE SAW: What do you think you're doing?
SPIDER-MAN: Staying away from you for three minutes.

Bone Saw's furious, leaps—

—but so does Spider-Man, across the cage, somersaulting to the opposite side. He clings there, drops to the ground.

CROWD: Yeahhhhhhh!!! Go Spider-Man!!!!

Go Spider-Man? He looks around, scans the cheering crowd. Turns back in time to see Bone Saw about to grab him. He leaps—

—does a one-handed hand stand on Bone Saw's head. He grins, confidence growing, fast.

SPIDER-MAN: Not a bad costume, what is that, Spandex? I used Lycra for mine and it itches like crazy.

Bone Saw swats him down, grabs his leg.

BONE SAW: I got you now, insect!

Bone Saw thrashes him about, pitches him against the cage. Spider-Man falls to the ground.

SPIDER-MAN: Owwww.

Bone Saw drags him out of frame.

SPIDER-MAN: *(cont'd)* You know, technically it's arachnid.

A shadow falls upon Spider-Man. He looks up, sees Bone Saw flying at him, prostrate, with a flying elbow. Spider-Man's eyes go wide. He flips his feet up, just in time to place them on Bone Saw's chest, kicking him into the cage.

Bone Saw slumps to the mat, knocked cold. The crowd freaks out. Flashbulbs pop.

CROWD: Spider-Man! Spider-Man! Spider-Man!

Spider-Man looks around the arena, raises his arms, triumphant.

SPIDER-MAN: Ahhhh... show biz.

INT. ARENA OFFICES—NIGHT

The administrative offices, upstairs at the arena. The PROMOTER puts a single hundred dollar bill into Spider-Man's palm (Peter is still wearing the costume).

PROMOTER: Now get outta here.
SPIDER-MAN: A hundred bucks? The ad said three thousand!
PROMOTER: Check it again, webhead. It said three grand for three minutes. You pinned him in two. For that I'll give you a hundred, and you're lucky to get it. You made my best fighter look like a girl out there.

Enraged, Spider-Man grabs the guy by the shirt and pulls him closer. A side of Peter Parker we've never seen before.

SPIDER-MAN: I need that money!
PROMOTER: I missed the part where this is my problem.

Spider-Man stares at him for a long moment, burning with rage, he wants to bust this guy right in the nose—

—but he turns and leaves instead, passing a squirrelly-looking GUY on the way in, his hair dyed platinum blond.

INT. HALLWAY—NIGHT

Spider-Man walks away down the corridor, clutching the lousy hundred dollar bill, muttering under his breath. He's nearly to the elevator when he hears a SHOUT from behind him.

PROMOTER: Hey! What the hell do you—

He turns, as the door to the Promoter's office BANGS open hard, shattering the glass, and the squirrelly-looking guy races out, clutching a canvas bag. He is a THIEF.

PROMOTER: *(cont'd)* Help! That guy stole the gate, he's got my money!

A SECURITY GUARD approaches from one end of the corridor. The elevator behind Spider-Man DINGS, its doors start to open, and the Thief takes off down the hallway toward it.

SECURITY GUARD: Hey, you! Stop that guy!

Spider-Man looks up, at the Thief racing straight at him, at the Security Guard giving chase, at the opening elevator behind him. He thinks, debates—

—and takes a step back. The Thief races right past him and into the elevator.

Thief: Thanks, pal.

The doors close and he gets away. The Security Guard arrives, SLAMS his fist on the elevator doors.

SECURITY GUARD: What the hell's the matter with you?! You just let him go!

The Promoter comes rushing up out of the office, a large red welt growing on his cheek.

PROMOTER: You coulda taken that guy apart! Now he's gonna get away with my money!

SPIDER-MAN: I missed the part where this is my problem.

He turns and walks away, down the corridor.

EXT. NEW YORK PUBLIC LIBRARY—NIGHT

As night falls, Peter walks down the street toward the library, dressed in street clothes again. He looks around for Uncle Ben's car.

Peter stands on the corner where Ben said he'd pick him up. Looks to the left, to the right. Not there yet.

A POLICE CAR races by him, SIREN wailing, and heads for the far corner. We hear an AMBULANCE'S SIREN in the BG.

He takes an interest, moves across the street. As he walks, his brow furrows, two and two coming together in his mind in a bad way.

He walks faster. And faster. He elbows his way through the back of the swelling crowd. Then the middle. As a desperate conviction grows in his mind, he thrashes, breaking through the front of the crowd and looking down at the ground—

—where police officers stand over a body. It's Uncle Ben!

PETER: UNCLE BEN!!

He lunges forward, but COPS stop him, pulling him back.

COP 1: Hang on, hang on!
PETER: My uncle! That's my uncle!
COP 2: That's not gonna help him!
PETER: What happened?!
COP 1: Carjacker. He's been shot.

Frantic, Peter tries to reach his uncle.

COP 2: Hold on, kid! You can't help the guy.
PETER: The guy? He's not the guy! He's my uncle.

He pushes in, moves to Ben, kneels, takes his head into his lap.

PETER: (cont'd) Uncle Ben! Uncle Ben! It's me, Peter!

Ben opens his eyes, his mouth forms a smile, then the word "Pete." He dies. Peter cries, holding him. Sirens continue in the BG.

Behind him, a THIRD COP turns around suddenly, radio in hand.

COP 3: They got the shooter! He's headed south on Fifth Avenue!

Very close on Peter—listens intently, stony-faced.

EXT. A DARK ALLEY—NIGHT

An exaggerated shadow falls on the brick wall of an alley. A man tears off his clothes, violently. The shadow grows bigger as the man starts to run, suddenly the shadow leaps, high into the air, sailing toward the building right in front of us.

The costume's still not right and he's not wearing a mask (or face paint), but make no mistake, this is truly THE AMAZING SPIDER-MAN. He climbs straight up the building. We climb with him, rising higher and higher until we burst out over the roof's edge.

Spider-Man jumps backwards, grabbing a flagpole, swinging on it, allowing his momentum to hurl him to the next building, which he scales quickly.

ON THE ROOF,
he scans the horizon. He sees a cluster of police lights, screaming down Fifth Avenue in pursuit. Spider-Man's right arm rises, palm up.

THWIP!

A silver strand of web fluid shoots out across the street. Spider-Man wraps his hands around it and leaps.

We leap with him, swinging out over the city, held aloft by the tensile strength of the web. We plummet down, in a graceful, terrifying arc, and as the ground races up toward us, Spider-Man's left hand rises—THWIP!

Another web strand rockets out into the night, the web-slinger shifts his weight to the second strand, abandoning the first, pulling himself back up in a graceful arc that leads him out into the avenue.

Well, above the avenue anyway. He's now swinging along directly above the chase, which is below him.

DOWN ON THE STREET,
Uncle Ben's Oldsmobile SCREECHES around a corner and SMASHES through a row of newspaper boxes. Three police cars follow, not far behind.

Above, Spider-Man follows, unseen. He webs—left, right, left, moving faster than the police cars—and THUMPS onto the roof of the Oldsmobile.

INSIDE THE CAR,
Spider-Man's fist SLAMS through the roof of the car and grabs hold of the Carjacker's face.

ON THE STREET,
the car swerves, bumps, scrapes through traffic. Cars SMASH into one another as it careens through an intersection.

GUNSHOTS erupt through the roof of the car, fired from within, missing Spider-Man by inches. He leaps off the roof, on top of a speeding truck.

ON TOP OF THE TRUCK,
Spider-Man stands up. Eyes on the Oldsmobile, he sees something else.

A low bridge! Stretching straight across the street, right about at chest level for Spidey.

He triple somersaults, up, over the bridge, and lands on the roof of the truck again. The truck starts to slow, so he leaps again, onto the roof of the Oldsmobile.

INSIDE THE OLDSMOBILE,
Spidey lands right in front of us, staring through the windshield and then smashing a fist through the windshield, spiderwebbing it.

EXT. MARINE BATTERY BUILDING—NIGHT

The Carjacker loses vision and control, the Oldsmobile SMASHES through the gates of a creepy-looking building near the East River, Spider-Man still on its hood.

The car SCREECHES toward the front door of the building, Spidey sees it coming, knows he'll be crushed, so he leaps, up, out of sight.

FROM UP HIGH,
we see the Oldsmobile crash through and barrel into the building. A second later, the police cars race up, radios SQUAWKING.

The camera tilts up to reveal Spider-Man on the wall above them, clinging there. The police cars' pulsating light reveals him, fades and Spider-Man is lost in the darkness. When the light again sweeps by, he is gone.

INT. MARINE BATTERY BUILDING—NIGHT

In a far corner of the building floor, the Carjacker cowers with his gun. The sweeping searchlight from the police boat, through the dirty, leaded windows, reveals only his outline.

Spider-Man descends, upside-down, from a web strand. He rotates, lands softly on his feet behind the Carjacker.

The Carjacker whirls around, BLASTS a shot at Spider-Man. Sensing it, Spidey leaps, onto the nearest wall. The shot SMACKS into the wall where he was.

The Carjacker, whom Spider-Man sees only as a silhouette, starts BLASTING at him, as Spidey leaps from wall to ceiling to wall to floor, just inches ahead of the bullets.

IN THE STREET,
the Cops hear the shots. Weapons are drawn, rifles steadied. They can see figures moving inside the building.

IN THE MARINE BATTERY BUILDING,
Spider-Man does an acrobatic leap and lands on the Carjacker's arm, kicking the gun free. It SKITTERS across the cement floor as Spidey holds the guy up, curls a fist—

SPIDER-MAN: This is for the man you killed.

—and punches the Carjacker in the jaw. The blow lifts the man right off his feet, knocks his stocking cap off, and sends him sailing into one of the unbroken windows, which SHATTERS. Spider-Man leaps into the window frame, grabs the Carjacker, pulls him to his feet.

Spotlights from outside swing around to frame the pair of combatants in the window.

CARJACKER: Don't hurt me! Give me a chance, man, give me a chance!
PETER: DID YOU GIVE HIM A CHANCE?! THE MAN YOU KILLED?! DID YOU?! ANSWER ME!

Suddenly, the Carjacker's face is revealed, brightly lit. His squirrelly face. And his platinum blond hair.

It is, God help him, the Thief who stole the money at the arena. The one Spider-Man stepped aside for.

PETER: *(cont'd)* No! No, not YOU!

Yes. Yes, him. Peter hurls him aside, the Thief CRASHES against a wall and falls to the floor. Peter starts to hyperventilate, trembling in horror, realizes the ghastly truth:

He failed to stop the very man who murdered his uncle.

Images flood back at him, fast:

INT. ARENA OFFICES—NIGHT (FLASHBACK)

The Security Guard, yelling at him:

SECURITY GUARD: Stop that guy!

INT. ELEVATOR—NIGHT (FLASHBACK)

The Thief, standing in the elevator, looking at him evilly as the doors close on his escape.

EXT. ARENA—NIGHT (FLASHBACK)

Uncle Ben's body, lying in the street.

INT. MARINE BATTERY BUILDING—NIGHT

Back in the building, the Thief stands up, not ten feet away from Peter. The Thief aims the gun at him. Blind with rage, Peter walks toward him. The Thief backs up. Peter advances. The Thief pulls the trigger and—

—CLICK. Empty. The Thief backs up even further, trips—

—and CRASHES through a window. Peter lunges forward, tries to grab him but misses, and the Thief falls fifty feet, SMASHING into a wooden dock below. Dead. The money flutters down around the body from the canvas bag.

OUT ON THE RIVER,
a police patrol boat CHUGS into view, swings a spotlight around toward Peter. They get just a glimpse of him.

COP: YOU, FREEZE! DON'T MOVE! WE'VE GOT THE PLACE COMPLETELY SURROUNDED!

The Cops raise their guns to fire, but Peter disappears from the window, headed up—

INT. THE MARINE BATTERY BUILDING

—and by the time the rest of the lights hit the window Peter is gone. Across the building floor, a DOZEN COPS SMASH through the door, shine flashlights everywhere.

The building is empty.

EXT. A ROOFTOP—NIGHT

Peter, still wearing the suit but not the mask, drops his head in his hands on top of a building nearby, alone. All sound drains away, all sound except Peter's soft voice—

PETER: Uncle Ben...

Still with his mask off, tears run down his face.

PETER: *(cont'd)* Oh God, I'm so sorry...

Pulling away, we see he's sitting on a stone gargoyle, jutting out from the roof of a lonely building, silhouetted by the full moon of the night he will never forget.

INT. PARKER HOUSE—NIGHT

Peter at the front door. Opens it. Enters. Through the window, we SEE Aunt May in her bathrobe (she's been waiting up). We watch Peter tell her the bad news. Her reaction. He moves to her, holds her.

EXT. QUEST AEROSPACE TESTING GROUNDS—NIGHT

An angled concrete surface fades up out of darkness. Headlights sweep slowly across bold letters painted there, BUNKER 6 QUEST AEROSPACE PROVING GROUNDS. A car arrives and General Slocum gets out and is met by Quest Aerospace's PROJECT COORDINATOR. They walk along the back of the bunker.

PROJECT COORDINATOR: Our exoskeleton's got real firepower, General Slocum.
GENERAL SLOCUM: If it does what you say it can, I'll sign the contract tomorrow.

As the men exit frame they reveal the Badger, Quest's military exoskeleton design, some distance from the bunker.

CLOSER SHOT,
Technicians unplug and scurry away from the war machine.

EXT. BUNKER—NIGHT

Through a set of observation slits we see General Slocum peering out. The Project Coordinator slides up beside him.

PROJECT COORDINATOR: And what about your commitment to OsCorp?
GENERAL SLOCUM: Nothing would please me more than to put Norman Osborn out of business. (Okay, let's see if this dog'll hunt.)

CLOSE UP ON TEST PILOT,

The TEST PILOT adjusts some knobs on the control panel.

TEST PILOT: Beginning mission profile, and...mark.

The Badger begins to rise as billowing smoke covers the frame.

EXT. BUNKER—NIGHT

Slocum and the rest of the delegation observe the action through the slits.

BUNKER P.O.V.,
We see the BADGER lift off in a cloud of exhaust, rotate.

CLOSE UP OF TEST PILOT,
A green glow reflects off his visor.

TEST PILOT: What the hell is that?

He looks down at his control panel, makes adjustments.

The Test Pilot's eyes go wide.

TEST PILOT: (cont'd) Oh my God...What is that!!! NOOOOOOO!

BUNKER P.O.V.,
The Badger explodes in a massive ball of flame.

EXT. BUNKER—NIGHT

Through the slits we see Slocum and the other inhabitants go pale, their faces illuminated by the explosion.

BUNKER P.O.V.,
The silhouette of the Goblin emerges through the fireball of the exploding Badger, and a missile WHIZZES beneath camera.

ROCKET P.O.V.,
The rocket races toward the observation slit in the bunker. Slocum's face fills with fear, realizes his fate.

EXT BUNKER—NIGHT

There is a massive explosion in the bunker. Fire and debris shoot through the observation slits.

A hideous CACKLE is heard disappearing into the night.

EXT. Outdoor Amphitheater—Day

Hundreds of mortarboards fly into the air and a great CHEER rises up from the bare-headed HIGH SCHOOL STUDENTS. Graduation day.

IN THE CROWD,
the GRADUATES swarm everywhere, hooking up with their jubilant PARENTS. Norman Osborn and Aunt May, separate from one another, searching for their kids.

Favor Peter looking for Aunt May. He sees Harry.

PETER: We made it buddy!
HARRY: Good news. My father owns a building downtown with an empty loft he said we could have. Why not move in with me when you get to the city?
PETER: I'm not sure I can afford the rent.
HARRY: We'll work something out.
PETER: (crossing his fingers) Gotta get a job first.

ANOTHER ANGLE,
Favor Aunt May and Norman Osborn still searching. Aunt May spots Norman.

AUNT MAY: Mr. Osborn...I'm May Parker, Peter's aunt. I've heard about you.
OSBORN: Aunt May. How do you do? Can't find my boy.
AUNT MAY: (spotting him) There's Harry.

Harry appears with his diploma. Norman looks at him, a tight smile.

HARRY: Hey, Dad.
OSBORN: You made it. It's not the first time I've been proven wrong. Congratulations.

He holds out a hand. Harry takes it, accepts the firm handshake.

HARRY: Thanks.
AUNT MAY: (hugging him) Congratulations, Harry.

Osborn's face suddenly lights up, noticing something over Harry's shoulder.

OSBORN: Ah hah! The winner of the science award.

Peter appears, carries his diploma and science award.

AUNT MAY: Here's our graduate. (she hugs him) You two looked so handsome up there.

Osborn puts his arm around Peter.

OSBORN: I know this has been a hard time for you, but try to enjoy this day. Commencement: the end of something. The start of something new.
PETER: Thanks Mr. Osborn.
OSBORN: And if you ever need anything...

Favor Harry watching his father and Peter. Harry spots MJ with Flash and her crowd. He moves toward her.

Flash puts his arms around MJ's waist, she pulls away. A few words between them. We see her remove something from one of her fingers, hand it to Flash. Flash is stunned, angry. He hurls it over the crowd and stalks off. Harry sees this, looks back over at Peter, still next to his father. Harry moves to console MJ

INT. THE PARKER HOUSE—DAY (LATE AFTERNOON)

Aunt May and Peter have just come in. Peter, carrying his gown, moves slowly to the stairs. Aunt May holds his diploma and his science prize. She watches him start up.

AUNT MAY: May I fix you something?
PETER: No thanks.

She watches him, recognizes the sadness.

INT. PETER'S BEDROOM—NIGHT

Peter sits on the side of his bed. His door left ajar. In a moment Aunt May appears at the door, knocks. Enters. She looks at him, then puts his diploma on his desk and his science prize on a shelf along with a few other awards.

She moves to the bed and sits beside him. Finally:

PETER: I missed him a lot today.
AUNT MAY: I know. I miss him too. *(takes his hand)* But he was there.
PETER: I just wish I hadn't—
AUNT MAY: Peter, don't start that again.
PETER: I can't help thinking about the last thing I said to him.
AUNT MAY: Stop it.
PETER: He tried to tell me something important and I threw it in his face.
AUNT MAY: You loved him. And he loved you. He never doubted the man you would grow into. How you were meant for great things. You won't disappoint him. Or me.

She waits another moment, then squeezes his hand and gets up. Moves to the door.

She leaves quietly, closing the door all the way. Peter gets up, opens a dresser drawer, moves some sweaters out of the way, digs all the way to the bottom of the drawer...

...where his Spider-Man costume is crumpled, the red sweatshirt lying on top of it. The spider outline, sketched on its front.

UNCLE BEN: *(v.o.)* Remember...with great power comes great responsibility.

We HEAR the approach of what will become a GREAT ROAR.

DISSOLVE TO:
EXT. MANHATTAN—DAY

A train ROARS out of a tunnel.

INT. TRAIN DAY

Peter sits in the train, staring at the skyline, a pile of college text books in his lap.

EXT. MANHATTAN—DAY

Manhattan is in the background as the train heads into the heart of the city.

EXT. DELI—DAY

A ROBBER races out of a Korean deli, gun in one hand, sack of money in the other. The GROCER chases him out, carrying a baseball bat. The Robber turns to shoot him, when suddenly—

—THWIP! A web-strand wraps around the gun and yanks it sharply out of the Robber's hand. Stunned, both Robber and Grocer turn.

A shadow disappears into the night, barely seen.

EXT. STREET—DAY

A CABBIE leans against his cab, talking to a couple other CABBIES.

CABBIE: *(heavy accent)* This is not a man. My brother saw it building a nest in the Lincoln Center fountain.

EXT. JEWELRY STORE—NIGHT

A POLICE CAR SCREECHES to a halt in front of a jewelry store, siren SCREAMING. TWO COPS race up to the glass doors, which have been smashed, the store's alarm WAILING.

The Cops suddenly look up, over the door, where they see THREE JEWELRY THIEVES and their bag of loot caught in a web-net, dangling from a lamppost, tied up neatly for them.

EXT. CONSTRUCTION SITE—DAY

TWO CONSTRUCTION WORKERS dangle their feet off a beam while eating lunch.

CONSTRUCTION WORKER: Have you ever seen his face? Neither have I. Wait until his wife figures out he's running around in tights.

EXT. DARK STREET—NIGHT

A WOMAN holds out her purse, huddling before a MUGGER, who's holding a gun on her—

—until he's suddenly gone, swept up into the air by the red and blue blur that flashes through the frame.

Her purse falls back into frame. She scoops it up. A Note attached reads, "COURTESY, YOUR FRIENDLY NEIGHBOR-HOOD SPIDER-MAN."

EXT. POLICE STATION—DAY

A UNIFORM COP talks excitedly with a couple other Cops.

COP: Never mind the vigilante thing, you seen all those webs he leaves all over the city? I'm gonna cite the guy for littering.

INT. DAILY BUGLE—DAY

> WHO IS SPIDER-MAN?
> Costumed Figure Saves Fire Victims

It's the headline of a tabloid newspaper, the Daily Bugle. *There's also a large photograph of a burning building and a fuzzy, indistinct figure crawling up the side of it.*

JAMESON: *(o.s.)* He's a criminal, that's who he is!

The paper lowers with a crumple, revealing the face of J. JONAH JAMESON, owner of the last flattop haircut in America.

JAMESON: *(cont'd)* A vigilante! A public menace! What's he doing on my front page?

HOFFMAN, an employee of the Bugle *enters the office, interrupting the meeting Jameson is having with his city editor, ROBBIE ROBERTSON.*

HOFFMAN: Mr. Jameson, we have a page 6 problem.
JAMESON: We have a page 1 problem. Shut up!
ROBBIE: He's news.
HOFFMAN: They're a major account, it can't wait.
JAMESON: It's about to.
ROBBIE: *(ignoring Hoffman)* He saved six people from burning to death.
JAMESON: —in a fire he probably started! Something goes wrong and this creepy crawler's there, what's that tell ya?
ROBBIE: Boss, he's a hero.
JAMESON: Then why does he wear a mask? What's he got to hide?

HOFFMAN: We double sold page 6. Both Conway and Macy's bought three quarters of it.
ROBBIE: We sold out all four printings, Jonah.
JAMESON: Sold out?!
ROBBIE: Every copy.
JAMESON: Spider-Man, page 1, tomorrow! With a decent picture this time!

Jameson turns to Hoffman.

JAMESON: *(cont'd)* Move Conway to page 7.
HOFFMAN: There's a problem with page 7.
JAMESON: Then move them to page 8 and tell 'em we'll give 'em an extra column inch. Get out of here!
ROBBIE: Can't get a picture. I've had Eddie on it for weeks, nobody ever gets more than a glimpse of him.
JAMESON: What is he, shy?! If we can get a picture of Julia Roberts in a thong, we can certainly get a picture of this nut. Put an ad on the front page! "Cash money for a picture of Spider-Man!" Doesn't he want to be famous?!

EXT. DAILY BUGLE—DAY

His voice continues over the exterior of the building:

JAMESON: *(o.s.)* Then I'll make him INFAMOUS!

EXT. CHELSEA STREET—DAY

We're looking through the glass doors of MOONDANCE, a seedy-looking diner downtown. Inside, we see Mary Jane Watson, wearing a hideous orange waitress uniform, being berated by a SURLY COOK. She punches a time clock, grabs a raincoat, and stalks out of there.

As the doors open, a blast of NOISE and grease washes out after her. She makes her way down the street. The guy passing her stops, checks her out. It turns out to be Peter.

PETER: Hey!
MJ: *(doesn't look up)* Buzz off! *(keeps walking)*
PETER: Mary Jane Watson?

She freezes. As if hearing her own name frightens her.

PETER: *(cont'd)* MJ It's me. Peter.
MJ: *(turns, lights up, pulls her raincoat closed)* PETER!
PETER: Hi. How have you been? What are you doing around here?
MJ: I live around the corner. I was...headed to an audition.
PETER: An audition. So you're an actress now.
MJ: Working steady. In fact I just got off a job.

PETER: That's great, MJ

MJ: Yeah, I've never been happier. It's like they say, it's all about the work, y'know, the work is everything...But how about you? How's the photography?

PETER: Great. *(beat)* Actually...I haven't done much with it. I've been kind of busy...going to college...*(holds up the classifieds)* looking for a job, saving the world. But you! Look at you. You're actually living the life you dreamed about.

Suddenly, the door to the diner opens and the Surly Cook steps out, clutching a pile of restaurant checks in his meaty fist.

SURLY COOK: Hey, glamour girl! Your drawer's off by six bucks! Next time I take it out of your check, y'get me? *(she ignores him)* Excuse me, Miss Watson, I am speaking words to you. You get me?

MJ: Yes, Enrique, okay? I "get you," Enrique.

He goes back inside, BANGING the door shut behind him. MJ looks down, can't look Peter in the face. By way of an explanation, she opens her raincoat, flashes him the uniform.

MJ: *(cont'd)* Some dream, huh? But it's just temporary. Few extra dollars.

PETER: Well that's nothing to be embarrassed about. (You think they need a waiter?)

MJ: Don't tell Harry.

PETER: ...Harry?

MJ: *(sees his look)* Aren't you guys living together? We've been going out. Didn't he tell you?

PETER: *(recovering)* Oh, yeah...right.

MJ: I think he'd hate the idea of my waiting on tables. He'd think it was low.

PETER: Well, Harry never has lived on a little planet I like to call Earth.

MJ laughs.

PETER: *(cont'd)* Probably half the people starring on Broadway were waiters or even dishwashers.

MJ: How come you always make me feel better?

He smiles. Shrugs. An awkward moment.

MJ: *(cont'd)* Well...*(she turns to go)* It's good to see you, Peter.

PETER: *(calls after her)* Maybe I'll come down and have a cup of your Moondance coffee some day. *(quickly)* And I won't tell Harry.

MJ: *(looks back)* No, don't tell Harry.

PETER: *(to himself)* No, I won't. I won't tell Harry.

Finally, he turns and starts off in the other direction. He walks alone.

PETER: *(cont'd)* Harry and Mary Jane. Wow. *(keeps walking, sad)* Don't tell Peter.

Walks on.

EXT. HARRY'S APARTMENT—DAY

A cool place in Tribeca.

INT. HARRY'S APARTMENT—DAY

The door opens. Peter enters, downhearted. He spots Norman pacing around, speaking on a cell phone. Norman nods to him, Peter nods back. He SEES Harry at the dining room table. College textbooks open. Harry turns, out of sorts.

HARRY: Stormin' Norman making his weekly inspection. Spends half of it on the phone. *(re: open books)* Man, am I glad you're here. I need your help, I'm hopelessly lost. What's wrong with you? Somebody run over your dog?

PETER: No. I, uh...I was late and Dr. Connors fired me.

HARRY: Late again? What is it with you? Where d'you go all the time?

PETER: Around.

HARRY: For a completely responsible guy, you're completely irresponsible.

Osborn hangs up his phone.

OSBORN: Peter Parker.

He turns. Norman Osborn is walking toward him, all smiles.

OSBORN: *(cont'd)* Maybe you can tell me who she is.

PETER: Who?

OSBORN: This mystery girl Harry's been dating.

HARRY: Dad...

OSBORN: I think he wants me to meet this one, and believe me, it's the first time that's hap—

HARRY: *(sharply)* Dad.

Osborn stops, looks at Harry—what? Peter looks at Harry too, but Harry avoids his gaze.

PETER: Sorry. Harry hasn't mentioned her.

HARRY: *(to change the subject)* Hey, Pete, you're probably looking for work now. Dad, maybe you can help him find a job?

Peter shakes his head, makes his way toward the kitchen.

PETER: Oh, no. I appreciate it, but I'll be fine.

OSBORN: It's no problem. I'll make some phone calls.
PETER: No. I couldn't accept it. I like to earn what I get. I can find work.
OSBORN: I respect that. *(making his way over to Harry)* You want to make it on your own steam. That's great. *(to Harry)* Interesting, isn't it? Peter is looking for work. As in, actively seeking, as opposed to strenuously avoiding.
HARRY: What do you want from me? I'm trying to keep my grades up.

Peter notices a copy of the Daily Bugle *on the kitchen counter. He picks it up, looks at the front page.*

OSBORN: What other skills do you have, Parker?

Peter looks up from the front page of the Daily Bugle, *which he's been studying intently.*

PETER: I'm thinking of something in photography.

He tosses the Bugle back on the counter, where we see the front page. There's a crude sketch of Spider-Man's face, under the headline:

> WANTED: PHOTOGRAPHIC PROOF
> Bugle Offers Reward!

EXT. BANK—NIGHT

A 35MM camera is suspended in the cornice on the third floor of a building. Peering in through the lens, we see a red light flashing.

THROUGH THE CAMERA LENS,
the words "Auto Shutter" flash in red in the lower right corner of the frame. We're looking through the viewfinder now, watching as THREE BANK ROBBERS emerge from a bank, guns drawn, hostage in tow.

A dark figure swings into view and does battle with the bank robbers. The camera on the cornice suddenly FLASHES, and in that flash-instance, we get our first good look at—

—THE AMAZING SPIDER-MAN, in his new, improved, extremely snazzy costume. The image freezes, changes to—

INT. DAILY BUGLE—NEWSROOM—DAY

—the resultant still photograph. A hand flips past it, to more pictures of Spider-Man, all good shots, swinging, flying, web-shooting. Robbie Robertson looks up, in the newsroom of the Daily Bugle.

ROBBIE: They're good. Very good. How'd you get 'em?
PETER: If I tell you, you'll send your own photographer. Am I hired?

ROBBIE: It's not up to me. Mr. Jameson hires all staff personally.

They hear SHOUTS from the office across the hall.

JAMESON: *(o.s.)* IS THAT WHAT I SAID?! IS THAT WHAT I ASKED?! I SAID A PICTURE, EDDIE, NOT AN INK BLOT! WHY THE HELL CAN'T ANYBODY BRING ME DECENT ART ON THAT FREAK?! GET THE HELL OUT OF HERE!
ROBBIE: He fires 'em that way, too.

EDDIE BROCK, another young photographer, comes out of Jameson's office. Brock is shabbily dressed.

EDDIE: *(locks eyes with Peter)* What're you looking at, greenhorn?

Brock walks away. Jonah Jameson appears in the doorway, shouts after him.

JAMESON: AND BROCK! WOULD IT KILL YOU TO GET A DECENT SUIT?!

He turns, sees Peter, inexplicably continues in shouting mode.

JAMESON: *(cont'd)* WHAT?!

INT. JAMESON'S OFFICE—DAY

Jameson sits behind his desk, flipping through the photographs. Peter is across from him, nervous, but Robbie gives him a wink—hang in there.

JAMESON: They're crap. *(flip)* Crap. *(flip)* Crap. *(flip)* Megacrap. I'll give you three hundred for all of 'em.
PETER: That seems a little low.
JAMESON: Then take 'em somewhere else.

Peter rises, starts to collect the photographs.

JAMESON: *(cont'd)* Sit down. All right...I'll give you five hundred. That's the standard freelance fee.

Jameson takes the photographs back and hands them to Robbie, muttering as he points to one in particular.

JAMESON: *(cont'd)* Tear up page one, run that shot instead.

Peter does a double take—page one?!

ROBBIE: Headline?
JAMESON: Spider-Man, Hero or Menace? Exclusive *Daily Bugle* photos!
PETER: Menace? Sir, he was protecting that bank from those—

JAMESON: Tell you what, Atticus, you take the pictures, I make the headlines, okay, that all right with you?
PETER: Yes, sir—I would like a job, sir.
JAMESON: No jobs! Freelance. Best thing in the world for a kid your age. Bring me more shots of that newspaper selling clown and I might take 'em off your hands. Come on, get out of here. I got deadlines.

MONTAGE:

EXT. NONDESCRIPT BUILDING—NIGHT

We see a web. A camera flashes.

INT. BUGLE—DAY (LATER AFTERNOON)

Jameson, Robbie and Peter in Jameson's office. Robbie hands Jameson a front page mock-up with a photo of Spider-Man in action. The Headline reads:

NY CHEERS COSTUME HERO

Jameson frowns. Crosses out "CHEERS" writes in "FEARS," crosses out "HERO" writes in "COWARD." Holds up the paper. Headline now reads:

NY FEARS COSTUME COWARD

Peter sees it.

INT. JAMESON'S OFFICE—DAY

Peter brings in an envelope, hands it to Jameson, who opens it. More Spider-Man photos.

INT. BUGLE—ANOTHER DAY

Robbie hands Jameson another newspaper mock-up with a Spider-Man photo on the front page and no headline.

ROBBIE: Headline?
JAMESON: *(thinking)* "Spider-Man: Super-Hero or Super-Zero?"

Peter reacts.

INT. BUGLE—ANOTHER DAY

Robbie, Peter, Jameson. A newspaper is lowered to his desk.

CLOSE SHOT—THE HEADLINE SHOUTS:

"BIG APPLE FEARS SPIDER BITE!"

Pull back—all.

PETER: Why are you so hard on him? He's on the side of the law.
JAMESON: He thinks he is the law. There's no place

in this society for vigilante justice. Once one person takes the law in his own hands, it's anarchy.
PETER: *(growing dissatisfaction of Spider-Man photos & headlines)* Mr. Jameson. How about an assignment? I'd like to shoot something other than Spider-Man.
JAMESON: No, you just keep doing what you're doing.
ROBBIE: J.J., we need someone to cover the World Unity Festival. Let's send Peter.
JAMESON: World Unity Festival! Another epic display of OsCorp self-aggrandizement. Fine, send him, but I never said you have a job! Meat! I'll give you a box of Christmas meat! Best I can do! NOW GET ME MORE PICTURES!

EXT. OSCORP CORPORATE HEADQUARTERS—DAY

A sprawling high-rise adorning the Manhattan skyline.

INT. OSCORP BOARD ROOM—DAY

Norman Osborn sits at the head of a long table in the OsCorp board room, concluding a meeting. The cat who ate the canary.

OSBORN: In addition, we've secured three major new government contracts and I'm pleased to announce that as of today, OsCorp Industries has surpassed Quest Aerospace as the principal supplier to the United States military. In short, ladies and gentlemen of the board, costs are down, revenue is up, and our stock has never been higher.

Simultaneously, they all close the leather-bound folders that were open in front of them. Balkan sits forward.

BALKAN: That's wonderful news, Norman. *(clears his throat)* In fact, it's the reason we're selling the company.
OSBORN: What?!
BALKAN: It took us ALL by surprise, but Quest Aerospace is recapitalizing in the wake of the bombing.
OSBORN: Fargas, what the hell's going on here?

Fargas doesn't respond.

BALKAN: Quest is expanding and they've made a tender offer we can't ignore.
OSBORN: Why wasn't I told about this?
BALKAN: The last thing they want is a power struggle with entrenched management...
FARGAS: They want you out, Norman. The deal is off if you come with it. The board expects your resignation in thirty days.
OSBORN: You...can't do this to me, I built this company. *(to Fargas)* Max...please...

Norman quickly scans the faces of the hostile board members.

FARGAS: The board is unanimous. I'm sorry. We're announcing the sale right after the World Unity Festival.

BALKAN: You're out, Norman.

OSBORN: *(Oh, yeah?)* Am I?

EXT. TIMES SQUARE—DAY

An enormous, multi-colored globe stands over Times Square, today the site of World Unity Festival, a festival of healing and unification.

ON THE STAGE,
Macy Gray entertains the crowd with a soulful rendition of "Why Didn't You Call Me."

IN THE MAIN STREET,
Peter Parker works his way through the crowd, taking pictures. Through the lens he spots a YOUNG MAN reading the Daily Bugle. Peter focuses on the headline that reads—

"Big Apple Dreads Spider Bite!"

Peter lowers his camera, shakes his head.

He takes in the spectacle before him, continues working his way through the crowd, taking pictures.

Giant balloons float in the air. Thousands are in attendance here, the vibe is sweetness and light.

A MOTHER buys her seven-year-old boy, BILLY, some cotton candy. Five stories up, a balcony on one building has been converted into

A REVIEWING STAND,
buttressed by two Hercules statues, one at each corner, which appear to be holding the reviewing stand aloft.

All this under a large banner that reads "OSBORN INDUS-TRIES WELCOMES YOU TO THE 3RD ANNUAL WORLD UNITY FESTIVAL."

NINE ANGRY MEN AND WOMEN, the OsCorp board of directors, sit in a row in suits and ties, chatting up other DIG-NITARIES. Balkan and Fargas are smiling, but it's sorta grue-some.

Harry is fixing a UNITY DAY pin to MJ He stands back to study her.

HARRY: Perfect. Except how come you didn't wear the black dress? I wanted to impress my father. He loves black.

MJ: Maybe he'll be impressed, no matter what? You think I'm pretty.

HARRY: Of course I do. You're beautiful.

ANGLE ON PETER IN THE STREET,
Peter raises his camera, squeezes off a few shots.

THROUGH HIS LENS,
Peter scans the balloons, the floating streamers, comes to a Hercules statue. He tilts his camera up the statue's torso, ris-ing up, to the balcony's edge, up past Harry and MJ, up fur-ther...

He sees Harry put his arm around MJ, leans in for a kiss. Time slows down, Harry's mouth approaches MJ's, the worst is about to happen, but at the last second—

—MJturns, giving Harry cheek when he wanted lips.

ON THE STREET,
Peter whips the camera down, pumps a fist in the air. Hope!

Harry, his cheek turned, is looking down at the street. He sees Peter, who looks back up and sees Harry. They each see each other seeing each other. Harry, caught in the act.

ON THE REVIEWING STAND,
Harry averts his gaze from Peter, puts his arm around MJ, ushers her away.

ON THE STREET,
Peter's expression suddenly changes, completely, his eyes widen. We leap outside him as—

HIS SPIDER-SENSE
goes off, slowing everything to a crawl. Spidey P.O.V. races all around him, searching the crowd for any sign of danger, but finding nothing.

BACK ON THE STREET,
things return to normal speed. Peter looks around, puzzled.

ON THE REVIEWING STAND,
Harry leads MJ through the balcony crowd, spots Balkan and Fargas, walks up to them.

HARRY: *(cont'd)* Have you seen my father?

The two board members share an uncomfortable look.

FARGAS: I'm not sure he'll be joining us.

Balkan and Fargas turn, hear something. So do the others around them. It's a high-pitched WHINING sound. Harry and MJ look for the noise, make their way to the balcony edge.

ON THE STREET,
Peter is really going crazy, certain there's a problem some-where, but not sure what it is. He looks up.

IN THE SKY,
something darts in and out of the clouds, something small and very, very fast.

ON THE REVIEWING STAND,
Fargas is squinting up into the sky, at the source of the whining.

FARGAS: *(cont'd)* What is that?

Balkan joins him.

BALKAN: Must be new this year.

He raises a pair of binoculars.

BALKAN: *(cont'd)* What the devil! Is that our wing?

IN MID-AIR,
we're flying, a first-person shot. A deranged CACKLE echoes over the whine of a jet-engine turbine.

ON THE STREET,
whatever-it-is comes through for another pass, lower this time. But it passes so fast, zigzagging through the floats, that we can't really get a handle on it.

ON THE REVIEWING STAND,
Balkan and Fargas look troubled. But the crowd APPLAUDS, all smiles. They like this bit.

IN MID-AIR,
whatever-it-is curls up into the sky, banks and hovers, turning right toward the reviewing stand.

From behind it, we see that it's a figure atop a flying thing, and the figure reaches down to his belt and detaches some kind of device, the size of a softball, with vertical bulges like those on a pumpkin. As he raises the device, we get our first look at...

THE GREEN GOBLIN!

He's clad in a form-fitting dark green suit densely layered with complicated circuitry, a suit we have seen before, in the OsCorp lab. Over his face he wears a grotesque, green demonic mask, and he has both legs astride a small flat flying wing, big enough for one—also the one we saw in the lab.

The Goblin CACKLES, a hideous laugh that echoes over the street.

ON THE STAGE,
Macy Gray, her background singers and dancers stop performing, look around. Weren't informed regarding this part of the "show."

And the crowd CHEERS! They love this guy!

The Goblin twitches and the Glider responds immediately, banking and plummeting—

—straight down toward the reviewing stand.

The Goblin detonates the device he holds (a pumpkin bomb) and hurls it toward one of the Hercules statues.

KA-BOOM! Hercules crumbles. The reviewing stand begins to collapse, lurches lower, sways, V.I.P.s topple, MJ is thrown forward, Harry backwards.

Debris showers the pavement below, nearly crushing terrorized CITIZENS.

ON THE STAGE,
Ms. Gray's security guards rush in, cover her, escort her to safety.

ON THE STREET,
Peter elbows his way through the crowd and takes off toward the mouth of an alley.

ON THE REVIEWING STAND,
there is a shudder, a CRACK, and the entire stand drops a few feet. MJ is splayed precariously on the dangling balcony balustrades.

Harry gets to his feet, goes to her. But his weight causes the balcony to shift.

Hercules CRACKS yet again. MJ is tossed further to the outer edge of the balcony.

THE GREEN GOBLIN
soars upward. Takes another pumpkin bomb from his pouch and hurls it.

ON THE REVIEWING STAND,
the bomb lands with a THUNK, bounces to a stop right in front of the members of the OsCorp board. The bomb WHIRS a few feet into the air, and then—

ZAP-FLASH!

It explodes in a brilliant orange, so bright and searing it irradiates half a dozen members of the board, turning them into X-ray images.

SCREAMS everywhere. They don't love this guy anymore!

The blast's concussion causes the balcony to separate yet again. Now MJ is really in trouble.

Harry crawls over to her...blinking to get the spots from his eyes, he reaches out his hand.

MJ reaches out her hand to him, when—

THE GREEN GOBLIN
rises up behind her, on his Glider. Malefic grin. MJ turns to him, SHRIEKS.

The Goblin lets out a blood-curdling CACKLE, revels in the mayhem unfolding, but cuts it short, hesitates, hearing something. He turns and

THE AMAZING SPIDER-MAN!
swings down from a building above and (POW!) smacks right into the Goblin, knocking the villain clean off his Glider.

The Goblin plummets, from six stories up, except that he lands on one of the passing floats, bounces off it, makes a nifty mid-air twist—

And crashes feet first into a large tent below, which breaks his fall.

IN MID-AIR,
the Glider comes sailing down after the Goblin, as with a homing device. It SMASHES through the globe replica, which is knocked off its perch, and comes out the other side, heading for the Goblin.

SPIDER-MAN
clings to the side of a building, overlooking the chaos. His eyes zip over to—

THE REVIEWING STAND,
where MJ is in big trouble. But then there are SCREAMS, and his eyes zip over the other way, to where the globe replica has begun to roll—

ON THE STREET
—crushing everything in its wake. And headed straight for Little Billy, who stares in frozen shock as it heads right for him. His Mother SCREAMS.

ON THE BUILDING,
Spider-Man fires a web at a billboard high atop a nearby building.

AND SWINGS
in a huge arc. Straight for Billy. He sweeps the child up, just as the globe rolls past, stamping out parking meters like matchsticks.

THE GREEN GOBLIN

is on the ground, stuck in the tangle of the collapsed tent and surrounded by COPS, whose guns are raised.

GREEN GOBLIN: I surrender! I surrender! Media violence made me do it!

The Cops hesitate, and in that moment the Goblin leaps, inhumanly, into the thick of them. They go after him, piling on, in a blizzard of flashing nightsticks.

NEARBY,
Spider-Man swings to the ground, depositing Billy in the arms of his Mother. He looks over to where the Cops have blanketed the Goblin, fists flying.

But with a shocking burst of strength, the Goblin hurls the Cops off him, and they go flying in all directions.

Spider-Man makes a leaping run. He hand-springs, somersaults, vaults himself in the air, and lands on his feet in front of the Goblin.

GREEN GOBLIN: (cont'd) How dare you interfere with me! What do you want?!
SPIDER-MAN: World peace. But I'll settle for your chin.

And he sends a FIST into the Goblin's chin.

The Goblin flies across the street, crashing into a brick wall. Spider-Man comes at him again, with another haymaker—

—which the Goblin catches in one gloved hand. Stopping it.

GREEN GOBLIN: See what I did there?

And now it's his turn to throw a massive punch.

Spider-Man goes ass over elbows, smashing through an ice cream cart and into a lamppost.

The Goblin touches something on his wrist, and a moment later his Glider comes whizzing down, right behind Spider-Man, who leaps up and over it at the last second.

The Goblin jumps on the Glider, CLICKS his boots into the wings, and he's off, into the sky.

IN MID-AIR,
the Goblin banks left, turns back. He hits a button and small machine guns appear from the Glider's tips.

ON THE REVIEWING STAND,
Harry reaches for MJ but she's out of reach, still trapped on the reviewing stand. She tries to climb to safety as it sways, CRACKS like ice in springtime. Rivets POP.

IN MID-AIR,
the Goblin FIRES at Spider-Man, raking the ground around him with bullets.

Spider-Man fires a web up to an enormous Rasta Man float. And he swings up, out of the gunfire's path, up and over the top of the float as the Goblin disappears into the sky.

FROM SPIDER-MAN'S P.O.V.,
we see MJ on the crumbling balcony, imperiled. A procession of floats hover between her and Spidey.

So Spider-Man leaps. A super jump, a tuck and roll, and he leapfrogs from float to float, one, two, three. He makes his final leap for the balcony when—

IN MID-AIR,
The Goblin zooms in behind Spider-Man, wraps him in a bear hug and drives him into the building above the balcony. Glass and debris rain down.

ON THE BALCONY,
Harry is struck in the head by a chunk of debris. His knees buckle and he crashes to the floor, unconscious.

IN MID-AIR,
the combatants trade blows. The Goblin rears back, delivers a crushing elbow to Spidey's jaw, sending him plummeting toward the balcony.

ON THE BALCONY,
Spider-Man, glass and chunks of the building come crashing down near MJ, causing her to roll out, to the very edge. She is saved by the balustrades, which break her fall. MJ watches as debris crumbles, falls five stories.

Spider-Man is just about to move toward MJ when the Goblin appears, rising up out of nowhere, HOVERING right over them.

He whirls toward Spider-Man. A weapon HUMS up out of the Glider, points at Spider-Man.

Spidey shoots a web, it SPLATS over the Goblin's face, obscuring his vision. A laser beam BLASTS into the wall next to Spidey.

Spider-Man reaches up into the Glider and pulls out a handful of wiring from underneath the wing.

The Goblin takes off, clawing the webbing out of his face, the Glider smoking and sputtering. Safe!

No, not safe! The building ledge finally crumbles and she falls, SCREAMING!

IN MID-AIR,
Spider-Man dives down after her, straight down, trailing a web behind him. He catches MJ just short of the street, the web pulls taut, and they bounce back up just before hitting the pavement, like at the end of a bungee jump.

They sail back up into the air, just as the balcony finally collapses behind them.

EXT. COLLAPSING BALCONY
Harry wakes. He's at the edge of the balcony and just then he sees Spider-Man swinging away with MJ

EXT. STREET—DAY

They SWOOSH by overhead. A CABBIE exits his cab, points, watches the duo swing away.

CABBIE: What the hell's that?
CABBIE: (alt) Look, it's Superman.

IN MID-AIR,
Spidey and MJ swing through the spectacular canyon of skyscrapers, she works up the nerve to ask him:

MJ: Who are you?
SPIDER-MAN: You know.
MJ: I do?
SPIDER-MAN: Your friendly neighborhood Spider-Man.

EXT. ATOP ROCKEFELLER CENTER—THE GARDENS

Spider-Man lands gracefully, deposits her gently on the grass, where two YOUNG LOVERS are making out on a bench.

SPIDER-MAN: Don't mind us. She needs to use the elevator?

Jaws drop. Spider-Man turns and leaps off the edge of the building, throwing in a double somersault before shooting out a web. Breathless, MJ watches him swing away into the city.

MJ: Spider-Man...

EXT. HARRY'S APARTMENT—NIGHT

A tenant walks out, hails a cab.

INT. HARRY APARTMENT—NIGHT

The door opens. Harry enters with cell-phone in hand. He's in a panic. Peter at window, drinking a glass of milk.

HARRY: Pick up! Pick up! If somehow you get this, call me right away. (hangs up, sees Peter—he's manic) Pete! Oh, man, I'm glad you're here. Any word? Has she called?

PETER: Not yet. She will.

HARRY: She will? How do you know, you don't know that.

PETER: Feeling I have. You okay? How's your head?

HARRY: They patched it up, it's nothing. Where did he take her? What would he do to her? Thank God my father wasn't there. That whole scene, where'd that thing come from? What was it? *(re: Peter's glass)* What is that? Milk?

PETER: Uh huh, got milk.

HARRY: Why aren't you worried?

PETER: *(remembering)* Oh. Right. I am worried.

HARRY: I've put it together. Spider-Man knows she's my girlfriend. He'll want a ransom from my father.

PETER: *(cocks his head)* Really? What could he get?

The PHONE RINGS. Harry picks it up.

HARRY: Hello?

MJ: *(v.o.) (in a state of bliss)* Hi ya.

HARRY: Oh, thank God! *(to Peter)* It's her. *(to phone)* Where are you? Are you all right? Did he hurt you?

MJ: *(v.o.)* Ohh, noo. He was incredible.

HARRY: He was what? What do you mean he was incredible?

Peter reacts. Smiles.

MJ: *(v.o.)* Oh, I don't know. You know.

HARRY: Are you sure you're all right? Are you drugged? Where did he take you?

MJ: *(v.o.)* To a beautiful roof garden.

HARRY: To a roof garden?

MJ: *(v.o.)* Have you ever been there? You should go.

HARRY: No, I've never been there. Listen, I'm coming over.

MJ: *(v.o.)* Why?

HARRY: Because you need to tell me everything, that's why. And what did you mean by incredible?

MJ: *(v.o.)* I'm going to sleep now.

HARRY: Well, then, call me in the morning. Are you sure you're feeling all right?

MJ: *(v.o.) (still blissed)* Incredible.

HARRY: STOP SAYING THAT! Call me when you wake up, we'll go for breakfast and I'll buy you something beautiful...

MJ: *(v.o.)* Why?

HARRY: Because I want to. It'll make you feel better.

MJ: *(v.o.)* G'night.

HARRY: All right, g'night, get some sleep, uh, sleep tight, don't let the—

She hangs up. One of those sloppy hang ups, a good three seconds for the receiver to set down.

HARRY: *(cont'd) (he hangs up)* She's still a little rattled.

Peter tips his glass of milk back, head back, finishes it to the last drop. Milk on his lip.

PETER: At least she's all right.

HARRY: Look...about MJ I know that was a picture you didn't want to take.

PETER: I didn't take it.

HARRY: I know I should've told you about us, but you have to understand, I'm crazy about her.

PETER: We're friends. You didn't have to lie.

HARRY: I always knew you wanted her for yourself, but you never made a move.

PETER: I guess I didn't.

HARRY: Look, I'm going to get some sleep. How about you?

PETER: I think I'll look out at the skyline. I'd like to pray for those people who died.

HARRY: What was that thing that killed them? It happened so fast.

PETER: I don't know. But somebody has to stop it.

HARRY: Right. Well...I'll pray in the bedroom.

He hesitates, then moves into another room. Peter moves to the window and looks out at the night sky, the skyline. The terror that lurks.

THE DAILY BUGLE
has a front page picture of Spider-Man and the Green Goblin, doing battle atop the Goblin Glider, next to the headline:

TIMES SCARE!
Spider-Man, Green Goblin Terrorize City!

We tilt up from the paper to see—

INT. OSBORN'S APARTMENT—ENTRY HALL—DAY

—Norman Osborn, who's been staring at the front page, standing in the still-open doorway of his apartment. He's dressed in rumpled clothes from last night; he must have slept in them. He's disheveled, bags under his eyes, looks like hell.

And there's this headline. He looks back down at it, uncomprehending, searching for meaning.

ON THE FRONT PAGE,
we zip down to a box at the bottom of the page, where there's another, less prominent headline:

OsCorp Board Members Killed

IN THE APARTMENT,

Osborn rubs his head, trying to make sense of it. He's starting to sweat. He SLAMS the door—

INT. ENTRY HALL—DAY

—and staggers away, across the entry hall. Somewhere, far in the distance, he hears a faint CACKLE.

He stops, looks around. Where the hell did that come from? Frightened now, he lurches across the foyer and up the stairs.

INT. NORMAN'S STUDY (MASK ROOM)—DAY

Osborn enters his study, paper in hand.

OSBORN: Somebody there? *(looks around room, to balcony, silence)* Of course not.

He moves to a small table, whisky decanters. Hands shaking, pours a shot, raises it to his mouth.

GREEN GOBLIN: *(o.s.)* Stop pretending, Norman...

He turns around, looks up sharply, the wobbling glass still in his hand, his face dripping, terrified. The VOICE—mirthful, other-worldly. We've heard before, it's The Goblin. Osborn stumbles to the middle of the room.

OSBORN: Who said that?

GREEN GOBLIN: *(o.s.) (his demonic monotone)* Don't play the innocent with me. You've known all along.

OSBORN: Who are you?

GREEN GOBLIN: Follow the cold shiver that's running down your spine. Look, I'm right here.

Norman turns to the mirror.

OSBORN: I don't understand.

GREEN GOBLIN: Did you think it was coincidence? So many good things...all happening for you...all for you, Norman.

OSBORN: What do you want?!

GREEN GOBLIN: *(o.s.)* To say what you won't...to do what you can't—*(shows Osborn paper in mirror)*—to remove those in your way.

OSBORN: *(holds paper, studies it)* The board members! YOU killed them?!

GREEN GOBLIN: *(o.s.)* WE killed them...

OSBORN: Oh, God! My God!

GREEN GOBLIN: *(o.s.)* Stop mewling...You sicken me...you ooze weakness...

OSBORN: I'm not a murderer, I'm a scientist, a respectable businessman. The police.

Norman scurries over to the phone, reaches for it—

—but The Goblin beats him to it.

GREEN GOBLIN: *(o.s.) (shrieking)* HYPOCRITE! LIAR!

The Goblin rears back, heaves the phone toward the balcony. Norman watches it fly through the air, sees The Goblin, now standing on the balcony, duck as it zips past his head. The Goblin stands there, looking down on Osborn.

GREEN GOBLIN: *(cont'd)* Now shut up and listen! Try to understand the beauty of all this. YOU are now in full control of OsCorp Industries. Your greatest wish, granted by me. Say thank you.

Osborn thinks, takes everything in.

OSBORN: Hmmm. And then what?

GREEN GOBLIN: *(o.s.)* We'll eliminate your rivals. OsCorp will become the most powerful military supplier in history. You'll have limitless wealth. Presidents and Kings will court your favor. So don't be shy. Take what you've always wanted. Power. The weak will serve you. The world will be yours and mine. Yes. You and I, we can have a hell of a time.

Osborn lurches to his chair.

OSBORN: I suppose the damage has been done, right?

GREEN GOBLIN: Yeah.

OSBORN: Can we do it alone?

GREEN GOBLIN: *(o.s.)* There's only one who could stop us.

OSBORN: *(a better thought)* Or...be our greatest ally.

GREEN GOBLIN: Exactly! We need to have a little chat with you know who.

OSBORN: But how do we find him?

With that he snatches up the Bugle *from the table top, looks at the front page picture of Spider-Man and the Goblin.*

INT. JAMESON'S OFFICE—LATE DAY

JAMESON: *(finishing the sentence)* "The Green Goblin."

Jonah Jameson is in his office, chewing a cigar and admiring the front page of his newspaper. Peter Parker stands opposite. (On the wall behind Jameson is a framed photograph of a handsome astronaut.)

JAMESON: *(cont'd)* You like that? Made it up myself. Ever since Spider-Man, they all gotta have a name. HOFFMAN! Call the patent office and copyright the name Green Goblin! I want a quarter every time somebody says it!

PETER: Spider-Man wasn't terrorizing the city, he was trying to save it! It's slander!

JAMESON: I resent that! Slander is spoken! In print it's libel.

He tosses his cigar over his shoulder, out the window behind him.

PETER: You don't trust anybody, that's your problem, Mr. Jameson.

Peter walks out of his office. Jameson yells after him.

JAMESON: I trust my barber! What are you, his lawyer? Let him sue me and get rich like a normal person! That's what makes this country—

His cigar flies back through the window and lands on his desk. Jameson looks at it, puzzled, turns around—

—and THE GREEN GOBLIN SMASHES through the window frame. He grabs Jameson by the throat with one hand and scoops him up off his feet, his glider hovering over the floor of the office.

INT. NEWSPAPER OFFICE OUTSIDE JAMESON'S OFFICE—LATE DAY

Peter's eyes pop wide as he looks into Jameson's office. Secretaries, reporters and other Bugle *employees scurry about to escape the mayhem. Peter quickly ducks into the hallway.*

INT. JAMESON'S OFFICE—LATE DAY

The Goblin's grip remains firm on Jameson's throat.

GREEN GOBLIN: Who's the photographer who takes the pictures of Spider-Man?! I need to talk to him about his favorite subject. Where is he?
JAMESON: He's a free-lancer, I don't know who he is! His stuff comes in the mail.
GREEN GOBLIN: You're lying.
JAMESON: *(choking)* I swear!
GREEN GOBLIN: This is your last chance!
JAMESON: Please...air...stop...
SPIDER-MAN: *(o.s.)* Hey.

The Goblin whirls. Spider-Man hangs upside-down in the window.

SPIDER-MAN: *(cont'd)* I wear the tights in this town.
GREEN GOBLIN: Speak of the devil.

He lets go of Jameson, who drops to the floor in a heap, gasping for air.

JAMESON: I knew it! You and Spider-Man are in this together! I knew that creep was—

THWIP! A bunch of webbing SPLATS across Jameson's mouth, shutting him up.

SPIDER-MAN: Hey kiddo, let mom and dad talk for a minute, will you?

The Goblin points his glove at Spider-Man and sprays gas directly from it, into Spidey's face. Everything goes black.

EXT. DAILY BUGLE—LATE DAY

Spider-Man, unconscious, tumbles from what used to be Jameson's window and plummets toward the ground below.

Right before he meets his demise, The Green Goblin swoops in, catches Spider-Man and zooms away.

EXT. MIDTOWN ROOFTOP—NIGHT

Spider-Man is regaining consciousness on the roof of a tall building in midtown. The Goblin Glider nearby, the Goblin standing next to it in the shadows. Spidey tries to move.

GREEN GOBLIN: Relax.

Spider-Man struggles, drags himself to a sitting position, against an abutment. Feels like he weighs a thousand pounds.

GREEN GOBLIN: *(cont'd)* My hallucigen gas slowed your central nervous system to a crawl, just for a few minutes. Long enough for us to have a talk. Don't worry, I didn't remove your mask. I'll respect your privacy, for the moment anyway. Because I respect you.
SPIDER-MAN: *(fighting to be alert)* Who are you?
GREEN GOBLIN: A kindred spirit. A fellow traveler...You've changed and now you want someone to tell you what to do, who to be. And there's no one who could possibly understand...*(leans in)*...except me.

Spider-Man looks down, at his hand. He can raise a few fingers, but they're trembling.

GREEN GOBLIN: *(cont'd)* They call us freaks. But we're not less than human, we are more than human.
SPIDER-MAN: I'm not like you. You're a murderer.
GREEN GOBLIN: Well...to each his own. I chose my path. You chose the way of the hero. And they found you amusing for a while...the people of this city. But the one thing they love more than a hero is to see the hero fail, fall, die trying. The truth is people don't like heroes. Who wants an example you can never live up to? Take my word for

it...in spite of all you've done for them, eventually they will hate you. Read the headlines.

In spite of himself, Spider-Man is listening.

GREEN GOBLIN: *(cont'd)* We are who we choose to be, but a day will come when you must ask yourself, did I choose wisely—why am I risking my life for ungrateful fools?
SPIDER-MAN: Because it's right.

The Goblin circles Spider-Man.

GREEN GOBLIN: Right? Wrong? Capital R, capital W? You're young, aren't you? You believe in truth, beauty, professional athletes as role models. Well, here's the real truth. There are fourteen million people in this city, and those teeming masses exist for the sole purpose of lifting a few exceptional people onto their shoulders. You, me, we are exceptional. I had problems, but I used my God given powers and poof, those problems vanished.

Spider-Man stares. He's thinking...

GREEN GOBLIN: *(cont'd)* Imagine what we could accomplish together. What we could create. *(loving this)* OR...we could destroy, cause the deaths of countless innocents in selfish battle, again and again. And again, until we both are dead.

He summons his glider. Hops aboard. Looks at Spider-Man.

GREEN GOBLIN: *(cont'd)* Think about it, hero.

He cackles and shoots off into the night.

EXT. MANHATTAN—DAY

The sun rises over the Manhattan skyline.

EXT. STREET CORNER—DAY

A Daily Bugle truck motors up to a newspaper stand. A bundled stack of papers tumbles to a stop at the feet of the newsstand proprietor. Citizens gather around, fish out their money. The proprietor bends down, cuts the twine bundling the papers revealing the headline—

Spider-Man, Green Goblin Terrorize City!

EXT. MIDTOWN BUILDING—NIGHT

Peter leans against the wall of a midtown television studio. He's glum. He's staring at a line of newspaper vending machines across the sidewalk. Each displays the headline: "Spider-Man, Time for a Bug-Free City!"

Mary Jane Watson comes out the side door of a television stu-

dio. As it SLAMS behind her, a little too hard, she turns and looks at it, notices the sign that says "ARTISTS ONLY." She laughs bitterly to herself, starts walking away. Peter's been waiting.

PETER: Hey!
MJ: *(turns)* Hey.
PETER: How was the audition?
MJ: How'd you know?!
PETER: The hotline. Your mom told my aunt who told me. We have no secrets from each other.
MJ: So you just came by?
PETER: I was in the neighborhood. I needed to see a friendly face. Took two buses and a cab to get in the neighborhood, but...
MJ: They told me I need acting lessons. A soap opera told me I need acting lessons.

A light rain starts to fall.

PETER: I'll buy you a cheeseburger. Sky's the limit, up to seven dollars and eighty-four cents.

She laughs. She smiles. But:

MJ: I'd like a cheeseburger, but I'm going to dinner with Harry. Come with us.
PETER: No thanks. *(a beat)* So how's it going? I mean, with you and, never mind, none of my business.
MJ: It's not? Why so interested?
PETER: I'm not, am I interested?
MJ: You're not?
PETER: Well...why would I be?
MJ: I don't know. Why would you be?
PETER: Y'know...just...I don't know.

She smiles.

MJ: Sorry you won't come with us.

It's raining harder.

MJ: *(cont'd)* Gotta run. *(runs)*

Disappointed yet again, confused. Did she want him to confess his love?

But he's suddenly jostled by FOUR PUNKS, walking past him from behind, bumping into him.

PETER: 'Scuse me.

They ignore him, keep walking in MJ's direction. Peter turns, walks away. Then turns back, furrows his brow.

EXT. DARK STREET—NIGHT

From high above, we see MJ turn a corner onto a dark street. The Four Punks catch up, surround her. They stop to admire her, heckle her, she says something to them...Now they're pissed. And Punk #1 goes for her purse.

DOWN ON THE STREET,

MJ's no pushover, she's mixing it up with them. She shin-kicks Punk #1, elbow-jabs Punk #2, punches Punk #3 and maces Punk #4 with the canister that dangles from her keychain.

MJ: What are you guys, from out of town or something?

Now they're really pissed. And bigger. And there's four of them. MJ is shoved into a wall, and Punk #1 SNICKS open a knife. It looks bleak.

Suddenly, THWIP-WRAP! all four Punks are slammed together as if lassoed, and they go flying up, out of frame.

MJ stands, slack-jawed, staring in wonder at something we can't see. Then, suddenly, she leaps out of the way as—

—Punk #1 comes flying back and SMASHES through a window next to where she was standing. Punk #2 SMACKS up against a brick wall, Punk #3 flies through another window and Punk #4 goes barreling into a trash can. They lie about on the ground, either unconscious or with the good sense to fake it.

MJ walks forward, staggers, and as we come around behind her, we see what she sees.

Spider-Man stands in the shadows, breathing hard after his exertions. She looks at him, can't make him out in the inky darkness. But we get closer to him—and he's not wearing his mask! Didn't have time to put it on.

Peter fumbles for it, pulls it from his waistband. But hesitates, knowing she can't see him fully.

PETER: You have a knack for getting in trouble.
MJ: You have a knack for saving my ass. I think I have a superhero stalker.

She walks closer. He retreats, further into the shadows, still no mask.

PETER: I was in the neighborhood.

She stops, squints at him. She's heard that before, and recently. Does she suspect?

MJ: You are amazing...

She's almost to him now—so Peter pulls the mask on.

SPIDER-MAN: Some people don't think so.

MJ: But you are.
SPIDER-MAN: Thank you.

He leaps up, onto the wall above her, clinging there upside-down. She steps up underneath him. He's right at lip height.

MJ: Do I get to say thank you this time?

She puts her hands on his mask...and starts to lift it. Spider-Man is paralyzed, can't stop her.

SPIDER-MAN: Wait...

But she doesn't lift it all the way up. Just so his mouth is exposed. And she kisses him. That is, she kisses him, rain streaming down both their faces and over their parted lips. She pulls back. Touches his lips with her fingertips.

MJ: That's so you'll remember where your mouth is..

She replaces the mask, tenderly. Spider-Man hesitates, then scampers up the wall and out of sight. She watches him go, eyes shining.

MJ: *(cont'd)* Yowza.

EXT. CITY SCAPE—DAY

"YOWZA" is HEARD again. But it's being DISTORTED into the SOUNDS of the sirens of fire trucks and police cars and ambulances.

EXT. CITY—DAY

Spider-Man swings through a city corridor.

SPIDER-MAN: Help is on the way! Yowza! Yowza!

CAMERA COUNTERS Spider-Man as he swings past lens and he heads towards a burning apartment house surrounded by fire trucks, police cars, ambulances. A crowd is there, including some people who have been rescued.

EXT. APARTMENT BUILDING—DAY

FEATURE a MOTHER, her two young sons holding on to her skirt, as she, against her will, is being forced out of the building by two FIREMEN. She fights to get back in:

MOTHER: Let me go, my baby's in there, somebody save my baby, let me go!
FIREMAN: It's too late, lady, the roof's ready to collapse.

The woman continues to struggle and scream.

ANOTHER FIREMAN reacts to something above.

FIREMAN #2: Hey! Up there! Look! It's him!

Above the crowd we SEE Spider-Man swinging his way to the burning building. He disappears inside. We BOOM DOWN to—

FIREMAN: What's he doing?

FIREMAN #2: He's crazy, he hasn't a chance.

MOTHER: Save my baby, please, please!

They wait. The building continues to burn. There is a loud CREAKING noise as the roof starts to collapse.

MOTHER: *(cont'd)* NOOOOOOOOO!!!!!

THROUGH A SMOKY, FIRE-ENCASED WINDOW, Spider-Man swings out, cradling a web-encased parcel. Behind him, a tremendous fireball. He descends towards CAMERA.

VOICES: He's alive! He's got the kid! I don't believe it!

The crowd applauds. Spider-Man drops into view, landing at the feet of the mother and her two boys. He still holds the parcel.

SPIDER-MAN: *(extends baby)* Here's your baby.

MOTHER: *(takes it)* Oh, God Bless you, Spider-Man. Bless you, bless you.

SPIDER-MAN: *(to the boys)* You children be good. Stop playing with matches. Don't start something you can't put out.

COP: *(O.S.)* Don't let him get away!

A COP bursts through the crowd, draws his gun, levels it on Spider-Man.

COP: *(cont'd)* Hold it right there. You're wanted in connection—

OLD WOMAN: *(O.S.)* Hellllpppp!! Helllppppp!!

Behind the COP, a YOUNG MAN raises a finger toward the building.

YOUNG MAN: Look! There's somebody else!

The crowd turns, sees an OLD WOMAN barely visible through a window dancing with fire.

The COP looks at Spider-Man, Spider-Man to the COP.

COP: I'll be here when you get back.

The COP lowers his revolver. Spider-Man leaps away.

INT. NEARBY SMOKY ROOM—DAY

Spider-Man flips through a window, lands, scans the smoky room, fire leaping about. He sees what appears to be an OLD

WOMAN, draped in a shawl, huddled in the corner.

SPIDER-MAN: Everything's going to be okay ma'am.

OLD WOMAN: *(V.O.)* Oh. Thank you sonny. You're my hero.

SUDDENLY WE HEAR:

The CACKLE!

GREEN GOBLIN: *(O.S.)* What's wrong with lighting up now and then? *(another CACKLE)*

The "OLD WOMAN" lets the shawl fall to the ground, turns.

SPIDER-MAN: *(sees Goblin through licking flame)* Goblin! YOU? You started this fire?

GREEN GOBLIN: *(moving closer)* You're pathetically predictable. Like a moth to a flame. *(then super serious)* What about my generous proposal? Are you in, or are you out?

SPIDER-MAN: It's you who's out, Gobby. *(preparing to attack)* Out for good!!

The Goblin reaches to his belt, hurls a razor bat at Spider-Man, who deflects it with his left arm. SNICK!

SPIDER-MAN: *(cont'd)* *(pain)* AHHH!

Spider-Man looks down at his arm. A deep gash oozes blood. He raises his arms, shoots a web to a burning beam above Goblin's head. Spider-Man tugs on the webs, sending the beam and debris raining down on The Goblin, obstructing his view.

The Goblin throws the beams and debris aside, looks around. Spider-Man is gone. A trail of blood leads out the window. The Goblin's body tenses, he howls with anger.

GREEN GOBLIN: I don't forgive and I don't forget. It breaks my heart. We could have been so good together. (ALT.) I don't forgive and I don't forget. You can consider my offer withdrawn.

INT. HARRY'S APARTMENT—DAY

A browning turkey is pulled out of the oven by a pot-holder.

Aunt May forks the turkey to test it. MJ, in her black dress and apron, helps. The signs of a full Thanksgiving meal are on the counter all around them, and the dining room table in Harry's apartment is set for five.

Harry is fastidiously checking the table, plumping pillows, straightening chairs. The doorbell RINGS.

HARRY: Okay... he's here.

Mary Jane comes out of the kitchen, takes off apron.

HARRY: *(cont'd)* You look great.

Harry opens the door. Norman Osborn stands in the hallway in a very nice suit, dabbing sweat off his forehead with a handkerchief. He carries a small, ribboned pastry box. Mary Jane comes out of the kitchen.

OSBORN: Sorry I'm late. Work was murder. Here's a fruitcake. Who's this young lady?
HARRY: MJ, I'd like you to meet my father, Norman Osborn. Dad, I'd like you to meet Mary Jane Watson. MJ

She flashes a radiant smile. Osborn steps closer, holding out a hand but also, unmistakably, narrowing his eyes. Studying her.

OSBORN: How do you do? I've been looking forward to meeting you.
MJ: *(senses badness)* Happy Thanksgiving, sir.
AUNT MAY: *(moves in)* Hello, Norman. We're so pleased you're here. Where's Peter? He better have remembered the cranberry sauce.

Behind them, a red and blue costumed figure WHOOSHES past the living room window, unnoticed, and lands—

EXT. APARTMENT BUILDING—DAY

—on the side of the apartment building. Spider-Man pivots and crawls down a few floors, to his window, opens it.

IN THE LIVING ROOM,
they hear the SMALL THUD, and all turn toward his room.

HARRY: That's weird, I didn't know he was here.
AUNT MAY: Peter?

INT. PETER'S BEDROOM—DAY

Peter crawls across the ceiling and drops onto the floor in his bedroom.

IN THE LIVING ROOM,
They hear a BIG THUD.

AUNT MAY: My goodness.

IN PETER'S BEDROOM,
He pulls off his mask and immediately tends to his injured, bleeding arm. He whips around and looks at the door, wild-eyed. He sees shapes moving through the frosted glass of his bedroom door, hears Aunt May's voice calling to him.

He still has his mask off, holding a bundle of street clothes.

IN THE LIVING ROOM,
Aunt May is nearly to the door, Norman, Harry, and MJ just behind her. She turns the handle, opens it, and they see—

IN PETER'S BEDROOM,
—nothing. The room is empty.

HARRY: Pete?
AUNT MAY: But there's nobody here...

Osborn comes in and glances around the room. Kind of a mess, clothes and books and science equipment scattered everywhere. But no Peter.

We look up. Peter, maskless, clings to the ceiling not three feet over their heads. A big, fat drop of blood is oozing from the cuts on his arm, right over Osborn's head.

OSBORN: Bit of a slob, isn't he?
AUNT MAY: All brilliant men are.

Osborn smiles, loves that Aunt May. They turn to walk out—and the drop of blood falls. It hits the light-colored carpet, right where he was standing. Osborn, the last in the doorway, freezes, tilts his head at the sound. Good hearing, man. Human Performance Enhancers will do that for you.

The others leave, but Osborn turns and walks back to where he was standing.

On the ceiling, Spidey's eyes widen—oh no. Osborn is directly below him.

Osborn bends down, studies the carpet. He sees the drop of blood. Quickly, he looks up at the ceiling above him.

There's nobody there.

He turns, looks at the open window. He walks to it.

FROM OUTSIDE THE WINDOW,
Osborn leans outside and looks in both directions. Camera pulls back to reveal Spider-Man clinging to the underside of the ledge.

Apparently satisfied, Osborn turns and goes back inside.

INT. HARRY'S APARTMENT—DAY
The front door to Harry's apartment opens again. Peter attempts a casual entrance, now dressed in street clothes and carrying a brown paper bag.

PETER: Hey everyone. *(kisses Aunt May)* Sorry I took so long, it's a jungle out there. I had to hit an old lady with a stick to get these cranberries.
AUNT MAY: Oh, Peter. Come on everyone, let's sit down and say a prayer.

They all move for the table. Norman reaches for the jellied cranberry log. Aunt May slaps his hand.

AUNT MAY: *(cont'd)*...and Norman...*(indicates turkey and carving knife)*...will you do the honors?

Norman picks up the knife. Aunt May reacts to blood on Peter's arm.

AUNT MAY: *(cont'd)* Peter, you're bleeding!

PETER: Yeah, I stepped off a curb and got clipped by one of those bike messengers.

AUNT MAY: Let me see.

She pushes his sleeves up, exposing the X-shaped slashes in his forearm.

AUNT MAY: *(cont'd)* What in the name of heavenly glory?!

Norman Osborn's eyes widen. He recognizes those slashes!

AUNT MAY: *(cont'd)* You've got to be more careful out there! This city has a lunatic on every corner.

We move in on Norman, holding the carving knife, his eyes focusing in like laser beams, staring at the distinctive cuts on Peter's arms.

AUNT MAY: *(cont'd)* Everyone sit down, I'll go and get the First Aid kit. And then we'll say grace. This is the boys' first Thanksgiving in this apartment and we're going to do things properly.

OSBORN: *(to Peter)* How did you say that happened?

PETER: ...Bike messenger.

As Peter turns to Norman, his breathing sharpens, his eyes widen and fill with fear, suddenly and inexplicably

HIS SPIDER-SENSE

kicks in like crazy. Everybody around him slows to a crawl, and his P.O.V. pivots around the room, rapidly scanning every nook and cranny for the source of the danger that must surely be nearby. He flips from frozen face to frozen face—Aunt May, MJ, Norman, Harry—all friends, right?

BACK IN THE APARTMENT,

Peter pops out of his Spider-Sense, confused, drops of sweat on his forehead, to find Osborn still staring at him.

PETER *(cont'd)* *(finishing)*...knocked me down.

OSBORN: You'll have to excuse me, I'm afraid I've got to go.

HARRY: What? Why?

OSBORN: Something...has come to my attention.

HARRY: Are you all right?

OSBORN: Fine, I'm fine. Thank you. Mrs. Parker. Everyone.

AUNT MAY: What happened?

He strides out of the apartment, throwing one last look back at Peter Parker.

HARRY: Dad!

IN THE HALLWAY,

Osborn leans against the wall in the hallway, eyes darting, thinking a mile a minute. Harry comes out behind him, leaving the door ajar.

HARRY: What are you doing? I planned this whole thing so you could meet MJ, and you barely even looked at her!

OSBORN: I've got to go.

He turns, starts down the hall. Harry grabs him by the arm, turns him around.

HARRY: Hey, I like this girl, this is important to me!

OSBORN: Harry, please. Look at her. You think a woman like that's sniffing around because she likes your personality?

HARRY: What are you saying, Dad?

OSBORN: Your mother was beautiful, too. They're all beautiful, till they're snarling after your trust fund like ravening wolves.

HARRY: Dad...This girl's not...

OSBORN: *(interrupts him)* A word to the not-so-wise about your little girlfriend. Do what you need to with her and broom her fast.

Osborn leaves.

HARRY: What?

IN THE APARTMENT,

MJ stands on this side of the door. Listening. Everyone else is in the living room or kitchen. They can all hear.

MJ turns away and grabs her coat. Harry comes back in. MJ storms past him.

HARRY: Where are you going?

MJ: Thanks for sticking up for me, Harry.

HARRY: You heard?

MJ: Everyone could hear that creep.

HARRY: *(suddenly angry)* That "creep" is my father! All right?! If I'm lucky, I've got the brains and the guts to become half of what he is, so you keep your goddamn mouth shut about things you don't understand.

AUNT MAY: Harry Osborn!

MJ: You're acting like somebody's father—mine! *(as she goes)* I'm sorry, Aunt May.

She storms out of the apartment, SLAMMING the door behind her.

PETER: Harry, go after her!
HARRY: I don't think so.
PETER: Harry, come on!
HARRY: No. I can't. *(to Aunt May)* Welcome to an Osborn Thanksgiving.

He storms into his bedroom and SLAMS the door.

PETER: Sorry, Aunt May. It looked great.

He jumps up, gives her a kiss, and hurries out of the apartment. Aunt May, shocked at all the discord, sits at the table alone.

AUNT MAY: We didn't even get to say grace.

EXT. STREET—DAY

Peter hurries out of the building. Looks for MJ, sees her sitting on a nearby step. She's crying. The chauffeur-driven Bentley drives past. MJ gives it the finger.

Peter stands by her. She looks up at him, mascara dripping. She needs a hanky. He has one. Holds it out to her.

PETER: Take it.

She hesitates, takes it.

PETER: *(cont'd)* Keep it, it's yours. Got a million of 'em. Aunt May, a dozen every Christmas.

She laughs through her tears. She blows her nose. "Honnnk." She laughs harder. Then starts to cry harder. He sits next to her.

PETER: *(cont'd)* That's okay. Good cry.
MJ: I'm sorry I acted like that, but I couldn't stay there. Being treated that way brings back bad stuff. I hate being thought of as if I'm not worth anything.
PETER: I understand.
MJ: I know you do. Your poor Aunt May. But I can't go back in there.
PETER: She'll be okay. She's tough. I've never seen Mr. Osborn act like that. I've never seen either of them act like that. *(a beat)* But I know Harry really loves you.
MJ: Sometimes I wonder why I ever went out with him in the first place. I guess because he asked me. Dumb, black dress.
PETER: However, you do look extremely beautiful in it.

She looks at him, smiles at him.

MJ: Thank you. You look very handsome yourself tonight.

An opportunity. He could kiss her now, but he doesn't make a move. He's more in love than ever. She puts her arm around his shoulder. Looks off. No move.

CAMERA angles up to SEE HARRY at the window looking down.

EXT. OSBORN'S APARTMENT—NIGHT

Norman Osborn's apartment building. Nighttime, drifting toward it. We hear a VOICE from inside. The Goblin.

GREEN GOBLIN: *(o.s.)* This changes everything...

INT. OSBORN STUDY—NIGHT

We see Osborn, huddled on the floor, cowering in a pool of light at the end of the hall. He's got something in his hand.

GREEN GOBLIN: *(o.s.)* Spider-Man is all but invincible...but Parker...Parker is flesh and blood...We can destroy him...
OSBORN: I can't! I've been like a father to that boy. He's the good son.
GREEN GOBLIN: *(o.s.)* Which is exactly what he wanted! He came to you, the greedy, open-mouthed, scheming little orphan...
OSBORN: He did...
GREEN GOBLIN: Plucked your heartstrings like a master... Connived his way into your heart, leaving no room for Harry, your TRUE son and heir...

Closer to him now, we see what he's got in his hand. It's the mask he has worn as the Green Goblin. He's clutching it in two hands, talking to it.

OSBORN: It's true...oh God...
GREEN GOBLIN: *(o.s.)* And now, after everything you've done for Peter Parker, after everything you've taught him, THIS is how he repays you?!
OSBORN: What have I done to Harry? What have I done to my own son?
GREEN GOBLIN: *(o.s.)* Betrayal must not be countenanced.... Parker must be...educated.
OSBORN: What do I do?
GREEN GOBLIN: *(o.s.)* Instruct him in the matters of loss and pain...Make him suffer, make him wish he were dead...
OSBORN: Yes!
GREEN GOBLIN: *(o.s.)* And then grant his wish.

OSBORN: But how?

GREEN GOBLIN: *(o.s.)* The cunning warrior attacks neither body nor mind...

We drift down, to the mask, which doesn't speak, of course. That's all in Norman's head. But we continue to hear his thoughts as we drift into its ghastly yellow eyes—

OSBORN: TELL ME HOW!

GREEN GOBLIN: *(o.s.)* The heart, Osborn...first we attack his heart.

—and the screen turns yellow.

EXT. PARKER HOUSE—NIGHT

The Parker house sits silent.

INT. AUNT MAY'S BEDROOM—NIGHT

Aunt May is getting ready for bed dressed in flannel pajamas. She moves to a photograph of Uncle Ben on the bedside table, touches it affectionately. Aunt May kneels by the bed. Her knees CREAK, it's painful for her. She rests her elbows on her bed, which is turned down for the night, folds her hands, and closes her eyes in prayer.

AUNT MAY: Our Father, who art in heaven, hallowed be thy name. Thy kingdom come, thy will be done, on earth as it is in heaven. Give us this day our daily bread, and forgive us our trespasses as we forgive those who trespass against us. Lead us not into temptation, but...

Suddenly the wall behind her EXPLODES, SHATTERED glass flying in all directions.

Aunt May spins around, horrified, and falls to the floor. The Goblin hovers over her and the room slowly fills with green vapor and the horrible BUZZ of the Glider's turbine engine.

AUNT MAY: *(cont'd)*...but...but...but...

Aunt May pales as she stares into the Goblin's inhuman eyes.

GREEN GOBLIN: FINISH IT! FINISH IT!

Her hands clutch her chest, she GASPS:

AUNT MAY: ...DELIVER US FROM EVIL!!

Her body arches, tenses, then goes limp. Her eyes close.

GREEN GOBLIN: AMEN, SISTER!

EXT. PARKER HOUSE—NIGHT

From across the street, the Green Goblin's horrible CACKLE fills the neighborhood night.

INT. HOSPITAL CORRIDOR—NIGHT

Peter races down a hospital corridor, frantic. He reaches the last room on the right, ducks inside, and sees—

INT. HOSPITAL ROOM—NIGHT

—Aunt May, in a hospital bed, hooked up to a variety of urgently BEEPING machines. DOCTORS and NURSES swarm around her, treating her. Peter rushes forward, to her bedside.

PETER: Aunt May!

She looks up at him, still conscious, but barely so.

PETER: *(cont'd)* What happened?! Is she going to be okay?!

NURSE: Sir, please! Let the doctors work!

The nurse leads Peter to the door. The doors start to close when Peter hears—

AUNT MAY: Those eyes...those horrible yellow eyes!

A Doctor hurriedly puts an oxygen mask over Aunt May's face. The door shuts in Peter's face.

INT. HOSPITAL CORRIDOR—NIGHT

Peter's own eyes widen as he realizes who she means.

PETER: The Goblin. He knows...oh God, he knows who I am...

INT. HOSPITAL ROOM—NIGHT

The middle of the night. Peter sits a lonely vigil in Aunt May's hospital room. He's brought a picture for her bedside, a framed shot of May, Ben, and himself.

He looks at the picture, at Uncle Ben. Gone. Back at Aunt May. Nearly killed, because of me. He leans down, kisses her forehead as he blinks back tears.

PETER: I'm sorry.

INT. HOSPITAL HALLWAY—DAY

MJ carries a bouquet of flowers, checks room numbers as she passes. She comes across Aunt May's room, peeks in.

Peter sits in a chair next to Aunt May's bed, his head in his hands. Open text books and fast food sacks lie scattered about. Aunt May is asleep. If it wasn't for the surroundings and the circumstances, it would be a beautiful sight.

MJ takes this in, moved.

INT. HOSPITAL ROOM—DAY

FAVOR PETER. There's a soft TAPPING from the door behind him. He turns. It's MJ He lights up.

MJ: Can I come in?

Peter nods. MJ looks at Aunt May. She comes to Peter, still holding the flowers, puts her arms around his neck, gives him a hug. He closes his eyes, almost can't bear it.

MJ: *(cont'd) (with arms around him)* I'm so sorry. I just heard about it.

She turns to the bed, moves closer to Aunt May. She lays the flowers on the bedside table, gently touches Aunt May's forehead.

MJ: *(cont'd)* Will she be okay?
PETER: We think so. She finally woke up this morning. For a while. Thanks for coming.
MJ: Who would do this to your Aunt May? Why would anyone want to hurt her?

Peter doesn't answer.

MJ: *(cont'd)* I'm sorry, Peter, I know you've asked yourself these questions.
PETER: It's okay, how about you? Are you all right about the other night?
MJ: I'm sorry about that. Makes things worse for everybody.
PETER: You were fine. Have you talked to Harry?
MJ: He called me. I haven't called him back.

She turns away from Peter, looks at sleeping Aunt May. She takes the time to tuck in her bed sheet.

MJ: *(cont'd) (without facing Peter)* The fact is, I'm in love with somebody else.
PETER: You are?
MJ: At least I think I am. *(turns to Peter)* This isn't the time to talk about this.
PETER: No, go on. Would I know his name? This guy.
MJ: You'll think I'm a stupid little girl with a crush.
PETER: Trust me.
MJ: I'm like head over heals, it's whacked...
PETER: Who is he?
MJ: It's funny. He saved my life twice, and I've never seen his face.
PETER: *(pleased)* Oh. Him.
MJ: You're laughing at me.
PETER: No, I understand. He is extremely cool.
MJ: But do you think it's true, the terrible things they say about him?

PETER: No way. That isn't Spider-Man, not a chance in the world. I know him a little bit. I'm sort of his unofficial photographer.
MJ: How do you always manage to find him?
PETER: Wrong place, right time, I guess.
MJ: You ever talk to him?
PETER: Sometimes.
MJ: Does he ever talk about me?
PETER: Uh...yeah...once. Once he asked what I thought of you.
MJ: What did you say?
PETER: *(searching for the words)* I said...I said, Spider-Man, I said the great thing about MJ is when...when you look in her eyes and she's looking back in yours and smiling, well, everything feels...not quite normal because you feel...stronger. And weaker at the same time and you feel excited and at the same time terrified. The truth is, Spidey—I call him Spidey sometimes—the truth is you don't know what you feel, except you know the kind of man you want to be and what it is, is, it's as if when you're with her, it's as if you've reached...the unreachable...and you weren't ready for it.

And he looks up, because these inner thoughts were said out loud, and MJ is staring at him, tears welling in her eyes.

MJ: You said that?
PETER: Uh...umm...ssssomething like that.

Aunt May opens her eyes...looks at them, unbeknownst to them.

Peter is embarrassed, he's said too much. To his surprise, MJ reaches out and takes his hand. Which, of course, is exactly when—

—Harry Osborn comes in the door, carrying a bouquet of flowers. His eyes go immediately to MJ and Peter, standing so close, holding hands, looking at each other in That Way.

HARRY: Hello.

And they confirm it all by hastily withdrawing their hands. Harry's face hardens.

EXT. OSBORN'S BUILDING—NIGHT

That night. We drift toward the rooftop colonnades of Norman Osborn's spooky apartment building.

INT. FIRST FLOOR—NIGHT

Harry comes in the front door.

HARRY: Dad?

No answer. But light spills from the staircase that leads up.

INT. UPSTAIRS HALL—NIGHT

Harry stands at the bottom of the stairs, he can faintly hear voices, ANGRY MURMURING. But he can't make out the words.

HARRY: Dad? Is that you?

The voices abruptly stop. A moment later, his father appears at the top of the stairs. They talk, from this great distance. Osborn is just a dark shadow.

OSBORN: What is it?
HARRY: You were right about MJ You were right about everything. She's in love with Peter.
OSBORN: *(pause)* Parker?

Osborn begins to move down the stairs toward Harry.

HARRY: Yeah.
OSBORN: And...how does he feel about her?
HARRY: Are you kidding? He's loved her since the fourth grade. He just acts like he doesn't. But there's nobody Peter cares more about.

Osborn's eyes light up at this information.

OSBORN: I'm sorry...*(pause)* I haven't always been there for you, have I?
HARRY: Well...you're busy...you're an important man, I understand that.
OSBORN: It's no excuse. I'm proud of you. And I lost sight of that somewhere. But I'm going to make it up to you. I'm going to rectify certain...inequities.

He comes into the light, slips an arm around his son. Hugs him. It'd be nice, if it weren't so creepy.

OSBORN: *(cont'd)* I love you, son.

INT. HOSPITAL ROOM—NIGHT

Favor PETER, his eyes closed, homework on his lap. Then, as if from a horrible dream, he opens his eyes, startled, looks around, trying to come awake.

WIDER SHOT
Aunt May, in her bed, looking at him. (MJ's flowers, now in a vase on the bedside table.)

AUNT MAY: Peter. Pete?
PETER: *(suddenly aware, sees her)* Huh? *(he stands quickly, his homework falls to the floor)* You're awake. That's good. Good. You okay?
AUNT MAY: I'm okay, but I think you should go home and get some sleep. You look awful.
PETER: And you look beautiful. *(a beat)* I don't like to leave you.
AUNT MAY: I'm safe here.
PETER: I should have been there. Maybe I could've done something.
AUNT MAY: Done something?

She gives a light-hearted chuckle.

AUNT MAY: *(cont'd)* You do too much. College, a job, all this time with me—you're not Superman, you know. *(Peter can't help but find that funny)* A smile, finally. Haven't seen one of those on your face since Mary Jane was here.
PETER: Hey, you were supposed to be asleep. What did you hear?
AUNT MAY: *(an enigmatic smile)* You know, you were about six years old when MJ's family moved in next door. And when she got out of the car and you saw her for the first time, you grabbed me and said, "Aunt May, Aunt May! Is that an angel?"
PETER: Gee, Aunt May, did I say that?
AUNT MAY: You sure did, Peter.
PETER: Harry's in love with her. She's still his girl.
AUNT MAY: Isn't that up to her?
PETER: She doesn't really know me.
AUNT MAY: Because you won't let her. You're so mysterious all the time. Tell me, would it be so dangerous to let Mary Jane know how much you care? Everyone else knows.

Peter considers this for a beat, the full meaning coming to him. A concerned look spreads across his face.

PETER: I'll be right back.

Peter rises, races out of the room—

INT. HOSPITAL CORRIDOR—NIGHT

—and snatches up a pay phone in the corridor of the hospital. He puts a quarter in, dials, waits while it rings.

PETER: Come on, pick up.

MJ's answering machine picks up, her recorded voice:

MJ: *(o.s.)* Hi it's me, sing your song at the beep.
PETER: MJ, it's Peter, you there? Hello? All right, well, I'm calling to check up on you, so call me when you get in...Uh...don't go up any dark alleys.

There is a CLICK as the phone picks up at the other end.

PETER: *(cont'd)* Hello?

No answer. Then, a sound. No...a CACKLE.

Peter's face pales.

The CACKLE grows louder. Finally, the Goblin's VOICE:

GREEN GOBLIN: *(o.s.)* Can Spider-Man come out to play?
PETER: Where is she?

We move in on Peter's face as he hears the most terrifying words of his life.

GREEN GOBLIN: Be of love, a little more careful, Spider-Man.

EXT. DARK PLACE—NIGHT

MJ opens her eyes, regaining consciousness.

She pulls herself to her feet, disoriented, holding her head in pain. She takes a step backward but stops, suddenly, wind-milling her arms for balance. Looking down, she sees—

—the roadway of a bridge, hundreds of feet below her!

She GASPS, takes a step back, horrified as she figures out where she is. Camera leaps back to reveal that she stands—

—ATOP THE WESTERN TOWER OF THE QUEENSBORO BRIDGE!

EXT. NEARBY BUILDING—NIGHT

Spider-Man lands on the side of a building. He sees the Goblin Glider soaring past, toward the top of the west tower of the Queensboro Bridge, where MJ is still stranded.

EXT. QUEENSBORO BRIDGE—NIGHT

MJ hears a WHINING sound and turns, just in time to duck as The Goblin zooms overhead. She watches as he rockets toward the Roosevelt Island Tram Station.

INT. TRAM—NIGHT

A red tram with ten EIGHT-YEAR-OLDS wearing New York Giants paraphernalia watch in awe as The Goblin zips by. They rush to the windows, as do the THREE DADS who are chaperoning them, for a better view.

EXT. ROOSEVELT ISLAND TRAM STATION—NIGHT

The Goblin CACKLES with glee as he races toward the tram station. A rocket launcher emerges from the glider. WHOOSH! The rocket launches, headed toward the station.

The Goblin peels off just as the rocket barrels into the tram station, obliterating it in a massive ball of flame and smoke.

EXT. QUEENSBORO BRIDGE—NIGHT

MJ lit from the fireball, takes in the carnage.

EXT. NEARBY ROOFTOP—NIGHT

Spider-Man watches as flame and smoke bellow out of what remains of the tram station. He leaps off the building toward the bridge.

EXT. QUEENSBORO BRIDGE—NIGHT

MJ watches in horror as huge chunks of debris from the tram station rain down on the roadway below her.

EXT. QUEENSBORO BRIDGE ROADWAY—NIGHT

Cars come to a screeching halt, others crash into one another, as flaming chunks of the tram station plummet from the sky.

EXT. QUEENSBORO BRIDGE—NIGHT

Spider-Man zips toward the bridge, sliding across a web he has shot.

EXT. 2ND AVENUE TRAM STATION—NIGHT

From inside of what remains of the tram station, a cable SNAPS, WHIPS LIKE A SNAKE, rockets past camera.

INT. TRAM—NIGHT

The EIGHT-YEAR-OLDS and the THREE DADS, suspended several hundred feet above the river, watch as the snaking cable whips toward them. The tram suddenly drops.

EXT. TRAM—NIGHT

SCREAMS are heard as the tram plummets toward the water below.

The Goblin rockets into frame, grabs the dancing cable and zooms away, halting the trams' descent.

EXT. QUEENSBORO BRIDGE—NIGHT

Spider-Man drops onto the vertical high-tension wires that hold the bridge aloft, takes a giant leap and lands on the bridge.

GREEN GOBLIN: Spider-Man!

Spider-Man looks up, sees—

—The Goblin, standing at the edge of the bridge tower, clutching MJ in one hand, the cable holding aloft the tram full of kids in the other.

GREEN GOBLIN: *(cont'd)* This is why only fools are heroes!

Spider-Man freezes.

GREEN GOBLIN: *(cont'd)* Because you never know when some lunatic will come along with a sadistic choice...

He shoves MJ further out, so her toes are actually over the edge. She looks down, almost loses her balance. Cars race over the bridge platform, two hundred feet down.

GREEN GOBLIN: *(cont'd)* Let die the woman you love...

The Goblin loosens his grip on the cable, lets it slip through his hands causing the tram to drop, a sickening dip. The children SCREAM.

ATOP THE BRIDGE,
The Goblin watches with glee, tightens his grip on the cable.

GREEN GOBLIN: *(cont'd)* ...or suffer the little children.

Spider-Man watches as the tram sways horribly, sees the pleading faces of the Children and their Fathers as they POUND on the glass, begging for help.

He looks back up, sees MJ teetering over the edge, the Goblin's hand in her back.

GREEN GOBLIN: *(cont'd)* Make your choice, Spider-Man, and see how a hero is rewarded!

Spider-Man is momentarily paralyzed, torn in half.

The tram quivers.

MJ teeters.

GREEN GOBLIN: *(cont'd)* This is your doing! You caused this! This is the life you have chosen!

Spider-Man looks, left, right, left, right, agonizes over his choice.

GREEN GOBLIN: *(cont'd)* Choose!

The Green Goblin lets go of MJ and the cable at the same time, sending them to their deaths below.

Spider-Man watches as the tram falls before him, MJ behind him. He looks back and forth, turns, sprints along the bridge toward MJ and leaps—

—grabbing MJ in mid-air. He shoots a web to the undercarriage of the bridge, swings underneath with MJ

SPIDER-MAN: Hold on!

He releases his web, grabs the cable to the tram dancing before him. The weight of the tram yanks Spider-Man and MJ down, out of frame.

IN MID-AIR,
Spider-Man, the cable in one hand, MJ on his back, falls with the tram to the water below.

Spider-Man uses his free hand to shoot out a web toward the underside of the bridge. The web sticks.

INT. TRAM—NIGHT

The tram comes to a halt, bounces up and down. KIDS, DADS and equipment tumble about.

EXT. BRIDGE ROADWAY—NIGHT

A crowd has formed atop the bridge. Some cheer at Spider-Man's heroics.

EXT. QUEENSBORO BRIDGE—NIGHT

Spider-Man's body is stretched to the limit, with one hand holding on to the cable, the other the web.

EXT. QUEENSBORO BRIDGE—NIGHT

Spider-Man looks at MJ

SPIDER-MAN: Climb down.

MJ turns, looks at him, confused.

SPIDER-MAN: *(cont'd)* The cable to the tram, climb down.
MJ: *(voice quivering)* I can't.
SPIDER-MAN: MJ, just do it.
MJ: I'm scared.
SPIDER-MAN: Trust me.

MJ looks him in the eyes, down to the water below, then back to his eyes.

SPIDER-MAN: *(cont'd)* Trust me.

She climbs down his body, then the cable.

Spider-Man watches MJ descend the cable. He hears a WHINE from behind and turns to see just as—

—The Goblin hauls off and cold cocks him in the jaw, zooms away.

The force of the blow causes Spider-Man to sway back and forth as he struggles to remain conscious.

ON THE CABLE
MJ barely manages to hang on as she is thrown side to side.

INT. TRAM—NIGHT

The tram dips again, causing bodies to go flying.

EXT. QUEENSBOR BRIDGE—NIGHT

The Goblin swings around for another assault. He CACKLES as he extends his arm, exposing the razor sharp blades that adorn it. Spider-Man watches, helpless as The Goblin delivers a crushing blow to his stomach. Pieces of flesh and Spidey suit go flying. He loses his grip on the cable.

WIDE SHOT OF TRAM & MJ PLUNGING TOWARD THE WATER BELOW

Spider-Man dangles from the web, grasping for the cable snaking past him. As the last of the cable whizzes by, he lunges for it, catches it. Spider-Man SCREAMS out in agony, blood gushing from his hand.

The cable goes taut, causing MJ to lose her grip. She falls, landing on the tram below. She raises her head and sees Spider-Man, head to the side, out of energy, holding on to cable and web. She hears the glider's engine and sees The Goblin circling in for a final blow—

—but he stops. Looks at Spider-Man before him, his body stretched to the limit, looking like a rag doll with his head to the side. He almost looks as if he feels sorry for Spider-Man. His hovering engine emits a light HUM.

Spider-Man raises his head, looks at the Goblin.

Sorry for him? Naah! The Goblin gives an evil grin and the glider races toward Spider-Man full throttle.

Spider-Man braces for the blow. The Goblin zeros in on his prey, cocks back a fist—

—but a huge chunk of asphalt clocks him in the side of the head, sending him spiraling out of control, past Spider-Man.

The Goblin regains control, looks around. Where the hell'd that come from? He raises his head just as he is pelted with more asphalt, bottles, shoes, etc.

We PULL BACK to reveal a bridge full of New Yorkers hurling anything and everything they can get their hands on.

GREEN GOBLIN: *(covering his face)* AAHHHHHH-HHHHHHHHH!

He zooms out of sight to avoid the raining debris.

EXT. BRIDGE—NIGHT

Spider-Man looks down, sees a massive mound of rock that spreads from the support piling. He eyes the cheering crowd and with newfound strength starts to lower the tram to the piling.

EXT. SUPPORT PILING—NIGHT

The tram touches down gently on the rocks. MJ stands, looks up. We push in on her face looking adoringly at Spider-Man.

EXT. BRIDGE—NIGHT

Suddenly, a line wraps around Spider-Man's waist.

The Goblin zooms by, holding the rope. It goes taut and yanks Spider-Man out of frame.

Spider-Man thrashes about as he spins out of control behind the glider.

EXT. SUPPORT PILING—NIGHT

MJ reacts in horror as she sees Spider-Man being dragged away.

EXT. APPROACHING ROOSEVELT ISLAND—NIGHT

The Goblin turns around and CACKLES, getting a kick out of watching Spider-Man struggle.

He's seen enough, holds out his arm, once again exposing the blades on it, and SNICKS through the rope. Spider-Man goes crashing into the abandoned hulking ruin of a condemned smallpox hospital on Roosevelt Island below.

INT. HULKING RUIN—NIGHT

From below, we watch as Spider-Man crashes through the termite-infested boards of the third floor. As he falls he shoots a web to a support beam, swings down and smashes through a wall of crumbling brick and rotten wood, knocking him out and ripping off the majority of his mask.

INT. HULKING RUIN—NIGHT—LATER

Spider-Man comes to. Can't quite make out where he is. Light streams in from the massive holes of the condemned structure. Dust dances about, making it difficult to see.

He looks up, hears the WHOOSHING of the Goblin's Glider circling about. He gets to his feet, staggers and falls down. Pulls himself back up. He looks at himself, covered in blood, costume in shreds.

He hears a strange bloodcurdling scraping noise. He looks around, spots the lone unbroken window in the structure, covered by a wooden shutter.

He approaches the window, still punch-drunk, and flings back the shutter. A horde of razor bats press against the window, flapping their wings against the glass. Suddenly they burst through, sending shards of glass raining down on Spider-Man. They encircle him, dive, SLICE and SLASH at the few parts of his body that remain unbloodied. He screams out, tries to swat at them but that only leaves massive gashes in his hands.

Spider-Man looks across at the wall on the far end of the room and races toward it. The swarm of razor bats follow.

He runs full speed at the wall, jumps, plants his feet on the wall and does a back flip. The razor bats fly under him, crash into the wall, crumple to the ground.

Spider-Man looks at the heap of razor bats on the ground. A cocky smile creeps across his face.

SPIDER-MAN: You ain't so bad.

His happiness soon fades as more bats come after him. He flips and tumbles around the structure to elude them, but is quickly overtaken as they revert to ripping him to shreds. He falls to the ground.

GREEN GOBLIN: (o.s.) Enough!

The razor bats fail to heed their master's call, and continue slicing and dicing.

GREEN GOBLIN: (o.s.) (cont'd) I SAID, ENOUGH!

The razor bats stop their destruction, meekly fly away.

Spider-Man rolls over in a daze, an outline of blood marking his previous spot. He looks up at The Goblin hovering over him, tries to stand. His legs turn to jelly and he crashes to the ground. The Goblin laughs, reaches down onto his glider and pulls out a rod. He presses a button and three blades pop out, giving the weapon a pitchfork/spear appearance.

GREEN GOBLIN: (cont'd) Ahhh, misery, misery, misery. Again and again I've tried to make my case, but you won't oblige. Had you not been so determined, your sweetheart's death would have been quick and painless, but now, now that you've really pissed me off, I'll see to it that it's slow and...painful. (moving in for the kill) ...just...like...yours.

The Goblin rears back with the spear, brings it down on Spider-Man's chest. At the last moment Spider-Man catches it, looks at The Goblin, his strength returning. He yanks the spear from The Goblin, SMASHES it against his head so hard it sends The Goblin flying back ten feet. He crashes to the ground.

Spider-Man rises, pissed, full of adrenaline, fury. He breaks the pitchfork over his knee, tosses the parts to the side. He grabs The Goblin by the chest, pulls him up from the ground, throws a haymaker to The Goblin's jaw.

The Goblin goes flying through a nearby wall. The Goblin rises, manages to advance. SMACK! Spider-Man delivers another devastating blow. The Goblin crumples against a nearby stone wall.

GREEN GOBLIN: (cont'd) Please...

Spider-Man picks him up yet again, his rage is barely controlled. He pulls his fist back for another blow, and knowing this one will put him down for the count, Goblin, to save himself, pulls off his mask to reveal Norman Osborn.

GREEN GOBLIN: (cont'd) Peter...

Spider-Man, his fist still in the air, ready to deliver the final blow, stares in the face of his best friend's father.

Shock. Disbelief. He rips off pieces of his own mask to make sure he's seeing right. He is. He lets go of Osborn, who slumps to the floor, looking up at Peter, pathetically.

OSBORN: (small voice) Peter...thank God for you.

Peter, his hands covered in blood, trembles, still with rage, shaken by the violence he feels inside.

PETER: Can't be...you're a monster.
OSBORN: Please, Peter, don't let it take me back. I need your help. I'm not a monster.
PETER: You killed those people on the balcony, you could have killed your son.
OSBORN: "IT" killed. The Goblin killed. I had nothing to do with it. Please, don't let it have me again. Protect me, I beg you. Talk to me about this—

Surreptitiously, Osborn brings his right hand around in front of him, unseen by Peter. On his wrist, the TOUCH PAD CONTROLS of the Goblin Glider flash patiently.

PETER: You tried to kill Aunt May. You wanted to kill Mary Jane.
OSBORN: But not you, I would never hurt you.

Osborn presses the RED BUTTON on the pad. Peter doesn't see. Behind Peter, the Glider rises up into the air without a sound. Osborn keeps talking, to keep him distracted.

OSBORN: (cont'd) I knew from the beginning if anything happened to me, you were the one I could count on, you, Peter Parker, would save me, and so you have. Thank God for you.

During this, Osborn pushes himself to his feet. With his back against the wall, holds out a hand in pathetic supplication.

OSBORN: *(cont'd)* Give me your hand. Believe in me as I believed in you. I was like a father to you. Be a son to me now.

PETER: I have a father. His name was Ben Parker.

Suddenly a look crosses Peter's face. Osborn begins to cackle. It grows louder, crazier, totally, happily insane.

HIS SPIDER-SENSE KICKS IN

OSBORN: God speed, Spider-Man.

Spider-Man's perception leaps outside his body and whips around, giving him a look behind him, just as—

—the Goblin Glider's SPEAR rotates into position on the front of the moving Glider, in ultra-slow motion, just a few feet behind Peter, headed straight for his back!

In sudden real time, Peter hurls himself to the side, twisting and bending in a near-impossible contortion—

—the Glider's turbine SCREAMS as it whistles just past him—

—terror creases Osborn's face—

—and his own Glider rockets right through him.

Norman Osborn slumps over, impaled by his own contraption, pinned to the wall. Peter rushes forward, but it's too late.

So dies Spider-Man's first, and most heinous, archfoe.

In the distance, Peter hears SIRENS, headed for the hulking ruin. He looks back at the body of Norman Osborn. Steps forward. He cradles him in his arms, lifts him—

INT. OSBORN'S APARTMENT —NIGHT

—and sets the body down again, this time on the floor of Osborn's apartment, beside wide-open French doors, curtains wafting in the breeze. Osborn's body is dressed again, no trace of the incriminating Green Goblin costume. Blood soaks through Osborn's shirt. He looks like the victim of a murder.

Spider-Man takes a few steps away, toward the open French doors, then hears a nearly-silent GASP from the door to the apartment. He whirls around.

Harry Osborn stands in the doorway, looking from his dead father to Spider-Man, aghast.

HARRY: You...

Spider-Man raises his hands to protest his innocence. He takes a step forward—but Harry takes a step back in fear.

SPIDER-MAN: No...
HARRY: MURDERER!

Harry lunges toward a table nearby, opens the top drawer, grabs a gun and turns.

But Spider-Man is gone. The curtains blow in the wind.

EXT. CEMETERY—DAY

Track a line of expensive cars parked along the narrow winding road. In BG, a fresh grave, a few people from the service, including Pentagon generals, are dispersing. Aunt May and MJ stand talking.

Harry and Peter walk toward the Osborn Bentley. Silent. Then.

PETER: I'm so sorry, Harry. I know what it's like to lose a father.

HARRY: I didn't lose him, he was stolen from me. And one day Spider-Man will pay. *(into Peter's eyes)* I swear on my father's grave, Spider-Man will pay.

They reach the Bentley. Norman's chauffeur opens the door for Harry and moves off.

HARRY: *(cont'd)* Look...about MJ I was just trying to please my dad. I thought he'd be impressed, me, with such a beautiful woman. I know she was never right for me. I wanted to make him proud, that's all. Now I'll never be able to. Thank God for you, my friend. You're all the family I have left.

Harry gives Peter a hug, then gets in the car. Closes the door. The Bentley drives off.

Peter turns and looks toward MJ and Aunt May on the hill by Norman's gravesite. As he turns, MJ locks eyes with Peter. Smiles at him.

VERY CLOSE ON PETER—V.O.—THE VOICE FROM THE OPENING SCENE

SPIDER-MAN: *(v.o.)* No matter what I do, no matter how hard I try. The ones I love are always the ones who pay.

EXT. CEMETERY—ANOTHER HILLTOP—DAY

Peter is walking towards another tombstone.

VERY CLOSE SHOT—MJ

Her bright smile. It fills and lights up the screen.

MJ: *(looking past camera—shouts)* HEY!

NEW SHOT—PETER
He turns. PULL BACK to show we are at Uncle Ben's gravesite. MJ enters frame.

MJ: *(cont'd)* Your aunt thought I'd find you here.
PETER: *(to "Ben")* MJ's here, Uncle Ben.

FAVOR THE TOMBSTONE—IT READS:
    BEN PARKER
    BELOVED HUSBAND AND UNCLE

MJ moves closer to Peter.

MJ: You must miss him so much.
PETER: He was a beautiful guy.

A pause. They begin to walk, heading up a small knoll. The skyline of New York in the background. MJ stops.

MJ: There's something I've been wanting to tell you. *(MJ pauses a beat. Peter stops, waits)* When I was up there and I was sure I was going to die, there was only one person I was thinking of, and it wasn't who I thought it would be. It was you. I kept thinking, I hope I make it through this, so I can see Peter Parker's face one more time.
PETER: My face?
MJ: *(she nods)* Sometimes what you want...you have to go to the edge of your life to find out it was right next door.

This is blowing his mind.

MJ: *(cont'd)* I've been so stupid for so long. There's only one man who was ever there for me, who has always been there for me...who makes me believe that I'm...more than I ever thought I was. That I'm just...me, and it's okay...The truth is...I love you. I really love you Peter.

During the last speech, CAMERA has moved slowly in for a TIGHT SHOT of Peter.

SPIDER-MAN *(v.o.)* Tell her you love her. Tell her who you are.
PETER: I...can't...
MJ: You can't what?
PETER: Tell you everything. I mean there's so much to tell.
MJ: Yes. So much to tell.
PETER: To tell the girl next door.
MJ: But is that all I am?
PETER: Oh, no, no, you're the amazing girl next door,

Mary Jane, the amazing, amazing girl, and I want you to know that I will always be there for you, I will always be there to take care of you. I promise you that. I wish I could give you more than that, but you must know...that you will always be safe.

She looks at him. She moves to him. Embraces him. He's about to be captured.

She kisses him. A gentle, little kiss. But full of magic.

PETER: *(cont'd)* *(dazed)*...can't.

Too late. The kiss is deeper. More passionate, and he can no longer control himself, brings her closer, kisses her as she's never been kissed before...except by the kiss she experienced with Spider-Man.

And when that extraordinary kiss is over, she moves her head back, breathless, looking into his eyes. She has just experienced that kiss again. Spider-Man. Her eyes wide open.

She wants more, so does he, but...he "can't." The music rises.

CLOSE ON M.J. IN LOVE.

BACK TO PETER, he forces himself to turn. WE STAY CLOSE ON HIM as he walks away, MJ receding in the BG.

SPIDER-MAN: *(v.o.)* *(sadder, wiser)* Can't say I didn't warn you. The story of my life is not for the faint of heart.

A wind kicks up. Peter pulls his coat tighter.

SPIDER-MAN: *(v.o.)* *(cont'd)* Like the man said, it's hard to be a saint in the city. But whatever life holds in store for me, I now accept. I will never forget these words again:

Peter looks over his shoulder at MJ, still standing by the gravesite.

SPIDER-MAN: *(v.o.)* *(cont'd)* "With great power comes great responsibility."

He continues on. We move in closer on his face.

SPIDER-MAN: *(v.o.)* *(cont'd)* This is my gift. It is my curse. Who am I?

Peter cracks a little smile.

SPIDER-MAN: *(v.o.)* *(cont'd)* Baby, I'm Spider-Man.

INT. JAMESON'S OFFICE—DAY

JAMESON: Spider-Man, I don't get it. First the town thinks he's trash, now he's a glamour boy.

ROBBIE: He's a hero, J.J.

JAMESON: Don't give me that line again, I don't trust heroes. They're nothing but criminals in disguise. Hoffman, where's Parker? I want some pictures.

HOFFMAN: He just left.

JAMESON: Left? He's always leaving.

HOFFMAN: He went to cover the hostage story.

JAMESON: Sure! Another hostage story. But where is he when The Green Goblin busted through my window? The Goblin and Spider-Man, in front of our noses! A golden opportunity and the photographer went to lunch. *(looking off)* And what's that?

He's looking at an OFFICE BOY holding up a pair of trousers.

OFFICE BOY: Peter Parker's pants, J.J.

JAMESON: What?

OFFICE BOY: They were in the closet.

JAMESON: Parker's pants?

OFFICE BOY: With his shirt and tie and shoes and socks.

JAMESON: What's going on here, who's he think he is, Tarzan? Where is he, running around the town naked? And who put flowers on my desk?

MISS BRANT: I did, sir. It's your birthday.

JAMESON: What're you looking for, a raise? I don't want flowers, I want Peter Parker, not his pants, I want pictures, I wanna sell papers, I want Spider-Man! *(He continues on as:)*

EXT. CITY—DAY
Spider-Man swings away, shimmering into the glass and stone canyons of his city.

FADE OUT